Faith, My
in Han China

Faith, Myth and Reason in Han China

by MICHAEL LOEWE

Hackett Publishing Company, Inc.
Indianapolis/Cambridge

Reprinted 2005 by Hackett Publishing Company, Inc.

11 10 09 08 07 06 05   1 2 3 4 5 6 7

For further information, please address:
   Hackett Publishing Company, Inc.
   P.O. Box 44937
   Indianapolis, IN 46244-0937
   www.hackettpublishing.com

Cover design by *Abigail Coyle, Deborah Wilkes* and *Lance Brisbois*
Printed at *Sheridan Books, Inc.*

Library of Congress Cataloging-in-Publication Data
Loewe, Michael.
   Faith, myth, and reason in Han China / by Michael Loewe.
      p. cm.
   Originally published: Allen & Unwin, 1982.
   Includes bibliographical references and index.
   ISBN 0-87220-757-9 (cloth)—ISBN 0-87220-756-0 (pbk.)
   1. China—Social life and customs—221 BC–960 AD. I. Title.
   DS747.42.L63 2005
   931'.04–dc22

                                             2004028487

Contents

Preface

Archaeological discoveries of the last decade have radically transformed the history of the Ch'in and Han empires. So far from remaining the preserve of specialists, this has now become a subject that arouses lively interest among members of the public who visit museums or see the popular reports of television or the press. For those who wish to pursue this interest, there exist both general works on the cultural development of China through the ages and specialist studies of the Han period. But most of these latter are concerned with institutional or political aspects of history and there is as yet no general survey of the religious and intellectual background of the period. The following pages, which are intended for non-specialist readers, attempt to fill this deficiency by describing the cultural context within which the recent archaeological discoveries should be placed.

So far from being restricted to Chinese civilisation, many of the themes that are under discussion here are of universal interest, recurring as they do in other cultures. The Chinese no less than other peoples were concerned with the nature of the gods and the ways that led to paradise. In seeking to understand the universe as a single system, they explained the processes of creation in terms either of myth or of reason. Their practice of divination became subject, as elsewhere, to intellectual considerations; in their cults of state they sought to link temporal with eternal power, by exhibiting the sacred character of kingship. Their beliefs and ideas stand revealed in philosophical essay and iconography, in symbolical action and religious observance alike.

Of necessity it has not been possible to include here an account of all aspects of Han religious and intellectual development. I have tried to explain matters of belief and theory before attending to practice, and to take subjects in the order of faith in the unknown, explanations of nature and the view of mankind. Some important topics, such as popular religion, medicine and alchemy, are conspicuous by their absence, for the reason that they require deeper research before a general statement can be framed, or treatment within another context than the one that is envisaged here.

My thanks are due to a number of friends, colleagues and

viii

pupils whose interest in Han history has stimulated thought on these matters during years gone by. I am particularly indebted to Christopher Cullen for guidance over astronomy and permission to cite from one of his articles on p. 54; to John Major for constructive criticism on a number of matters; and to Derk Bodde and the Princeton University Press for permission to print a passage from *Festivals in Classical China* on p. 142. I am also glad to acknowledge the help of Anthony Raven who read the typescript and corrected a number of errors.

M.L.

Preface to the Hackett edition

Considerable changes in the scope of historical studies of early imperial China and the ways in which its problems can be handled have become apparent in the twenty years that have passed since the publication of this book in 1982. While there is no call for a drastic revision of the book, it is open to supplementary information and modification in some respects.

Such changes derive from the rich, and at times dramatic, archaeological discoveries, which are now said to comprise at least 30,000 tombs of Ch'in and Han times, of which no more than a few have been excavated. Some of these are major edifices, built below ground or hewn into the cliff; symbolic devices engraved or painted upon the artifacts found within show the force of religious belief or the prevailing attention to mythology and folklore. Some of the many wooden and silk manuscripts that have been found bring unknown written works to our attention, with a religious, philosophical, literary, administrative or technical content. Some provide new information for the authenticity of texts well known hitherto; some may be cautiously identified with works whose titles have been preserved but whose texts have long been lost.

In fastening on such evidences scholars have reached a deeper comprehension of many aspects of the times. Research that takes into consideration both literary and material sources of information has led to a more refined understanding of both religious beliefs and practice and of intellectual concepts, and to the correction of assumptions that have been maintained over decades or even centuries. At the same time the new evidence has opened up new questions; and as in all historical studies there remain the difficulties of assessing the pace and extent of change and identifying moments or incidents that are crucial. If two examples may be cited, we cannot claim to follow precisely the places taken by *Tao* in the many strands of Chinese thought, or to comprehend exactly what a concept such as *ch'i* may have implied in the development of scientific ideas.

As research has developed, so has greater discredit fallen upon a facile view that Chinese thought can be neatly categorised in a few identifiable types. Some of the new documents show how a practice of divination could be reduced to a somewhat mechanical consultation of a written guide in place of a trust in the powers of a seer. Legal prescriptions dated in 217 and 186 BC show how, for all the claims to the contrary, the Han government inherited and practised the orders and punishments of Ch'in, mitigated as some of their severities would be; and the same documents show how greatly the force of these laws affected the conduct of daily life. Questions have been raised regarding the adoption of a patron element or phase in Former Han times. At the same time it is now seen that more importance is due to the intellectual changes of Wang Mang's time and their place in China's traditions. Other questions concern the authority ascribed to early masters and their writings and the validity of arguments based on such premises; doubts have been raised over the significance of a distinction long held between a 'modern text' and an 'ancient text' school.

Attention is due to a few detailed problems or matters that call for correction. The edict dated in 178 BC (see p. 86) would seem to be framed somewhat anachronistically (see the author's *The Men who Governed Han China*, pp. 152–54). Representations of the 'god' *Tai-i* (see Chapter 12 below, p. 130) now found show him in anthropomorphic guise. It now seems improbable that Tung Chung-shu relied on the theory of the Five Phases to explain the operation of the universe (see pp. 85, 149, 217). There were two men called Ching Fang, each concerned with the *Book of Changes,* dated respectively at c. 140 to c. 80, and 79 to 37 BC; references here (see pp. 78, 88) are to the second of these men. The effective beginning of the Western Chou Dynasty may now be taken as 1045 BC.

M.L.

Faith, Myth and Reason
in Han China

Introduction

Considerable advances have taken place in the study of Chinese history in recent years. The rich store of Chinese historical writings and the heritage of Chinese scholarship have been supplemented by the spectacular finds of archaeologists and the application of critical canons of history, evolved in the western tradition. For the Ch'in and Han periods (221 BC to AD 220), attention has fastened hitherto on the sequence of political units, the evolution of institutions and the incidence of social and economic change. For the evidence has applied most directly to such matters, and by clarifying those aspects of the Ch'in and Han empires an overall picture has emerged of the initial stages of the Chinese imperial tradition.

Nevertheless historians have been well aware that such considerations cannot be separated from other aspects of that tradition, which include the religious or mythological background from which those institutions sprang, and the intellectual framework within which they were formulated. However, the literature has lent itself more readily to an analysis of dynastic motives and political trends than to the shared beliefs and intellectual assumptions of the Ch'in and Han peoples. While considerable strides have been taken in analysing the systems of thought or the writings of a few individual authors, it has yet been too early to distinguish the strands that together make up Han thought and religion in a systematic way. It is, however, now becoming possible to identify the growth of certain concepts and to examine how they gave way to new modes of thought and the impact of new faiths; and indeed it has fast become essential to do so. For we are concerned with a world which maintained no strict distinction between sacred and secular, or between political issues and intellectual problems. If we are to understand the motives for political change, we must also comprehend the hopes that inspired the hearts, and the reasons that controlled the minds, of Han China.

It has been convenient and customary to consider the history of China in terms of the dynastic changes and chronological divisions adopted in the Standard Histories (*cheng shih*). Such distinctions frequently blur sequences of a more important nature or mask certain key developments that have affected the growth of Chinese culture. Nevertheless some force is lent to the division of Chinese history in dynastic terms, if it can be maintained that dynastic changes reflect intellectual innovation. As political frameworks can rarely, if ever, exist without a philosophical basis, it would be improper to disregard dynastic changes entirely when considering religious or intellectual history. This principle is particularly true of the Ch'in and Han periods which witnessed the initial and experimental establishment of imperial government, and the steps taken to represent such government as the normal and respected way of organising mankind; such achievements depended no less on China's philosophers than on her statesmen.

The period of time that is under consideration – no less than four centuries – must be regarded as long in any examination of intellectual development. In many ways the four centuries may be deemed to be formative. Before they had closed, China had received the effect of a new religion, brought by intrepid Buddhist venturers from the west. The last century of the Han dynasty saw the formulation of spiritual disciplines and bodily exercises, and a clerical authority, that together provided Taoist religion with a framework. Shortly after the Han dynasty, Wang Pi (226–249) gave Chinese philosophy a new dimension in his metaphysical speculations. These major developments will not feature in the pages that follow; for they herald the start of new stages in Chinese religious and intellectual activity, which came to fruition in the succeeding centuries. Attention will, however, be paid to the earlier stages of Chinese cultural development that took place before the imperial dynasties had been created, for a large measure of Han belief and practice may be traced to those centuries that preceded political unification. On the one hand, continuity may be traced between the art and literature of western Han (202 BC to AD 8) and its predecessors; on the other, the theories and observances of eastern Han (AD 25 to 220) lead forward to the view of life expressed so vividly in the Sui and T'ang periods.

The four centuries under consideration witnessed a conspicuous change in Chinese views of the world and man's place therein. Officials who lived around 150 BC could well have been astounded had they encountered the principles entertained by their successors of AD 150. They could hardly have understood their assumptions regarding the universe or approved of the practices in which the court took part. By AD 150, the emperors had for some time been offering services to different powers from those worshipped by their ancestors of western Han. There was a new explanation of the workings of the heavens and their wonders; a new view was taken of the miracles wrought on earth and amongst men, as the consequences of an all-embracing order of nature. Men and women saw new ways of attaining a life of eternity beyond the grave and relied on new types of talisman to achieve those ends. The emperor's authority had won a new respect which derived not from the results of conquest by force, but from the legitimate power bestowed by a superior. The institutions of state now depended on a common acceptance of a series of holy books, whose texts and interpretation had passed through a lengthy process of controversy.

These changes and developments may be charted in religious practice and philosophical essay, in the call exerted by mythology and in the symbols of iconography. Evidence of three types is to be found. There are the artifacts interred with the dead, many of which have been brought to light only recently. There are the extant texts of literature whose transmission has been subject to two millennia of editing. There are also newly found fragments of texts that have remained unknown, unsung or deliberately suppressed for perhaps as long and which are yet to be examined fully.

Insufficient time has elapsed in which to assess the value of recent archaeological discoveries fully. Most of the attention paid to these finds has concentrated on explaining their artistic, symbolical and technological significance. Sites that may illustrate a sequence of different stages of human occupation in the Ch'in and Han periods still await investigation. A further limitation is presented by our ignorance of the context of many well-known objects; for although our museums display a rich variety of mortuary bricks, bronze mirrors and pottery or lacquer vessels, it is only exceptionally that we know the provenance of such treasures, or the particular times or places of burial to which they can be related.

These difficulties are currently being reduced by a number of developments. State-sponsored archaeology, promoted by the government of China since 1950, has resulted in controlled excavation and the regular publication of reports of discoveries.

It has become possible to draw up schemata for the chronological sequences of a number of types of artifact (e.g. coins, mirrors or brick-built tombs). The identification of the occupants of a number of tombs or of the date of their completion, ranging from 210 BC to AD 182, sometimes adds a degree of precision to Ch'in and Han artifacts and sites which may excite the envy of archaeologists in other fields. Nevertheless, a great deal of work remains to be done by way of establishing sequences for artifacts, discriminating between regional styles and relating such distinctions to the sequences demanded by texts or suggested by art historians.

Fortunately the Standard History of the Han dynasty (*Han shu*) includes a list of the titles of books which formed the imperial collection of writings at about the beginning of the Christian era. The list had been compiled as part of a major project, undertaken at the imperial command. An edict had entrusted two famous scholars, Liu Hsiang (79–8 BC) followed by his son Liu Hsin (died AD 23), with the task of collecting and classifying literature that came from all parts of the empire.

Originally the list was accompanied by short descriptions of the books that are named and some account of the different versions in which copies had been preserved at the time. Had such descriptions survived in more than fragmentary form, it would be possible to trace the intellectual achievement of early China in some considerable detail. Unfortunately only a few of the notices remain. Nevertheless we possess an impressive list of the works committed to writing at that time, and we can form an idea of the wide variety of their subjects. The titles range from interpretations of classical texts, or scriptures, to historical records; from statements of ethical philosophy and tracts on political theory and statecraft to textbooks of mathematics and the sciences (e.g. astronomy, agriculture, medicine and divination). In addition to collections of poetry, there are accounts of idealised institutions and rituals, and descriptions of practice and protocol.

Unfortunately these writings were subject to the major hazards of warfare, fire and looting, which the capital cities of Ch'ang-an and Lo-yang suffered respectively in AD 26 and 190. As a result of these and other incidents only a small proportion, less than a quarter, survives of the 677 entries included on the list. Moreover, in reading the received copies of such works, we are necessarily subject to several limitations. For it cannot be assumed that the printed copies that lie before us are identical with the books assembled by Liu Hsiang and Liu Hsin to be placed on the shelves of the imperial library. In a number of cases it can be demonstrated that the texts collected at that time included material that has now been lost. Alternatively it is known that some of the most famous books of early Chinese civilisation, that allegedly date from before the Christian era, now include the interpolations of later editors; some may have been fabricated *in toto* at a later stage and ascribed to authors of the Han period or before.

A special difficulty attends the use of early texts as a source of Chinese mythology, for by the time that the imperial library was being formed and its catalogue drawn up, Chinese officials were deliberately attempting to promote the values of a sophisticated intellectual culture and to deprecate the influence of spontaneous religious impulses. A measure of standardisation had set in, that was designed to reduce the faith attached to the myths, images and symbols of the past, and to replace them with an appeal to the preferred doctrines of the empire and its intellectual basis. Somewhat exceptionally, two major texts survive which draw in part on the religious and mythological background of China that dates from a time before this process had affected the editing of texts. These are the *Songs of the South (Ch'u tz'u)*, whose poems derive from the practice of shamanism and the religious motifs of the Yangtse river valley; and the *Classic of the Mountains and the Lakes (Shan-hai ching)*, which acts as a guide to the holy mountains of the gods. But even these books demand considerable care in handling, in view of their inclusion of some material that had been affected by secondary considerations and intellectual motives. Much research yet remains to be completed in relating the descriptions of the deities, strange beasts and practices mentioned there to the depictions of Han iconography and the observances of religion and folklore.

1

Four attitudes of mind

The questions posed by Han philosophers, the observances kept in Han shrines and the themes that run through Han mythology reflect some of the fundamental attitudes and ideas that informed the Chinese heart and mind. These derived in part from a search for permanence in a highly volatile world. There was a deep concern to maintain the perpetual operation of those natural cycles whereby the world had been created and was continuing to exist, and a desire to regulate thought and behaviour so as to conform with those cycles. There was a common acceptance that unseen powers may affect human fortunes, and that communication is possible with such powers, either to attract blessings or to preclude disaster. Above all, the universe was regarded as being unitary; there was no essential division between sacred and profane, and the creatures of heaven, earth and man were seen as members of a single world. Similarly there was no rigid separation between religious and intellectual categories, in the way that has become accepted in the west. For in Ch'in and Han, heart and mind complemented one another, and the results of scientific observation or philosophical speculation were by no means necessarily kept apart from the beliefs, hopes and fears of mythology.

The principal problems that beset the Han mind were in all probability little different from those that were faced in other cultures such as those of Israel or Greece. They concerned the nature of superior powers and the question whether they could be identified, contacted and worshipped. The Chinese were anxious to determine the destiny of man after death and the best means of providing for his future welfare. Some sought to understand the extent of the world in which man is placed and its mode of operation; or they asked about the place of man in the universe and his relation to other created things. There were those who sought to avert the worst effects of unseen evil influences; others sought ways of organising man to the fullest extent of his abilities. Some asked how the standard of human behaviour could be improved; others asked how authority could best be conceived as a legitimate instrument for exercising government.

The intellectual history of early China has frequently been bedevilled by the loose and ill-disciplined use of terms such as Taoist, Confucian or Legalist, in respect of periods before such categories applied. Certainly these terms featured among the six principal schools of thought listed by Ssu-ma T'an, who died in 110 BC; but it is unlikely that at that time it would have been possible or suitable to classify certain thinkers exclusively within the groups of Confucian (*ju*), Taoist, Legalist (*fa*), Yin-Yang, Mohist or Nominalist (*ming chia*) that he neatly distinguished. Such groups shared a great deal of ground in common and precise definitions were hardly possible.

Nor was a neat distinction appropriate at the time of the next important event in the description of Han thought. This was the classification of literature by Liu Hsiang and Liu Hsin (see p. 4, above). Such a classification was not intended in the first place as an analysis of Chinese philosophy; it was essentially the work of scholars charged with the bibliographical task of collecting literature and ordering the array of books in a library. However, in such work there were obviously cases where classification could hardly be avoided for practical reasons, for it was necessary to insert the title of a piece of writing in the list of works that were being assembled, however difficult it might have been to determine whether a particular author's book should be labelled in one way or another. The categories established by Liu Hsiang and Liu Hsin corresponded in part to the six schools brought to the fore by Ssu-ma T'an. But the writings with which they were concerned stretched back for a number of centuries, perhaps eight or nine, before his time, and included a number of later productions. Liu Hsiang and Liu Hsin had necessarily to create many more categories than the six upon which Ssu-ma T'an had fastened in his account of the major philosophical schools.

For all these limitations, it has been the traditional practice of Chinese scholars to accept the categories that were followed in the work of the Lius, and in many cases to apply them retrospectively over a wide range of Chinese literature. The results have been false in the sense that they have imposed distinctions according to criteria which may not have been applicable in the earlier stages of Chinese writing.

There is a further reason why these categories cannot be accepted without reserve. A number of the most fruitful sources of information for Chinese thought before the Christian era did not derive from the hand of a single author. They were the results of the corporate work of a number of writers, whose names are usually unrecorded. This was partly due to the prevailing custom whereby men of prominence tried to add to their distinction by inviting a body of learned men to attend their court, in order to advise on theoretical and practical matters of concern and to compile an account of their deliberations. It follows that the contents of some works can only be eclectic, deriving from different attitudes of mind; such differences may sometimes, but are by no means always, distinguished clearly. One of the most obvious examples of such an anthology is the *Spring and Autumn Annals of Mr Lü* (*Lü shih ch'un-ch'iu*), which includes anecdotes, prescriptions for behaviour and statements of philosophical principle. The work was compiled in the middle of the third century BC, and includes ideas that are later classified variously as Taoist, Confucian or Legalist.

From such materials it is possible to discern four principal attitudes to life, which were centred respectively on nature, man, the state and reason.

Those who stressed the importance of the order of nature sought to conform with the universal rhythms and cycles that they believed to inform the universe. They saw man as being but a part of the major order of existence and subordinate thereto. Man should therefore be encouraged to co-operate with the processes of nature; and he should be prevented from destroying the resources of nature solely to gratify his own greed. Many of these ideas can be traced to, or were deliberately fastened upon, early works such as the *Tao-te ching* or the *Chuang-tzu*; and we know from recent archaeological discoveries that the message of the received text of the *Tao-te ching* is substantially identical with that of copies which were circulating in the second century BC. It was upon such writings that the concepts later known as 'Taoism' came to depend; for example, the mysterious system of nature, which may be comprehended by means other than those of reason; the fallibility of ephemeral human values; and the folly inherent in organising mankind to excess.

For the Han period, these ideas were expressed in a book known as the *Huai-nan-tzu*. Like the *Lü shih ch'un-ch'iu* this was compiled by a group of writers serving at a court. The contributors to the *Huai-nan-tzu*, which was completed half way through the second century BC, applied these principles to the observed operation of natural forces, and sought to explain the universe according to the regular cycles of creation, death and rebirth. It is noticeable that some of the ideas and principles of this type of attitude are also seen in the writings of Tung Chung-shu, to whom reference will be made shortly in connection with another mode of thought. It may also be observed that although the *Huai-nan-tzu* is usually classified as 'Taoist', it attributes considerable powers to heaven (*t'ien*) in a manner that is characteristic of 'Confucianists'.

To some thinkers the prime concern of man was man, his leadership and his organisation. They believed that man's first duty lay in improving his behaviour and his potential for ethical conduct; by such means he could best improve his way of life and increase the measure of his happiness. Such improvements involved education, the acceptance of political hierarchies and social organisation, and conformity to generally accepted patterns of civilised behaviour. But it was also maintained that, if such results were desirable in the interests of mankind as a whole, they must also permit full scope for individual improvement and the exercise of individual aptitudes; for the sacrifice of such qualities for the mere sake of ordered government would not be acceptable.

The ethical principles upon which such concepts were based had been enunciated by K'ung Ch'iu (Confucius: 551–479 BC), his disciples and his disciples' disciple Meng K'o (Mencius: 390–305 BC); and for this reason this attitude to life is described as Confucian. However, these ideas were by no means limited to that school. Some of them were promoted by other thinkers, such as Mo ti (480–390 BC) or Hsün Ch'ing (340–245 BC) who encompassed them as part of their own doctrines. Practical rules for the guidance of man in attaining these goals, in ordering his own conduct and in his relations with different ranks of society were laid down in several compendia of propriety (*li*), perhaps before or during the Han period.

In addition, the ethical ideals of K'ung Ch'iu and his immediate followers formed an important part of the syncretism promoted by Tung Chung-shu (*c.* 179–*c.* 104 BC), who has sometimes been described as the formulator of Han Confucianism. His system of values differed from that of Confucius in so far as it coupled a theory regarding the order of nature and creation with Confucius' ethical ideals. Moreover, Tung Chung-shu's concepts of the state and of the order of mankind applied to the united empire of his own day; they could hardly have suited the political situation in which Confucius had lived some three centuries previously.

According to Chinese tradition, the empire of Ch'in had been formed (in 221 BC) as a result of a rigorous discipline of state, the imposition of a stern code of laws and the successful prosecution of warfare. Such measures and policies rested on the formulation of political theories which saw the enrichment and strengthening of the state as the prime object of government. Any measures designed to provide material benefits for mankind as a whole could be justified, regardless of their effect on individual aspirations. Reliable protection against external enemies and the dedicated service of the people were the true goals of government rather than the provision of opportunities for moral improvement; so far from attempting to conform with the rhythms of nature, man should set about the conquest of nature so as to extract as great a store of riches as was possible. This attitude is generally described under the term 'Legalist'.

A statesman of the fourth century BC named Shang Yang was one of the first men to formulate these theories in writing, and the direct tradition of his teaching is preserved in the book that bears his name (*Shang chün shu*). Other texts which promote the same doctrine, i.e. that of government for the sake of the governors rather than those who are governed, and which have been of prime importance in the growth of Chinese thought, include the *Han-fei tzu*; and there is considerable common ground with the philosophy of Hsün Ch'ing who is, however, usually classified as 'Confucian' rather than 'Legalist'.

The insistence on the rigorous application of the laws of state formed a fundamental feature of this way of thought. In political terms, this involved the institution of hard-and-fast rules for the punishment of criminals or deserters, and for the encouragement of others to render positive service, either on the field of battle or by undertaking the arduous and unrewarding work of transporting and delivering grain over long distances.

Chinese historians have attributed the successful establishment of the Ch'in empire to the imposition of a discipline based on these principles; they have attributed the collapse of Ch'in, after a few years, to the excessive demands that such a discipline forced upon a suffering population. However valid these explanations of imperial rise and fall may be, it remains true that Ch'in had succeeded in forging a framework of institutions and imposing a call for corporate action without which imperial government could not have been created. Despite the claim that the succeeding regime of Han had relieved the population of China from oppressive government and harsh legislation, many of Ch'in's institutions and theories remained in force during the Han dynasty, and many acts of the Han governments were directed towards achieving the same ends.

This view of government and the aims of the state is hardly contested in the essays of Chia I (200–168 BC), who has often been regarded as an outspoken critic of Ch'in. It seems rather that he was urging his contemporaries not to prejudice the agreed ends of government, chosen by Ch'in and adopted by Han, by excessive and mistaken demands on the population. The memorials of Ch'ao Ts'o, a statesman who died in 154 BC, are likewise directed towards strengthening China's internal and external security; they assume that the importance of the state overrides that of the individual. The same opinions are voiced in a remarkable document (the *Yen-t'ieh lun*) of perhaps 60 BC; this purports to record a debate held in 81 BC, regarding the role of the state and the justification of some of its policies. Finally, in assessing the importance of a 'Legalist' view in the Han period, during the second half of the second century AD social disruption, political corruption and loss of imperial purpose led some statesmen such as Hsün Yüeh (148–209) to issue a call for rededication, on the basis of a renewed sense of corporate discipline (see p. 15 below).

By the beginning of the first century AD two important developments were becoming manifest in Chinese thought. The results achieved by men of science were more accurate and dependable than they had been hitherto. Secondly, political and dynastic leaders had been exploiting and abusing current beliefs to show that superhuman powers were supporting their own exercise of temporal authority. The efficacy of the one trend and the intellectual deceits inherent in the other together induced a reaction in the form of an appeal to reason rather than dogma, and in a demand for an explanation of natural phenomena that would withstand systematic enquiry, without requiring an act of faith. This intellectual approach to the work of nature was likewise applied to human achievements and ambitions, and to contemporary beliefs in occult powers. It was expressed most fully in the writings of Wang Ch'ung (AD 27–c. 100), whose scepticism, rejection of religion and demands for rational explanation have often led to a comparison with Lucretius.

Wang Ch'ung was by no means the first or the only rationalist of his age. His immediate predecessors included Yang Hsiung (53 BC–AD 18) and Huan T'an (c. 43 BC–AD 28), but it is thanks to the preservation of most of Wang Ch'ung's trenchant writings that he has been regarded as an innovator in Chinese thought. He tried to show how rational and systematic modes of enquiry that had been successfully applied, e.g. to astronomy, could be adapted or adopted in examining other phenomena of nature. He argued from analogy, sometimes forcefully, sometimes improperly. He insisted on the importance of observation and experiment, and on the weakness of accepting unproven dogma. Wang Ch'ung's principles led forward to the scientific and technological innovations of men such as Chang Heng (78–139), best known for his construction of a seismograph and an armillary sphere. It may, however, be noted that, unlike Wang Ch'ung, Chang Heng retained a profound sense of mystery in his concept of the universe; he recognised that by no means all things would respond to rational explanation.

Wang Ch'ung's methods of enquiry and argument may be exemplified in his treatment of thunder, where he seeks to disprove a supernatural origin and to demonstrate that it is the result of natural conditions. His motives and reasoning bear a marked resemblance to those of Lucretius (c. 100–55 BC) who likewise desired to liberate his contemporaries from the dread that thunder inspired, as a manifestation of divine wrath. Lucretius starts his argument (Book VI, 96f.) with a well-known lyrical passage describing the phenomenon: 'First of all the blue of the sky is shaken by thunder because the clouds in high heaven, scudding aloft, clash together when the winds are fighting in combat.' He continues by explaining thunder as being due to the movements and interactions of clouds, winds, rain and lightning; he firmly rejects the view that thunderbolts

were weapons, manipulated arbitrarily by an enraged Jupiter.
Wang Ch'ung starts his essay as follows:

At the height of summer, thunder and lightning follow one
after the other at speed, smiting and smashing trees, destroying buildings and from time to time injuring or killing human
beings. It is usually explained that when trees are struck and
houses destroyed, heaven has been 'collecting its dragon', and
that human beings who are harmed or killed are guilty of faults
that may not have been seen; or that, when people are given
impure things to eat or drink heaven grows angry and strikes
to kill them. The low reverberations of thunder are said to be
the sound of heaven's wrath, like the grunts or growls of a
man. Wise men and foolish men, wherever they are, all accept
these views. But when we discuss thunder in the light of
human activity we can see how nonsensical they are.

Wang Ch'ung spends a lot of effort in disproving the obvious
fallacies of the belief, and in demanding that its assumptions
should be thoroughly examined and their necessary consequences sought out. For example, he asks what is the nature of
heaven that it should be willing and able to produce thunder for
the reasons alleged, and he points to the illogicalities in assuming
that it does so. When he treats the question constructively, he
does so by way of analogy, examination of the evidence and
experiment; he calls on the forces of Yin and Yang as natural
forces that control the world:

Try pouring two litres of water into an iron-smelter's furnace;
the steam will explode and burst out with the sound, as it were,
of thunder; and if anyone happens to be nearby he will
certainly get his body burnt. Now, let us suppose that heaven
and earth form the furnace (and very spacious it will be); that
the force of Yang makes the fire (and very intense it will be);
and that the clouds and the rain form the water (and very
abundant it will be). If these elements are in discord; if they
explode and hit one another, how can violence be avoided? If a
man is struck or injured, how can he avoid being killed?
    Or, take the case of a smelter who is casting iron; he makes
his mould of clay, and once this is set hard by heat, the iron is
held down; but if it is not, the iron may hit somebody by

bursting out, and that person's skin will be scorched and peel off. Now, the heat of Yang's energy has far deeper intensity than that of a smelter's furnace; when the force of Yin stimulates, it does so with far greater humidity than that of clay; and if Yang's force hits a man, he will suffer far more than the pain of being scorched or flayed.

In the remainder of the essay, Wang Ch'ung draws attention to the verifiable evidence that may be observed on the bodies of those who have died as a result of thunder or lightning; he refers to experiments made by casting red-hot stones into a well, and seeks some analogy in terms of human fever and colds. He ends his argument, perhaps somewhat smugly (but no more smugly than Lucretius), by writing: 'There are thus five reasons for verifying the hypothesis that thunder derives from fire, while those who maintain that it derives from the anger of heaven cannot adduce a single proof; we may therefore conclude that their statement is nonsense.'

As the centuries passed, more and more attention was being paid to the set forms of society and behaviour, and to the value of precedents in determining decisions of state. The process is sometimes termed the 'Victory of Confucianism', and it marks a characteristic difference between the frame of mind of the western and the eastern Han periods, i.e. between the last two centuries BC and the first two centuries AD. At the outset of the Han dynasty there is detectable a freshness of outlook, free of inhibition, with a sense of innovation; by the middle of the first century AD there was a conscious reliance on forms of the past, and a search for support in tradition. The intellect was taking first place, before the call of mythology. Hopes of immortality were no longer expressed only in imaginative paintings of a blessed land, but in the highly sophisticated symbols of a cosmic scheme. In art, the contrast may be seen by comparing the iconography of the third century BC with the more polished, but often more mundane, creations of the third century AD.

These changes accompanied further signs of a greater attention to the intellect, as may be seen in the growth of the volume of literature and the increased number of literate men in government service. Since 124 BC the state had been taking deliberate steps to encourage learning, as a means of recruiting and training men as officials. By the end of western Han such policies had already achieved marked results; by the middle of the second century AD familiarity with select works of literature was forming a hallmark of that class of men who were to control China's destinies. The cleavage in the attitudes of western and eastern Han is seen alike in dynastic terms. Four hundred years separated the political inexperience and experiments of Ch'in from the sophisticated institutions of imperial government of the closing decades of Han. A new view of the state and its sovereign powers had emerged, that drew on traditions of the deep past as a means of reforming contemporary abuses. The process reached culmination in the expressions of faith by Wang Mang, single emperor of the Hsin Dynasty (AD 9–23). His protestations looked to the old kingdom of Chou (traditionally 1122–256 BC) for political and social ideals; he sought to substitute these for the appeal to material force and worldly success that had characterised the Ch'in empire and the first century or so of western Han. In doing so, Wang Mang left a heritage for the restored emperors of eastern Han to enjoy and transmit to the future.

But by the closing decades of the dynasty a further change may be detected, in the prevalent views of a number of learned writers. Few could fail to note how the traditional values, espoused in eastern Han, had failed to prevent social and political instability; this weakness was shortly to give rise to the split of China into the Three Kingdoms. At this time, Hsün Yüeh (148–209), to name but one man, had recognised the need to reconcile Confucius' ethics with 'Legalist' principles, in order to preserve the essential features of the body politic. Under the leadership of Ts'ao Ts'ao, virtual founder of the kingdom of Wei (AD 220–65), it was the emphasis on discipline rather than ideals that was most strongly marked.

In the treatment of individual topics which follows, an attempt will be made to describe the approaches of naturalist, humanist, authoritarian and rationalist thinkers. In so far as Wang Ch'ung's views will usually appear towards the close of each chapter, they may seem to carry greater weight than is their due. For, being couched in a more systematic and logical way than those of other philosophers, they may appear to have been attractive and persuasive; being placed chronologically after the opinions of others, Wang Ch'ung's critique may seem to have been the final pronouncement on a particular problem or subject. But it should

16

by no means be supposed that Wang Ch'ung's opinions were received with general approbation. So far from being accepted by his contemporaries, he remained exceptional; so far from attracting support, he was relegated to obscurity for several centuries.

2
The gods

During the Ch'in and Han periods the Chinese served a multiplicity of gods and spirits. There were the holy spirits (*shen*) attached to particular localities; there were the lords of natural forces such as wind and rain; and there were the gods who presided over occupational skills such as those of the kitchen or the spinning wheel. In addition there were the *kuei*, sometimes identified as the spirits of the dead that derived from human beings (see Chapter 3). Superior to all these categories there were the *ti* of the various divisions of the universe, and *t'ien*, or heaven, who came to be regarded as the highest power of all. At the close of the second century BC the state also instituted worship to the two major powers of *hou t'u* (lord, or queen, of the earth) and *t'ai i*, the Grand Unity or unifier (see Chapter 12).

It is immediately apparent that the Chinese were not bound by a sense of exclusiveness. Rather than a monotheistic belief, there was a faith in a whole hierarchy of beings, any of whom could be worshipped simultaneously for different purposes. The motives for such service were eudaimonistic, to procure blessings and to avert calamity. There seems to have been no conscious sense of gratitude to a god or spirit in return for unsought blessings or for benefits received as a result of prayer. The nearest approximation to such impulses is perhaps seen in two respects; first, in a sense of honour due to an ancestor's spirit, rendered in proportionate measure as if he were still living; and secondly in the account that the emperor would very occasionally render to heaven of the stewardship entrusted to him on earth.

Just as the Chinese conceived human relationships in terms of a hierarchy, so too did they classify their gods in a series and conduct their worship according to such terms. Such restrictions are particularly noticeable once a temporal authority found itself involved in offering services to a variety of superior powers; of necessity it had to define its objectives and lay down its forms of worship.

Of all these deities, *ti* appears earliest in the sources of Chinese civilisation. He was the supreme god of the Shang people, whose practice of divination by means of bones and shells (see Chapter 9) led to the production of China's earliest written records (*c*. 1700 BC). To the peoples and king of Shang, *ti* was conceived as a single power, sometimes described as *shang ti* or God on High. In the literature that dates from a thousand years later, it seems that he was conceived in anthropomorphic and not in animal terms. There are references to sites on earth where *ti* 'feasted the spirits' and allusions to his abode in heaven, behind the Ch'ang-ho gate. He is credited with the powers of a supreme ruler over the world of nature and man, and he is regarded as being willing to help man.

But the concept of a single supreme power known as *ti* or *shang ti* was accompanied by that of a whole multiplicity of lesser gods, also described as *ti*. There was a belief that, once dead, those who had reigned as the kings of Shang on earth became *ti* and shared an existence with *shang ti*, as participants in the same order of creation. In so far as these lesser *ti* had previously been members of the human world, there remained a direct link between them and the realm of man. Communication could be achieved partly through the descendants of these *ti* directly and partly through specialist intermediaries blessed with occult powers.

At this early stage the animal world possessed a special function in mythology and in art which it was destined to lose from perhaps 700 BC. Until then the higher animals served as members of the same order of existence as that of *ti* and the spirits of the deceased ancestors. They were admired for their nobility and grandeur, and they too acted as a link between the two worlds. This was at a stage before animals came to be depicted in conflict with man or at the mercy of man, or as objects whom man wished to propitiate.

At a later stage, perhaps in the fourth century BC, a new concept of *ti* enters in. This was due in part to the impact of a philosophy which saw the universe in terms of five orders (see Chapter 4), which comprehended all things, spiritual and temporal, earthly and heavenly. To suit the growing urge to conceive and classify all beings in such terms, five *ti* were named for special honour. They were associated with the five colours, likewise conceived as being characteristic of the five orders of the universe; in this way the five *ti* of green, red, yellow, white and finally black came into special prominence. In time these became the objects of worship in the cults of state during the second and first centuries BC. Of these five *ti*, the god or power of yellow (Huang ti) appears conspicuously in mythology, religion and philosophy in a number of significant ways, of which two deserve mention. In mythology Huang ti is named as the earliest ruler of the world in the remote past; and just before 100 BC we hear of Huang ti being invoked as a means of acquiring immortality.

T'ien, or heaven, had been regarded as the supreme deity by the house of Chou, whose kings had ruled in part of China after the Shang dynasty (traditionally from 1122 to 256 BC). Conceived anthropomorphically, *t'ien* was regarded as a power which was distinct from that of the spirits of the deceased kings. Whereas the kings of Shang had enjoyed a direct association with the world of *ti*, heaven was an external power which could, if it wished to do so, confer authority on a new house and its kings. These in turn claimed to be the Sons of Heaven. Such a belief was encouraged as a means of supporting the authority of those kings. However, from the eighth century onwards, China saw the rise of a large number of leaders and rulers of small domains, whose powers depended on their exercise of force to conquer their rivals. In such a situation the claims that the kings of Chou were acting as the nominees of *t'ien* rang hollow. However, as none of the contending kings or rulers of the other states could exercise unchallenged dominion or rule over more than a portion of Chinese territory, they could no more convincingly assert that they had received a mandate from a supreme authority. It was only from the first century BC that it became both possible and appropriate for an emperor of a united China to revive the concept of ruling thanks to the authority conferred by *t'ien*. Probably from 31 BC onwards the worship of *t'ien* was introduced as part of the cults observed by the emperor and his officials.

Heaven thus became an integral part of the superhuman support upon which the emperors of China rested their claim to rule. It was seen as the patron deity of the old kings of Chou, whose example came to be held in respect and admiration, as indeed it had been by Confucius and his disciples. Heaven also featured in the scheme of cosmology formulated by Tung Chung-shu. It was a power which maintained a fatherly interest in the activities of man and kept the conduct of the ruler of man, heaven's own son, under constant surveillance. Heaven thus stood in a special place both in the ethical precepts of Confucius himself and in the system which found a place for imperial government within the universe, and which has been known as Han Confucianism.

Our knowledge of the Chinese concept of the *shen*, or holy spirits, derives from sources of very different types. The first five chapters of the *Classic of the Mountains and the Lakes* (*Shan-hai ching*) call on pre-Han traditions and consist of a list of the holy sites inhabited by these beings. But in the *Huai-nan-tzu*, of the latter half of the second century BC, we read of the holy spirits in a completely different context. Here the authors were attempting to explain the wonders and workings of the universe partly in terms of mythology and partly in terms of scientific hypothesis. Their outlook was that of the school which assigned greater importance to conformity with the order of nature than to the need to organise mankind. In general, widely differing as these sources may be in time and purport, the concept of the *shen* is similar.

The holy spirits are conceived in multiplicity. They are associated with special sites on the hills, and the powers that they exercise may be localised. Some of them may be conceived as acting within or controlling natural forces and phenomena such as wind or rain. They are described as being of hybrid forms, in which the bodies of, e.g., bird and dragon, or horse and dragon, are combined. In many cases they possess human heads or faces surmounting the bodies of ox, sheep, snake or bird. The following citation may serve as an example of how the holy spirits are described in the *Classic of the Mountains and the Lakes:*

> Altogether there are fourteen mountains in the third stage, south, stretching for 6530 leagues, from Mount T'ien-yü to Mount Nan-yü. The holy spirits of those hills all have dragons' bodies with human faces; they are worshipped with the sacrifice of a white dog and with prayer, and with rice used for the offering of grain.

Or else:

Altogether there are nine mountains in the third stage, east, stretching for 6900 leagues from Mount Shih-hu to Mount Wu-kao. The holy spirits are of the form of human bodies with rams' horns and they are worshipped with the sacrifice of a ram and with millet. When these spirits appear, there will be a disaster brought about by wind, rain or flood.

Similarly, in the *Huai-nan-tzu*'s account of the topographical characteristics of named districts, we read of spirits with human faces and dragons' bodies, but without feet; or there are those with human heads and dragons' bodies who beat upon their bellies to make music. In the more prosaic chapters of the history of the Han dynasty there is a long list of the shrines which existed at the outset of the Ch'in period, with some references to the services that were rendered there. In addition to the shrines attached to special localities, at many of which blood sacrifices were offered, there were shrines dedicated to the sun, moon and planets, to the lord of the winds and the master of the rain.

Many of these spirits are as capable of visiting mankind with evil as with good. Man can attempt to assimilate himself to their persons, by consuming part of their flesh or donning some of their fur. If such measures or forms of worship are acceptable, a man may obtain freedom from disease, fear or bewilderment, or he may be saved from the evils of hunger. Positive blessings may even ensue, such as a promise of descendants, or the general benefit of peace and stability. Evil results that can be brought about by the holy spirits may include floods of such immensity that they affect a whole province; or they may make it necessary to call upon the whole population to serve as labourers or in the armed forces and suffer consequent hardships. In one particular case, the mere sight of such a spirit or creature is dangerous. This one is described as being a large serpent with a crimson head and white body, whose sound is that of cattle; the merest glimpse can reduce the whole district to drought.

The holy spirits are thus manifest in the form of hybrid animals. Man may serve them or pacify them by worship, such as the offering of grain or the sacrifice of living creatures; the potential harm that they can perpetrate may be exorcised by specialists such as shamans. The extent of the services rendered at their shrines could vary considerably, depending on the motive, wealth or status of the worshipper. A critic who was writing towards the middle of the first century BC drew a contrast between the humble, but sincere, offerings of the past and the lavish, but ostentatious, ceremonies of his own day. He looked back to an idealised past in which ordinary folk presented their offerings of fish or beans, attending to their religious duties in spring and autumn. In those days the number of shrines and religious occasions was restricted, corresponding with social rank, and people did not undertake journeys beyond their homes for these purposes. But in his own time things had altered, very much for the worse. Rich folk voiced their prayers at holy mountains and to the rivers, slaughtering their cattle, striking up music from their drums, or with a show laid on by their actors or by puppets. Those who were not so well off served the lords of the south or the roads, or worshipped at the terrace of the clouds, over above the water, where they sacrificed their sheep or dogs, and enjoyed the music of strings and pipes. The poorest classes of all offered their chickens and pigs or aromatic herbs.

In a document that was written shortly after the establishment of the Han dynasty we find a criticism of the habits and austerities practised by those who sought mystical experiences or other benefits in the mountains. A fairly late text, of the fourth century AD (the *Pao-p'u-tzu*), refers to the powers possessed by the spirits of the mountains. It describes the nature of the ascent to holy mountains and their attendant dangers; for precautions are necessary so as to conform with the ways of these spirits:

> All those who desire to compound drugs, to avoid the turmoil of the world or to live the life of a hermit make their way into the mountains, but if they do not understand the right way of doing so they will often meet with disaster. That is why the proverb tells us of the white bones that lie scattered at the foot of Mount Hua. It is referring to those who comprehend only one aspect of a problem, and are not able to take account of a comprehensive scale; although they are trying to find a way of life, they in fact die a death of violence.
>
> For, whether they are large or small, all mountains are informed by the divine powers of holy spirits, great or small in proportion to the size of the mountain. Calamity unerringly follows for those who enter the mountains without knowing the correct means of doing so. They may fall a victim of disease, or injury and be terrified; or they may see lights and

shadows, or hear strange sounds. Or it may so happen that large timbers will of their own accord fall upon them, at a time when no winds blow; or mighty rocks will hurtle down and crush them, without apparent cause. Or else a man may wander around in a daze, and tumble into a pit; or he may fall a victim to tiger, wolf or wild beast, or to men of evil intent. So the mountains should not be entered without due thought. You should choose the third or the ninth months, which are the times when they are properly open; and within those months you should choose a day that is propitious and an hour that is felicitous. If you cannot wait for one of these months, then at least choose the right day and time. And all those who enter the hills should first purify themselves for seven days; they should not pass through filth or corruption, and they should carry with them the talismans for the ascent of the hills.

There is also the idea of the hierarchy of the spirits. In the *Huai-nan-tzu* we read of two holy spirits who acted on behalf of *ti*, by linking their arms and keeping watch over the night. A number of other passages likewise suggest that the *shen* and the *kuei* were of an inferior order of being to *ti*, and a writer of the second century AD distinguished a series of *shen* whose hierarchy corresponded with human hierarchies. Thus some holy spirits were entitled to be worshipped by the son of heaven or by noblemen; others were said to be the preserve of shamans; and there were those who could be the object of prayer, hope or fear on the part of lesser mortals.

At an earlier stage the hierarchical concept had been formally enshrined in one of the compendia that laid down the correct procedures for all types of behaviour and conduct. These rules specified at which shrines the son of heaven should worship, and which could be approached by noblemen or prominent officials. It may be noted that a formal approach of this type, whether idealised or real, is a product of that school of thought which accorded first priority to the organisation of man and regulation of his relationships.

Particular attention should perhaps be paid to twelve special *shen* who were regarded as having powers that were peculiar to each of the twelve months. Either these spirits themselves, or the intermediaries who were capable of making contact with them, were depicted around the edge of the earliest surviving Chinese manuscript to be preserved on silk (probably of the third or the fourth century BC). Despite the obscurities of the manuscript it seems clear that some of the figures are of hybrid form.

Reference will be made below (see Chapter 5) to the concept of twelve as divisions of the heavens or the universe; one of the major ceremonies of state of the first and second centuries AD also concerned this idea. This took the form of a battle, enacted by twelve spirits who were presented in animal garb; their function was that of exorcists who devoured ten baleful influences, thus affording protection to mankind.

The ideas of the holy spirits spring from ancient Chinese mythology. In their worship there participated the emperor and his officials, intermediaries such as shamans, and undistinguished members of society, whose wanderings in the hills could often bring them face to face with these powers. References to these deities and their depictions suggest that two principles affected the growth of the belief. First, mankind was feeling an impulse to identify itself with the animal world; secondly, man was transforming his image of mighty beings from animal into human form. Suggestions of both of these motives appear in literature, mythology and ceremonial practice.

3

The life hereafter

There is no complete statement of the beliefs that the Chinese
entertained regarding a life hereafter. Allusions and fables
abound in mythology, but there is no solemn drama or saga of
sacred literature which corresponds with the conquest of death
that is enshrined in the Christian tradition. Nor is there a logical
presentation of the arguments for a future life or a visionary
description such as may be found in the *Phaedo*.

Our information derives from the literature of the learned and
the creations of artists that adorn the tombs of the rich. Both of
these types of evidence necessarily reflect only a part of the whole
tradition of Chinese belief, and they cannot be expected to state
explicitly the assumptions that were generally accepted by the
majority of the population. The literature of the Han period was
in the main compiled for the sake of men of letters rather than for
those who tilled the fields; and although the culture of Han China
drew on widely disparate elements from different ethnic traditions, a marked tendency towards standardisation had already set
in. The embellishment of tombs and their symbols were chosen
to suit the outlook of the educated official who prided himself on
his connections with the capital city of the north. The more
earthly faith of those who inhabited swamp, forest or mountain
may be identified in some elements of Chinese mythology; but
in the mortuary art of the higher classes of Han society such
beliefs have been weakened in the face of accepted dogma.

It is therefore likely that we know of only some of the many
beliefs of the Han period regarding death and the cults directed to
ensuring survival. In these, a general distinction may be drawn
between several objectives. First, there was a wish to prolong the
life of the flesh on earth as long as possible. Secondly, there was a
desire to effect the entry of one element of a deceased person's
soul into another world or paradise; this was sometimes
conceived as a world of the *hsien*, or immortal beings. A further

concept envisaged the need to provide as effectively as possible for a second element of the soul, whose destiny was somewhat different.

The two different elements of the soul of man which the Chinese distinguished were known as the *hun* and the *p'o*. By informing the material body and maintaining it in a state of harmony, they served to keep a human being alive; death occurred when the three elements of *hun*, *p'o* and body were separated. During life, the *hun* and the *p'o* had different functions. The *hun* corresponded to a power that could direct activity and was capable of spiritual experience and intellectual energy. The *p'o* enabled the body to take action and exercise its limbs, for it infused strength and movement into its various members.

Normally the *p'o* and the *hun* would separate at death. The immediate reactions of a dead person's relatives would be to attempt to restrain the *hun* from embarking on a journey that was regarded as being somewhat perilous. Only when such attempts had been shown to be ineffective would the mourners accept the inevitable and proceed with another type of service, designed to escort the *hun* to its destination as expeditiously and safely as possible. That destination was probably identified as the realm of *ti*.

Alternatively it could be regarded as the world of the *hsien*. The character and habits of these immortals are explicitly described in inscriptions made on a certain type of bronze mirror used as a talisman for the soul. They lived aloft, impervious to old age, slaking their thirst on the springs of jade and assuaging their hunger on the fruit of the jujube tree. They floated aloft below the heavens and roamed around all quarters of the globe; in their wanderings over famous mountains they would pluck the Herb of Life. The world of the immortals is sometimes depicted in the fresco paintings of Han tombs.

If all was well, the *p'o* was thought to remain with the body; services were designed to ensure that it was provided with all the comforts that might be needed to maintain a reasonable style of existence; these comforts were envisaged in terms of human and material values, e.g. utilities or consumable stores. Such measures were designed to discourage the *p'o* from leaving the body once it had been laid to rest. For, were the *p'o* to leave the body and return to the scene of its previous incarnation, it might be given to venting its anger upon living persons, in order to procure a more active and diligent service than had been its lot. Souls or ghosts who returned to the land of the living in this way were sometimes called *kuei*, or demons. This term conveys a *double entendre*, as a pun; for a different word, also pronounced *kuei*, means to return to one's home; the expression can be regarded as an equivalent of the term 'revenant'. The strength of the belief in the ability of souls to interfere violently in the lives of the living is testified by Wang Ch'ung's strong reaction and arguments (see p. 35 below).

In certain circumstances the *p'o* was thought to leave the body for another abode, which was known as the Yellow Springs (*huang ch'üan*). In that case it would find itself in the company of 'that multitude which no man can number' already arrived at another shore. To enable it to retain its identity, the *p'o* could be provided with symbols of the status that it had previously enjoyed during its co-existence with the *hun* and with the body. Such symbols could include the seals that proclaimed the titles of honour or the offices that the dead man had held; or there would be figurines of attendants who had escorted him in life in accordance with the dignity of his station or his wealth.

Different means were necessary to achieve these different objectives, but it is possible that some confusion occurred in practice. Thus, it could be hoped that life on earth might be prolonged by bodily exercises or disciplines that included the ingestion of elixirs or drugs. These could either be gathered straight from the creations of the natural world or artificially compounded by man. At the same time the virtues of the elixir appear in a totally different context, that of searching for an entry to the world of the future. Similarly, the provision of valuable material goods as funeral furnishings may have been designed to achieve several of the purposes that are mentioned above. (For the services rendered to the dead, see Chapter 11 below.)

One further concept which enters into the Han views of the life hereafter will be considered in greater detail below (see Chapter 6). This is the idea that one type of living creature can be transformed into another and thereby attain a renewed form of existence. The concept sometimes features in the symbolism or iconography of funerary furnishings.

In general, it is possible to distinguish four ideas of paradise or the life after death. One approach was by way of the Blessed Isles of the East; a second way was explained in terms of the whole structure of being that underlies the universe. A third idea, which is in parallel to the paradise of the eastern isles, was that of the magical realm of the west, over which the Queen Mother of the West presided. Finally there was the somewhat vague notion of the land of the Yellow Springs with its host of underworld officials, to which the *p'o* might find itself relegated.

By the Han period the belief that the Blessed Isles of the East could provide an entrée to the next world included a number of the elements that have already been mentioned. The elixir of long life could be tasted there; the islands could also act as a route towards renewed existence in the world of *ti*. Different traditions give the number of the islands as three, four or five. That their names sometimes include the word *hu*, i.e. vase, may indicate some basic idea of the symmetrical shape of these magical mountains that arose from the sea. The best-known name of one of the islands is P'eng-lai, which subsequently came to do duty as a general term for paradise; it appears in Japanese mythology under the guise of Hōrai.

From a number of passages something may be learnt of the qualities and virtues of these islands, and of P'eng-lai in particular. They were magical islands, where the buildings and the trees were made of precious jewels. Living creatures were marked off from those of this world conspicuously, for they were all clothed in pure white; and they lived from everlasting unto everlasting. But the difficulty lay in achieving access to these islands which tended to disappear, mysteriously, the nearer that an intrepid mariner approached. Of some importance is the connection between these islands and the authority of *ti*, as may be seen in the following passage, taken from a collection known as the *Lieh-tzu*; while being compiled in perhaps the third or fourth century AD it certainly drew on a much earlier tradition and mythology.

> East of P'o-hai, we know not how many thousands and millions of leagues away, there is a mighty abyss, in truth the bottomless vale, with no base beneath, and named 'The way to the void'. The waters from the eight corners and the nine divisions of the universe and the River of the Milky Way all flow into this valley which grows neither larger nor smaller. There are five mountains there, called Tai-yü, Yüan-chiao, Fang-hu, Ying-chou and P'eng-lai. These mountains measure

thirty thousand leagues in height and in girth, and there is a flat plane at the summit which stretches for nine thousand leagues. They lie at a distance of seventy thousand leagues from one another, but they may be thought to be like neighbours. The terraces and the towers at the top are all made of gold and jade; the animals and the birds are all pure white. Trees of pearl and precious gems flourish there, with flowers and fruit of a delicious taste. None of those who eat of them grow old or die, and the persons who live there are all of a breed of immortal beings or holy men. In the course of a single day and night they fly from one island to another, times without number.

But there is nothing to which the roots of the five mountains are linked or fastened, and they wander up and down and here and there following the tides and the waves; not for a moment are they able to stand firm. The immortal beings and the holy men found this troublesome and laid a plaint before God (*ti*). And God was afraid that the islands would float away beyond the western limits of the world, and that he would lose the homes of all these saints. So He commanded Yü Ch'iang to order fifteen giant turtles to hold the islands fast by raising their heads. The turtles took their turns at this duty; they formed themselves into three teams and relieved each other once in every sixty thousand years; and for the first time the mountains stood firm.

Whatever the form of this myth may have been, we hear of kings of the fourth century BC who set out to find these islands and procure the drug of immortality therefrom. But it was always said that the islands would recede and disappear, like a mirage. The First Ch'in emperor had heard about the islands from a number of specialists in the occult. Rather than risk a personal failure and the humiliation of setting out and not finding them, he had a number of youngsters, of both sexes, despatched on his behalf; they blamed the winds for their failure to find the islands.

It may seem strange that the First Ch'in emperor should have been said to entertain hopes of this type, for he is depicted as a man of highly practical motives, who stopped at little in order to forge his empire and impose a ruthless government on his subjects. Possibly the Chinese historians were deliberately trying to represent him as being nonetheless gullible, and subject to charlatans.

They provide a similar record for Wu ti, who reigned as Han emperor from 141 to 87; he is shown as being highly susceptible to the pretensions of a number of specialists who claimed to be masters of secret arts. Li Shao-chün, who was one of these, counselled the emperor to seek the blessings of P'eng-lai, of which he claimed first-hand knowledge and experience. He advised Wu ti to render due service to the god of the stove, in order to persuade certain strange creatures, possibly of a spiritual nature, to come to him. With their help, cinnabar could be transformed into gold; from that precious metal there could be fashioned vessels for eating and drinking; and the years of the emperor's life would be prolonged. Once that had been achieved an approach could be made to the immortal beings of P'eng-lai, in the ocean; and once he had seen them he could perform certain major ceremonies and sacrifices, with the result that he would not die. Li Shao-chün continued:

> Once when I was travelling by sea I saw the master An-ch'i, who feeds on outsize jujubes that are as large as gourds. An-ch'i is one of the immortals who is in direct contact with P'eng-lai, and who admits strangers to his presence at his own whim.

In all fairness, the remainder of the story, as related in the Standard Histories, must be added. When, shortly after this interview, Li Shao-chün died, the emperor refused to believe the news, trusting as he did that the maestro's skills could preclude such a demise. He declared that he was sure that Li Shao-chün had been transformed into another creature and moved elsewhere, and he immediately ordered a provincial official to be trained in Li's arts. There were also other occasions when we learn that Li's advice to seek the joys and blessings of P'eng-lai had not been lost on Wu ti, despite Li's death. From about 130 to perhaps 98 BC Wu ti sent several expeditions to find the islands of the eastern sea; on one occasion he personally visited the east coast of China in the hope of catching a glimpse of those magical sites. Reference will be made below (see Chapter 11) to the depiction of P'eng-lai in a painting which probably acted as a talisman to convey a spirit to a world of eternity. That painting was found in a tomb which was sealed shortly after 168 BC, and may illustrate the strength of the belief at that time.

It seems reasonable to suppose that the eastern way to paradise features in Chinese thought and imagery in the centuries before the institution of the Ch'in empire in 221 BC. There is no way of determining how widespread the belief was, or for how long it occupied a significant place in Chinese intimations of immortality. Certainly it should not be supposed that other concepts, which will be described immediately, displaced a faith in P'eng-lai and its properties.

From perhaps 50 BC, or somewhat earlier, other considerations enter into the question of the life after death. By then several attempts had been made to formulate a major concept of the universe and its constituent elements, which were regarded as the interlocking parts of a whole. It will be shown below (see Chapter 4) how these theories concerned the nature and shape of the world and the sequences of observed movements in the universe. They derived from observation and they gave rise to speculation; they were concerned with the relative positions of heaven, earth and man, and their relationships. However, these theories did not of their own accord hold a place for the dead. Herein lay perhaps their greatest weakness, for those whose view of man was not limited to the life of the flesh.

Evidence that at present goes back to about 50 BC shows how some Chinese were deliberately seeking to forge a symbolical link between this concept of the universe and the life of human beings after death, in the realm of the immortals. The talismans that were used for the purpose depended on the acceptance of ideas that will be described below (see Chapter 4); it is therefore necessary to defer a description of these beautiful objects until later (see Chapter 11). It may be noted here that not only did these talismans seek to provide a bridge for the passage of the soul from the seen universe to the unknown world. They also sought to reconcile conflicting concepts of cosmology; they may also have acted as a symbolical means of placing a deceased person within the most favourable cosmic concept that could be imagined.

The search for paradise in the realm of the Queen Mother of the West (Hsi wang mu) is an even later development. Although the Queen features in Chinese literature from the fourth century BC, and is mentioned as a donor of the elixir by a poet of the second century BC (Ssu-ma Hsiang-ju), it is not until the first century AD that Chinese iconography regularly alludes to this means of attaining immortality.

A number of elements are mingled in the mythology and cult of the Queen, which was destined to be taken to much greater lengths after the Han period. In the early stages she presides over a magical world situated where the sun sets; she fills a role as a partner with privileged kings of the earth and later with her own consort, King Father of the East. Her meetings with those partners parallels other fables of Chinese mythology which show how the seasonal meetings of certain pairs of individuals are essential for the continuation of the world order. The Queen is portrayed as a donor of the elixir of long life or of immortality; in iconography she is depicted with certain characteristic attributes and attendants.

In the earliest texts the Queen Mother of the West is mentioned along with other primeval figures who were associated with the creation of the universe and man, such as Fu Hsi or Huang ti. She is timeless, none knowing her beginning or her end. Sometimes she is described as a hybrid creature, with the tail of a leopard and the teeth of a tiger. She wears a crown, which is the symbol of her power to maintain the continuity of the universal cycles of being; she commands some of the constellations.

The realm of the Queen is described in vivid imagery, as the 'mountains of jade' or the 'mountain of the turtles'; it is linked with the magical site of K'un-lun. Somewhat exceptionally, the Queen is described in the following passage as dwelling in the bowels of the earth. Although this text did not reach its present form until the fourth century AD, it is probably based on much earlier material:

South of the western lake, by the shores of the flowing sands, behind the Red River and before the Black River there is a great mountain called 'The heights of K'un-lun'. There are spirits abiding there with human faces and the bodies of tigers, striped and with tails, white in all cases. Below, there are the depths of the Jo River which encircles the spot. Without, there is the mountain of the flaming fire, and when an object or creature is cast therein it is immediately burnt. There is a person who wears a crown (*sheng*) on the head, with the teeth of a tiger and the tail of a leopard; she dwells in a cave and is named 'Queen Mother of the West'. On this mountain there are found all manner of living creatures.

There are various forms of the myth of the Queen's meeting with her partners. In the earliest versions, a king of part of China (Mu, king of Chou) journeys to the far west to meet her and is so enthralled with the joys of her world that he is strongly tempted to forswear his kingdom and his earthly responsibilities and to stay with her for ever and ever. In the later versions of the story, which were not compiled until the latter part of the third century AD, her meeting was with no less a monarch than Wu ti, of Han, who, as has been seen, was an avid seeker of immortality. Here the tale has been elaborated in a number of significant ways. In these versions it is the Queen who undertakes the journey to earth, rather than the other way about. In the earlier stages of the myth the king of Chou had been beguiled by banquets and the two partners had exchanged songs and gifts. In the later versions she is received by Wu ti, after considerable preparation and a ritual of cleansing. She arrives at the tryst upon the appointed hour, attended by her trusted birds, to be greeted with the kindling of a nine-branched lamp. Of considerable importance is the dating of the meeting, which is fixed at the seventh day of the seventh month; for this day is marked in other elements of Chinese myth and religion as one of the most important annual festivals, that heralded a new phase in the regular cycle of the world's growth (see p. 62).

Sculptures from a tomb in east China, of perhaps the third century AD, provide further details of the Queen. Here she is partnered by a consort who may be identified as the King Father of the East and thus stands apart from humanity, along with the Queen. The two are depicted at the heads of columns or mountains, which perhaps serve two purposes. First, they may emphasise the seclusion of these beings and the difficulty of access; for the columns are so shaped that ascent by normal means is well-nigh impossible. Secondly, the depiction may symbolise the axial tree that links the realms of earth and heaven, springing from K'un-lun, the centre of the world. The portrayal of the Queen at the summit of a column or mountain may be contrasted with the reference cited above to her dwelling in a cave.

One of the earliest references to the Queen's gift of immortality is anything but complimentary. A poet who was writing in 130–120 BC sees no joy in living for ten thousand generations in the manner that is ascribed to her. But at about the same time there is a tale of a self-defeating attempt to steal the drug of deathlessness from the Queen. It is possible that a tomb which may be dated to the second half of the first century BC (that of Pu Ch'ien-ch'iu) includes in its paintings the earliest known attempt to portray the Queen for symbolical purposes. By the second century AD she had won a firm place in iconography, whether in mirrors, sculptures, or, in one case, a screen made of jade (dated 174). Characteristic features of her depiction will be described below, with reference to the practical steps taken by way of service or to seek for the blessed gift of immortality (see Chapter 11).

Ideas of the Yellow Springs (*huang ch'üan*) are somewhat vague. The expression is used by a few authors to indicate underground sources of water that provide refreshment for various species of vermin. There are also two early references in which the Yellow Springs feature as a home for the dead, where meetings may take place. As opposed to the other ideas of immortality, the concept of the Yellow Springs thus seems to include the idea of a corporate existence shared by human beings after death. A Han poet wrote of the dead, lying asleep below the Yellow Springs, never to awake in a thousand years.

Possibly life in the Yellow Springs was regarded as being somewhat dismal, in a gloomy abode that knew no joys. There may even be hints that it was thought to be peopled by a society of a human type, with its normal degrees of hierarchy, with officials whose leave was requisite for certain activities, and a presiding Queen or ruler who required propitiation. It is also possible that it was the afterworld of the Yellow Springs that one or two statesmen, of whom anecdotes are told, had in mind. In one such anecdote, one senior official was urging his colleague to proceed with steps to depose a newly acceded emperor. The latter had shown himself to be unworthy of his charge, owing to his profligate and dissolute behaviour. 'If you fail to take the necessary steps,' the statesman asked his colleague, 'how will you face the previous emperor "below the earth"?'

One further idea regarding life after death occurs in connection with the services that an emperor performed; this will be mentioned in that context below (see Chapter 12). This was the belief that Huang ti, the Yellow Emperor, had achieved immortality himself and was able to act as an intermediary on behalf of others who desired it.

These beliefs were often merged. There developed a number of ways of seeking either for life everlasting or for immortality in another world, or for satisfying the spirits of the dead with suitable comforts. There was no reason why an individual should limit his precautions to those that served a single purpose or followed from one particular belief. Many Chinese would take steps to meet a number of eventualities or to provide for a continuity of existence in several of the realms whose existence was postulated.

Some of these beliefs could lead to costly funeral rites as a necessary part of the precautions that were due. There were those who rejected the beliefs either on grounds of the expenses that were thus incurred or on grounds of reason. Before the imperial period there had been philosophers such as Mo ti who had argued against the wisdom of providing expensive funeral services, on the grounds of economy; such views were reiterated at times throughout the Han period. But we must wait for Wang Ch'ung (AD 27–c. 100) for a sustained argument that springs from scepticism and an attempt at objective examination. Like Lucretius, Wang Ch'ung was in part setting out to free his contemporaries from their fears; in this particular case he was concerned with fear of the harm that spirits of the dead (*kuei*, or revenants) might wreak on their return to earth, to walk in the company of men.

Wang Ch'ung discusses the question on a number of occasions, and his chapter 'On the nature of death' (*Lun ssu*) forms the fullest expression of his views, set out in logical, workmanlike fashion. He endeavours to disprove the commonly accepted belief that on death a human being becomes a spirit, that the spirits of the dead possess the power of cognition and communication, and that by these and other means the spirits of the dead can harm living persons.

What evidence, Wang Ch'ung asks, is there to show that anything is left after the corruption of the body, and if there were, could it be recognisable?

Take a sack and fill it with grain; it will then be rigid; you can stand it on end, and from its shape it will be recognised as

36

being a sack of grain from a distance. But suppose that the sack is pierced. Out trickles the grain; the sack is spoilt and the grain lies abandoned, and nobody will be able to recognise it even if they do see it again.

Wang Ch'ung expostulates that the claims made by human beings to observe the spirits of the dead cannot be substantiated. If indeed the dead can become spirits, he argues, and can be observed, then they would become visible not in single numbers as is claimed but in their thousands and myriads at every turn of the road. Finally he writes:

The nature of heaven and earth is such that while it is possible to renew a living fire, it is not possible to set an extinguished fire alight again. While it is possible for a living person to be revived, it is not possible to bring a dead person into existence again. Since it is not possible to rekindle extinguished ashes, we have considerable doubts whether a dead person can be restored again, in the body. As, once a fire is extinguished it cannot be set alight again, it is clear, *a fortiori*, that a dead person cannot become a spirit.

Wang Ch'ung is equally insistent that the dead can possess no power of cognition, any more than human beings can do so before birth. Body, vital energy and strength are together needed to sustain life and maintain the power of comprehension and utterance. If that power is enfeebled by illness, it can only be expected that it is eliminated by the body's demise. Similarly, in order to inflict violence, a man depends on material agents, strength of limbs and other forces which a child cannot muster, let alone the sick, the decrepit or the dead.

Wang Ch'ung's arguments are by no means always sound. There are occasions when he draws conclusions *ex silentio*. For example, as a proof that the dead have no power of cognition or communication, he points to the failure of those who die by violence to arraign their murderers before authorities on earth. If the dead have the powers with which they are credited, he asks, why do we not hear of the spirits of a deceased husband or wife giving vent to anger or jealousy at their former spouse's remarriage?

Perhaps the last thoughts about death may be left to two speculative or mystical philosophers. One of the contributors to the *Huai-nan-tzu*, which was presented to Wu ti in 139 BC, discusses the whole question of life and death within the context of creation and the evolution of the human race. He asks who can really say whether life or death should be regarded as the more happy state of affairs; for it may be that, while hard service is the lot of the living, it is the dead who lie at rest. Accept your destiny, he urges, and do not seek either to bring the life that is given you to a close or to prevent the occurrence of death. He writes:

> When I am alive, I possess a seven foot long body, and when I die I occupy as much ground as my coffin. In my life I am just like all those beings who possess a body, in the same way as when I die I am submerged among those who have none. If I am born to live, the number of living creatures is not thereby multiplied, and when I die the earth is not enriched thereby. So how may I comprehend in which of these states there may be found joy or hatred, benefit or injury?

The second example comes from a poetic work of Chang Heng (78–139), which is entitled 'Thoughts of the mysterious' (*Ssu hsüan fu*). This was written some two and a half centuries after the passage from the *Huai-nan-tzu*, by a man who is known to history for his contributions to astronomy and the evolution of scientific instruments. His poem reveals another side to his personality, wherein there is ample room for those mysterious aspects of the universe that cannot be observed, measured or manipulated. The poem demonstrates the faith that Chang Heng reserved for irrational modes of enquiry, such as divination, and for the skills of shamans. He sees himself tracing out the principal ways to paradise that we have been considering. In the east, he climbs P'eng-lai and sojourns in the neighbouring island of Ying-chou, to pluck the Herb of Life; he sees himself undertaking this journey in the terms of a mythology that had been current for centuries. And just as others chose to take no risks and to perform the services required to procure immortality according to several creeds, so too Chang Heng sees himself visiting the Queen Mother of the West on her silvery terrace where the immortals dwell. But, wonderful and beautiful as the delights of the flesh that she provides for his entertainment may be, tempting as the chance of immortality may be, Chang Heng's heart is set elsewhere; he cannot tarry to indulge his whims or his fancies.

4

The order of nature

By the Ch'in and Han periods, the Chinese view of the order of nature comprehended three major principles: that of the Five Phases, which regulated the cycles of growth, change and decay; that of the complementary forces of Yin and Yang which interacted with those phases; and that of the single overriding presence of *tao*. The three ideas arose from different origins, which cannot be traced precisely. They recur in a number of contexts with different connotations to suit the intellectual developments of the age. Writers of most schools of thought use the expressions, without defining their terms of reference.

The term *wu hsing*, which is variously rendered as the 'Five Phases' or 'Five Elements' or 'Five Agents', is mentioned in some of the earliest texts of Chinese literature. Writing in about 100 BC, Ssu-ma Ch'ien tells of the contemporary view of the origin of the idea. Nothing, he implies in a famous passage, is known of the ideas that were current in the remote past during the time of Shen nung, who was one of the earliest lords of the world. It was Huang ti, the 'Yellow Emperor', who examined the movements of the stars, worked out their cycles and initiated the concept of the five phases that comprehend universal activity. One of Ssu-ma Ch'ien's contemporaries, who contributed to the *Huai-nan-tzu*, credited human beings of a somewhat superior type with having discerned the principle. 'The materials grown in heaven and earth are basically limited to five categories,' we read; 'the saintly men recognised the distinction of the Five Phases; as a result their efforts to keep things in order were not wasted.'

Whatever its origin may have been, the theory had gained recognition among most writers of the Han period, including rationalists such as Wang Ch'ung. By the beginning of the Christian era, it had so impressed itself upon the Chinese mind that it was taking its place in the characteristics of Chinese iconography. Traditionally, in the fourth or third century BC it was being fused with a further concept of Yin and Yang, by a naturalist philosopher named Tsou Yen; but there is no surviving text that can substantiate this claim. Certainly by the Han period it is necessary to consider the two concepts as separate aspects of a single theory.

Yin and Yang are the two complementary forces of dark and light, rest and activity, cold and heat. Each of these forces moves forward in time, progressing to a point when it is dominant; it then gives way before the advance of the other; and together they contrive by these repeated movements of ascent and descent to bring about the perpetual cycle of birth, death and rebirth. The cycle is seen as taking place in five phases or stages before repeating itself. While the translation of the expression *wu hsing* as Five Phases conveys this idea of a *perpetuum mobile*, the term *wu hsing* also carries within it the idea of five activating powers or agents, each one being imbued with its own characteristic. For reasons that will be apparent below, the term is sometimes translated as Five Elements.

It was common ground among all thinkers save the rationalists to regard the universe as a unity composed of three interacting members. The unity of these three, i.e. heaven, man and earth, was such that the universe could be viewed as a living organism, and the destiny of any one of those members was regarded as affecting that of the others. The overall pattern of Yin and Yang and the eternal cycle of the Five controlled all activities, whether in the heavens, on earth or within the realm of man. Only by comprehending such principles could one hope to understand how the heavenly bodies move in their orbits; how the produce of the earth is created and decays; and how human affairs prosper, decline and are restored. The theory was thought by many to apply to man's own artificial creations, as well as to the circumstances in which he lives or the destiny imposed upon him. The institutions that man evolves for his own benefit or to govern himself, and the organs that he creates for the exercise of temporal power, are subject to the same overriding rhythm.

The theory of Yin-Yang and the Five Phases may be regarded as a philosopher's answer to the search for permanence in a highly volatile world. Where all that can be observed is subject to change, either rapid or slow, human beings can be reconciled to their destiny, and accept that their fate is that of playing a minor role within a major whole, provided that they can discern a pattern that outlasts everything. When the only permanent feature of the universe is change, man can draw comfort if he sees himself and his destiny as parts of a universal change. In the theory of *wu hsing*, combined with Yin-Yang, Chinese philosophers were providing an answer to heart-searchings that could complement the patterns and the tales of traditional mythology.

The powers of Yin and Yang were conceived as two trends which followed one another in alternation; there was therefore no difficulty in determining their order of succession. But complexities entered in as the idea of the Five Phases developed, and difficulties arose for several reasons. The idea of the Five was applied to the rhythms or distinctions of the natural world, such as the sequence of the seasons or the spatial directions of earth. In such cases it was awkward to reconcile a fundamental series of five units with a natural series of four members. Later the scheme of the *wu hsing* was adopted as a means of classifying objects of other categories, such as the organs of the human body, or sensory perceptions. In such cases it was no less awkward to reduce all members of a category to five alone; this result was achieved by a selection of five particular colours, flavours, or odours, etc. In addition, the five material elements of wood, fire, earth, metal and water were adopted as symbols which represented each of the five phases or categories.

In time, the symbols assumed a greater degree of prominence than the phases of development themselves, and different opinions arose regarding the order in which they should properly be placed. Of the total number of possible ways in which five objects may be arrayed, two principal ones were selected; they reflect two principal attitudes towards the natural development of the world.

One school of thought saw the movements of the world of nature as the advance and decline of Yang, followed by that of Yin, in a total of five phases. In the first, Yang grows up, and in the second it enjoys its moment of maturity. In a third phase, when Yang's force has been spent and Yin's force is not yet moving, there is a moment of equilibrium. There then ensue the fourth and fifth phases, when it is the turn of Yin first to grow to maturity and then to exercise its full strength. Thereafter the cycle is repeated, apparently without allowance for an interlude of balance, before Yang's rise begins again.

This scheme is sometimes described as the 'order of mutual production', as may be illustrated by reference to the material elements adopted to symbolise the five:

Yang	rising growth	wood	green dragon
	maturity	fire	scarlet bird
Equilibrium	tranquillity	earth	(no animal symbol)
Yin	rising growth	metal	white tiger
	maturity	water	serpent and turtle

Fire arises from wood, and in turn produces ash, or earth; from earth there is produced metal, which in turn becomes liquid; and it is from the sustenance of water that wood grows.

In the foregoing scheme, each of the Five Phases is seen as an integral part of the major process of nature. In the second main sequence to be adopted by some thinkers, stress was placed on the individual strength of each of the material elements. Each one, and the phase that it symbolised, was explained as coming into existence by conquest of its predecessor, and the order of the Five is sometimes described as that of 'mutual conquest'. Thus, metal conquers wood; in its own turn it is reduced by fire. Fire is extinguished by water, whose force is dammed up by earth; and earth is subject to manipulation and control by implements made of wood. The order is thus:

> wood
> metal
> fire
> water
> earth

This order of the symbols cannot immediately be reconciled with the overriding rhythm of Yin and Yang's pulsation; if the order is interpreted in terms of nature, it implies a perpetual conflict among the elements of the material world.

In whatever order the Five Phases were understood to operate, the theory admirably suited the Chinese love of classification and hierarchy. All manner of things, whether natural or man-made, soon came to be classified in fives, so as to suit this overall scheme; to achieve such a result a certain measure of intellectual manipulation may be detected. In some cases a correlation was relatively easy, for example with the five planets, which were assigned as follows:

wood	Jupiter	east	spring
fire	Mars	south	summer
earth	Saturn	centre	
metal	Venus	west	autumn
water	Mercury	north	winter

But with other categories, whose members did not conveniently number five, distinctions had to be drawn and selections made, sometimes arbitrarily. Thus, a correlation may easily be suggested between east, south, west and north on the one hand, and wood, fire, metal and water on the other; and the four seasons fall naturally into their places. But it becomes necessary to name a fifth direction, or distinguish a fifth season, if the correspondence is to be complete. In other instances it may not always be so self-evident why five particular flavours, smells, types of grain, domestic animals or dynastic houses have been selected for assignment to one or other of the Five Phases or symbols.

It will be seen below (see Chapter 13) how the theory of the Five Phases was applied to dynastic questions and even exploited so as to harness support for a particular imperial house. It is also of some importance to note how the Five Phases affected iconography, from perhaps the middle of the first century BC onwards. The theory is seen conspicuously in the choice of four animal devices as symbols of the two phases of Yang (the green dragon, and the scarlet bird) and the two of Yin (the white tiger, and the serpent and turtle). These four symbols were usually placed correctly by artists and craftsmen, in the order whereby one phase was believed to grow naturally from its predecessor. They are incorporated in talismans designed to secure blessings of a universal nature; in some cases they may be accompanied by what may be a fifth symbol, of a mound. This may stand for earth, or for the phase which intervenes between the decline of Yang and the growth of Yin.

The Five Phases and Yin-Yang feature in the statements of view of a variety of writers of the Han period, whether they were of the persuasion that stressed the importance of nature, the duty of man or the essential role of the state. A school of Yin-Yang thought forms one of the six types of philosophy that were singled out by Ssu-ma T'an for description and comment. That author has been praised for the objective view that he took of the school; for while he agreed that it was quite correct in insisting on the inexorable effect of the cycles and rhythms of the world of nature, he criticised the excesses of fancy that could follow. Rigorous adhesion to the theory's rules, and attempts to regulate life accordingly (e.g. by insistence on a choice of actions deemed suitable for a particular season of the year), could only inspire fear. By the beginning of the Christian era, there were sixteen separate works in the imperial library which were classified as deriving from the Yin-Yang school; they amounted to 249 chapters or fascicules.

The Five Phases and Yin-Yang are also related to the Han idea of *tao*. This expression has been used by Chinese and other writers to cover a wide variety of meanings and concepts, and it is a matter of some importance to note that use of the term or even acceptance of *tao* as a principle does not necessarily imply that a particular writer or work should be classified as 'Taoist'.

Tao is known first and foremost in writings such as the *Tao-te ching* and the *Chuang-tzu* as the rule that underlies the universe and which a mystic may be able to apprehend. The *tao*, or way, is majestic, and brings into question the value of human assumptions, judgements and aspirations. The books in which this message was expounded were certainly current during the Han dynasty, and surviving manuscript copies show that there is no vital difference between those texts and the versions that are extant today. It is also known that some of those who were placed highly in the land were followers of the *tao* and its mystical path (e.g. the empress Tou, consort of Wen ti, who reigned 180–157, and mother of Ching ti who reigned 157–141).

There is a further way in which *tao* came to be used, with very different implications, which does not affect Han thought until the second century AD. This arose from the growth of a number of cults that were designed to save mankind from the immediate sufferings of the flesh. Some of the leaders of those cults exercised a commanding influence over their followers, to whom they promised relief from bodily pains, or drugs that would secure long life. Their connection with *tao* is not immediately self-evident. It was forged with the deliberate intention of defining intellectual authority for the cults' beliefs; in the search for such authority, the leaders of the cults claimed that they were following the teachings of Lao tzu or the *Chuang-tzu*. The exercises, disciplines and practices of these cults, which are sometimes described as 'Popular Taoism' or 'Taoist religion' acquired somewhat different values from those of the mystical searcher of the way.

To those who thought in terms of the Five Phases and Yin–Yang, *tao* was the order of nature within which those rhythms operated. *Tao* was an inbuilt system believed to inform all manner of created things, such that they could be regarded as possessing an intelligence of their own. The *tao* of this type, so far from being restricted to the apprehension of a mystic, could be understood by intellectual processes. It was the Five Phases, combined with Yin and Yang, that explained the operation of this *tao*, as may be seen in works such as the *Huai-nan-tzu*; and herein the message is plain. The efforts of human beings will only succeed if they conform with *tao* and refrain from contravening its principles. So far from attempting to master nature, man must realise that he too is but a part of the natural order; if he rebels against its canons he does so at his peril. Such dangers obtrude once man begins to impoverish the natural world in order to satisfy his own material ambitions, and a majestic passage of the *Huai-nan-tzu*, which is better rendered by paraphrase than by translation, sets out the theme in universal terms.

> The age of perfect purity was marked by a silence and a tranquillity in which all things responded to the natural order. Basic qualities remained unimpaired with no wasteful dispersal of energy; conformity with the order of nature was matched by rightful conduct. Actions, decisions, pronouncements conformed with the natural order; in the prevailing state of harmony and concord there was no room for pretence or deceit.
>
> In this state of affairs, man did not need to choose a supposedly favourable occasion for an action nor did he practise divination in order to secure the successful outcome of an event. There was no scheming or prudent calculation of what was to be started or what brought to an end …
>
> Man's bodily frame formed an inherent part of heaven and earth; his essence was of the same substance as Yin and Yang.

Being one, they were in harmony with the four seasons of the year; being bright, they were lighted by the sun and the moon; and they were paired as male and female to match the creative forces of the world. In this way heaven formed a covering above to whose qualities man could aspire; and earth provided a firmament below for the joy of living. The four seasons followed one another without loss of due order; the winds blew and the rain fell without excess or violence. Sun and moon shed their light in serenity and purity; the five planets kept to their orbits without missing their regular movements. It was a time of favourable omens of many sorts, such as the appearance of the phoenix or *chi-lin* animal, or the fall of honey-dew; and there was no place for design or deceit in the heart of man.

But there followed an age of decline; when tunnels were drilled in the rocks to seek treasure; gold or jade were cut about and carved, to form the implements of man; clams and oysters were forced apart so as to yield their pearls. Man smelted copper and iron, and the myriad living creatures did not reach their full growth. From the wombs of animals man cut out beings as yet unborn; they put to death young animals; and the *chi-lin* animal who comes at an age of bliss never walked the earth. Man overturned the nests; the eggs were smashed; and the phoenix who foretells a time of happiness never took wing. Man drilled with metal or stone to take fire; he laid a structure of timbers to build his edifices; he burnt down the forests to trap the animals; he drained the lakes to catch the fish . . .

The passage continues with other examples of the way in which man had come to despoil nature, with catastrophic consequences that attend the imbalance wrought in Yin and Yang. The four seasons of the year do not follow their regular order, and climatic violence follows with destruction and death. These sad results are accompanied by the distress and quarrels of humanity amidst a welter of suffering.

It has been remarked above that Ssu-ma T'an, for one, protested against the consequences of an excessive faith that was sometimes pinned to the theory of the Five Phases. Such consequences followed not only from the habit of automatically and artificially classifying objects, emotions or natural forces in fives, but also from the conscious efforts to regulate human behaviour so that it would correspond with such a scheme. Above all, the theory could be used for purposes of political propaganda. It was coming to fruition at a time when the idea of imperial government had not yet been fully accepted, and when contending parties were striving to show their right to exercise rule over others; as a result the Five Phases are incorporated in the Chinese view of history. The following passage, from the *Lü shih ch'un-ch'iu*, shows how the theory could be used for this purpose. It is noticeable that it is directly linked therein with an undefined power which is called *t'ien*, or heaven. The order of the phases, or their symbols, is that whereby each one achieves dominance by conquering its predecessor.

Whenever a sovereign or king is about to rise to power, heaven will certainly manifest a favourable sign to mankind in advance. At the time of the Yellow Emperor [a mythological ruler], heaven had displayed creatures of the earth, such as worms, beforehand. The Yellow Emperor said that the energy of earth was in the ascendant; and in those circumstances he singled out yellow for prominence among the colours and modelled his actions on earth. In the time of Yü [founder of the Hsia dynasty] heaven had displayed grasses and trees that were not killed off in autumn or winter. Yü said that the energy of wood was in the ascendant; and in those circumstances he singled out green for prominence among the colours and modelled his actions on wood. In the time of T'ang [founder of the Shang dynasty] heaven had first shown how metal blades were produced from liquid. T'ang said that the energy of metal was in the ascendant; and in those circumstances he singled out white for prominence among the colours and modelled his actions on metal. In the time of king Wen [effective founder of the Chou dynasty] heaven had displayed fire, with scarlet birds holding texts inscribed in red in their beaks, and assembling at the altars of Chou. King Wen said that the energy of fire was in the ascendant; and in those circumstances he singled out red for prominence among the colours and modelled his actions on fire.

It will of course be the energy of water that must displace that of fire, and heaven will make a display of water in advance, so that the energy of water will come into the ascendant. When that occurs, the ruler will single out black for prominence among the colours and model his action on water.*

---

* The 'texts inscribed in red' were books which were thought to describe the ways of antiquity. King Wu of Chou had been informed that they included information regarding the Yellow Emperor and other mythological rulers and wished to consult them. Their description as 'red' implies that they were written in imperishable materials.

While the date of compilation of the whole passage is not known for certain, it may be placed shortly before the foundation of the Ch'in dynasty (221 BC). This was later alleged to be living under the dispensation of water, and to have taken appropriate symbolical steps, such as the choice of black for colours of the court.

5

The universe and the shape of the heavens

A number of texts that survive from the Han period or earlier are imprinted with the rich imagery of Chinese mythology. These are not books that were later enshrined in the classical tradition or chosen as educational manuals for recruits to the civil service; nor are they the writings of those wishing to see truth entirely as a set of verifiable facts. Rather are they the winged words of poets and mystics who have caught a glimpse of ultimate reality and are trying to express that glimpse in symbolical form.

A mythological view of the universe appears in three principal sources. It is seen in the poems of the *Ch'u tz'u* (Songs of the South), and in the guide to holy places of the *Shan-hai ching* (Classic of the Mountains and the Lakes). The imagery of both of these works springs from the landscapes of central or south China. The third source is to be found in one of the chapters of the *Huai-nan-tzu*.

We may first consider a view of the universe that appears in the poem *Yüan-yu* or 'The Far-off journey', in the *Ch'u tz'u*. This was probably compiled not long before 100 BC. As the poet's theme is that of a mystic's journey to a better world, there are some features that are also seen in a search for immortality. The poem starts:

> Grieved at the parlous state of this world's ways,
> I wanted to float up and away from them.
> But my powers were too weak to give me support:
>   What could I ride on to bear me upwards?
> Fallen on a time of foulness and impurity,
> Alone with my misery I had no one to confide in.

During his journey the pilgrim reflects on those men of the past who had likewise sought to escape from the world of the flesh;

but he fears that he cannot achieve similar results. It is in the continuation of the journey that he passes through realms that lie beyond those of earth and man:

> I met the Winged Ones on the Hill of Cinnabar;
> I tarried in the ancient land of Immortality.
> In the morning I washed my hair in the Valley of the Morning;
> In the evening I dried myself on the coasts of heaven.
> I sipped the subtle liquor of the Flying Spring,
> And held in my bosom the flower-bright *wan-yen* jewel.
> My jade-like countenance flushed with radiant colour;
> Purified, my vital essence started to grow stronger;
> My corporeal parts dissolved to a soft suppleness;
> And my spirit grew lissome and eager for movement.

Such are the delights that enabled the pilgrim to reach the walls of heaven and enter the house of God. But his journey was by no means over, as he seeks asylum and guidance from protecting deities such as Kou Mang of the east. He commands mythical creatures such as Fei Lien, the god of the wind, to clear his way; he summons Hsüan wu, the spirit of the north, to his service. He is able to order certain goddesses to play their zithers, and their music eases him on his way to the Gate of Coldness, at the world's end. Eventually he arrives at the point where earth has become invisible and the sky cannot be seen; and the poem ends with the pilgrim's successful attainment of a state of purity.

Another poem in the same collection, which reflects the ideas of the fourth century BC, is entitled *T'ien wen*, 'The heavenly questions'. This is in the form of a catechism or set of riddles, which are inspired by a mythological view of the universe of a less ethereal type than that of *Yüan-yu*. Many of the questions relate to the stars and their origins, and their relative positions:

> How did the Mother Star get her nine children without a union? Where is Po Ch'iang, the Wind Star, and where does the warm wind live?

Some of the riddles concern the sun and its course:

> The sun sets out from the Valley of the Morning and goes to rest in the Vale of Darkness. From the dawn until the time of darkness, how many miles is his journey?

There is also a reference to the story of the ten suns of the Fu-sang tree, the damage they inflicted and their destruction by I the archer. Other questions concern the wondrous deeds of man, beast or god:

> When P'ing summons up the rain, how does he make it come? When those different parts were assembled and joined on to a deer, how were they fitted into shape? When the Great Turtle walks along with an island on his back, how does he keep it steady? If he leaves the sea and walks over dry land, how does he move it?

or:

> King Mu was a breeder of horses. For what reason did he roam about? When he measured the circuit of the world, what was he searching for?

Chapter Four of the *Huai-nan-tzu* has been described as a mythical geography; its contents partake partly of scientific observation and partly of mythological imagery. The chapter sets out to describe the universe in systematic terms which are verifiable and quantifiable. Drawing on the rich sources of fable and folklore, it fits these into a systematic exposition of the theme, which concerns the shape of the world.

The chapter, which has sometimes been described as the 'Treatise on Topography', is entitled *Ti hsing*, the body or shape of the earth. From the outset, the text shows how Chinese thought was tempted by the love of classification and enumeration:

> All things that are borne upon the body of the earth lie within the confines of the six dimensions and the limits of the four extremities. It is the sun and the moon that illuminate them, the stars and the planets that regulate them and the four seasons that keep them in order; they are controlled by the Great Planet of the Year [Jupiter]. Between heaven and earth lie the nine continents and the eight extremities; on the dry land there stand the nine mountains with their nine passes; and there are the nine lakes, the eight winds and the six rivers ...

There follows a catalogue in which all these features are given names. Many of these derive from mythological fable and persist in the later stages of Chinese religion (e.g. Mount T'ai). Some are well known as the names of administrative units of imperial history (e.g. Chü-lu), or serve as place-names even today (e.g. Yün-meng or Chü-yung). Exact distances are quoted to measure the expanses lying between these features of the known world; but the passage soon draws on the mythological aspects of the universe, referring to unknown or magical features such as K'un-lun. Many of the names cited in this connection are also mentioned in the *Shan-hai ching*. Details, such as the profusion of trees made of jewels, cannot be proven; they are set down from the brush of the believer, and the reader is expected to accept these statements with the same validity as that accorded to the numbers of mountains, rivers and winds.

A further feature is seen in this description. Not only are places such as the Hanging Gardens, the Cool Breezes, or Ch'ang-ho, the Gate of Heaven, mentioned; there are also references to the work accomplished by culture heroes in controlling the forces of nature and fashioning the shape of the earth so as to guide it towards its present form. Further on in the chapter we are led to the link that may be seen in the magical places that are named and the world of the holy spirits and god:

All these four streams are the holy springs of god; they may serve to compound the medicines of the plants and to water all manner of created things.

Ascend twice the height of Mount K'un-lun; the height is called the 'Mountain of the Cool Breezes', and if you climb it you will not die. Climb twice as high, and you are at a spot named the Hanging Gardens; climb that and you will then possess magical powers with which you may command the winds and the rain. Climb twice as high again, and that is heaven in the highest; if you ascend there you will be a holy spirit, for that is the abode of god on high.

The Fu-sang tree stands in Yang continent, illuminated by the sun, and the Chien tree stands at Tu-kuang; this is how all the many gods go up and down. No shadow falls from the sun, and no echo reverberates from sound; for this is the centre of heaven and earth.

It need occasion little surprise that the *Huai-nan-tzu* includes a concept not unlike that of the *axis mundi*; for this idea recurs in the mythologies of many quarters of the world. There is also one further feature which deserves recognition as playing a significant part in the *Huai-nan-tzu*'s concept of the universe. This is the mythological explanation of the tilt of the celestial axis as related to the horizon, or perhaps the obliquity of the ecliptic. In a different chapter we read:

> Long, long ago, Kung Kung was fighting with Chuan Hsü in a struggle to become god. He grew angry and struck the mountain of Pu-chou. The column that supported heaven was sundered and the cords that held the earth tight were severed. Heaven was tilted towards the north-west, so that sun and moon, stars and planets were moved there. Earth did not fill up the void in the south-east, and as a result the press of waters and the dust of the world found their home there.

The *Huai-nan-tzu* here gives an explicit answer to the riddle which was included in a poem of the *Songs of the South* to which reference has already been made. The text of the question is worthy of citation, to show how the subject featured in a poem that called upon the same mythology as that of the *Huai-nan-tzu*:

> How are the Ladle's Handle and the Cord tied together? How was Heaven's Pole raised? How do the eight Pillars of Heaven keep it up? Why is there a gap in the south-east?

Two basic assumptions appear in the *Huai-nan-tzu* regarding the shape of the universe: first, that the heavens are round and the earth is square; and second, that time and space are divisible into twelve parts. 'The order of heaven is termed round and the order of earth is termed square', we read unequivocally; and elsewhere, 'Being circular the heavens have no edge and that is why they cannot be observed; being square the earth has no limit and that is why none can spy out her gates.' As happens in other aspects of Han thought, an idea that has been accepted as true in respect of one element in the world of nature is regarded as being applicable to others, and an attempt is made to demonstrate that this is so. We therefore read again, in the *Huai-nan-tzu*, 'Man's head is round, for it is shaped like heaven; man's foot is square, for it is shaped like earth'.

The idea recurs in the symbols of Han art and in talismans.

Excavations coupled with literary evidence have made possible the reconstruction of a religious building that had been erected to the south of Ch'ang-an city. The complex comprised a circle which enclosed a square building, used for ceremonial and worship. The same device appears on some of the early styles of bronze mirrors, and it formed an essential characteristic of what were perhaps the most powerful of all Han mirrors, i.e. those with the TLV pattern that attempted to link man's destiny with the permanent features of the universe (see Chapter 11). In addition, the circle that encloses the square is found imprinted repeatedly in many of the bricks of which Han tombs were sometimes constructed. This result was achieved by the very simple means of impressing coins into the clay before the baking; for Han coins were themselves cast as circular discs, guarded by a raised rim, with a square hole left in the centre.

Several numbers featured in early Chinese speculation as forming a key to understanding the cosmos, and importance had been attached to the number twelve long before the time of the *Huai-nan-tzu*. Already in the Shang-Yin period, two series of written characters were being used to denote certain phenomena or to enumerate the days as they passed in the month. One of these series comprised twelve terms, and one ten; the two were used in combination, to form a cycle of sixty terms altogether. The application of the two series and the cycle to Han thought and calendrical reckoning will be seen below.

An early reference to twelve divisions of the universe may be found in the *T'ien wen* poem of the *Songs of the South*:

How does Heaven co-ordinate its motions? Where are the twelve Heavenly Houses divided? How are the sun and moon connected with them, and the stars spaced out over them?

By the time of the *Huai-nan-tzu* the order of twelve appears in scientific discussion and explanation. Twelve years marked the cycle of the heavenly year, as may be demonstrated in the orbit of Jupiter. The division of the year into twelve months was in one famous instance at least linked with twelve guardian spirits; this is depicted on the earliest silk manuscript that survives, from perhaps the third or even the fourth century BC. The *Huai-nan-tzu* reminds us that just as there are twelve months whereby the 360 days are regulated, so too does man, for his part, possess twelve limbs or organs with which to control his 360 joints; and twelve musical modes give rise to sixty notes. The acceptance of the order of twelve as a division of universal significance may be seen again in the symbols of the TLV mirrors; here the square centre is marked with twelve equal divisions, each being identified by a character of that age-old series of twelve terms, known from the Shang-Yin period.

In addition, by the time of eastern Han if not earlier, the twelve members of the series had been assigned animals to act as their emblems: Rat, Ox, Tiger, Hare, Dragon, Snake, Horse, Sheep, Monkey, Cock, Dog and Boar. In at least one of the major ceremonies of the court, the Great Exorcism, the ritual was enlivened by twelve palace attendants who impersonated these animals; their use as the characteristic symbols of successive years of the calendar survives today.

There were at least three explanations of the shape of the heavens and the earth's relation thereto. The theory of the covering heavens or 'Dome of the universe' (*Kai t'ien*) is probably the earliest of the three to have been formulated; although it is not known precisely when it originated, it may probably be accepted as being the principal view held during the second century BC. The theory conceived the heavens as a wheel that carried the sun and the moon with them, despite their own efforts to move in a contrary direction; the Dipper remained at the centre. According to one interpretation of the theory, both earth and heaven are flat, or perhaps slightly convex. As one writer has put it:

> In both cases heaven rotated once daily about an imaginary axis (usually held to be vertical), carrying with it the heavenly bodies. The Chinese observer was some distance away from this axis, and hence the pole-star was not overhead. Rising and setting of the sun, moon and stars was explained as an optical illusion caused by their entering and leaving the observer's allegedly limited range of vision.

There is a reference to the theory in the *Lun-heng* of Wang Ch'ung:

> The men of letters hold that, while the sky revolves towards the left, the movements of the sun and the moon are not fixed

to the sky, each one revolving independently. But objections may be raised to this view. Suppose that it is assumed that the sun and the moon move independently, without being fixed to the sky, and that the sun travels for one degree while the moon travels for thirteen degrees; it would follow that at the time when the sun and the moon rise, they would be revolving eastward in their forward motion; how is it that they turn about and start revolving towards the west? But if it is assumed that they are fixed to the sky, their revolutions will follow the four seasons of the sky. They may be compared with ants crawling on the top of a mill-stone; while the sun and the moon travel slowly, the sky travels at speed; and the sky carries sun and moon along with it as it revolves. As a result, while the sun and the moon are in fact travelling east, they are *per contra* revolved towards the west.

A second theory, named *Hun t'ien*, saw the heavens as extending continuously in space and surrounding the earth on every side, rather than being poised as a cover or lid above it. Possibly the *Hun t'ien* theory may have been evolved by the beginning of the first century BC, but for a description we must wait until at least the time of Chang Heng (*c.* AD 130), to whom the following passage is attributed:

> The heavens are like a hen's egg, though round as a bullet, with the earth lying in the centre and forming, as it were, the yolk. Being larger than the earth, the heavens enclose it in the same way as the shell encloses the yellow substance within. The heavens stand firm, riding upon vapour; the earth floats about, supported by water.
>
> The circumference of the heavens extends for 365 and a quarter degrees. This space may be divided into two equal parts, with 182 and five eighths degrees covering the earth on top, and 182 and five eighths degrees encircling it below. As a result, half of the twenty-eight lunar lodges are observed and half are hidden.
>
> The two extreme points are named the south and the north poles, with the north pole forming the centre of the heavens. This lies due north, 36 degrees above the earth; with the result that if a circle with a diameter of 72 degrees* is described

---

* That is, a polar declination of 72 degrees. I owe this explanation to John Major.

therefrom it will be perpetually visible and never hidden. The south pole forms the centre of the heavens, lying 36 degrees below the earth. If a circle with a diameter of 72 degrees is described therefrom, it will be perpetually hidden and un-observed. Something more than 182 and a half degrees separate the two poles.

The heavens revolve like the axle of a carriage; there is no terminal point to their revolution; their shape is boundless, and they are termed the *Hun t'ien*, or continuous heavens.

The latest of the three theories to be mentioned is that which saw the heavens as an infinite space (*Hsüan yeh*), wherein the whole company of the heavenly host move around at will, and quite independently of one another, with the Pole Star always keeping his place. This theory cannot be traced for certain to before the latter part of the eastern Han period, and its introduction may be regarded as another sign of the cleavage between the intellectual attitudes of western and eastern Han which has been noted elsewhere.

It is hardly surprising that thinkers and writers of the Han period paid considerable attention to the heavens and the movements of the bodies therein. For, of all observed objects, the stars and the planets are the least ephemeral, and the most regular in their behaviour. An understanding of their habits and their orbits can do much to answer the call for permanence in a highly volatile existence. In so far as the heavenly bodies are regarded as being members of the same universe as man and the creatures of the earth, a sense of human impermanence could be diminished, if it could be believed that some of the creatures of that universe enjoyed a relatively permanent status. It is partly owing to this striving for unity, and the desire to demonstrate the connection between the more permanent habits of the stars and the briefer activities of man, that it is difficult to distinguish between astronomy and astrology in Han thought. Astronomers demon-strated how the stars were a part of eternity; astrologers linked human fortunes with that eternity.

An idea of the interest that astronomy evinced may be gathered from the extent of the writings on the subject known to exist at the beginning of the Christian era. In the abbreviated catalogue of the works in the imperial library, there is a total of twenty-two entries for astronomy and astrology, comprising over four hundred sub-divisions. The titles of the books, which are now lost, indicate that the subject matter was concerned with the sun, moon and planets, with comets, and with other phenomena that may be classified under meteorology. Some books specialised in verifications of predictions supplied in respect of certain movements of the stars or the behaviour of comets. It is possible, or even likely, that a high proportion of these works were accompanied by illustrations. To support the evidence of these entries in the catalogue, it is now possible to call on manuscript copies of books that are of this very type, as will be seen below in connection with planets and comets.

Developments in astronomy may be traced in the evolution of new instruments and the known achievements of a few named men. The practical value of their work may be seen in the refinements introduced in the calendar, which resulted from more accurate observations and calculations. Major changes in the calendar, which indicate the main stages of advanced techniques and knowledge, took place in 104 BC, AD 1–5 and AD 85.

The earliest instruments of which there is knowledge were the gnomons of the fourth and third centuries BC; these were used to measure the length of the sun's shadow and to fix the occurrence of the summer and winter solstices, for purposes of calendrical reckoning. The earliest *clepsydra* of these centuries served only to measure equal, defined periods of time, with which to divide the night into its five watches. Some time before 105 BC there was evolved a water-clock proper which could measure the continuous period of the day and night, and divide it into twelve double hours, of a hundred parts altogether. The earliest example of a bronze gnomon to have been found dates from perhaps AD 100.

Perhaps the earliest definable instrument known to have been used to observe the stars and to measure their movements was the *Ch'ih tao i* (Instrument of the Red Path, or Equatorial Instrument). This was evolved by Keng Shou-ch'ang, a statesman known for the advice that he tendered on the problems of China's economy between 57 and 54 BC. He is also known as the author of a treatise on the movements of the moon, which ran to over two hundred chapters. The instrument that he evolved was in use in the imperial observatory in the second half of the first century AD. It measured the movements of the heavenly bodies with reference to the equator of the heavens (the Red Path), which was graduated in 365 and a quarter degrees. The more accurate and precise measurements that it produced were presumably available to Liu Hsin, who was responsible for the calendrical adjustments introduced in AD 1–5.

A significant improvement occurred with the construction of the *Huang tao i* (Instrument of the Yellow Path, or Ecliptical Instrument) in AD 102. This was achieved by the astronomer Chia K'uei, largely on the basis of work done by Fu An, a specialist in eclipses, some twenty years previously. The new instrument facilitated direct measurements of the true motions of the sun, moon and planets, which in reality follow the ecliptic (Yellow Path) rather than the equator.

At much the same time (AD 103) a still more refined type of water-clock was introduced, which provided for more precise regulation so as to correspond with the changing length of daylight. These instruments were used independently of sundials, which were made as circular discs, graduated in one hundred divisions. These dials were mounted in the plane of the celestial equator, and the passage of time was marked by the fall of the sun's shadow from a post placed centrally on the instrument. The last invention of Han astronomers to be mentioned is that of the armillary sphere, which followed logically from the work of Keng Shou-ch'ang, Fu An and Chia K'uei. The new instrument was highly complex; it is attributed to the hand of Chang Heng in AD 124.

From very early times, at least the fifth century BC, observers had distinguished a series of twenty-eight lunar lodges of varying size which could be identified by certain guide-stars or constellations. These twenty-eight lodges are named on an artifact found in a tomb of 433 BC. For the Han period, they first appear in material form as names inscribed on a circular dial, found in a tomb of 165 BC. By the start of the Christian era, the sizes of the twenty-eight lodges were calculated as varying between 2 and 33 degrees. As a result of the concern felt to relate the heavens and the earth to each other as members of the same universe, a correspondence was drawn between the twenty-eight lodges and territorial divisions that could be identified on earth.

The great circle of the ecliptic, or path taken by the sun, moon and planets, was known to cut obliquely across the celestial equator. Fu An is the first Chinese astronomer known to have calculated the obliquity of the ecliptic, in *c.* AD 85; it was with reference to the equator that Chinese astronomers measured the positions and movements of the stars, either in terms of degrees or according to a scale marked in feet and inches.*

A further way, of dividing the heavens into twelve segments, dates from at least the fourth century BC. These segments were calculated to extend for as near equal parts as was possible in a circle divided into 365 and a quarter degrees (i.e. seven segments were regarded as extending for 30 degrees and five for 31 degrees, totalling 365 degrees). The twelve segments, or Jovian Stations, were based on the observed movements of Jupiter. Yet a further system saw the heavens as comprising five palaces, corresponding with the emblems or symbols of the Five Phases, and being named accordingly.

Four principal points are defined on the sun's path as the two solstices, when the sun reaches its extreme northern and southern positions, and the two equinoxes, when the ecliptic crosses the equator. As yet the precession of the equinoxes had not been discovered; this achievement is credited to Yü Hsi, of the fourth century AD. Just before the Christian era, Liu Hsiang was referring to the nine routes taken by the moon, and it is the same scholar who is credited with the first certain knowledge of the cause of eclipses. Although this explanation was acceptable to Chang Heng in the middle of the second century AD, eclipses were still regarded in general as a matter of surprise, warning and danger, rather than as deriving from the regular motions of the heavenly bodies. Eclipses feature in Han as oddities or strange phenomena that require explanation (see Chapter 8).

It is hardly surprising that the five planets whose movements were observed were associated with the Five Phases and their symbols:

Jupiter	Wood	East
Mars	Fire	South
Saturn	Earth	Centre
Venus	Metal	West
Mercury	Water	North

A number of technical terms were evolved to describe the different types of planetary movement, some of which were to all appearances retrograde, and their speed. The meticulous

---

* One foot (Han) equalled approximately 23 cm, and was divided into ten inches.

nature of astronomers' observations and the degree of accuracy achieved has recently been demonstrated in the discovery of a silken manuscript, which was buried in a tomb in *c*. 168 BC. The text tabulates the times and locations of the rising and setting of the planets over the years 246–177 BC; the calculations of the planets' periods compare very well with those of today (e.g. the period for Saturn is given as 30 years; the modern calculation is 29.46 years).

The treatise on astronomy and astrology which was incorporated in the standard history of the Han dynasty (*Han shu*) was probably compiled by Ma Hsü, sometime before AD 150; it duplicates much of the material carried in the corresponding treatise of the *Shih-chi* of Ssu-ma Ch'ien. In the *Han shu* there are listed 118 named constellations and 783 stars which are identified and placed within the five palaces of the heavens. The constellations are divided into two categories, of which one is related to the areas, events and destinies of the world of earth and man. There are indications that β Ursae Minoris was taken by some Han writers as being the Pole Star.

The fortunate discovery of another manuscript, in the same tomb of *c*. 168 BC, and its comparison with literary references, permits a close appreciation of how much was known, and what was thought, about comets. The manuscript includes diagrams of twenty-nine different types of comet, which result from sustained observation and accurate depiction. Each diagram is accompanied by a text which gives a name to comets of that type; there is also a statement of which events its appearance may foreshadow. The names are largely botanical (e.g. bamboo, thatch, artemisia) and may have been selected as mnemonics; the consequences of a particular comet's appearance often concern military fortunes. Some of the specific records of observed comets in the Standard Histories may be identified with verifiable events, such as the appearance of Halley's comet in 12 BC and probably that of its predecessor in 87. The origin of comets was ascribed by some writers to the dissipation of energy or matter by the planets.

The study of the stars was actively promoted by the imperial government, which included a complement of official astronomers. The site of the imperial observatory of Lo-yang that served the later Han emperors and their successors in later dynasties has been identified. Astronomers' work was essential to the administration of China, in so far as the regulation and promulgation of the calendar depended on their observations and calculations.

The calendar was luni-solar, with some months of the year long, at thirty days, and some short at twenty-nine days. Adjustment was needed to ensure that the length of each month would fit as closely as possible with the cycle of the moon. So that the cycles of the sun and the moon could be reconciled overall, it was necessary to include an intercalary, or thirteenth, month to the year, after every thirty-two or thirty-three months had passed. It was part of the government's responsibility to determine when these changes should be introduced, and what length should be given to each one of the months. Copies of the resulting calendar were then distributed to officials.

Reference is made below (see Chapter 14) to the means adopted for designating years. For the later Han period, days of the month were identified by a numerical series, beginning afresh for each month. Previously they had been identified by the successive terms of the cycle of sixty members formed by combining the terms of the two series of twelve and ten that have been mentioned above. The importance of retaining a place for both of these series in Han usage and harmonising them may be seen in a number of respects, such as the ceremony of the Great Exorcism (see Chapter 12). In addition the cycles of twelve and ten both feature in the Han division of time (see p. 5 above). The difficulty of retaining provision for twelve hours, which were in all subdivided into 100 parts, needs little stress; but an experiment that was made in 5 BC to change to a system of twelve hours and 120 parts was short-lived, lasting only for a few months. It seems that ideological considerations were of greater importance than practical convenience.

Evidence for the Han calendrical system and the calculation of time depends on both literary and material sources of information. While the reconstruction of the Han calendar and its adjustments has long been possible on the basis of references in the standard histories, this has now been supported and modified by the discovery of official documents drawn up in the course of the administration of the empire. The earliest virtually complete calendar to be discovered so far is for the year whose greater part corresponded with 134 BC.

Quite apart from the attention paid to observing the heavenly bodies, calculating their movements and constructing the calendar, there are other ways whereby the stars in their courses exercised an influence on the heart and mind of Han China. There are several examples of tombs whose decoration included a chart of some of the stars, usually painted on the vault; their presence was presumably intended, like that of other talismans, to place the deceased person in the eternal context of the cosmos. In addition, two constellations, which are known as the Weaver and the Oxherd, feature in one of the best-known tales of Chinese mythology. The two constellations, the one male and the other female, lie on opposite sides of the Milky Way, separated from one another and frustrated in their attempts to form a union. This had been forbidden, owing to the failure of the Weaving Maid to persist in her mundane tasks and duties. Only on one occasion in the year, the night of the seventh day of the seventh month, are the two partners permitted to meet; and it is from that single, but essential, union that the web of the cosmos continues to be spun. Some of the artists who decorated Han tombs included figures of these two constellations, which may be identified as the Lyre and the Eagle, among the furnishings; they perhaps intended to demonstrate that, just as the union of these two partners was being manifestly achieved, so too was survival secured for the loved one who was interred beneath.

6

The earth and its creatures

It cannot be known how deeply the Chinese were concerned with the problem of how matter comes into being or what agent is responsible for creation. It may only be surmised that, like other peoples whose livelihood depends primarily on the nurturing and harvesting of crops rather than on the destruction of animals, the Chinese were well aware of the need for the regular processes of natural growth to continue; they may well have been many who pondered on questions such as the source of creative power or the results of discontinuing those processes.

Mythology and iconography suggest that some answers were being found to these questions, and Han philosophers were showing their awareness of the problems. In mythology we hear of creation that follows the presence or activities of a semi-divine figure which may be somewhat dramatic; or sometimes a conflict may be necessary, or an initial act of disruption. Alternatively there are tales of an essential union that is achieved by two partners. In speculative terms, such an act of union is transferred to primeval natural forces; or creation is explained as the operation of cycles set in motion by complementary powers and proceeding according to identifiable rhythms.

As all manner of things, in heaven and on earth, were regarded as being members of the same order of being, there was no specific hierarchy whereby matter was created and classified; man was seen as but one of the myriad objects of the world of nature. In general terms, creation was regarded more as a continuing process than as a single act. There was no idea of a personified purposeful creator worthy of worship, in the manner of the west, and no sharp distinction between creator and created. As a result there was no insistence on the thanks or services due to an identified being, in return for the gift or life or natural wealth. No linear concept of time develops from the need to identify or establish a single beginning from which all other processes followed.

In neither mythology nor philosophy can there be found the idea of *creatio ex nihilo*; creation is a process of transforming one substance into another but not one of manufacture. The nearest approach that we may find to the Psalmist's joyful cry that the heavens declare the glory of God may be seen in the following passage from the *Huai-nan-tzu*:

Heaven has set out the sun and the moon and arrayed the constellations; it has regulated Yin and Yang and it has stretched out the four seasons, giving heat by day and rest by night, with the winds to dry out the world and the rain and the dew to give it moisture. When it brings creatures to life, none see that they are nourished, but they yet grow; when it brings creatures' lives to a close, none see that they are destroyed but they yet perish. This may be called the divine intellect, and the holy men take this as their model.

The emergence of a world which possesses finite shape from a state of primeval chaos, in which heaven and earth were still formed as one substance, is mentioned in a number of myths, whose origin can hardly be traced with certainty. According to one, possibly late, account the original inchoate mass was like a chicken's egg, and from that agglomeration there was brought to life the semi-human being P'an-ku. Heaven became separated from earth, and as the distance between the two increased, so did P'an-ku, who existed between them, grow in girth. According to one account, that may be quite late, it was from P'an-ku's body that the physical features of the earth, its rivers and hills, its strata and its vegetation came into being.

According to another account the reduction of chaos to order was brought about by Nü-kua, who appears later as the female partner of Fu Hsi. The *Huai-nan-tzu* credits Nü-kua with this great work in the following terms:

Long, long ago the four extreme pillars of the world lay in disorder and the nine continents were split apart. The heavens did not form a complete covering above and the earth did not give full support below. Fierce fires flamed without abatement; mighty waters flowed without cease. Wild beasts devoured mankind, birds of prey seized the old and the weak in their talons.

So Nü-kua fused the five-coloured stones together, to fill up the gaps in the azure skies. She severed the feet of a turtle, and with these she set up the four extreme pillars of the world. She slew the black dragon, to save the province of Chi, at the centre of the world. She collected together the ash of burnt reeds to stem the uncontrolled rush of the waters.

The gaps in the azure skies were filled up; the four extreme pillars stood straight; the mighty rush of the waters was dried up; the province of Chi lay flat. Wild beasts and reptiles lay dead, and mankind lived.

The myth retains elements of an initial stage of destruction or disruption and it is reminiscent of the story of the destruction of Pu-chou, one of the supports that held the heavens in place (see p. 52 above). That act of destruction had been the result of a conflict fought between two prominent deities or persons, and it is possible that other stories which concern the reduction of chaos to order may also involve just such a conflict. For example, a Chinese version of the primeval flood involved the failure of Kun to stem the waters, his discomfiture and his punishment. Finally he was replaced by his son, Yü the Great. The tale may well mark the last stages of a quarrel and conflict.

A more persistent element in Chinese mythology, to which reference has already been made, is that of the seasonal meeting between certain partners. Such meetings follow periods of separation; they are essential to generate or regenerate the process of growth and birth. As has been seen (p. 62) they are sometimes ascribed to constellations. In other forms they take place between semi-divine persons, and human beings may be involved.

This myth is seen both in literature and in iconography. The annual meeting of the two constellations, the Weaver and the Oxherd, was specifically timed to take place on the seventh day of the seventh month, which is one of the turning points of the year. In tales that are told of the meeting between the Queen Mother of the West and sovereigns of China such as Han Wu ti (reigned 141–87), a search for immortality constitutes a vital element. In versions of the story that emerge from perhaps the second century AD, the partnership is between two semi-divine persons, the Queen Mother and the King Father of the East. This meeting is sometimes portrayed as that of the essential union between the two forces of Yin and Yang.

Iconography illustrates the theme in two ways. First, the Queen Mother of the West is regularly depicted with a characteristic crown as one of her necessary attributes. The crown is to be explained as a symbol of the power that she possesses to weave the web of the cosmos and thus keep life going. Secondly, the theme of union appears frequently in other forms, either as a depiction or as a symbol.

In the well-known painting from Ma-wang-tui, of 168 BC, two dragons are interlaced together, linked by a jade ring. At later stages of art development, but well within the Han period, there are many examples of figures whose serpentine bodies and tails are linked together inextricably, and which are surmounted by human heads. These two figures sometimes appear without attributes; sometimes they carry in their hands the emblems of creation, i.e. the bird that represents the sun and the power of Yang, and the toad or hare that represents the moon and the power of Yin. Alternatively, they may carry the tools whereby creation is accomplished, i.e. the pair of compasses and the set-square. The motif is explained as that of the union between Nü-kua and her male partner Fu Hsi, which was believed to bring about the generative power of creation.

In some instances the two figures are shown clinging to a circular device which effects that union; the same theme, of the ring clasped by two figures, sometimes links animals together. In addition, many of the medallions or decorative cartouches of Han reliefs are surrounded by a decorative border formed by a series of circles that are crossed by diagonal lines. It is possible that that device was itself intended as a symbol of the essential union of two figures, without which the process of birth and rebirth could not be accomplished.

From mythology we turn to attempts to explain or understand creation in terms that move towards natural science. The association drawn between Nü-kua and Fu Hsi on the one hand and Yin and Yang on the other is an indication of what some Chinese had in mind. The theme is propounded in a somewhat mystical manner in the following passage from the *Huai-nan-tzu*.

Long ago, before heaven and earth existed, there was form

but no material substance. All things were remote and dark, inchoate and indistinguishable, in their primordial state and vast. None knew of the gates that led within.

Two spirits were born, mingled together; they measured out the heavens and laid the plans of the earth. The abyss was so deep that none could fathom out where it ceased; the space was so vast that none could comprehend where it would come to an end.

Thereupon there was a separation into Yin and Yang, and a division into the eight extreme corners; hard and soft were formed from one another and the myriad creatures then took shape. Brute force was made into beast, pure force into man; and for this reason pure spirit is what is owned by the heavens, and that which is of bone is possessed by earth. Pure spirit enters into the gates [of heaven]; bone goes home to the roots [of earth]; and as for man, how may he still survive?

This is the reason why the holy saints took heaven as their model; in conforming with its nature they were not held fast by common ways, nor were they led astray by man. They looked to the heavens as their father and to earth as their mother. Yin and Yang formed the bonds and the four seasons the threads; heaven stood serene in its purity and earth lay stable at her rest. Those of the ten thousand created things that lose sight of these truths die; those that take them as their model live. For that which is tranquil and vast forms the home of the holy spirits; that which is empty and has nothing is the abode of the way of nature [*tao*].

This is why those who perchance seek these things without lose them within; and those who preserve them within lose them without. It is like the roots of a tree and the tips of its branches; by drawing themselves forth from the roots, a thousand twigs and ten thousand leaves will each one follow after the nature of the tree.

Pure spirit is that which is received from heaven; material substance is that which is given from earth. Therefore is it said that the one produces the two, the two produce the three and the three produce the ten thousand created things. The ten thousand things of creation bear Yin upon their backs and enclose Yang within their bosoms; by keeping the two forces in balance they maintain a harmony.

Whatever the implications may be of the creation of all things from unity, the *Huai-nan-tzu* refers in several passages to a creative force. This is the *tsao-hua-che*, the person who or the agent which forms and transforms, or 'the creator'. Thus:

> The creator chooses and fashions his material in the same way as a potter works his clay. He picks it out from the earth and it is made into a vessel; but it is no different from what it had been before it had been separated from the earth. The clay is formed into a vessel; the vessel is broken into fragments and returned to its old home; and it is no different from what it had been when it had been formed as a vessel.

The same metaphor is applied directly to the creation of man. Elsewhere in the *Huai-nan-tzu* we read of the holy saints whose qualities are such that they naturally accommodate to eternal values and can be partnered with the *tsao-hua-che*. In one passage we are told how the *tsao-hua-che* is superior to all material forces such as fire or metal and impervious to their powers of destruction. However, in none of these passages is there a hint of a creator who is an identifiable person; nor is the concept necessarily one of unity. Early commentators, of the third century AD, seem to have been at a loss to explain this rather vague idea, which they tended to identify with heaven and earth, or with Yin and Yang.

In addition to the treatment of the problem of creation in this way, a somewhat later text, which may well be drawing on earlier sources, carries a dialogue that is of a speculative or even metaphysical nature. This is seen in the opening passages of Chapter 5 of the *Lieh-tzu*, the 'Questions of T'ang'. A discussion of the nature of time and space and how these may be limited soon leads into a mystical consideration of the different parts of the cosmos. Part of this dialogue has already been cited above, in connection with the islands of the eastern ocean (see p. 28).

Whatever explanation is given of the *tsao-hua-che*, one Han philosopher at least forcefully rejected any idea that creation was intended or controlled by a master mind. This was Wang Ch'ung, who devoted the best part of a chapter of his major work to disparaging the myths that have been mentioned above, of the destruction of Pu-chou or Nü-kua's part in the act of creation. Wang Ch'ung seems to have recognised heaven as a power that is capable of providing a life-giving force which, for example, will produce vegetation; but he cannot accept that heaven brings about such results purposefully, let alone for the benefit of the human race. For Wang Ch'ung, the growth of matter, be it animal, vegetable or mineral, as well as the occurrence of inexplicable events or strange phenomena in heaven or on earth, all take place spontaneously and without deliberate intention. The actual power of growth is generated by *ch'i*, a term which has a variety of meanings and usages, and which is difficult to comprehend in its entirety.

Ch'i conveys the idea of creative energy or life-giving force; while the term sometimes denotes the physical form in which such energy is manifested, such as steam, *ch'i* can be very different from the bodily substance of which matter is formed. *Ch'i* is a quality or property which is dispensed to the members of the created world from external forces such as heaven and earth. Being an acquired property of such creatures from the moment of their existence, it serves to keep them alive and growing. The principle is stated in the opening sentence of Wang Ch'ung's chapter on 'Spontaneity' or 'natural growth':

> When the vital energies of heaven and earth are joined together the myriad things of the world of themselves come to life, in the same way as when the vital energies of a man and a woman are joined together children are of themselves brought into being.

In developing his theme, Wang Ch'ung demonstrates that neither heaven nor earth possesses the necessary physical organs with which to bring about creation. He writes of the strength of spontaneity almost with a feeling of awe, in a passage that is perhaps a counterpart to the injunction to consider the lilies of the field. This follows his scornful refusal to believe the traditional tales that certain babies had been born with Chinese characters implanted in the palms of their hands, thereby disclosing something of their future destiny and determining what their names should be.

> When the grasses and the trees come to life, their flowers and their leaves grow fresh and thick, all with the twists and curls that indeed resemble the decorative strokes of written

characters. Now, if we are to say that heaven created the written characters in the hands of the babies must we not also say that heaven deliberately created the flowers and the leaves? Remember the story of the man of Sung who set out to carve a mulberry leaf in wood and took three years to complete it. Confucius commented 'If heaven and earth were to take three years to make a single leaf, there would be precious few creatures of nature that would possess leaves!' From Confucius' remark we may infer that leaves are created of themselves, and that for this reason they may be formed simultaneously. Whereas, were heaven to create them, the process would be as tardy as that of the man of Sung with his single mulberry leaf.

Consider the fur and the feathers of the animals and the birds with their hues and colours, and ask how these could have been created deliberately. Had this been so, neither birds nor animals would have been able to reach their state of completion. Or consider how the myriad creatures of nature are born in spring and become mature by autumn; and ask whether heaven and earth created them deliberately or whether they came to life spontaneously. If we are to say that heaven and earth made them deliberately, they would have used hands to do so; how could heaven and earth possess millions and millions of hands such that millions and millions of creatures could be made at the same time?

The creatures of nature are placed between heaven and earth in the same way as a babe lies within its mother's womb. The mother encloses the life-giving energies of the child which is born alive after ten months, with nose, mouth, ears and eyes; with hair, skin, down and veins; with blood, arteries, fat and bones; with sinews, nails and teeth. Did all these grow of their own accord within the mother's womb, or was it the mother who deliberately created them?

Reference will be made below (see Chapter 7) to the more sophisticated concept of creation and change as part of a cycle of sixty-four stages. But attention must first be given to the place of man as this was conceived within the order of created things. To many, man occupied a middle position placed between heaven and earth, and he was seen as bearing responsibility for co-operating with the order of nature, and thereby taking care of the earth and its manifold gifts. To those whose view of life was centred on the qualities and proper occupations of man, who are often described as Confucians, each man bore responsibility for so organising his own efforts that they would be beneficial to as many members of the human race as possible. Ideally the leader of man would report to heaven periodically, giving an account of the stewardship that he had discharged on earth.

By those whose philosophy was centred on the state and its capacity for acquiring wealth and strength, and who are sometimes classified as Legalists, it was thought right and proper that men should be organised and even coerced so that they would exploit the riches of the earth to fullest advantage, in the interests of state or empire. For those who, like Wang Ch'ung, sought to explain the workings of nature on rationalist grounds, man must be regarded as being but one of nature's creatures, whose existence comes about no differently from that of other creatures. As he remarks in one famous passage, man is comparable with the 'lice that grow among men's clothing'. The statement bears no moral overtones and implies no qualitative judgement; it is simply concerned with the fortuitous way of man's creation and ambience.

But if we look at what was conceived as man's relations with the animal world, complexities enter in. Two distinct stages may be traced in the attitude expressed both in mythology and in some of the creations in bronze of China's early artists. Initially, animals held pride of place as awe-inspiring creatures, being regarded with admiration and affection. But in a later stage, from perhaps the eighth century BC, the animals are no longer the friend and protector of man or the object of his worship. They have become his potential enemy; the artistic creations of these centuries show man challenging the animal world and acquiring dominion. The change in iconography possibly reflects a change in man's way of life. With development of agriculture as a primary occupation, man had become dependent on conserving and protecting the riches that he had wrung from the earth; some members of the animal world had become natural predators of such resources; mythological tale and decorated bronze bring out the ensuing conflict.

It has been shown above (see Chapter 2) that some of the holy spirits that were worshipped shortly before and probably during the Han period were conceived in animal form, or as hybrids. It was also believed that certain animals, whose forms could not necessarily be recognised in nature, would appear from time to time as harbingers of good fortune that was about to attend human destinies. The rare appearances of the *chi-lin*, often mistranslated as 'unicorn', or the phoenix were to be welcomed; for they came in response to human conduct, and assured man that his way of life was in harmony with the order of the universe.*

There is a further assumption that lies behind Chinese ideas of creation. This was the belief that it was perfectly possible, or even regular, for one living creature to be transformed into another, of a different type. The prevalence of this belief is perhaps not surprising among a people whose familiarity with the life-cycle of caterpillar, cocoon and moth had enabled them to master the art of sericulture, from the second millennium BC. The idea of transformation obtrudes in mythology and in rationalist speculation. Kun, father of Yü the Great, had himself failed to save mankind from the floods; by poetic justice he was transformed into a turtle. Heng O, who stole the drug of immortality and fled equipped with it to the moon, was changed into a toad and lived there for ever. In the opening passage of the *Chuang-tzu*, with its vision of a universe that was not bound by human values, we read of the fish of immeasurable size that was transformed into a bird of similar dimensions.

From such imagery we may turn to the studied logic of Wang Ch'ung, who recognises that the principle operates in the animal world, between frogs and quails, or sparrows and clams, and even between man and other living creatures. He even accepts the principle in one of his most sceptical chapters, wherein he sets forth a whole series of reasons to disprove that man survives death and can reappear as a 'demon' that will injure mankind. 'There are cases,' he writes, 'wherein a live body is turned into another live body, but there are no instances in which a corpse is transformed into something living.'

---

* The guises in which the *chi-lin* appears in Chinese art vary considerably over the centuries, and no single form can be taken as characteristic or definitive.

7
The cycle of change

From a very early stage in Chinese civilisation a particular means of divination was being practised that was destined to give rise to profound and extensive intellectual consequences. Precise information regarding the earliest forms of the method are lacking. Probably it was used to seek answers to questions of a simple type, that could be given in the form of 'yes' or 'no'; and it seems that such answers were manifested in the material production of a visible pattern, achieved after a random process. This pattern was probably in the form of a single straight line, either complete, for 'yes', or split into two halves for 'no'.

From such beginnings there grew a highly complex system of divination which, as will be shown below (see Chapter 9), was practised extensively during the Han period. It is with the intellectual implications that we are concerned now.

Long before the Han age the original simple procedures of this type of divination had given way to a complex process marked by ritualism. The change is seen in two ways. First, in the initial stages the questions had been put to a seer, whose visionary powers had enabled him to seize intuitively upon the answer that was inherent in the single line; but in the later stages, the answers were forthcoming after the consultation of written guides, or precedents, rather than by the immediate apprehension of eternal truth. Secondly, from the production of a single line which would suffice to inspire a seer's reaction, there developed a lengthy ritual which led to the deliberate production of a more complex pattern. This comprised six parallel horizontal lines, either complete or split. The total number of possible hexagrams was sixty-four; the answer to the problem that was posed depended upon which one of these sixty-four figures emerged, after completion of the whole divinatory process, which was still random.

The change from the spontaneous utterances or prophecies of

a seer to the pronouncements of a learned consultant is seen in the production of special documents that came to be used during the mantic process. These documents were presumably designed to act as guides on which consultants could rely in cases of difficulty, or as an *aide-mémoire* to the predictions that had been made in the past. One of these manuals, whose text may date from perhaps 800 BC, survived the hazards of literary loss to be incorporated in the classical, or scriptural, texts upon which Chinese education rested during the imperial age. This was the *Changes of Chou* (*Chou i*) which now forms an integral part of the *Book of Changes* (*I ching*).

The *Chou i* provided a set of sixty-four names by which each one of the hexagrams could be identified. As many of those names are of physical objects, either natural or man-made (e.g. the *ming-i* bird, the well, the cauldron), it is possible that they had been chosen in the first instance as mnemonics. In addition, the *Changes of Chou* includes statements of two types: first a general idea of what bearing each hexagram is likely to have on a general problem; and secondly a more specific interpretation that applied to each one of the six lines of the pattern, should special attention have been called to it during the process of divination.

This old text was couched in language that was obsolete or in formulae whose meaning had long been forgotten by the beginning of the Han period. Such a loss of knowledge, however, had not prevented the use of the book in a somewhat different way from the original intention. From the sixth century BC at least it was being used, according to our records, not as a set of guide-lines to accompany an act of divination, but as a source of wisdom in its own right, which possessed the authority of dogma. However, there were some who could not rest content with using a set of ancient sayings blindly and who required an explanation. As a result a number of written amplifications or interpretations of the original texts of the *Chou i* came to be written down, and it is some of these that form the other, and larger, parts of the *Book of Changes* that we possess today. Some of these expositions, which are known together under the evocative title of the *Ten Wings*, date from various times before the Han period and from the Han period itself. They reflect a view of life and reality that was currently acceptable.

By now several complications had entered in. The ritual of divination provided not only for the interpretation of the original hexagram produced during the process; in certain instances it involved the interpretation of a second hexagram, developed very easily from the original one by means of a minor transformation (e.g. by substituting a single complete line for a split line, or vice versa). In addition, while all the sixty-four hexagrams retained their own identity, with their names perhaps suggesting something of their characteristics, they were also being regarded as consisting of two trigrams, superimposed one upon the other. The total number of trigrams that can be formed is eight, and these (known as the *pa kua*) came to be regarded as symbols of the primeval forces that controlled the workings of nature. They too were assigned names that identified their character, i.e. heaven, thunder, water and mountain, and, corresponding these to, earth, sun, fire and lake. The hexagrams were being regarded as combinations of two of these elemental forces. The eight were themselves classified in various ways and lent themselves to interpretation as symbols of the states brought about by Yin and Yang.

From the random production of the linear patterns, from the identification and classification of those sixty-four patterns, and from the recognition of the eternally volatile nature of creation there arose a sophisticated set of concepts. The sixty-four hexagrams came to be adopted as symbols of a series of situations, of which one was thought to prevail at each successive moment of time. Each of these situations was thought to be imbued with its own properties and qualities; the combination of conditions pertaining to each situation was thought to determine the suitability of certain activities.

The sixty-four hexagrams had developed into a series of signs of great subtlety. Thanks to this more sophisticated way of considering them and their philosophical overtones, the whole system of divination by this means had undergone a change of purpose. At the outset, as far as we may comprehend, it had evolved in order to determine the answers to simple questions. These required a short, restricted answer, either by way of encouragement to undertake an action or by way of discouragement to refrain from doing so. But with the new concept of the sixty-four hexagrams as symbols of cosmic situations, divination had become addressed to a much deeper type of enquiry. It sought to identify the prevailing situation of the cosmos and to ascertain whether it was suitable for a proposed project. It asked whether that project would fit harmoniously with the conditions of heaven, earth and man.

This new aspect of the sixty-four hexagrams follows reasonably enough from the ideas that had been gaining ground in the centuries before the imperial period. These comprised a belief in the single, unitary nature of the universe, in which the actions of any single part are associated with and affect those of the other parts. It was also recognised that the universe, of which certain parts only were open for immediate observation, was subject to continuous change. These beliefs were now combined with the classification of cosmic situations into sixty-four known and identifiable types.

From such considerations a major consequence followed. If by the exercise of mantic powers and processes it is possible to determine how the current situation of the cosmos can be classified, and what type of situation is due to be its successor, it is equally possible to regulate one's behaviour and actions in such a way that they will be appropriate to those situations and thus be likely to be crowned with success. In the prevailing view of the sixty-four hexagrams as symbols of major change, it had become possible to predict the likely effect of proposed actions, whether they were launched on a personal scale or initiated on behalf of the state.

These were the philosophical principles that lay behind the production of texts such as the 'Ten Wings' and the teachings that were associated with the *Changes of Chou*. They sought to interpret the long-forgotten meanings of the original pithy statements in the light of contemporary thought. Much of contemporary thought stressed the transitory nature of existence; part of the purpose of the 'Ten Wings' was to demonstrate that behind that apparent transience there existed one overriding permanent principle. This was nothing less than the fact that change itself is continual, pervasive and unavoidable. The significance of the sixty-four hexagrams and the amplifications of the 'Ten Wings' lay in showing how the observed changes of the material world, while being explicable in immediate terms according to the agreed rhythms and cycles of Yin-Yang and the Five Phases, could nonetheless form part of a regular, systematic and cosmic whole. Once that system was comprehended, there would be little difficulty in accommodating to the apparent ruptures in the normal sequences of the natural world, which could otherwise occasion surprise or fear. Eventually the series of sixty-four stages would be used to explain the intellectual problems of creation and to show how a balance could be retained between the three estates of heaven, earth and man. This development occurred after the Han period.

The following citation from the 'Ten Wings', long included as an integral part of the *Book of Changes*, gives some indication of how the sixty-four hexagrams and their system had developed:

> The *Changes* are vast, they are great; however remote the matter for which they are cited, they will not demur; however close the matter to which they are cited they stand upright in tranquillity; and if they are cited in respect of that which lies between heaven and earth they will be applicable.
>
> Consider *Ch'ien** the creative; when at rest it is comprehensive, and when activated it stands upright; and herein is the greatness of the *Changes* created. Consider *K'un** the receptive; when at rest it is closed upon itself; when activated it lies opened wide; and herein is the vastness of the *Changes* created.
>
> Being vast and great the *Changes* match heaven and earth; by embracing the permutations they match the four seasons; by comprehending the principle of Yin and Yang they match the sun and the moon; by virtue of their simplicity they match the noblest qualities that may be attained.

But despite these majestic protestations there were difficulties in accepting that the sixty-four stages exercised a permanent and overriding influence over the world. For while some philosophers had been exploring the meaning of the hexagrams and their symbolical values, others, of a more scientific frame of mind, had been stressing how other cycles of nature operated, for example those that were bound to 5, 12, 28 or 365¼. While metaphysicians could insist that all could be explained in terms of sixty-four, men of science would need to reconcile that cycle with the Five Phases of birth, death and rebirth, the twelve divisions of the year and the heavens, the regular movement of the sun, moon and planets through the twenty-eight lodges

---

* *Ch'ien* and *K'un* are the first two of the sixty-four hexagrams. In addition to the all-important symbolical force of each one, they also signify the two series, each of thirty-two hexagrams, that together make the sixty-four, the one series deriving from the creative principle of Yang and the other from the receptive principle of Yin.

and the sun's own annual cycle of 365¼ days. In addition, whatever protestations might be made regarding the majestic and overriding influence of the sixty-four changes, it was very often difficult to sustain such a conviction in the practical terms of daily life, in face of the disruptions wrought by freaks of nature.

One of the philosophers who addressed himself to these problems was named Ching Fang (probably dated 79–37 BC). His views on strange phenomena or natural outrages will be considered below (Chapter 8), and no small part of his contribution to Chinese thought lay in his attempt to combine a consideration of such matters with the idea of the sixty-four hexagrams. As a man of public affairs, Ching Fang provides a good example of how intellectual developments were bound up with political considerations, and how far achievements in philosophy could sometimes conflict with the success of a career in public life. Ching Fang held pronounced views regarding the contemporary conduct of government and the professional standards of those in high places of society. In the course of debate he antagonised a number of prominent statesmen and suffered the death penalty for his outspokenness at the age of forty-one.

One of the achievements with which Ching Fang was credited was the foundation of one of four schools of expositors of the *Changes*. Each one of these four schools attempted to explain the text of the early document by means of word-for-word or phrase-by-phrase interpretation. This method is to be distinguished from the totally different expositions of those who tried to produce a synthesis, i.e. to explain the meaning of the ancient text and its lessons by a systematic statement of principles, as in the 'Ten Wings'.

From early days Ching Fang's school was regarded as possessing individualist characteristics which distinguished it from the other three schools with which his is generally grouped. He had paid considerable attention to matters such as the origins of climatic changes and their overall message; he had studied the subject of musical harmonies and their relation to the rhythms of nature; and he was known only too well for his accurate prediction of phenomena such as eclipses. In a memorial of 37 BC, which was motivated by political considerations, it seems that he was attempting to show how the cycle of the sixty-four changes can be reconciled with that of the sixty terms which marked the changes of season in the observed world of nature. Citations that are preserved from some of his writings show Ching Fang attempting to formulate general principles from particular cases and to validate the principles at which he had arrived.

Ching Fang sought universal truth in the system of the sixty-four changes and their symbols. But at least one of his contemporaries was of a sufficiently radical frame of mind to reject the *Changes* and their centuries-old authority as being unsatisfactory for such a purpose. This was Yang Hsiung (53 BC to AD 18), well known as a man of letters; parts of his prose and poetry still survive. Feeling that it was not possible to provide for all permutations of the cosmic situation within the scheme of sixty-four stages, Yang Hsiung evolved his own set of symbols, which, while being similar to those of the *Book of Changes*, numbered eighty-one instead of sixty-four. Yang Hsiung's symbols took the form of tetragrams in which each of the four parallel lines took one of three forms: they were either whole, or split into two parts, or split into three parts. In setting out this scheme, in a document entitled the 'Classic of the Great Mysterious' (*T'ai hsüan ching*), Yang Hsiung clearly had the *Book of Changes* in mind as his model. His eighty-one figures are explained in terms of their constituent lines, each with its own implications and with an assessment of the general universal situation that it represents. Like the *Changes of Chou*, the *T'ai hsüan ching* was designed as a guide to be used in divination; for Yang Hsiung believed in the value of such processes to reveal truth. Unlike the *Changes of Chou*, the *T'ai hsüan ching* incorporated intellectual as well as intuitive elements. By substituting his own scheme of linear figures in place of the sixty-four hexagrams, he intended that the process of divination would be both more subtle and more sophisticated.

Like Ching Fang, Yang Hsiung was trying to reconcile a universal scheme with the observed and verified rhythms of parts of the natural world. He met with considerable criticism, on the grounds that he had no right to claim authority for his own scheme that could in any way be comparable with that of the hallowed text of the *Changes of Chou*. He had to wait for a thousand years before his genuine attempt at this type of metaphysics received due praise. This came from the brush of the remarkable historian Ssu-ma Kuang (1019–86).

8

Omens and miracles

The foregoing chapters have been concerned with attempts to explain the positive aspects of the universe and mankind either in mythological or in philosophical terms. We have considered the early views of the heavens and the earth and of the creation of matter. We have noted theories that account for events witnessed on earth as parts of a normal, regular sequence, whose cyclical repetition is essential for the continuation of the world. We have observed the emergence of a series of figures deemed to symbolise all situations and stages of existence.

These attempts have focused on the explicable and constructive acts of nature; but a satisfactory understanding of nature must also provide for events of the opposite type, that are violent or destructive and which defy reconciliation with the accepted scheme. These are the apparent disruptions of the natural order, or strange phenomena that are seen in the heavens, felt on earth or suffered in the world of man. Their size and strength (e.g. of an eclipse or an earthquake) is such that they cannot evade observation or be dismissed as being meaningless. If certain recurrent events of the years, such as the burgeoning of flowers in spring, are taken to be comforting signs that the cycle of nature is operating constructively, so too must unexpected, disruptive and unexplained events constitute omens that strange and possibly alarming or destructive consequences may be due to follow.

The term 'omen' is applied here deliberately to these strange events and their forecasts. It is used to denote the messages believed to lie behind those occurrences of nature that cannot be avoided, and it will be seen below that the term is used in a distinct way from 'divination' and 'oracle' (see Chapter 9). 'Divination' is used for those processes whereby man deliberately produces or manufactures signs whereby he can espy an answer to his problems. 'Oracles' is used of signs that are already inherent in natural objects, which man can see for himself if he takes the trouble to look.

Several attitudes were adopted towards these strange and violent events, or omens. Some regarded them as the deliberate acts of heaven; others believed that they were nature's own response to man's misbehaviour. They were used by some as a means of supporting a political authority, or of criticising an emperor. Others explained these events by looking for precedents; on some occasions a strange occurrence in the natural world formed an excuse for a political measure. Finally we shall see how Wang Ch'ung's attitude, as might be expected, was one of profound scepticism.

Some Chinese of the Han period regarded these events, which had apparently brought about a rupture of the order of nature, as miracles. They were due to direct intervention by a superior power, which was intended to bring benefit to mankind; the superior power was denoted as heaven. This idea formed an integral part of Tung Chung-shu's explanation of the universe and its three interlinked elements of heaven, earth and man, and it will be seen below that these miracles were explained as warnings given by heaven to his son, i.e. the emperor or ruler of man.

In order to maintain support for his own exercise of authority, an emperor needed to show that it was part of the normal working of the universe. If his rule failed to be blessed by tranquillity but was in fact cursed by violent catastrophes, the emperor could not claim that he was an effective ruler within the framework of a beneficent universe; both he and his officials would become subject to suspicion, protest or threat of removal. By explaining untoward events as providential actions which could be expected in certain circumstances as a means of assisting an emperor, Tung Chung-shu lent support to the emperor's position as an integral and essential part of the cosmic scheme.

As this scheme of the universe and the place of temporal power therein served the purposes and hopes of those who wished to govern the empire, violent and catastrophic events inevitably involved political questions. Officials had necessarily to explain the occurrences of natural outrage; faced with such a necessity, they were at times tempted or obliged to exploit these incidents for dynastic or political purposes.

The emperor had to take note of these events and it is thanks to the activities of officials and their reports that our evidence is due. Not only was it the duty of officials who were established within the central government to record and report events such as the aberrations of stars or planets; it was also the duty of provincial officials to submit descriptions of strange occurrences within their areas of administration. For the western Han dynasty alone the histories incorporate reports of between three and four hundred such events. In addition, the histories include the comments and interpretations that were put on these events, i.e. the omens as these appeared to leading statesmen and intellectuals of the day. There are also records of the actions that were taken in response to these reports. Comments were incorporated in the solemn edicts proclaimed by the emperor on these occasions.

A number of strange events were regarded as portents of evil which affected the life-span of an emperor or the destiny of the dynasty. An eclipse which was observed on a day corresponding with 4 March 181 BC caused consternation for the Empress Lü, who had seized control of the empire. 'This is meant for me', she is reported to have remarked; and the histories duly recorded her death in the subsequent year.

The following example shows the detailed nature of the reports that were submitted and finally found their place in the histories. It discloses the attention allegedly paid to the events by one of China's leading intellectuals, and the attempts to draw an analogy between the events reported and precedents of the past:

On the day *ping-hsü* in the second month of the third year of Ho-p'ing [28 March 26 BC] there were landslides on Mount Po-chiang and Mount Chüan-chiang in Csien-wei. The course of the river was blocked and the stream ran in the reverse direction, damaging city-walls and killing 13 persons. Earthquakes were felt, extending for 21 days and registering 124 tremors. On the day *ping-yin* in the first month of the third year of Yüan-yen [12 February 10 BC] there was a landslide at Mount Min in Shu commandery. The course of the River was blocked and the stream ran in the reverse direction, three days elapsing before passage through became possible.

Liu Hsiang took the view that when, in the Chou period, there had been a landslide at Mount Ch'ih and three rivers had dried up, the Yu king had met his end. Now, Mount Ch'ih was the place where Chou had arisen. The Han dynasty had arisen in Shu-Han; landslides were now taking place and the rivers were drying up in its place of origin. In addition there had been a comet, extending from She-t'i to Ta-chiao, starting from Shen and reaching Ch'en.* These events could hardly fail to signify the end of the dynasty.

Three generations subsequently there was no successor to the imperial throne and Wang Mang usurped that position.

Reports of this type referred to activities in the heavens such as eclipses or the fall of meteorites which, though not unprecedented, are out of the normal order of nature. Sometimes they referred to extraordinary phenomena such as the simultaneous appearance of two moons. Some officials reported accidents of nature on earth, such as an unexplained outbreak of fire in a holy place. Other incidents that drew attention included rarities or acts of violence on earth, such as a snowfall which took place in summer, a display of dancing by brown rats, typhoons, swarms of locusts or earthquakes. The birth of prodigies or freaks; accidents that befell man-made objects, such as the collapse of buildings; and references to general calamities such as a succession of poor harvests likewise feature in these records, as do reports which concern man himself (e.g. dreams; apparitions or hallucinations, such as the sudden sound of a multitude of voices or bells, or the spontaneous utterance of a significant truth in children's ditties).

But not all the phenomena that were reported as rarities or unexplained incidents were of a catastrophic or a destructive type. News of the appearance of mythical beasts such as dragon or phoenix was received with acclaim. Examples of *ex post facto* reporting may perhaps be seen in the supernatural circumstances alleged to have ushered in the birth of prominent individuals such as emperors. Edicts welcomed events of a felicitous nature and good augury such as a fall of honey-dew or the choice of the palace as a roosting place by certain spiritually blessed birds. The following account is included in an edict which was proclaimed in 109 BC:

Whereas the magical herb of life has burgeoned within the inner part of Our palace of the Sweet Springs, bearing nine

---

* These are names of constellations or stars.

stalks and interlaced leaves, so are We aware that God on high is immanent in all places, omitting not Our lowly mansions from His care, and bestowing His omnipresent blessing upon Us. We therefore order that a general amnesty be proclaimed throughout the world; and We command that gifts of meat and wine shall be distributed to each group of one hundred households who reside at Our capital site of Yün-yang.

To those of a 'Taoist' frame of mind whose values depended above all on the maintenance of cosmic harmonies, the reasons for the appearance of strange phenomena and for the violent disruptions of nature were not far to seek. They sprang from the imbalances that were brought about in the world largely through man's greed. In a Chinese version of the story of the fall, we may read of the beginning of life as a time of unsullied purity and tranquillity, with no extraneous or artificial considerations to mar the ideal image of a simple state of creation. Such a state of existence comprised its own virtues, and there was no scope for deception. With no deliberate effort or design, man lived at one with the physical structure of heaven and earth, with the essential being of Yin and Yang and with the rhythms of the four seasons; and there was no scheming, contrivance or deception in the human heart or mind.

But there came an age of decadence and decline. This was marked by man's excessive efforts to extract precious stones and minerals from the earth; by his indiscriminate slaughter of young birds and animals; by his extravagant use of timber for building and his clearance of forests to make way for the hunt. This sacrifice of nature's wealth to human greed was still insufficient to satisfy the ambitions of the rulers of men. At a time when material goods were in too short supply for the growing numbers of human beings, strife and discord soon followed. It was in the upset balance of Yin and Yang and the loss of seasonal regularity that natural forces such as lightning, frost or hail wrought destruction on the ten thousand creatures of the earth.

Violent acts of nature were thus the result of man-made disturbances of the universal order. To those whose frame of mind is represented in the *Huai-nan-tzu* they occurred as the spontaneous consequence of such disturbances, without the direct intervention of an identified power. But a different view, that was taken by Tung Chung-shu, soon came to be adopted as part of the orthodox 'Confucian' dogma and to be exploited for dynastic or political purposes.

Tung Chung-shu's thought combined an understanding of the natural way of the world with attention to ethical principles and the improvement of man. He saw that the processes of birth, decay and rebirth follow one another according to the Five Phases, and he believed that human institutions followed the same pattern. To the view that the three estates of heaven, earth and man form parts of a single unity and cannot operate independently, he added or revived the concept of heaven as a superior authority, capable of giving guidance to man and of superintending his destinies. Heaven remained undefined; but it deliberately participated in human affairs, and conferred its blessing on a ruler of man, provided that he conducted himself appropriately, without abusing the great charge and gifts with which he had been endowed.

Tung Chung-shu held fast to one further principle, that the lessons of the past may be applied to an understanding of the present. In seeking to establish a sequential view of history, he held to the idea of a golden past followed by the fall. But to Tung the fall was somewhat different from the view of the *Huai-nan-tzu* to which reference has been made above. He saw his historical sequences in political and ethical terms, as the benign rule of the early kings of Chou, followed by the disunity of China and the suffering of the Chinese people during the periods of the *Spring and Autumn Annals* and the *Warring States* (i.e. from 770 to 221 BC). Tung Chung-shu's main source of knowledge for this period was a document entitled the *Spring and Autumn Annals* (*Ch'un-ch'iu*), which tersely records events that took place between 722 and 484, and which was believed to have been compiled or edited by Confucius.

To Tung and the author of this chronicle the rule of the early kings of Chou had been exemplary, being blessed by the authority of heaven; no less a teacher than Confucius had time and again praised those kings for their beneficent example. Much of Tung Chung-shu's philosophy was an extension of the teachings of Confucius as applied to his own time. For this reason and others Tung is regarded as the founder of Han Confucianism, as this came to be accepted during the imperial period.

Tung Chung-shu fastened on historial instances wherein the

order of nature had been subject to upset or violence, and related
them to the political disturbances that attended instability in his
own day. He believed that strange phenomena were to be
explained as being due to the direct intervention of heaven, being
designed to show a ruler the error of his ways in time for him to
repent. The warnings that heaven chose to give were in the form
of disorders in the skies or on earth that were analogous to the
disorders brought about by the ruler's own errors of omission or
commission; the connection could be traced without difficulty.
Initially, examples of this type of event and its lessons were
found in the history of previous ages, and Tung Chung-shu and
others applied their interpretations retrospectively. As a later
development, they were applied in like manner to contemporary
events. Fortunately the *Han shu* includes a statement of the
principles that are involved, which is ascribed to Tung Chung-
shu (*c.* 179–*c.* 104 BC) himself:

> On the day *ting-yu* in the sixth month of Chien-yüan in the
> reign of Wu ti [i.e. a day corresponding with 9 July 135 BC], a
> disastrous fire broke out in the shrine dedicated to Kao ti in
> Liao-tung. On the day *jen-tzu* of the fourth month [25 May]
> there was a fire in one of the halls of rest in the park maintained
> in honour of Kao ti. Tung Chung-shu commented as follows:
> 'The method of the *Spring and Autumn Annals* is to cite events
> of the past in order to explain those of the future. For this
> reason, when a phenomenon occurs in the world, look to see
> what comparable events are recorded in the *Spring and Autumn
> Annals*; find out the essential meaning of its subtleties and
> mysteries in order to ascertain the significance of the event;
> and comprehend how it is classified in order to see what causes
> are implied. Changes wrought in heaven and on earth, and
> events that affect a dynasty will then all become crystal clear,
> with nothing left in doubt.

An edict which was proclaimed just at the start of Tung
Chung-shu's life, in 178 BC, shows that he was in fact drawing
on assumptions that had already been accepted. The occasion
was the solar eclipse of 2 January 178 BC, and the edict read as
follows:

> We are informed that when heaven gave life to the human race

it instituted rulers to look after its members and to keep them
in order. When a ruler of mankind is not possessed of the
appropriate qualities or when his measures of administration
are not fair, heaven points out these failings by means of a
calamity so as to give warning of the disorders.

Throughout the Han dynasty there were times when officials
reported the occurrence of strange events, and a study of these
occasions reveals that the incidents had been selected on anything
but a regular basis. They served as a means of voicing criticism
against a government without infringing the majesty of the
emperor; for all failings could be attributed to those who
surrounded him. A conspicuous instance of outspoken criticism
is reported for the events of 5 January 29 BC, when a solar eclipse
was accompanied by earth tremors that were registered within
the imperial palace itself that same night. The court and
government were deeply impressed, or even frightened, by this
possibly unique coincidence, of phenomena that appeared in
heaven and on earth within the same day. Tu Ch'in, a prominent
man of letters, submitted a lengthy comment which included the
following passage:

The solar eclipse occurred on the day *mou-shen*; ... that night
there was an earthquake which was felt in the buildings of the
Wei-yang Palace. These events must surely foretell disasters
that will follow a struggle for favour between the empress and
the other consorts and the injury that they wreak upon one
another. I ask Your Majesty to take due heed of this
warning....
It is for Your Majesty to regulate relations with the empress
and the other consorts; to control the favours extended to
women; to prevent extravagance; to forego indulgence in idle
enjoyments; to cultivate personal parsimony; to take a personal interest in the manifold affairs of state....
But if attention is not paid to these various matters; ... if the
resources of the world are wholly spent so as to support a life
given over to licentiousness and extravagance; if the strength
of the whole population is used solely to satisfy material
indulgences; if the court finds room for men who are given to
flattery while excluding those who are marked by integrity;
and if it trusts those officials who spread calumnies while

punishing those who are stamped by loyalty; it will then happen that men of wisdom seek a refuge from public life in caves, their talents unused, and senior ministers of state will feel aggrieved that they are not given office; and even though there may be no strange events, the homeland will suffer damage....

The incidents of 29 BC provoked another statesman, Ku Yung, to attribute these dire events to heaven's criticism of the personal conduct of the emperor, which was unworthy of his station and likely to bring disgrace to his position. Ku Yung specifically advised the emperor to reform his ways and to concentrate more on matters of state and less on affairs with women.

The phenomena of the heavens and the earth and their dire warnings feature in reports from officials and edicts that were issued throughout the remainder of the Han dynasty. They played a particularly conspicuous part in the attempts made by Wang Mang to demonstrate that the establishment of his own dynasty in AD 9 had received the blessing of heaven. The doctrine remained unquestioned by Liu Hsiang and Liu Hsin, two highly intelligent men of letters, whose work contributed markedly to the formation of the Confucian tradition as is shown elsewhere (see p. 187). Finally, in AD 166 a brave critic named Hsiang K'ai based much of his virulent attack on the eunuchs on the evidence of strange phenomena and their significance in the affairs of men.

We have had occasion above to note the views of Ching Fang in connection with the cycle of change (see p. 78). A large number of citations from 'Mr Ching's amplifications of the Changes', which are quoted in the Standard Histories, have in fact to do with strange events and their value as portents. These are short statements, of the form 'given situation x, its portent is y', e.g.:

In the third month of the first year of T'ien Han [100 BC] there was a rain of white hair from the sky; in the eighth month of the third year [98 BC] there was a fall of white coarse hair from the sky. According to Mr Ching's amplification of the Changes, 'Joy first, sorrow later; the portent for this is a rain of feathers from heaven'. There is a further saying, 'Bad men up in front, good men take to flight; down falls the hair from the skies'.

A study of meteorology had enabled Ching Fang to forecast the appearance of certain climatic conditions with accuracy, and he had earned a correspondingly high reputation. In addition he expressed the view that portents for good or evil are the direct consequences of human decisions. It was on this basis that he tried to persuade his emperor (Yüan ti) to eliminate some of his advisers. These were men who were at enmity with Ching Fang; for his failure to make his point with sufficient conviction, the latter forfeited his life.

As a final example of the effect of this belief in omens on imperial policy, let us quote an edict of the year 60 BC, which is concerned with events of an auspicious nature:

> The following edict was proclaimed in the second month of the second year [of Shen-chüeh, i.e. 60 BC]:
> On the day *i-chou* of the first month just passed [5 March] phoenix assembled and honeydew descended in the capital city, accompanied by flocks of birds numbered by the ten thousand. Unworthy as We are We have frequently received in this way the benediction of heaven, 'merely attending to Our duties without indolence'.* We command that an amnesty be declared throughout the world.

But there were those of a rationalist frame of mind to whom these notions had no appeal. The best-known example is Wang Ch'ung, who, as we have seen, insisted that the creation of matter comes about spontaneously and without deliberate intent. He likewise reacted strongly against any suggestion that phenomena such as eclipses, earthquakes or the birth of freaks owe their origin to a deliberate decision reached by heaven. He could not conceive that heaven possesses a special purpose of warning mankind or the rulers of men of their errors. Nor could he see any consistent pattern in human history that would verify that heaven was actually doing so. He asked how it could be supposed that these incidents could be purposefully activated:

> Now, as we know, heaven takes no deliberate action and therefore does not speak. Calamities and changes of nature come about in their own time, being caused by vital energies.

* This is a short citation from the *Book of Documents*, for which see Chapter 16.

In so far as heaven and earth are not able to take deliberate action, so are they likewise unable to attain cognition.

There may be a cold within a man's stomach which will then suffer pain; but it is not the man who has brought this about, it is the vital energies of their own accord. The space between heaven and earth is comparable with that between a man's back and his stomach.

If we are to say that heaven causes calamities and natural changes, are we also to suppose that all manner of strange phenomena, small or great, mild or grave, are in each case the work of heaven? Suppose that a cow gives birth to a foal, or that a peach tree bears plums. According to what our friends say, are we to believe that a spirit of heaven has penetrated the cow's womb to make the foal, or implanted plum seeds within the peach tree?

9

Divination and oracles

A distinction has been drawn above between the use of the terms omens, divination and oracles. Omens are the lessons inherent in the mighty disturbances of nature which none can avoid observing; divination results from the deliberate steps taken by man to induce signs from which a message may be learnt; and oracles are the signs already present in natural objects, plain for man to see if he takes the trouble to find them. While this distinction may serve to clarify our understanding of these matters, there is no reason to suppose that it was consciously borne in mind by the Chinese masters of these techniques or the seers, philosophers and officials who have left their interpretations and comments behind them. Nor is it necessary for us to adhere too rigidly to these distinctions, particularly that between divination and oracles. For 'divination' as defined here includes the manipulation of shells and bones in order to procure a message or a sign. However, the term 'oracle bones' has become so well entrenched in western usage that it would be excessively pedantic to abandon it.

Divination has a long history in China which may be traced back to the first evidences of civilisation and the emergence of the earliest known records of connected writing. It arose from the hope of ascertaining the appropriate nature or value of a proposed activity, and it started as a spontaneous process brought about by a seer and his instinct. But with the passage of time dependence on the natural powers of the seer gave way to some measure of artificiality; intellectual considerations overlaid prophetic utterances; and standard regulations were written down to ensure that the processes were carried out correctly and with economy.

There were two principal methods of divination; first with the use of shells and bones, and secondly with the use of stalks. The origin of the processes was necessarily affected by religious beliefs, and most of the early exercises were directed to ascertaining the will of *ti*, or God on high. But at an early stage of Chinese thought and belief there enters in the basic idea of lucky (*chi*) and unlucky (*hsiung*), as qualities which were inherent in particular days or sites. By the Ch'in and Han periods the majority of the questions put to divination were intended to find out those circumstances of time and place that would be suitable for a proposed action, or whether an action could be planned so as to fit in with an appropriate stage of the cycle of being.

One characteristic of divination and oracles as practised in China is the value placed on linear patterns as the signs of a message. This is apparent in both of the principal methods, those of shells and of stalks, where lines were induced to appear by man. It is also found in the concept of geomancy as this came to be developed, from origins that can be traced at least to the Han period. It may be noted that the stress on linear patterns is by no means limited to China; divination and oracles of other cultures fasten equally on such patterns, whatever the medium in which they are seen.

Different types of evidence suggest that divination and oracles were matters of considerable importance in Han China. The Standard Histories record incidents in which divination was practised, either for an individual's sake or on behalf of the emperor and his government. Sometimes these accounts include opinions that were voiced by statesmen regarding the validity of the proceedings. In addition there are the *Han shu*'s lists of manuals and books that had been compiled on these subjects and which formed part of the imperial library at the beginning of the Christian era. One of the chapters of the *Shih-chi* itself sets out prescriptions for the use of divination with shells and bones, in the form of guidance for practitioners. The institutions of state included an establishment for specialists in divination along with those who were masters of other arts or sciences such as astrology, medicine and music. The opinions of philosophers of different schools are expressed in memorials submitted to the throne, in compilations such as the *Huai-nan-tzu* or in tracts such as the chapters of the *Lun-heng*. Finally, evidence for the practice of divination is found in a number of manuscript copies of manuals made for experts and their pupils. Archaeology has also revealed a few examples of instruments which may be identified as the ancestors of the magnetic compasses that were used much later in geomancy (*feng-shui*).

Turtles' shells and animals' bones formed the regular medium for divination during the Shang dynasty (traditionally 1766–1122 BC) and previously; and the method was still employed during the Han period. The early practice had comprised a long and solemn rite in which the Shang kings themselves sometimes took part. The shells or bones were first weakened by the application of a poker or similar instrument; they were then exposed to intense heat. The seer or specialist would await the emergence of cracks in the material, and from their frequency, shape or other details he would pronounce the answer to the question that had been raised. Essentially, the method consisted of the deliberate production of a linear pattern by artificial means.

Once the bone cracking had been completed, an account of the incident was engraved on the bone or shell, with the question that was posed, the prognostication that the cracks suggested and, sometimes, a factual record of the outcome. It is thanks to this practice that the earliest forms of Chinese writing have been preserved. The remains of the bones and shells that were used show that before the end of the Shang period some measure of standardisation had set in. In a number of cases the poker or instrument had been applied successively in a neat and regular fashion, thus ensuring that the material could be used as economically as possible. The style of the inscriptions also testifies to the orderly minds of those who engraved them in a regular, systematic fashion.

No remains have yet been found of shells or bones used during the Han period, but literary evidence shows that the practice continued at that time and that it became subject to an increasing degree of standardisation. A chapter of the *Shih-chi* (no. 128), part of which was inserted from about the start of the Christian era, includes prescriptions for the ritual. There is also a complete scheme of the types of mark which might be expected to appear on the plastra of the turtles, with rules for their use and interpretation. The same chapter carries a list of the types of question that may be put, regarding matters such as illness, the prospect for the crops or climate, the likely outcome of commercial transactions or the expediency of searching for robbers. There is also a description of thirty types of crack that can be discriminated on the shells or bones.

The best type of turtle was rare, with a certain mystique attached to its provenance; this may be seen in the *Shih-chi's* account of a somewhat strange ancient rite. This assumed that the tortoise or turtle and the yarrow might be associated together, with the plant growing above and the tortoise lying below. After a fresh shower of rain, when the skies were clear and no wind blew, certain specified plants were cleared from the undergrowth by night; bonfires were set alight, and a particular note was taken of the spot where they were extinguished. This spot was then encircled with a length of forty feet of new cloth, and digging could start the next day. A magical plant described as the root of the thousand-year-old pine could be found at a depth of 4–7 feet but not beyond; and those who ate this plant would not die. In a manner that is not entirely clear the text associates this rite with the yarrow plant; for it adds the further information that, provided the yarrow plant bears its full complement of 100 stalks, there must be a divine tortoise guarding it below. Elsewhere in the same chapter we read that shells used in divination were preserved as sacred relics, in the shrine dedicated to the memory of the first of the Han emperors.

The other principal method of divination was the deliberate formation of a linear pattern of six lines, by casting or manipulating the stalks of the yarrow plant. This had been practised for some centuries before the Ch'in and Han dynasties. Like the turtle, the yarrow was believed to possess magical properties that derived partly from its longevity. According to some accounts the turtle was believed to live for as long as three thousand years, and it was during that long period that it had acquired its store of wisdom. The yarrow plant also lived to a great age, maturing slowly; one stalk was grown every seventy years, and after seven hundred years there would be ten stalks. According to another ancient tradition, when the whole world lies at peace and harmony, and when government that is in accordance with the true principles of kingship prevails, the stalks of the yarrow grow to a length of ten feet, and they will number no less than a hundred.

Casting the stalks included a random element. During the ritual they were divided into small groups by chance; and depending on the numbers of the stalks thus cast, so was the diviner entitled and obliged to construct each of the six lines of the pattern and thus form his hexagram. Although it is not known for certain in what way this manipulation took place during the Ch'in and Han periods, there is a suggestion that the method was similar to that which is used today, with a cast of forty-nine out of an original fifty stalks. The cast of the stalks determined whether the line that emerged was complete or split, and whether it was fixed in that form or on the point of changing into the other.

The original process of divination by stalks and hexagram depended on the seer's immediate recognition of how the resulting hexagram applied to the problem that was under consideration. By the Han period, as has been seen above (see Chapter 7), the process had been accompanied and even superseded by the consultation of ancient texts or manuals that served as guides; the difficulty of understanding those manuals had led to the formation of a whole branch of literature and philosophy, from which profound intellectual consequences stemmed. But an element of mystery survived, as may be seen in the following remarks of Ssu-ma Ch'ien, apropos of divination by turtle shells and yarrow stalks:

When I travelled south of the Yangtse river, I observed the practices there and questioned the old men. They told me that once in a thousand years the turtle will crawl over the leaves of the lotus and a hundred stalks will grow from a single root of the yarrow. Moreover, when these things come to pass, there will be no wild beast such as tiger or wolf among the animals, and nothing in the undergrowth that is venomous or will sting. Families living on the banks of the River have always nurtured the turtles, fed them and given them to drink, in the belief that they will be able to induce a flow of vital energy, and thus serve to succour the weak and keep the old alive. All this must surely be true.

As in most cultures, so in China there was a deep-seated belief that certain periods or moments of time and certain regions or localities possessed inherent qualities that made them fit or unfit for particular activities. The incidence of good or ill fortune depended partly on the correspondence between such properties and the circumstances of the individual who was most intimately concerned; for there must be no conflict between the timing of actions in terms of the year or the calendar and the chronological cycle of that individual's own fortunes. As with the principles of divination, so here the beliefs were in the first instance instinctive and irrational; it was only in the secondary stage that they became subject to intellectual categorisation and the inhibitions of a written manual. Unlike divination, there was no question of deliberately inducing signs which would reveal the nature of a proposed activity; a professional could ascertain this from natural observation and the application of his esoteric power.

The belief may be illustrated most directly from a text that is slightly later than the Han period but which may nonetheless be regarded as being applicable to that time. This is the passage which has been cited (see p. 22) above in connection with the mysteries and the dangers of the mountains:

> So the mountains should not be entered without due thought. You should choose the third or the ninth months, which are the times when they are properly open; and within those months you should choose a day that is propitious and an hour that is felicitous. If you cannot wait for one of these months, then at least choose the right day and time. And all those who enter the hills should first purify themselves for seven days; they should not pass through filth or corruption, and they should carry with them the talismans for the ascent of the hills.

The strength of the beliefs, in practical terms, is illustrated in an anecdote that is related of Ming ti (reigned 57–75). It is said that he was once somewhat surprised to learn that the presentation of reports to the throne was forbidden on certain days of the calendrical sequence so as to conform with these beliefs; he abolished the ban without delay.

Literature of the Han period includes a number of references to the expression *k'an-yü*. The full meaning of this term had already eluded some writers of the third century AD, and much later it was re-adopted to denote the practice of geomancy with the use of a magnetic compass. For the period under consideration the term seems to denote a system for choosing the right days for a particular purpose. At least one manual on the subject was available for consultation on the shelves of the imperial library at the start of the Christian era. In addition, fragments of a manuscript text found quite recently can almost certainly be identified as parts of just such a work. This was found in a tomb of north-west China that was probably sealed in the time of Wang Mang's reign (AD 9–23) or a little later. The following sentences serve as examples of the manuscript's prescriptions:

> On *chia* days do not build a house; you will not live there and it will certainly run to waste.
> On *i* days do not bring materials home; you will not keep them and they will certainly perish.

Such prescriptions designate days according to the terms of the two cycles of twelve and ten, which were regarded as regulating the operations of the universe (see p. 53). When the principle of *k'an-yü* was applied to matters of personal choice, it was likely that these general rules were reconciled with similar considerations of the key days or dates that affected an individual's life.

There are also indications of a strong belief in a similar principle, i.e. the inherent suitability of certain places for a proposed purpose, be this the erection of a house, the orientation of a building or city or the choice of a burial plot. This was one of the principles that led later to the widespread practice of geomancy (*feng-shui*) that has so affected the face of Chinese cities and landscapes. For the Han period little is known of the underlying principle or the techniques that were applied. There are some suggestions regarding the 'veins of the earth', and there survive a few specimens of instruments that were in use in the second century BC and which may be concerned with later developments.

The veins of the earth were natural channels or properties of the earth which could only be ruptured at one's peril. It is hardly surprising that a belief in their integrity appears in the *Huai-nan-tzu*'s naturalist view of the universe. They are comparable with the underlying principles which maintain the integrity of heaven and of man; they may be observed by careful inspection of the topography of a region; or they may be apprehended by a seer gifted with special powers. To eliminate disaster and to assure a successful outcome of a venture, it is essential to avoid interfering with these life-lines.

The idea appears in a somewhat surprising anecdotal context. The famous general Meng T'ien, who had served the Ch'in empire valiantly and succeeded in protecting north China against the incursions of alien raiders, eventually fell a victim to professional and political jealousies and received orders to commit suicide. In searching his mind and conscience to determine in what way he could rightly be judged guilty of disloyalty, the only fault with which he could blame himself was that of severing the veins of the earth, in the course of constructing his defence lines. In rational terms, the veins are explained as life-lines along which the vital energy that is needed to keep the earth alive proceeds. In choosing a site for a house or a grave it is necessary to ensure that it will be fed with a sufficient supply of such energy and that constructional work will not endanger the smooth distribution of such energy elsewhere.

Instruments (*shih*: diviners' boards) known to have been used from at least the second century BC were designed to ensure that the cycles of the heavens and the earth had reached a point that was suitable for a proposed action. From such instruments there eventually developed the magnetic compasses that were used for purposes of geomancy from perhaps the eleventh century; but in the initial stages the boards were used to ascertain the answers to a variety of questions, and not necessarily those which concerned the choice of a site for a house or a grave. The instruments were set to show the position reached by the sun in the heavens and to orientate the observer with the directions of the earth. Once these settings had been found, it was possible to read off from a set of symbols on the boards whether a proposed action would be successful or not. The boards served to combine intellectual and intuitive approaches to the problems of life.

Other forms of oracle are exemplified in the inspection of the inherent qualities or signs of natural conditions such as clouds, winds, rainbows or comets. A recently found manuscript of before 168 BC bears text and diagrams used for consultative purposes in this respect.

Chinese of the Han period cracked their shells and bones, manipulated their yarrow, or milfoil, stalks or set their diviners' boards for a variety of purposes. They raised questions of probability, such as whether a patient would be cured of an illness or what would be the outcome of a battle. There were some who asked for direct advice, e.g. should a child be raised or not; should a military leader surrender to a conqueror? Sometimes specialists in divination were asked to enquire whether a proposed time would be suitable for a funeral or for a wedding, or whether a specified site was suitable for habitation or for burial. Some of the questions were matters of choice between several alternative candidates for advancement, either for selection as an heir or for a high-ranking appointment of state.

A number of instances are recorded in which questions such as the dynastic succession are said to have depended on divination. In 180 BC the king of Tai (known as Wen ti) consulted the turtle before deciding whether he should accept the invitation to become emperor; at the close of the Han period in AD 220 the future Wei Wu ti had the stalks cast before agreeing to a similar suggestion. Similarly, at a moment of crisis in 74 BC a senior statesman suggested consultation of the turtle and the stalks before inviting a candidate (the future Hsüan ti) to become emperor. In eastern Han there were cases of divination by a cast of stalks and the *Book of Changes* to determine the likely character and destiny of a girl, before settling that she should become an imperial consort.

Divination featured among a whole host of precautions taken by the Han government before embarking on the expensive campaign of military advance to the west in 102 BC. We are told that the hexagram which emerged (*Ta kuo*: no. 28) and the appropriate passage in the *Book of Changes* yielded an encouraging interpretation; in addition, the choice of the general who was to lead the campaign likewise depended on the cast of the stalks. In the event the campaign was costly and hardly successful, and an imperial edict had perforce to admit that 'the prognosticators have all been gainsaid and confounded'. On a different level, but still within a military context, the *Huai-nan-tzu* records a custom whereby, on receiving titular appointment from the emperor to take command of military forces at a time of emergency, a general officer would give orders for his religious aides to fast and keep vigil, and then to divine by use of the turtle to determine a favourable day for the formal acceptance of his commission.

In the same text there is a description of a regular act of divination whose origin can probably be traced back to the Shang period, and which persisted until the nineteenth century. On the day of the winter solstice the emperor led his senior statesmen in solemn procession to the sacred sites of worship, on the north side of the city, there to greet the incoming year. As part of the ceremonies of this month he ordered his chief functionaries to divine by turtle and yarrow, so as to ascertain the fortune that would characterise the new year.

Finally, we read of a case of divination or prognostication whose results were by no means unanimous or clear. There was an occasion when Wu ti (reigned 141 to 87) called together specialists in all types of divination and other techniques to determine whether a certain date would be suitable for him to take a wife. The masters of the Five Phases advised that he could do so; but specialists in *k'an-yü* and other varieties of the art were far less encouraging, even to the point of definitely prognosticating misfortune of a high order. The experts in the service to the Grand Unity, however, pronounced that the event would be followed by the greatest of good luck. Others were indecisive. According to the edict of the day, the emperor chose to come down in favour of the masters of the Five Phases. Unfortunately the identity of the consort in question is not revealed; it remains unknown how far these specialists were vindicated.

The frequency with which divination was practised is suggested by recorded criticism of its excesses and abuses. One of the poems of the *Songs of the South*, which may be dated around the middle of the third century BC, makes the point that neither the turtle nor the stalks form appropriate means of seeking answers to questions that involve principle or ethics. In a tract that was probably written between *c.* 60 and *c.* 50 BC, a critic of the contemporary political and social scene drew attention to the rarity with which, he alleged, divination had been practised in the golden past, in contrast with the prevalent custom of trusting regularly and blindly to the choice of a day, for good or ill. An even stronger view was expressed by a writer in the middle part of the second century AD. Wang Fu noted how the acknowledged masters and sages of the past had consulted shells and stalks properly and appropriately; but he castigated the practice of doing so as a means of furthering personal schemes or ambitions.

We have noted several references to divination in the *Huai-nan-tzu*, and as we might expect in that compilation the general view of these processes reflects the nature–centred attitude to the world of 'Taoist' thought. In the state of primeval bliss, when mankind still lived in natural harmony with his surroundings and his fellow creatures, there was no need to practise divination by shells or stalks, or to take deliberate steps to choose a suitable

day for an activity; for successful results would be achieved
without artificial effort. It was only after the fall (see p. 44) that it
became necessary and commendable to do so, for by then human
greed and ambition were beginning to damage the order of
nature. A famous passage of the book carries a great paean of
praise to the institution of the order of nature on the skies and on
earth, in contrast with the puny results of human skills and
intellect. Those men who were really great did their best to
achieve harmony with the qualities of heaven; to achieve that
result it is justifiable for ordinary mortals to offer prayer to those
spirits that cannot be perceived in material form, and to practise
divination before taking decisions.

The *Shih-chi* records an anecdote in which the validity of
divination was first brought into question and then vindicated.
Two men of letters, including the famous poet and philosopher
Chia I (200–168) paid a visit one day to Diviners' Row in
Ch'ang-an city. They had been arguing about the place and
purpose of divination, and, sharing a carriage to drive there, they
fell in with a practitioner called Ssu-ma Chi-chu. It so happened
that there were few people around in the streets that day, as it had
just been raining, and they found the master at leisure with a
mere handful of pupils; they were discussing the order of heaven
and earth, the orbits of the sun and the moon, and basic questions
of Yin-Yang, and good and ill fortune.

The two visitors were greatly impressed with Ssu-ma Chi-
chu's discourse and expressed their surprise at the humble way of
life that he obviously led. Ssu-ma Chi-chu burst out laughing,
and roundly asked them what they did regard as humble or
honourable. He claimed that by real standards his own way of life
was in no way to be despised. He agreed that according to the
generally accepted view of the world his own occupation could
not be compared with that of high-ranking officials such as his
two distinguished visitors; but he insisted that, so far from being
contemptible, his profession was bound by a considerably
greater degree of integrity than an official's career. For, he
argued, many officials so lacked integrity that they would stop at
nothing to promote their own interests, whatever the detriment
might be to the public; whereas specialists in divination set about
their work according to the highest professional standards, in
deep consideration of the major principles of the universe. In
addition, divination brought notable benefits to the world, such

as the placation of holy spirits and demons, or the cure of the sick; and it encouraged all the virtues of loyal service in state and family. The incident closes with the discomfiture of the two officials by Ssu-ma Chi-chu's eloquence.

It is hardly surprising that Wang Ch'ung voiced a different opinion from that of the *Huai-nan-tzu*. In his usual rationalist frame of mind he set about the task of exposing the fallacies inherent in the contemporary belief that certain days or times were likely to be lucky or unlucky occasions for certain activities. By way of example he criticised the way in which funerals were so arranged that they would accord with this principle. He argued that obedience to the principle was subject to inconsistency, and that it therefore rested on false premises. He asked why it should be thought right to make a point of choosing suitable days for some activities but not for others; and he criticised the failure to seek a real connection between cause and effect.

But there were those of Wang Ch'ung's contemporaries who took a different and more moderate view, and we must cite the qualified approval of divination by two men, as well known for their practical turn of mind as Wang Ch'ung was for his rationalism. From about AD 60 Wang Ching had earned a reputation as a successful irrigational engineer, and in 82 he was given a responsible post in provincial administration. In his youth he had been trained in the *Book of Changes*, and he is described as being skilled in astronomy and mathematics, with a deep understanding of technical details. According to Wang Ching's biography, he had had occasion to note the frequent references to divination in some of the 'scriptural' texts (see Chapter 16), and had observed some discrepancies in the manuals that concerned these techniques. These, however, did not suffice to destroy his faith in the validity of the processes; for he set about assembling all the writings that he could collect on these subjects and drew up his own compendium to show how they were applicable to the problems of daily life.

A belief in the efficacy of divination is also apparent in the case of Chang Heng (78–139) who is well known for his construction of scientific instruments. Chang Heng's practical mind retained considerable respect for the mysterious. His keen sense of criticism rejected outright a dogmatic belief in some of the contemporary writings that had acquired a pseudo-scriptural authority; and in attacking such texts he may well have had in mind some of the writings that purported to explain the mysteries of the *Changes*. But as against the falsity of such texts he draws attention to the frequent validation of forecasts derived from divination or the consultation of oracles; the latter included prognostications based on the movements of the stars or the behaviour of the winds. It seems likely that Chang Heng accepted these phenomena and revelations as signs of impending events. If these forecasts could not be understood on scientific grounds, they must nonetheless be accepted, for reasons that lie beyond the power of human understanding.

10
Shamans and intermediaries

According to one of the earliest passages in Chinese literature to mention shamans, long ago there was no communication between ordinary mortals and the holy spirits; but there were some specially favoured persons, incapable of deceit, whose wisdom encompassed a natural sense of right and wrong. Their qualities were such that they spread a radiance around and they could hear and understand everything. It was upon such persons that the holy spirits would descend. The passage notes the use of two terms to describe these individuals, one for men and one for women; the terms are usually rendered 'shaman'.

A number of other passages which likewise date from the pre-imperial period help to fill out the idea of the shaman or intermediary in early China. The distinction of sex does not seem to have been maintained as a matter of great importance. The shamans were not only concerned with invoking spirits and acting as intermediaries between gods and men; they also possessed specialist powers as physicians who could prevent or heal diseases. They could also stimulate fertility and assist in childbirth. They could sometimes bring down spirits by means of impersonation; they performed ritual dances to promote marriage, and by dance and music they invoked rain. They may even have made themselves invisible as part of the invocation, during which they would hold or brandish instruments or symbols of jade.

In several passages the *Classic of the Mountains and the Lakes* names shamans whose activities were connected with the holy places listed in that mythical catalogue. In the land of Wu Hsien, or the Shaman Hsien, there are those who brandish green or blue snakes in their right hands and red snakes in their left hands. This is on Mount Teng-pao, where a whole host of shamans move up and down. Another part of the book, probably of a later date, names six shamans whose arms encompass the body of Yeh-yü, a hybrid creature with a snake's body and a human head. They are also said to stand possessed of the elixir that forfends death. Yet another chapter describes the 'mountain of the snakes and the shamans upon which there are men who clasp wooden staves and stand facing the east'.

In addition to the *Classic of the Mountains and the Lakes* there is other evidence which illustrates the view of the shaman in early China. The silk manuscript which dates from perhaps the third or fourth century BC bears twelve figures at its periphery that may well be interpreted as shamans acting in their capacity as invokers of holy spirits. Moreover there are allusions to the subject in some of the manuscript medical treatises found at Ma-wang-tui, in a tomb dated at 168 BC. These not only include prescriptions for dealing with observed and diagnosed symptoms; there are also references to invocations that could be used to eliminate disease, presumably through the medium of specialists or shamans who possessed the necessary powers.

It is noticeable that these references derived from the culture of central and southern China, that grew up around the Yangtse river valley. From the same area, the *Songs of the South* likewise sheds light on the belief in the powers of the shaman and his practice. The two principal poems to be considered in this connection, the *Summons of the soul* and the *Great Summons* (*Chac hun* and *Ta chao*), were probably composed in the second half of the third century BC. They consist of invocations, one of which is specifically put into the mouth of the Shaman Yang; they are designed to lure back the souls of recently deceased persons and thus restore them to life. The poems or invocations describe the terrible dangers attendant on those who venture into the unknown world beyond the grave, and hold out hopes of a return to the delights and pleasures that may be enjoyed in a life on earth.

In a further series of poems, the *Nine Songs*, that are included in the collection and probably date from the third century BC, shamanism has acquired a particular form, in which the shaman's relationship with the spirit is represented as a kind of love-affair. Arthur Waley writes of this as follows:

> In the Nine Songs the typical form is this: first the shaman (a man if the deity is female, a girl if the deity is male) sees the Spirit descending and goes out to meet it, riding in an equipage

sometimes drawn by strange or mythical creatures. In the next part of the song the shaman's meeting with the Spirit (a sort of mantic honeymoon) is over. The Spirit has proved fickle and the shaman wanders about love-lorn, waiting in vain for the lover's return. Between these two parts may have come the shaman's main ecstatic dance.

A number of named shamans appear in the pages of the standard histories that cover the Han period, and there is considerable evidence to show that a belief in the shaman and his powers was widespread. It was particularly prevalent in the Yangtse river valley, the home of the old state of Ch'u whose rich mythology has been noted above. Another region singled out for mention in this connection lay further north, along the Huai river. This had been the old state of Ch'en, where women were held in high esteem and there was a deep love of religious observances. Further east, in the Shantung peninsula (the former state of Ch'i) we hear of a special practice which had survived from long previously.

There was a general ban imposed there on the marriage of the eldest daughters of an ordinary family. These girls were singled out for other purposes; they were termed the 'children of the shaman' and became responsible for the religious rites conducted on behalf of each family. The association of shamans with the observance of worship and sacrifice to deities is also known from another reference. At the outset of the Han dynasty a complement of religious officials and women shamans was established at Ch'ang-an city. Many of these shamans were assigned specific responsibilities, e.g. for the worship of the Five Powers, or the Lord of the East. At the time of the great religious reforms of 31 BC this complement of officiants was disbanded.

The *Huai-nan-tzu* alludes to the powers possessed by the *ling*, an expression that sometimes denotes the shaman, that enabled them to control the winds and the rain. In addition to being able to observe ghosts, they also invoked the presence of spirits. According to one report, in the *Hou Han shu*, a named shaman who came from Ch'i served with the rebel forces who rose up in AD 18 and became known as the Red Eyebrows. This shaman practised dancing and music in the course of worship to one of the local deities of Ch'i; he was hoping to procure happiness and help thereby. But there were those in the camp who scoffed at the utterances that the shaman produced, as from the god, and which enjoined the army to fight for the imperial rather than the rebel cause. The sceptics were immediately struck down by illness, and not unnaturally some confusion reigned in the rebel camp.

In one passage the *Huai-nan-tzu* groups the powers of the physician with his needle and stone together with those of the shaman. According to one anecdote a shaman could exercise powers to cure a disease when she was herself afflicted with illness. This is reported in connection with Wu ti, who fell ill in 118 BC. Despite the attendance of every physician and shaman who could be found, there was no improvement in his condition, until it was suggested that he should summon a special shaman from the north. It was said that when she herself fell ill, spirits would descend into her person. In due course she contracted an illness and the emperor was duly cured through her powers of intercession.

Other reports remark on the relations of shamans with individuals in the normal conditions of everyday life. Huang Pa, who rose to the high office of chancellor in 55 BC, was once out riding in a carriage with an expert who specialised in assessing a person's destiny on the basis of his or her physical characteristics. The expert pronounced categorically that a woman whom they had just observed was destined to become rich and to attain high honours. When Huang Pa examined her he found that she was a daughter of a shaman's family, and immediately took her to be his wife. Possibly Huang Pa enjoyed some measure of his wife's good fortune vicariously; he was one of the few senior ministers of the time to die without violence. On a somewhat different note we hear of a dedicated man of letters named Kao Feng, in eastern Han. He feared that he could not evade a call to serve in an official capacity, but managed to avoid the duty by claiming that he came from a shaman's family and was therefore not qualified to hold office. It is not known how strictly such a ban was imposed.

The histories remind us that shamans were also employed for purposes of malefaction, principally the invocation of a curse. During Chao ti's reign (87 to 74), a son of the previous emperor (Wu ti) named Hsü entertained pretensions to the throne, and employed a female shaman from the old land of Ch'u to bring the spirits down and curse the reigning emperor. She maintained that the spirit which duly descended came from no less a person than Wu ti himself and that he had given instructions that Hsü should become emperor. She was handsomely rewarded and ordered to maintain her prayers at Wu shan (Shamans' Mountain) in her own home region. Opportunely, Chao ti died quite soon, and she acquired a reputation for efficiency. Similarly, when Ai ti lay ill in 4 BC accusations were raised that shamans had been commissioned to curse him, and a similar instance is recorded during the reign of Ming ti (reigned AD 57 to 75). In another context, an imperial edict reported that the Hsiung-nu had been laying curses on Chinese armed forces and using shamans for the purpose.

It is hardly surprising that such practices led to criticism of the shamans and attempts to suppress them. At a time of political instability and nervousness in 99 BC a ban was imposed on those shamans who performed their services on the roads. We next hear of steps taken by a provincial official named Luan Pa, in c. AD 140. His region was especially given to the worship of the spirits of the hills and the rivers, to the point that common people were being forced to contribute to the upkeep of such services. Luan Pa, however, was himself a master of certain esoteric arts with which he was able to bring spirits under control. He had the shrines that had been erected for worship destroyed, and the corrupt shamans punished, possibly by shaving the hair from their heads.

The records also report a case of firm, merciless treatment undertaken by Pan Ch'ao, who is best known for his highly successful military campaigns in central Asia in AD 73. In one of the states that lay across his path, Khotan, the king had become subject to the influence of the Hsiung-nu, and was by no means willing to treat the Chinese general with the respect that he claimed to be his due. In addition the king had a strong belief in the efficacy of shamans. Some of these advised him that the gods would be angry if he were to make overtures to the Han envoys; he should rather seek horses from them which could then be used in sacrifice. The king's messengers duly presented a request for horses to Pan Ch'ao who, however, knew exactly where it had originated. He tricked the king into sending the shamans themselves to take delivery of the horses and promptly had them executed.

The religious reforms of 31–30 BC came about largely thanks to the efforts of K'uang Heng, who spared little criticism of the contemporary scene that he saw around him in Ch'ang-an. He believed that the age was sadly marred by a devotion to material ends and by its subsequent corruption; he argued for a return to the moral principles and practices ascribed to the golden age of the kings of Chou. K'uang Heng's main efforts were directed to a reform of the cults of state, as will be seen below (see Chapter 12), but in the course of one of his tirades he referred to an unsavoury aspect of shamanism. In giving examples of how a people will be affected by the example of a leader or his character, he pointed to the case of one man who had favoured the shamans and the consequent readiness of the common people to indulge in *yin ssu*.

The precise significance of this expression may not be known for this period of time (*c.* 30 BC). It implies practices of an impure or lewd nature, or religious abuses such as sacrifices to deities who were not acceptable. For later periods the term may imply sexual practices, but there is no direct evidence to prove that these were involved in shamanist exercises of the Han period. The subject is mentioned by the histories in connection with Sung Chün, who was serving as a county magistrate.

Sometime after AD 25 Sung Chün found that the area to which he had been sent, in the upper Yangtse river valley, was prone to a belief in shamans and spirits, and somewhat negligent of book-learning. It was for this reason that he established schools in his county, and banned the practice of *yin ssu*, to the general relief of the population. Later in his career Sung Chün was promoted to be governor of Chiu-chiang commandery. He found (*c.* AD 56) that in one of the counties it was customary to sacrifice to the two holy mountains of T'ang shan and Hou shan. The shamans collectively chose women and men from among the general population to become the brides and bridegrooms of the mountains. These were changed, year in year out; and once a person had been wedded in this way, he or she did not venture to enter into a normal marriage. Before Sung Chün's time none of the provincial officials had dared to ban this practice, but it was brought to an end when he ordered that all those chosen for marriage to the mountains should be taken from shamans' families, without disturbing persons of normal status for this purpose.

A further type of malevolent practice sometimes associated with shamans was termed *ku*, or *wu-ku*, and has been rendered as black magic or witchcraft. Originally *ku* signified the concoction of poison by the collection of various types of vermin and allowing them to devour one another; parts of the survivor were then administered to wreak bodily harm to a victim. But it seems that there was also a belief in a type of malevolence that could be brought about by magical processes involved in *ku*, although this may not necessarily have taken the form of actual poisoning. Sometimes *ku* was linked specifically with imprecation, and a charge of practising these black arts was sufficient to bring about the deposal of an empress (130 BC) or the downfall of others (91 BC). Suspicion of the practice also led to the institution of an official search for incriminating evidence from time to time. The most dramatic and widespread case of *ku* that is recorded is that of the alleged practices of 91 BC, which ushered in a short spell of violence and bloodshed in Ch'ang-an, with the suicide of the empress and the crown prince.

Han writers expressed varied opinions on the validity of the shamans' performances. Chang Heng has already been mentioned in connection with astronomy; it has been noted how this distinguished man of science held to a belief in mysterious powers which could not be wholly understood. To his acute mind the utterances of the shamans were worthy of just as much respect as that due to other forms of enquiry and revelation, such as astronomy or divination. He drew a sharp contrast between such matters and a dogmatic belief in the virtue of writings which had acquired a meretricious credibility as would-be scriptures.

Wang Ch'ung, on the other hand, was more critical, as might be expected. He refers scathingly to the custom whereby the shaman, dressed in black robes, would call down the spirits of deceased persons and act as the medium through whom they could make their utterances. In other passages he mentions the spontaneous, uncontrolled mouthings of the shaman and the belief that these are imbued with the vital energy of Yang. In his chapter on exorcism he takes a definite stand in seeking to show that shamans possessed no powers of eliminating evil or appeasing a god.

The written account of the great debate that was staged in 81 BC included a few uncomplimentary remarks about shamanism, as part of its diatribe against contemporary *mores*. These views were reiterated and expanded in a tract written in much the same spirit by Wang Fu, towards the middle of the second century AD.

Wang Fu was describing the faults that he could name in his own time, when morals were lax, society corrupt and government lacking in scruple. Among other matters he singled out the devotion given to shamans and their invocations, their musical performances and their dances. Intended as these were as a service to the gods, they ended by being a gross deceit of the populace, as did the shamans' claims to effect cures for illness. Too many persons abandoned the physicians and their medicines and in vain sought to find a cure with the shaman.

As a final comment on shamanist practice we may cite the remarks made by one of the historians whose opinions are appended as comments to the chapters of the *Hou Han shu*. He commended Lang I and Hsiang K'ai (fl.166), whom we have already met in connection with omens, for their skilful interpretation of strange phenomena; but he suggests that the partiality that these two learned gentlemen entertained for shamans constituted a weakness in their intellectual attitude.

No account of the Han view of shamans and intermediaries would be complete without referring to three individuals who claimed to possess powers of this type and with whom Wu ti is said to have had dealings. The first was Li Shao-chün, who came from a small kingdom to the north-west of the old land of Ch'i, where, as we have seen, the eldest daughters of all families had at one time been initiated as shamans. Li Shao-chün claimed to be able to control matter and to command spiritual beings, and to withstand the onset of old age. He had in fact astonished some of his contemporaries with faculties that appeared to be those of second sight. For example, when Wu ti had once shown him an ancient bronze vessel, he immediately identified its place of provenance and the date of manufacture to an exact year; his statement had been duly verified when the inscription on the vessel was read. It was with such a reputation behind him that Li Shao-chün claimed to be able to attract spirits; there were even those who regarded him as being a spirit himself. He also claimed to be able to transform base metals into gold. In this connection he maintained that the proper use of vessels made of gold would prolong the life of the user and enable him to make contact with the immortal beings of P'eng-lai.

Early in his reign Wu ti was sufficiently well impressed by Li Shao-chün as to take his advice. He sent specialists in various techniques to sea, to find the island and inhabitants of P'eng-lai, just as the First Ch'in emperor is reported to have done some ninety years previously. He also experimented in the production of gold from base metals. Eventually, when Li Shao-chün fell ill and died, the emperor refused to believe this melancholy fact; he insisted that Li had been transformed into another being and gone away elsewhere.

Li Shao-chün had clearly made Wu ti receptive of these and other ideas, as may be seen in connection with Li's successors. Shao Weng, who came from the land of Ch'i itself, entered the scene in 121 BC. Wu ti had just lost one of his favourite consorts, and Shao Weng so contrived his arts and devices that he was able to make her reappear in the palace, where the emperor was keeping watch from behind a curtain. The success of this venture delighted Wu ti, who rewarded Shao Weng generously.

Shao Weng was now faced with the problem of demonstrating the efficacy of his further powers. He recommended measures that could be taken to attract the holy spirits to come down to earth. Care should be taken to decorate the furnishings of the palace with suitable designs and representations of the deities, and the necessary equipment should be laid out in readiness for services and sacrifice. After about a year it transpired that Shao Weng's arts were a failure, as no spirits had appeared. In desperation he fed a piece of inscribed silk to an ox; feigning ignorance, he let it be known that a remarkable piece of writing would be found within the animal; and this was of course discovered within its belly when it was slaughtered. Unfortunately the emperor recognised the handwriting, and the gaff was blown. Shao Weng was put to death in secrecy, presumably to avoid revealing how the emperor had been imposed upon and duped.

Finally (113 BC) we hear of Luan Ta, who also came from the Shantung peninsula (i.e. the land of Ch'i). He had been introduced into the palace at a time when Wu ti was regretting that Shao Weng had possibly been put to death before he had had full opportunity to take his arts through to their logical completion. Luan Ta's claims were essentially identical with those of his predecessors, but his demands were somewhat more pretentious. He had made contact with some of the immortal spirits from P'eng-lai. He assured Wu ti that, subject to certain conditions, one of his major problems of government (the rupture of the Yellow river's banks) could be solved, the elixir of deathlessness could be obtained and the immortal spirits could be induced to appear. To achieve these results, it was necessary to assure the intermediaries that they would not suffer the fate of Shao Weng; and they must be provided with material symbols which would show that they enjoyed sufficiently high status with which to confront the spirits on terms of equality.

Wu ti reassured Luan Ta about Shao Weng's untimely death – due, he said, to poisoning after eating horse liver. He provided Luan Ta with all the necessities that he suggested, which included the rank of a general officer, seals of office and a title of nobility. Such were the gifts and privileges conferred upon Luan Ta and the marks of imperial favour that he enjoyed, that he was entertained and banqueted by the highest in the land. However, his reputation was vain and transitory. Despite the sacrifices with which he invoked the spirits each night, none deigned to appear, and the emperor realised that, once again, he had been duped. Luan Ta was brought up on a charge of having deceived the emperor and was cut in twain at the waist.

Wu ti had thus suffered a series of disappointments at the hands of men who promised him the gifts and blessings that their knowledge of the occult could bring. It may be noted that the emperor's final disillusionment and his fury with Luan Ta coincided with attempts of an entirely different nature to communicate with sacred powers. Reference will be made below to the cults of state which were being established at exactly this time and to the hopes of achieving deathlessness through the help of Huang ti, Power of Yellow, or the Yellow Emperor.

11

Services to the dead

Attentions paid to the dead derived from mythology, religious observance and philosophical theory. Literature of the pre-imperial period reveals something of the early beliefs and practices, many of which survived until the Ch'in and Han ages. The imagery of early poetry, principally that of the *Songs of the South*, may be matched with the symbols of iconography. The standard histories include a number of descriptions of burials; and although the motives for recording such details were doubtless biased, the fruits of archaeological work confirm that the historians were not necessarily guilty of exaggerating the splendours of funerary practice simply for purposes of propaganda. As the greater part of the archaeological evidence for the period in question derives from tombs, one of the most important results of such work lies in its disclosure of this aspect of Han religion and intellect.

There are doubtless many motives that lay behind Han funerary practice that are not yet understood, and many subtleties that still elude us. In discriminating between recognised motives it is of some importance to realise that the Chinese themselves did not necessarily believe that they were mutually exclusive. Different types of belief were sometimes contradictory and gave rise to very different observances; but the Han Chinese saw no difficulty in maintaining cults of several types simultaneously. Some of the practices were designed to prolong life on earth for as long as possible; others were intended to provide for an existence in another world, populated by different types of being. Many attempted to furnish the deceased with material symbols that would guide one element of the soul (the *hun*) to paradise, whether in the realm of *ti*, in the east, or in that of the Queen Mother of the West. Other practices were intended to serve the other element of the human soul, the *p'o*, so as to ensure that it would remain appeased and that there would be no danger of its reappearance as a harmful revenant. Other precautions would, it was hoped, preserve the body from corruption as long as possible, for motives that cannot be determined for certain. Towards the end of the Han period we learn of contracts that were solemnly drawn up to make sure that the deceased person had a right to the plot of land where he or she lay buried.

Many of these practices hark back to long before the imperial period. During the Han centuries they became imbued with beliefs and theories that were gaining a wide appeal and which were being actively promoted for purposes of state policy. Iconography thus discloses the growing attention paid to Yin-Yang and the Five Phases in Han thought, and the Standard Histories show how the practice of divination or an appeal to intermediaries came to affect procedures for burial. To some extent it is possible to suggest a chronological sequence which marks the impact of new ideas; but it must be noted that the introduction of new motifs and practices did not necessarily result in the withdrawal of others that had been intended to procure much the same results. Perhaps the most marked changes in burial practice occurred from the late second and the third centuries AD, when Buddhist beliefs began to take a firm hold of the Chinese mind, and practices which derived from Taoist exercises and disciplines acquired a religious fervour. Throughout the Han period, and indeed previously, the expenses that were involved in some funerary practices drew sharp criticism from philosophers, historians and statesmen.

It is unlikely that any formal definition of death can be found in early Chinese literature, but many might well have agreed that death was marked by the separation of the *hun* from the human body. Very often the first steps that were taken, when it appeared that this had occurred and that life was extinct, were designed to tempt or persuade the *hun* to return to its mortal coil and thus to defer the moment of death. This seems to have been the motive that lay behind a number of rituals of invocation. It is best illustrated in the two poems of the *Songs of the South* to which reference has already been made, the *Summons of the soul* and the *Great Summons*. It has been seen above that those poems were bound up with shamanist practice (see Chapter 10).

From some of the treatises on correct behaviour, which derive from the entirely different tradition of Chinese thought that may be generally classified as Confucian, we learn of the rite that was performed for this purpose. At the moment of death the official robe of the deceased person was carried to the roof of the house and an invocation was made to the *hun* to return to the body that it had apparently deserted. The appeal was made by an official or attendant whose rank suited that of the deceased person; he faced north and proclaimed the invocation three times. It has been suggested that the robe of the deceased person acted as a substitute for the body, should the *hun* be induced to make a return then and there.

Once it had been accepted that these measures were of no avail, that the *hun* would not return and that the fact of death must be recognised, elaborate procedures and ceremonies were set in motion. At this stage a different motive predominates, that of wishing to make sure that the *hun* would proceed to its appropriate destination. For this purpose different types of talisman were provided by way of decoration or furnishing within a tomb.

One of the most remarkable examples of such a talisman is the silk painting found in tomb no. 1 Ma-wang-tui, in central China. The tomb dates from 168 BC, and it is notable not only for the painting, which was in excellent condition when it was found, but also for the preservation of the corpse of the woman buried in the tomb, without decay. There was also a rich find of funeral furnishings, which enable the deceased person to be identified as the countess of Tai.

Several interpretations have been put forward as a means of understanding the painting, which had been laid face downward and forward on top of the innermost of the coffins. It seems most likely that it was a symbolical representation of the journey that it was hoped the *hun* would undertake in peace and safety. On this journey the *hun* of the countess passes through the island of P'eng-lai, shown in the shape of a vase that lies anchored in the sea. Within that island the soul receives the necessary sustenance of the elixir to prepare it for the next stage, whereby it is led to the gates of paradise. The talisman ensures that the soul of the countess is able to pass through the portals of Ch'ang-ho (see p. 5) which are guarded by human warders and animals. Once it has survived their scrutiny the soul is able to take up its position in the land of eternity, flanked by sun and moon and other symbols, at the very apex of the painting.

This interpretation of the painting is supported by the evidence of mythology as seen in the *Classic of the Mountains and the Lakes* and the poems of the *Ch'u tz'u*. The identification of the central figure within the vase as that of the deceased countess is supported by the funerary furnishings. It is also possible that a painting from a nearby tomb serves the same purpose; although this is considerably damaged it can be seen that some of the features that have been described above recur. It may be noted that, apart from the portraiture of the deceased person, the iconography of the painting from tomb no. 1 is entirely symbolical, being drawn from mythological subjects. There are no purely decorative features such as appear on later funerary furnishings, or scenes of household occupations, entertainment or amusement.

From about 50 BC talismans imbued with a different type of symbolism begin to appear. By that time greater attention had been directed by Han philosophers to the ideas of Yin-Yang and the Five Phases, and the purpose of these new devices reflects the new emphasis. It was intended that suitable material symbols would not only place the deceased person in the most favourable situation of the cosmos; they would also provide a path for the journey to the life hereafter.

There is thus a whole series of bronze mirrors, denoted on account of their characteristic design as TLV mirrors, which were made to serve this purpose. The mirrors combine in perfect harmony the two views of the cosmos, seen either in twelve divisions or as the product of Five Phases. They provide a necessary link between such a universe and a life after death; and they suggest that the physical situation of the deceased person has been determined after due regard has been paid to the appropriate processes of divination.

The most perfect examples of these beautiful mirrors are marked by a characteristic pattern of a square set within a circle, or the earth surrounded by the heavens; between the circle and the square the T, L and V markings are prominent. Within the square are set the twelve written characters of the series used to enumerate the twelve divisions of the natural order. These are faced by the four animal symbols of four of the Five Phases, i.e. the green or blue dragon of the east, the scarlet bird of the south, the white tiger of the west and the dark warrior (snake and turtle) of the north. The positions of these four are correctly contrived, so that, for example, the scarlet bird of the south faces immediately the seventh of the twelve characters written within the square, which marks the most southerly of the twelve divisions. In this way the two sets of symbols correspond with one another and there is harmony rather than conflict between the two schemes. It is possible that the prominent protuberance at the exact centre of the mirror, which certainly has a practical function, also serves as a symbol for the fifth of the Five Phases; it may be the mound which characterises earth (see p. 42).

Inscriptions set around the circles of these mirrors make it abundantly clear that the symbols of the Five Phases are intended to provide the deceased person with the correct guardians of the four directions. They also make it explicit that the beautiful scroll which encircles the extreme edge of the mirrors likewise bears a symbolical meaning and is not purely decorative. It is intended as a bank of clouds upon which the soul may mount in order to join the world of the immortal beings, whose habits are sometimes described in the wording. It has long been recognised that the characteristic T, L and V markers bear an affinity with similar marks on diviners' boards and other instruments. They may be intended on the mirrors to suggest that the diviner's board has been duly consulted, and has indicated how the most felicitous disposal of the deceased person may be attained.

These symbols are likewise installed in tombs and on funerary furnishings, in the form of carvings or paintings. Other ways may also be detected of indicating the way to the life of the immortal beings. The TLV mirrors themselves often carry images of elf-like creatures or mythical animals, probably conceived as inhabitants of that far-off land. Similar figures appear in rich profusion on the coffins in which the countess of Tai was buried. Like the imagery of the painting, they too may well have been intended to bring the deceased person into close contact with that world.

There also survive a few examples of paintings which depict the dead person actively undertaking the journey. The earliest of these to be found so far comes from a tomb in central China, of about 300 BC; as at Ma-wang-tui, the conditions of burial ensured its preservation in an excellent state. The painting shows the dead man riding aloft on a dragon, on his way through wind and wave to a better realm. Another example takes the form of a fresco painting from the north-eastern part of the Han empire (the modern province of Liao-ning). Here a suppliant adopts a series of postures of prayer and eventually reaches the land of the immortal beings, be they of animal, bird or human form, who greet him with a friendly welcome.

The same function, of indicating the path to the next world, may be recognised in a number of examples of a hybrid creature, in paint, relief work or sculpture. These figures combine elements of bird and man, either with a bird's body that is surmounted by a human head or face, or as a man or woman's body upon which wings have sprouted. These figures demonstrate to a deceased person how the journey may be taken through the Empyrean to the life everlasting.

Should it be desired to waft the soul towards the paradise of the Queen Mother of the West, similar measures could be taken. The Queen is shown in all her majesty in fresco, on stone reliefs and on bronze mirrors. As material evidence of this type is found in tombs that lie scattered in many parts of China, it cannot be assumed that the cult of this particular form of the life hereafter was necessarily concentrated in a particular region.

A roof painting in the tomb of Pu Ch'ien-ch'iu, in central China, may well form the earliest known example of this type of talisman, at perhaps 50 BC. Elsewhere, most of the evidence is in the form of stone carvings or moulded bricks, of which a large number were found in the east (Shantung province). Both these examples and a magnificent specimen from the west (Ssu-ch'uan province) probably date from the end of the first or from the second century AD. It is only from about AD 100 onwards that the theme of the Queen and her realm features on the bronze mirrors then being fashioned in deep relief, with a rich variety of decorative detail.

Well-known and easily recognisable attributes identify these figures as the Queen Mother, into whose presence the deceased person was to be guided. The Queen herself was portrayed with a distinctive type of headdress, or crown, that may have derived from her function as weaver of the web of the cosmos. A further connection with this aspect of the Queen's creative powers may be seen in the combination of dragon and tiger upon which she is occasionally seated, thus symbolising the union of Yin and Yang. The Queen is regularly attended on the reliefs by servants directly engaged in providing the elixir of long life or immortality. These include the hare who compounds the herbs that he and his companions have collected, and the toad, who was a well-established symbol of the process of birth, death and rebirth. A splendid fox with nine tails stands beside the Queen as a member of the blissful world of the hereafter. She is also served by a three-legged bird; this attribute may have derived from the early myth that the Queen was attended by a flock of three birds; later it became a symbol of the sun. Several depictions of the Queen include a suppliant, rendering service and praying for the gift of immortality.

A further feature which enters into some of the later depictions of the Queen reflects some of the references in literature written after the Han period. She is shown with her partner, the King Father of the East, with the suggestion that the two leaders are meeting in union and thus maintaining the eternal rhythms of the cosmos. This function of the Queen is also seen in a few indications that her position is situated aloft upon a cosmic tree or pillar which links the different parts of the universe.

The cult of the Queen Mother appears in an entirely different form in a remarkable incident that is reported for 3 BC. This was a popular movement which originated in the east and swept through China until it reached the capital city. There was a general expectation that the Queen was about to appear; fanatics were preparing for her advent by transmitting emblems up and down the land, to the accompaniment of highly stimulating music. There were those who behaved in a thoroughly undisciplined manner, regardless of other persons' property; many were terrified. Services were held in honour of the Queen, who was worshipped with singing and dance; a written promise was transmitted, assuring believers that they would not die. This movement, which is partly characterised by the search for immortality, is one of the earliest known examples of a popular cult in China. It is a forerunner of a whole series of such movements that sprang up from the second part of the second century AD and which are closely associated with the exercises of Taoist religion.

Different measures were taken in Han burials for the benefit of the *p'o*. These were designed to provide for its comfort while it still remained with the corpse and for an after-life that might have been passed in the sombre existence of the Yellow Springs. Miniature houses, granaries, farmyards, well-heads and boats were buried for this purpose, together with equipment of a more personal nature, such as articles of toilet, vessels, platters or bowls needed for eating a meal, clothes or rolls of silk required for clothing. Some tombs were equipped with basins used for washing, or incense-burners needed as purifiers; some of the most remarkable examples of early Chinese lamp-stands derive from the same motive.

In addition to utilities, the deceased person was provided with valuable goods such as precious vessels of bronze or lacquer, or jewellery cut from jade. These objects had perhaps been the owner's pride and joy during a lifetime spent on earth. Officials and noblemen were buried with their seals to indicate the status that had been theirs and the style of living which they would expect in the Yellow Springs. Other ways of indicating the status of a deceased person included the provision of replicas of the attendants and servants who had lived at his command. Sometimes these take the form of wooden manikins; sometimes they are painted in fresco, whether they were subordinate officials, guardsmen on duty, or personal servants. In addition the dead were sometimes equipped with figures of those who could amuse them in the next world, either as musicians or as acrobats. Very often the musical instruments were interred alongside such figures.

Some of the articles buried in tombs, such as swords or diviners' boards, may have been intended for the use of the *p'o* should it find itself in trouble or in need of advice and guidance. Of particular interest are the manuscript copies of texts interred in this way. These included a wide variety of literary or technical writings (e.g. copies of philosophical and historical works), which may have been included for the enjoyment or edification of the soul. Others (e.g. treatises on medicine, divination or the disciplines of war) were possibly intended for consultation at moments of practical difficulty. Towards the end of the Han period there are a number of examples of contracts drawn up for the purchase of the plot of land where the deceased person lay. Possibly these are to be associated with the large sums of money that were sometimes buried and which may have been intended as the purchase price or as rent due for the land.

Recent excavations reveal how attempts of a very different nature were sometimes made to provide for the well-being of the dead. These were designed to preserve the body intact as long as possible, presumably so that the *p'o* could live there happily, and not be tempted to return to the world of the living and wreak harm upon mankind for wrongs that had been suffered. The measures in question were of two types. In some cases the body was enclosed in a tailor-made suit, made up of rectangular pieces of jade. These were sewn together to fit the body, and it was hoped that by being encased in this life-giving substance the body would survive unimpaired. Regrettably, it must be recorded that in none of the cases of burial where this method was adopted was it successful; but this was not so with other methods, as has been dramatically demonstrated at the tomb of the countess of Tai, at Ma-wang-tui. Here effective results were achieved by encasing the body in no less than four massive timber coffins, at the foot of a deep pit; the surround had been dexterously sealed with layers of clay and charcoal. A further example of the discovery of a well-preserved corpse was found in a tomb of 167 BC. In addition there is a literary reference to the discovery of an undecayed body in about AD 225, which was identified as that of one of the Han kings who had died in 202 BC.

A further type of funerary furnishing takes the form of a talisman with a deep significance. There is a series of figures carved usually in wood which have been found at various sites in central China, in the valley of the Yangtse river. They are equally redolent of the rich mythology of that area as are the poems that spring from the south and other products of the local craftsmen. The figures are crowned with long, elaborate antlers; their faces bear protruding tongues that would reach to the waist if the figures had been extended that far; and occasionally they are studded with a pair of prominent goggle eyes.

Of equal importance is the detail that these figures sometimes grasp and devour a snake, and it is for this reason that comparison has been drawn with some of the elf-like creatures who embellish the coffins of Ma-wang-tui. It has been suggested that these were protector figures, whose function was to ward off evil influences from the deceased person. Possibly they are to be identified with T'u po, Lord of the Earth, who is described in one of the *Songs of the South* as being 'Nine-coiled, with dreadful horns upon his forehead'. The presence of a snake-devouring figure was perhaps considered desirable as a means of protecting the body from consumption by vermin.

There were also other symbolic designs which appeared on tombs, such as the sheep's head which would induce good fortune or happiness. Less frequently an artist would engrave designs of certain magical plants or animals whose appearance on earth was thought to prognosticate the golden age (see Chapter 8). A particularly fine example of such designs is seen on the reverse side of a stele erected in AD 171. This shows the white deer and the golden dragon, the ear of grain of plenty, and the magical Mu-lien-li tree, which grows from twin trunks. At the side there is a suppliant, standing ready to receive the gift of honey-dew as it drops from the skies.

Before a body was committed for burial considerable care was taken to make certain that a suitable time and place had been chosen for the ceremony. As with other religious ceremonies and formal occasions of state, so here there was scope for a ritualist approach. Those whose approach to life was that of the 'Confucians', who looked to the proper organisation of man as the prime necessity of a civilised existence, conceived a set of procedures and stipulations for the conduct of these matters. The surviving regulations lay down that in divining so as to choose a suitable day for a funeral one should look beyond the immediate future. In addition there were detailed prescriptions for the correct type of clothing to be used by those who took part in the ceremony. Wang Ching, whose concern with divination has been noted above, included the choice of a lucky site for burial among its proper objectives. The situation of the imperial tombs of the western Han emperors leaves no doubt that the sites had been chosen with great care.

The irrefutable evidence of archaeology for the construction of tombs in a grand manner is supported by a number of literary descriptions of especially important funerals. Necessarily such evidence is confined to the most prominent, privileged and wealthy persons in the land, but there is reason to believe that their habits were emulated lower down the scale, and we shall see how they attracted criticism.

The mausoleum built for the First Ch'in emperor before his death (210 BC) is described in the *Shih-chi*. Recent excavations of part of the extensive site used for the purpose confirm that the account of the tomb and its extravagant furnishings cannot be dismissed as mere exaggeration designed for propagandist purposes by a critical historian. The size of the project may be appreciated by the large number (six to eight thousand) of pottery figures buried at the perimeter of the site. These were life-size statues of warriors, horses and chariots, intended to act as guardians for the deceased emperor. Further excavation may disclose traces of the rivers of mercury and the mechanical devices reportedly fixed to the structure of the tomb.

The rock-hewn tombs of the king of Chung-shan (died 113 BC) and his consort (died 104 BC or before) provide good examples of the way in which members of the Han imperial family were laid to rest. This site (Man-ch'eng, Hopei province) yielded the collapsed remains of two jade-suits used for the burial and now skilfully reconstructed in their original form. In addition there was a profusion of splendid equipment in the form of bronze vessels, lamps and jewellery of jade. The three pit graves of the noble of Tai (died 186 BC) and his relatives, at Ma-wang-tui, reveal that the funeral furnishings for members of the nobility, who ranked immediately below the kings, were equally lavish.

Exceptionally it was ordered by imperial command that the luxuries and appurtenances usually reserved for the imperial family should be conferred on a special favourite of the emperor or a highly placed official. Huo Kuang, who died in 68 BC at the end of a long career as an official and statesman, was accorded the privilege of a jade-suit and a coffin of highly valuable catalpa wood; his tomb was constructed with a special arrangement of blocks of timber, specially shaped and placed for durability. Ai ti gave orders for similar preparations to be made to reward his favourite Tung Hsien, but the turn of political fortune robbed the latter of the chance of enjoying so honourable a privilege and forced him to commit suicide (1 BC). A further gift of this sort is recorded for the successful general Keng Ping who died in AD 90.

There are several examples of elaborately planned tombs built with a series of chambers, or even an architectural complex. These derive mainly from the second part of the second century AD and their occupants are not identified. They include the magnificent mausoleum of I-nan (Shantung province) and the site of Ho-lin-ko-erh (Inner Mongolia). The latter example is of particular value in view of its extensive frescoes, whose subjects include a rich variety of social activities as well as motifs designed for purposes that are described above. However, structures such as these are rare exceptions among a majority of tombs that were built on a much more modest scale.

The total number of Han tombs excavated since 1949 has been estimated at over 10,000. They lie scattered over the face of China, and are to be found in areas of Han colonial activity, such as the Korean peninsula. They were built as brick structures, either singly or in clusters; in some cases such clusters may comprise several hundred examples. Various styles of tomb emerged. As the habit of burying a man and wife together in the same structure grew, so did there evolve a design which allowed for a secondary burial to take place, with the minimum of interference or destruction. The combined evidence of tombs that were grouped together in large numbers (e.g. the 225 tombs at Shao-kou, near Lo-yang) has yielded stylistic distinctions which are of considerable value for purposes of dating.

Reference is also due to a very different type of cemetery made as a burial ground for convicts. A site south of Lo-yang contains a grid-like arrangement of graves, dug in neat rows on a modest scale, that accommodate over 500 convicts. These are accompanied in some cases by roughly inscribed bricks that record the barest details of the occupant – name, domicile, type of punishment and date of death. These inscriptions form a stark contrast with the highly decorated epitaph stele erected to commemorate the lives of successful officials and speaking grandiloquently of their ancestry, achievements and qualities.

The provision of extravagant funerals was no new practice introduced during the Ch'in and Han periods. It had already excited the criticism of the philosopher Mo ti (fl. 479–430 BC) by reason of the waste of material resources and human effort that was involved. He felt that this would be far better directed to serving the immediate needs and welfare of the living population. In Han times, the practice was condemned by an adviser of Wen ti (reigned 180 to 157). Of all Han emperors, Wen ti has been credited with the greatest desire to refrain from imposing demands for tax and service on his people. For that reason he is reported as ordering considerable reductions in the style of burial intended for his own person.

But it is in the *Discourses on Salt and Iron* that we find the clearest and most stringent criticism of contemporary practice (i.e. for the decades around 50 BC). One of the chapters of that book presents a diatribe against the wasteful and extravagant practices of the day, as compared with the frugal habits of the ideal past. Funerary practices rank high on the list of such habits. The critic points to the use of elaborate coffins, of several layers, that were made of valuable timber, as against the shells and planks of a former age. In the same spirit he condemns the burial of real equipment and valuables with the deceased person, in place of valueless replicas. He sees a further contrast with former practice in the way in which high mounds were being piled over tombs, with trees planted in neat rows alongside and an array of terraces, turrets and watch-towers. The critic also maintains that the contemporary practices that he was castigating had become completely separated from the real purpose of funerary cults:

Of old when a man served his living parents he did so with his full love, and when he followed their bones on their last journey he did so with unmitigated grief. So the saintly leaders of old drew up regulations to prevent the senseless elaboration of these practices. But now, while their parents are still alive, sons cannot bring it upon themselves to render them the love and respect that is their due; but once a parent dies, the children vie with one another in their extravagances. They may suffer no feelings of grief or sorrow, but by virtue of the luxurious funeral and the rich furnishings that they provide so will they win a name for fulfilling their duties. Their reputation will stand out among their contemporaries and their fine deeds will become a matter of common knowledge; and we then find ordinary members of the public imitating the ways of the rich and ruining their households or selling their inheritance in the process.

Many of these strictures recur in a similar essay written during the second century AD. Wang Fu adds colour to his argument by elaborating on some of the practical difficulties that were involved, for example in the transport of rare, expensive woods from the forests of the south over the long journey to Lo-yang city. Wang Ch'ung mentions the subject and argues on completely different grounds. To that rationalist it was offensive that practices should be observed which had no proper intellectual backing; he believed that there was no satisfactory statement of the issues involved, in the writings of either the Confucian or the Mohist schools of thought.

12

The imperial cults

The inscriptions and texts of the Shang and Chou periods show that a belief in *ti* or *shang ti* (God on high), and later in *t'ien* (heaven), formed an important element in the religion of early China. According to writers of later periods, service to *t'ien* almost formed a characteristic function of the kings of Chou, who insisted that the authority which they bore derived from the gift of that supreme power. The term *T'ien tzu*, or Son of Heaven, which appears in some of the earliest surviving Chinese literature and denotes the sovereign king of Chou, stresses the importance of this claim.

But a change came about following the weakening of the temporal power and moral leadership that those kings are said to have exercised. Such a change may be dated from 770 BC, on the occasion when the king of Chou was forced to move the site of his capital city. In the succeeding centuries independent rulers arose in several parts of China, sometimes arrogating to themselves the title and functions of a king. Most of these leaders had acquired their authority by force and could not claim to possess the individual blessing of heaven. In place of the worship of *t'ien*, that of the ancient deities known as *ti* came into prominence. Whereas the kings of Shang had worshipped the single supreme god, known as *shang ti*, the kings of the *Spring and Autumn* and the *Warring States* periods were at times worshipping several lesser *ti*, whose powers were somewhat more circumscribed.

This had become the practice of the kings of Ch'in, worship of the *ti* retained its prominent place in the cults of state after the establishment of the Ch'in empire in 221 BC. For nearly two centuries thereafter imperial services continued to be directed to these powers, until a renewed faith in *t'ien* as the supreme arbiter began to supplant that of the *ti*. This process began to affect imperial practice from 31 BC; the worship of heaven continued to be observed until the end of the imperial age in 1911.

The long history of the services paid to the various *ti* may be traced to the eighth century BC. The ceremonies are sometimes described as those of the four sacred sites (*ssu chih*) dedicated to the worship of the white, blue-green and yellow *ti*, and the *ti* of fire. From an early time these sites had grown up at Yung, which lay close to the places where the early kings of Chou, and later the emperors of Ch'in, established their centres of rule. Such proximity and its consequent significance did not, however, preclude the establishment of many shrines at other sites that were likewise dedicated to those deities.

The kings of Ch'in had attended some, but not all, of the services performed at Yung, which were accompanied by blood sacrifices and offerings of valuables. During the Ch'in empire officials of state maintained the cult, and immediately after the foundation of the Han dynasty, the new emperor took steps to retain continuity. Informed that the rites were held in honour of the white, blue-green, yellow and red *ti*, he asked why the fifth (i.e. black) had been omitted, and immediately ordered its inclusion. The incident perhaps reflects the growing influence of the theory of the Five Phases on religious practice.

As yet the Han emperors refrained from attending these services in person; but they reaffirmed the establishment of special officials responsible for their performance. The first recorded occasion of an imperial visit to the services at Yung is that of Wen ti in 165 BC. An interesting statement that is attributed to an official on this occasion draws an explicit association between the worship of these five powers and the earlier worship of *shang ti*. In the following year a further set of five altars was established in honour of these five gods at Wei-yang, which lay nearer to Ch'ang-an, and the emperor again attended in person. His successor did so in 144 BC, as did Wu ti in 134. Thereafter it was intended that the services of the bounds, as they were to be known, should be carried out every three years. Wu ti attended somewhat irregularly, for a total of nine times, between 123 and 92.

The *Han shu* includes the text of nineteen hymns which were sung at the services of the bounds. The translation of the first, which follows, was published by James Legge in 1871:

> Having chosen this seasonable day,
> Here we are expecting.

We burn the fat and the southernwood,
Whose smoke spreads all around.
The nine heavens are opened.
Lo! the flags of the Power,
Sending down his favour,
Blessing, great and admirable.
Lo! the chariot of the Power,
Amidst the dark clouds,
Drawn by flying dragons,
With many feathered streamers.
Lo! the Power descends,
As if riding on the wind;
On the left an azure dragon,
On the right a white tiger.
Lo! the power is coming,
With mysterious rapidity.
Before him the rain,
Is fast distributed.
Lo! the Power is arrived,
Bright amid the darkness,
Filling us with amazement,
Making our hearts to quake.
Lo! the Power is seated.
And our music strikes up.
To rejoice him till dawn,
To make him well pleased.
With the victim and his budding horns,
With the vessels of fragrant millet,
With the vase of cinnamon spirits,
We welcome all his attendants.
The Power is pleased to remain,
And we sing to the music of all the seasons.
Look here, all,
And observe the gemmeous hall.
The ladies in their beauty,
With wonderful attraction,
Lovely as the flowering rush,
Ravish the beholders;-
In their variegated dresses,
As from out a mist,
Gauzy and light,
With their pendants of pearls and gems;
The Beauty of the night interspersed,
And the *chin* and the *lin*.

With quiet composure,
We offer the cup of welcome.

Meanwhile two major innovations were being introduced in the imperial cults. The first was the worship of Hou t'u, lord of the earth, who may have been conceived as feminine. On the advice of officials, the new worship was conducted on five altars, which were erected on a circular mound, and the mound itself rose from within a lake. The service included an offering of calves and the major sacrifice of ox, sheep and pig. After their immolation, the bodies of the victims were buried, presumably to make certain that they would be received by the deity that was being addressed. The site chosen for these services lay at Fen-yin, in a commandery situated east of the metropolitan area. The emperor attended the inaugural ceremony in person in 114 BC, and on five other occasions between 107 and 100.

The second innovation in the state cults of Han was the worship of t'ai-i or Grand Unity. It had been suggested that this was a traditional ceremony that had fallen into abeyance, but which had been conducted at the south-eastern corner of the city, with a full sacrifice of animals. Wu ti gave orders for the necessary altars to be built near the Kan-ch'üan palace, the seat of his summer retreat. He attended the inaugural act of worship on the day of the winter solstice in 113 BC, and the ceremony was like that of the bounds, at Yung, with a special invocation. He himself was clothed in yellow robes; a row of lighted lamps filled the altar, by whose side there were ranged the sacrificial instruments. Natural lights were expected to appear at the crucial points of the ceremony, during which officials offered their jade rings, and the victims were presented for sacrifice. As with other religious ceremonies it was envisaged that the emperor should make a personal appearance every second or third year; Wu ti is known to have done so in 106, 100 and 88 BC.

In 110 BC there occurred a religious event of considerable importance; this was Wu ti's ascent of Mount T'ai (in Shantung province). T'ai shan was the most renowned of China's five major holy mountains and had long acquired a deep significance. Very few of the early monarchs of Chinese tradition had succeeded in carrying out the pilgrimage to the mountain, which involved two services, known as the *feng* and the *shan*. Throughout the imperial age the ascent by an emperor is recorded only rarely. Such visitors included the First Ch'in emperor in 219 BC and Kuang Wu ti in AD 56. Although information regarding the conduct and character of the ceremonies is far from complete, it is possible to trace the growth of different motives for this type of worship during the Ch'in and Han periods.

A variety of reasons may be suggested to explain why the idea of an ascent of Mount T'ai came to the fore in 110 BC. It was a time that was conducive to the initiation of imperial cults, as has been noted in the establishment of altars to the lord of the earth (114 BC) and Grand Unity (113 BC). At the time the emperor and his statesmen were paying close attention to the sacred aspects of sovereignty and the emperor's function as a religious dignitary. In addition it was a time when the leading statesmen of the empire were conscious of the success of their government. This had been demonstrated conspicuously in the expansion of Han influence in ever-widening areas by 111 BC, and the victory parade of that year in which the emperor celebrated his generals' triumph over the Hsiung-nu. A sense of achievement, leading to a rededication or renewal of imperial pride and purpose, is seen not only in the ascent of Mount T'ai in 110 BC. It is also manifest in the adoption of a new patron element (see p. 153 below), a new calendar and a new regnal title (T'ai ch'u, the Grand Beginning, in 105–104). Finally it was just about at this time that the emperor's faith in the intermediaries and their claims was meeting disillusion (see Chapter 10).

The most recent occasion when a sovereign of China had made the ascent of the mountain had been in 219 BC. The First Ch'in emperor had been making a series of imperial progresses throughout his provinces to demonstrate the strength of his regime and the certainty of the unification. The same motive led him to climb the mountain, where he is said to have performed the *feng* and the *shan* ceremonies. He had received somewhat contradictory advice from learned men as to the manner of proceeding, and as the ceremonies were conducted in secret no details are recorded. However, the *Shih-chi* incorporates the text of an inscription that the emperor is said to have cut on stone to commemorate the occasion. From that text it is clear that the object of the journey had been to proclaim the successful achievement of Ch'in rather than to seek blessings from a superior power.

The inscription recounts how in the twenty-sixth year of his reign (i.e. his reign as king of Ch'in, 221 BC) his imperial majesty had for the first time taken unitary control over all that lies below the heavens, where there was none that did not submit to his commands. In the course of an imperial progress that he made to visit the inhabitants of distant parts, he had climbed Mount T'ai, thereby encircling the eastern extremity of the world. The thoughts of those officials who accompanied him were bent on following his example and emulating his achievements, in praise of the services that he had rendered. The nature of the order that he imposed upon the world corresponded with the cycle of being, with all creatures obtaining their deserts, and all things being subject to a regular model and pattern. His great reign of right would form a shining example to which generations of the future would conform without change. Blessed by his saintly qualities, his imperial majesty knew no rest from the task of keeping the world in order once it had been pacified. Rising at dawn, and going to his rest only in the deep recesses of the night, he laid plans that would be of long-lasting benefit to the world, bestowing particular care on the provision of instruction. The principles that he enjoined penetrated widely to all parts, so that near and far all accept their rule and receive his holy will.

Different motives were dominant when Wu ti made his ascent in 110 BC. Three years previously a shaman had made a somewhat unusual discovery at Fen-yin, in the form of an ancient bronze tripod. In due course this was brought before the emperor who first satisfied himself that the discovery had not been faked and then asked his advisers for an explanation of the sudden appearance of this highly auspicious object. He was persuaded that it was an instrument intended for communication with sacred powers. In particular it was associated with the activities of Huang ti, the *ti* of yellow, or, in personified form, the Yellow Emperor. It was suggested to Wu ti that he was himself destined to possess comparable powers to those of Huang ti, and that the emergence of the tripod would enable him to conduct the *feng* and the *shan* sacrifices, just as they had been performed by Huang ti on Mount T'ai.

So far from there being a contradiction here with the established forms of worship, it was explained that Huang ti had himself performed the services of the bounds, addressed to *shang ti*, at the holy site of Yung. In addition there was one further characteristic or achievement of Huang ti that doubtless appealed to Wu ti. It was said that his immortal spirit had ascended to heaven; if Huang ti could achieve deathlessness in this way, so also, was it urged, could his successor. There was apparently every reason why Wu ti should begin his emulation of Huang ti's achievements by making the ascent of Mount T'ai and performing the *feng* and *shan* rites.

As a preliminary step for the ceremonies Wu ti also sacrificed at the tomb of Huang ti. It is reported that he expressed surprise at the existence of a tomb for someone who had gone straight to heaven; in response to his enquiry he was told that the tomb had been built solely for the burial of his hat and robes. When he enquired how the *feng* and the *shan* sacrifices should be conducted he met ignorance, as these ceremonies had been carried out too rarely for a living tradition to have been formulated. On the basis of some early texts he was advised that he should perform the rite at some distance from the summit of the mountain, and that a bull should be slain by arrows. The account of the discussions shows that Wu ti was more amenable to the advice tendered by specialist advisers such as Kung-sun Ch'ing than by the regular scholars who represented the established tradition; he rejected their advice on precedent outright.

The emperor's next step was to ascend the central peak of the range where he instituted a special sacrifice. He imposed a ban on felling the trees on the mountainside, and set up a religious community of three hundred households. These bore the sole duty of maintaining the worship, and were exempted from other obligations of state. He was then ready to make the ascent of the mountain itself. It was still in the third month of the year, before the leaves and plants had begun to sprout; so the emperor used the opportunity to have stone transported for the erection of a commemorative stela at the summit. It was in the next month that he performed the *feng* sacrifice; already he had offered minor oblations to various deities and he had ordered his officials to slay the bull, as the rites required. For the *feng* ceremony he adopted forms used for sacrifice to the Grand Unity. A large mound had been built, measuring twelve feet in width and nine feet in height; below there were stowed the tablets of jade to be used for inscribing a record of the occasion; but the contents of that record remained secret.

Later, Wu ti ascended Mount T'ai a second time, to perform the *feng* ceremony once again. The following day he performed the *shan* service at the north-east corner of the foot of the mountain, according to the ritual used in worshipping the lord of the earth. In each case the emperor made personal obeisance, clothed in yellow robes; and throughout there was a musical accompaniment. A set of holy matting was woven from specially chosen plants, and soil of five colours was heaped into the mound, mingled together. Rare beasts and birds from distant regions and white pheasants were used as an adjunct to the rites; but although rhinoceros and elephant were present at the mountain they took no part in the ceremony and were withdrawn. On the night of the sacrifices it seemed that a light shone; and in the daytime a white cloud arose above the mound.

A number of points call for comment in connection with Wu ti's ascent of Mount T'ai in 110 BC. First, as yet there was no direct association between the *feng* sacrifice and the worship of heaven. It will be seen below that by the time another Han emperor made the ascent, in AD 56, marked changes had been introduced into the imperial cults which concerned the object, style and place of worship; and in AD 56 heaven is specifically linked with the ceremony held on Mount T'ai. Secondly, Wu ti's failure to obtain clear advice from scholars may possibly cloak their disapproval of the project; it is possible that, trained as they had been in a traditional frame of mind, they would not have been willing to give their unqualified support for services of this type, unless they were specifically dedicated to the worship of heaven. Thirdly, the histories record a further visit which Wu ti paid to the mountain in 107 or 106. It is possible that it was intended that the cult should be permanently maintained by designated officials and a complement of households, with the emperor attending in person at stated intervals, in the same way that he honoured the shrines of the five *ti*, the lord of the earth and Grand Unity every few years.

Finally, the edict which was proclaimed after the ascent of 110 BC reveals something of the official attitude towards the cult of Mount T'ai. This was coupled with the services rendered to Grand Unity. The spiritual blessings that were sought were matched by signs and portents of a terrifying nature that all but discouraged the emperor from proceeding. Despite this he persisted with his act of rededication. In material terms it was recognised that the burdens laid upon the inhabitants of those areas which had had to bear the expense of the imperial progress should not pass unrequited. Lastly, the event was considered worthy of commemoration in the Chinese calendar. The term Yüan feng, 'the prime *feng* ceremony', was chosen as the regnal title whereby years should be enumerated from 110 BC.

In 109 Wu ti constructed an edifice named the *T'ung t'ien t'ai*, or 'Terrace for communication with heaven'. However, this was not built specially for the worship of that deity; it was but one of several towers which were erected with the avowed intention of attracting the presence of the immortal spirits of the world to come.

Shortly after his ascent of Mount T'ai (either in 109 or in 106), Wu ti took a further significant step in formulating the imperial cult. This was the construction of the *Ming t'ang*, or Hall of holiness. In addition to linking the dynasty with the traditions of the past, this combined in one form elements of the worship of the five *ti*, the lord of the earth and Grand Unity; and the association with the 'Yellow Emperor' showed the connection with the hope of immortality. We are told:

At the time when the son of heaven had made his first ascent of Mount T'ai he had recollected that in ancient times there had existed a hall of holiness at the foot of the mountain, on the north-east side. This had been in a site that was somewhat constricted and far from conspicuous. The emperor decided that he would like to build a hall of holiness by the side of Feng-kao, but he had no idea of the correct specification for such a building. It was now that Kung-yü Tai, a man from Chi-nan, submitted a plan of the Ming-t'ang that had existed in the time of the Yellow emperor. In the plan there was an edifice placed centrally with four outer sides unwalled and a roof made of thatch. A watercourse encircled the outer fence of the site; there was a covered way, surmounted by a tower, which led in from the south-west. This had been named K'un-lun, and it was from here that the son of heaven had made his entry to carry out his obeisance and sacrifice to god on high [*shang ti*].

Wu ti thereupon ordered Feng-kao to build a Ming-t'ang on the banks of the river Wen, in accordance with Kung-yü Tai's drawings. On the occasion when he renewed the performance of the *feng* ceremony (106 BC) he sacrificed to Grand Unity and the five *ti* on the upper storey of the Ming t'ang. He gave orders that the place for the worship addressed to Kao ti should be on the opposite side, and sacrificed to the lord of the earth on the lower level, with an oblation of twenty victims of the first order. The son of heaven duly made his entry by way of the road from K'un-lun; and he made his first obeisances in the Ming t'ang according to the approved procedure for the services at the bounds. When the rituals had been completed he had the victims burnt at the foot of the hall.

Over twenty-five years elapsed after the death of Wu ti (87 BC) before a Han emperor again attended personally at the imperial cults dedicated to the five *ti*, the lord of the earth or the Grand Unity. From 61 BC Hsüan ti (reigned 74 to 49) and his successor (Yüan ti, reigned 49 to 33) paid a total of four visits only to the shrines of Yung and five to those at Fen-yin; but their devotions at the shrine of Grand Unity, at Kan-ch'üan, were more regular, amounting to ten occasions between 61 and 37.

Shortly afterwards a major change was introduced in the imperial cults, for a variety of motives. It was a time of considerable changes in other aspects of Han policy and practice, thanks to a major intellectual reassessment that had been developing for some decades. By now the prevailing mood had moved conspicuously away from a 'Modernist' towards a 'Reformist' frame of mind. Statesmen saw Han no longer as the successor of Ch'in by right of conquest, but as the successor of Chou by virtue of moral scruples. In place of the enrichment and strengthening of the state that had been the prime motive of many of Wu ti's statesmen, the officials and advisers of Yüan ti and Ch'eng ti (reigned 33 to 7 BC) were striving to emulate the ethical ideals and moral purposes ascribed, rightly or wrongly, to the early kings of Chou.

In the practical terms of government this change was manifest in both domestic and foreign policies. A measure of retrenchment and economy was introduced in the running of the palace and the court; there was an unwillingness to become involved in foreign ventures and a desire to disengage from unnecessary entanglements. Such a reduction to plain essentials was also manifest in respect of religious practices, which were reformed by a purge of excesses, a reduction of expenditure and a return to the gods of Chou in place of those of Ch'in.

One of the moving spirits behind the reform was K'uang

Heng, who rose to be chancellor of the empire from 36 to 29 BC. He had emerged from a scholastic background and had expressed some sharp criticism of the lax habits of the time, the oppressive administration of officials and the prevalence of crime. Throughout his memorials he pointed to the good examples of the kings of Chou, and a number of measures taken in these years (47 to 44) derived from the views that he had been voicing.

K'uang Heng's suggestions for religious reforms were presented shortly after the accession of Ch'eng ti. He showed that it had been the practice of earlier sovereigns to worship heaven and earth at the bounds of their domains, rather than the five powers or other deities. In so doing he drew a distinction between earth, the corresponding partner of heaven, and Hou t'u, lord of the earth, who had been worshipped hitherto. He also suggested that the earlier form of worship had been consonant with the ideas of Yin and Yang. K'uang Heng objected to the effort and expense involved in the lengthy progress of the emperor to attend sites that lay at a distance from the capital city, and he suggested the replacement of those traditional sites by shrines which were to be set up at the southern and northern bounds of Ch'ang-an city. He also asked for the elimination of elaborate and expensive procedures in favour of a more simple and less costly form of worship.

On a day corresponding with 17 February 31 BC Ch'eng ti attended for the first time at the new form of worship that was conducted at the newly constructed altars at Ch'ang-an. But as yet the change had not been accepted finally and a reaction soon set in. No less a person than Liu Hsiang entered a plea for a return to the rites at Yung, Fen-yin and Kan-ch'üan, where previous acts of worship had evoked a definite response from the deities served there. It was also noticed that the change of 31 BC had not resulted in the birth of an heir to the throne as had been hoped; and it was recalled that on the very day that the old services had been suspended some highly inauspicious portents had occurred. So, in 14 BC, the state worship reverted to Grand Unity, at Kan-ch'üan, and the Lord of the earth at Fen-yin, and Ch'eng ti attended regularly. But seven years later (7 BC) the cults were transferred to the new sites of Ch'ang-an, only to be returned to their former homes in three years' time.

The final change in these matters took place after the presentation of a series of memorials by Wang Mang, from AD 5. This much-denigrated statesman and emperor should in fact be credited with providing imperial China with some of its most enduring principles, and the reversion to the state's worship of heaven and earth, which can be traced to these memorials, formed a characteristic element in subsequent imperial practice. Wang Mang reiterated the strength of the tradition of Chou and the importance of a sovereign's worship of heaven. In calling for the restitution of the cults to Ch'ang-an's altars to heaven and earth, he suggested a number of changes in the ritual, so as to emphasise the symbolic correspondence between imperial institutions and the ordinances of heaven.

The same stress on the importance of heaven's will and the force of the kings of Chou and their ideals is apparent in the procedure whereby Wang Mang rose to become acting emperor under the dispensation of Han (AD 6) and then emperor in his own right of the Hsin dynasty (AD 9). It will be seen below that when a Chinese emperor next embarked on the ascent of Mount T'ai for religious purposes, it was heaven that formed the objective of his devotions.

In the meantime other changes had attended the major reform initiated by K'uang Heng from 31 BC. In the preceding decades the number of shrines served by authorities of the central, provincial and local governments had grown out of all proportion. K'uang Heng and his colleagues claimed that there was a total of 683 sites of worship, addressed to a whole variety of spirits of the hills and the rivers, or the constellations. Of these they regarded 208 only as conforming with approved conventions. They rejected the remaining 475 as being improperly established and serving no useful purpose; and they suggested that these should be suppressed. As a result of this reduction, of the total number of shrines at Yung, which is given variously at 203 or 303, only 15 survived.

Somewhat inconsistently, as compared with his attention to the worship of heaven, Wang Mang permitted the restoration of a large number of cults to other spirits, and even some types of worship that were 'unacceptable' (i.e. *yin ssu*; see Chapter 10). By the end of his reign (AD 23) there were no less than 1,700 places of worship under the protection of the state; these were dedicated to all manner of deities and served by blood sacrifices of animals or birds.

With the restoration of the Han dynasty (AD 25) it was decided to establish the capital at Lo-yang. This was a city that occupied an honoured place in the tradition of the kings of Chou. Its ideological implications were those of a regime known for its cultural achievements and moral example, and they were very different from those of Ch'ang-an; for by its situation and past history Ch'ang-an had been associated with Ch'in's military conquests of its rivals and its rule through strength.

In AD 26 and 57 the new government had sites erected for the worship of heaven and earth to the south and north of Lo-yang. The forms of worship were those that had been practised by Wang Mang in AD 6. At the same time the masters of the newly restored dynasty recognised the call of the 'old religion' and the influence of Yin-Yang theory by providing for services to the five *ti*, at the site built on the southern side of Lo-yang city. At his accession, Kuang wu ti included the lord of the earth among the powers whom he invoked, and services are recorded to that deity in 42 and 57.

Thirty years after the restoration of the Han dynasty the first of the eastern Han emperors decided to emulate the example of Wu ti by embarking on the ascent of Mount T'ai and the performance of the *feng* and the *shan* sacrifices. He took particular care to consult the men of learning so as to ascertain the correct procedures, and he received detailed advice for the minutiae of the rite (e.g. the precise dimensions for the altars and the tablets of jade that were to be used). One counsellor told him that the whole rite of the ascent and the *feng* sacrifice was intended as a means of notifying heaven of the achievements that had been accomplished and of providing an everlasting inheritance for the future generations of man.

The *Hou Han shu* includes the text that was inscribed by imperial order on a stela to be erected on the mountain. From this it is clear that the dominant motive of the ascent of AD 56 was different from that of 110 BC. For whereas on the earlier occasion a direct link had been drawn with the search for immortality through the agency of Huang ti, in AD 56 the purpose was to commemorate dynastic success and to lay the foundations for its continuity in the future. At the start of the ceremony a pyre was kindled for sacrifice to heaven, at the foot of the mountain (on the south side). The record includes the somewhat enigmatic statement that 'all the holy spirits (*shen*) were in attendance'. The musical accompaniment was that of the type performed for the services held at the southern bounds of the city. After sacrificing to Mount T'ai itself the emperor made his ascent.

At the summit he changed his robes and took up his position at the altar, facing north. This stance was presumably chosen as a means of obeisance; for the normal direction for an emperor to face was south, in order to receive homage. The officials, courtiers and attendants in waiting were drawn up in lines, according to their degrees of precedence. The jade tablets that had been inscribed with the emperor's undisclosed notification were sealed by the emperor in person; they were then deposited within the stones of the altar, which was thereupon covered with further courses of stone. The emperor made his statutory double salutation and orders were given for the erection of the commemorative stela. After his descent from the mountain the emperor conducted the *shan* ceremony, in honour of earth. An amnesty was proclaimed throughout the empire, and a change was introduced in the reckoning of years, so as to record the event for all time.

A further aspect of the imperial cults is seen in the devotions paid by an emperor to the memory of his ancestors. These formed a significant means of enhancing the dignity due to the emperor's person and position and linking dynastic stability with religious considerations.

The construction of shrines for this purpose dates from the earliest days of the Han dynasty. When the founding emperor's father died (197 BC) orders were given to all the kings of the empire, who were in fact his descendants, to set up shrines in their kingdoms; similar steps followed the death of Kao ti himself (195 BC). In a statement made just before he acceded to the imperial throne in 180, the future Wen ti observed that the maintenance of these shrines was an important function of the emperor, and he referred to the matter again in an edict of 166 BC. As the years passed, shrines were erected to succeeding emperors in increasing numbers.

Responsibility for the physical upkeep of the shrines and the continuity of services was vested in special officials, who were subordinate to the Superintendent of Ceremonial (*T'ai ch'ang*). The emperors themselves visited the shrines regularly on the occasions of their accession. In one instance (117 BC) the investiture of some of the emperor's sons as kings took place in these solemn surroundings; and in 77 BC Chao ti paid a state visit to the shrines on attaining his majority. In addition, certain types of formal notification were made to the imperial ancestors in these shrines, such as the failings of Liu Ho as an emperor and the need to depose him (74 BC).

The inviolability of these shrines stands revealed in an order that dated from the time of the empress Lü (188–180): those who submitted proposals on the subject which were not supported by due authority would be punishable by death. In addition stringent punishments awaited those convicted of stealing robes or equipment from these holy sites. The outbreak of fire in one of the provincial shrines dedicated to Kao ti and in one of the parks dedicated for the same purpose (135 BC) was regarded as an alarming portent and drew serious comment from Tung Chung-shu. Similar incidents were reported for AD 48 and 139.

A sign of the elaboration of these services is seen in an order of 72 BC to honour the shrine of Wu ti with a set of three ceremonial dances, one of which was named *wu hsing* (Five Phases). But a halt was called to the steady growth of these cults during the reformist days of Yüan ti's reign, under the influence of statesmen such as K'uang Heng. It was realised that the expense of these services had risen out of all expectation and beyond all proportion. It was reckoned that the total annual expenditure amounted to 24,455 offerings made in the 167 shrines of the provinces, the 176 sites at the capital city and the 30 sites dedicated to the memories of certain empresses. These devotions depended on the provision of 45,129 men as guards and 12,147 priests, cooks and musicians, not to speak of those servicemen who were engaged in looking after the animals.

Such extravagance drew bitter comments from statesmen who were reducing expenditure in other respects and attempting to eliminate ostentation in favour of economy. By about 40 BC their protests were beginning to be effective; they secured the abolition of services at almost 200 of these shrines, and the suspension of services to the memories of the empresses. Some of these were restored temporarily in 34, and again in 28; but in the eastern Han period services were maintained only to the two emperors who were regarded as the founders of the dynasty, i.e. Kao ti and Kuang wu ti. The shrines fulfilled the same functions as previously; on several occasions records of significant events were deposited there, as e.g. at the ascent of Mount T'ai in AD 56.

The chapters which describe the ritual occasions for the

142

eastern Han period list a number of ceremonies that were conducted mainly by officials. Sometimes the emperor or the empress took part, or the rite was of such importance that it may be regarded as an imperial cult, even though the emperor was not necessarily present. Some of these occasions marked turning points in the calendar, such as the start of the four seasons. Some were concerned with the practical needs of China's way of life, such as the first ploughing of the year, in which the emperor and all officials participated. Similarly the empress led the way in an annual ceremony to mark the beginning of the year's sericulture, and the emperor led his officials in a maundy service for the elderly. Some of these occasions are described below (see Chapter 14), and this chapter will close with an account of a symbolic rite about which we possess considerable information, the Great Exorcism.

This rite was performed at the court as part of the New Year's Festival (*La*). The chief dignitary of the ceremony was the *Fang-hsiang-shih*, or Great Exorcist; he was clothed for the occasion in a bearskin, which was studded with four golden eyes. It will be seen from the description that follows that he led a troop of attendants in the ceremony, which was designed to free certain designated places from evil influences and to drive out pestilences, whether of a material or a psychological type. The description appears in the treatise on ritual in the *Hou Han shu*, and the translation is that of Professor Bodde:

> One day before the La there is the Great Exorcism (Ta No), which is called the 'expulsion of pestilences'. In this ceremony, one hundred and twenty lads from among the Palace Attendants of the Yellow Gates [a designation for the palace eunuchs], aged ten to twelve, are selected to form a youthful troupe. They all wear red headcloths, black tunics, and hold large twirl-drums. The Exorcist (Fang-hsiang-shih), [his head] covered with a bear skin having four eyes of gold, and clad in black upper garment and red lower garment, grasps a lance and brandishes a shield. Palace Attendants of the Yellow Gates act as twelve 'animals', wearing fur, feathers and horns, and the Supervisor of the Retinue leads them to expel evil demons from the palace.
> When the water is yet high in the night water-clock,* the

---

* High in the night water-clock: i.e. at an early hour of the night.

court officials assemble, with Palace Attendants, Masters of Writing, Imperial Clerks, Internuncios, and Generals of the As-Rapid-As-Tigers and Feathered Forest Gentlemen all wearing red headcloths. The Emperor with his escort drives to the Front Hall [of the palace], where the Prefect of the Yellow Gates [a eunuch] memorializes, saying: 'The youthful troupe is in readiness. We beg permission to expel the pestilences.'

Then the Palace Attendants of the Yellow Gates start a chant in which the troupe joins: 'Chia-tso, devour the baneful! Fei-wei, devour tigers! Hsiung-po, devour the Mei! T'eng-chien, devour the inauspicious! Lan-chu, devour calamities! Po-ch'i, devour dreams! Ch'iang-liang and Tsu-ming, together devour those who, having suffered execution with public exposure, now cling to the living! Wei-sui, devour visions! Ts'o-tuan, devour giants! Ch'iung-ch'i and T'eng-ken, together devour the *ku* poisons! May all these twelve spirits drive away the evil and baneful. Let them roast your bodies, break your spines and joints, tear off your flesh, pull out your lungs and entrails. If you do not leave at once, those who stay behind will become their food.'

As this takes place, the Exorcist (Fang-hsiang-shih) and the twelve 'animals' dance and shout, going everywhere through the front and rear palace apartments. They make three rounds, holding torches, with which they send the pestilences forth out of the Meridional Gate.* Outside this gate, mounted horse-men take over the torches and go out of the palace through the Guard Tower Gate,† outside of which horsemen of the Five Barracks Guards in turn take over the torches and hurl them into the Lo river.

[Meanwhile,] in the various official bureaus, each official wears a wooden animal mask with which he can act as a leader of those participating in the Exorcism.

When this is all over, peachwood figurines of [Shen Shu and] Yü Lü with rush cords are set up. When this has been done, the officers in attendance upon the throne stop their efforts. Rush spears and peachwood staffs are bestowed upon the [Three] Lords, the [Nine] Ministers, the Generals, the Marquises of Special Merit, the other Marquises, and so on.

---

* The Meridional Gate was the main south gate of the palace.
† The Guard Tower Gate was at the south of the entire palace complex.

13

Imperial sovereignty

From 221 BC until AD 1911 the emperor formed the supreme instrument of authority in the government of China. The principle was accepted whether a regime stemmed from a native or an alien house, whether its power was extended over all or only parts of the land, and whether it survived for centuries or for decades. Both the theory and the practice of imperial sovereignty were based on a variety of concepts which derived either from fact or from fiction and which were asserted in correct or in anachronistic terms. Ironically enough, some of the essential elements of imperial sovereignty evolved largely from the principles of two short-lived and greatly denigrated regimes, Ch'in itself and Wang Mang's dynasty of Hsin. Successors who owed their strength to the initial achievement of these two dynasties have often treated them with scorn and hatred.

During Ch'in and Han, imperial sovereignty developed from a reliance on force to a dependence on belief and theory; from the seizure of control by armed strength to an initiation of rule backed by religious sanction. At both the start and the end of the period under consideration a new authority arose in China, but there is a marked contrast in the statements issued at those times and the concepts that they expressed. In 221 BC the new masters of Ch'in felt no need to support their claim by an appeal to a higher authority; in AD 220 the first of the rulers of Wei received the instrument of abdication from the last of the Han emperors with a grave show of reluctance, as a solemn duty imposed upon him by heaven.

By the time of the *Warring States* (403–221 BC), there was a general acceptance that in the remote past the world had been governed by a series of rulers. These included mythical figures such as the three sovereigns or the five monarchs, culture heroes such as Shen nung, the founder of agriculture, and paragons of ethical ideals such as the blessed Yao and Shun. Some of these, it was thought, had acquired their positions owing to their saintly characters or individual merits, and the principle of hereditary succession, within a single royal family, is ascribed to a comparatively late stage in the tradition. It was said to have originated with the Hsia dynasty (traditional dates 2205–1766 BC), founded by Yü the Great. We still await confirmation that the Hsia dynasty existed in fact, but there can be no doubt that hereditary kingship was practised by the ruling houses of Shang and Chou (traditional dates 1766–1122 and 1122–256).

The chief function of the kings of Shang was probably that of a religious leader. In the tradition that was formed before the imperial period and fostered from Han times onwards, the kings of Chou were revered for their moral influence rather than for their practical administration. Unfortunately, hard evidence is scanty, and in the absence of original documents little can be said regarding the effect exercised by those kings in the period when they were thought to be strong (i.e. before 770 BC); but it is maintained by at least one scholar that their rule was enforced systematically and effectively. From 770 BC onwards the political history of China may be summarised as the rise of a succession of small states or estates, which gradually merged into larger units. By the beginning of the fourth century these had resolved themselves into seven major kingdoms, each ruled by kings who succeeded on an hereditary basis. The situation was dramatically and radically changed by the kings of Ch'in who set in motion and completed a long process of unification. The foundation of the Ch'in empire, as the sole political regime that claimed power over the whole land, began a new era for China in 221 BC.

The Ch'in empire had been established by military force, and although this example was repeated on numerous occasions in Chinese history, Ch'in's contribution to political theory was far wider. It showed how imperial government must depend, among other factors, on efficient discipline, the imposition of laws and the organisation of the population on behalf of the community. The emperor himself stood at the apex of the administrative structure whereby authority was devolved from the highest to the lowest in the land.

In an edict which was proclaimed shortly after the final act of unification, the man who was to be the first of the Ch'in emperors expressed his pride of achievement. The edict itself was primarily concerned with determining the title whereby he was to be known, and it followed the advice proffered by his loyal supporters. In their submissions they had included the following appreciation of the contemporary state of affairs:

> In the past the area over which the five sovereigns ruled extended for a thousand leagues. Beyond that area lay the domains of either Chinese or of alien lords, some of whom paid homage to the five sovereigns while others refused; and the son of heaven was not able to keep them under his control. But now his majesty has raised up forces to fight for the cause of right; he has punished by death those who practise oppression or live by crime, and brought peace to all places beneath the skies. The area within the seas is organised in the administrative units of commandery and county, and the laws and ordinances proceed from a single co-ordinating authority. This state of affairs never existed previously, even in the times of remote antiquity; it was never attained by the five sovereigns.

The distinction between the new regime and its predecessors, whether mythical or historical, was underlined by the choice of terminology used in court procedure and the title for the ruler. The adoption of 'First emperor' (*Shih huang ti*) was deliberate, and it was spelt out that in time this would be followed by a second and then a third successor, with the line lasting for ten thousand generations.

For all its much-vaunted strength, the Ch'in empire survived only one change of emperor and had ceased to exist in less than twenty years. Although it was subsequently criticised and cursed for the stark rigour and ruthlessness whereby it had governed, Ch'in bequeathed an example to its immediate successors of the Han dynasty, who had likewise risen to power by the exercise of armed strength. Whatever justice there may have been in the protests levelled against the political principles of Ch'in, the Han empire started by adopting its authoritarian way of life with little change. The first of the Han emperors retained a position that was little different from that of his predecessor of Ch'in, and had himself taken an active part in the fighting whereby his dynasty had been established (202 BC).

However, there are signs that for some decades yet the idea of imperial sovereignty had not been finally accepted as the normal way of governing China. There may well have survived those who failed to appreciate the grandeur of the imperial concept or to understand its difficulties. Others may have entertained a feeling of nostalgia for the old kingdoms of pre-imperial days and retained a sense of loyalty to the surviving members of their royal families. In Han several moments of crisis demonstrated that the new imperial regime was far from stable, and that it was subject to controversy aroused by political theory or rivalries that concerned the imperial succession. Incidents such as the effective seizure of power by the empress Lü (from 188 to 180), the armed conflict of 91 BC, and the deposal of an emperor in 74 reflect a basic intellectual void. If imperial sovereignty was subject to dispute and its possession rested on superior force, on what grounds could it be claimed that any contender had a better right to its exercise than his rivals? It was becoming essential to show that a legitimate emperor, who was entitled to accept obedience from his inferiors, could draw his rights and privileges from a superior and transcendent power, and not simply from victory on the field of battle or the mere right of heredity.

Support for the concept of imperial sovereignty was forthcoming from the philosophers; it was reinforced by religious practice and the interpretation of human history. Before considering these developments, it is necessary to look briefly at the practice of sovereignty by the emperors themselves.

By perhaps 120 BC it is apparent that the emperor was losing any function that he may have had as a director of human destinies in practical terms; he was acquiring a symbolical function. Traditionally Wu ti, who acceded in 141 BC while in his sixteenth year, is credited with initiating an age of expansion and activity in which the Han empire reached new heights of achievement. But on inspection it appears that such results should be attributed to others than the emperor himself. The military successes of his reign were due to his generals; the only occasion in which the emperor took part was that of a victory parade, held after the fighting, in 111 BC. Political initiative was in the hands of his statesmen, whose rise to prominence was due more to their relationship to an imperial consort than to the trust they had inspired directly in the emperor. In short, it was becoming exceptional rather than normal for a Han emperor to take an active or decisive part in government; at the same time we observe a renewed and deeper attention to the religious cults in which he took part (see Chapter 12).

A further development suggests that the emperor was becoming a figurehead rather than an active governor. This was the accession of infants to the imperial throne, at times when the succession was in dispute or subject to manipulation. Thus, Chao ti succeeded Wu ti in 87 BC while still in his eighth year, and a number of similar instances occurred throughout the remainder of the dynasty. It would seem that the continued existence of an emperor had become necessary, even though he was sometimes incapable of taking any part in the government of China. The reason is perhaps not far to seek. Without an emperor the whole structure whereby power was devolved and orders were transmitted could collapse, as there would be no fundamental source from which authority sprang. The presence of an emperor, however ineffective as a person, was essential in practical terms so as to maintain the legitimate continuity of a regime; the need to support the emperor's position in intellectual terms was correspondingly strong.

We may now consider the religious and philosophical influences which lent support to the concept of sovereignty and affected its development in Ch'in and Han. We may start with a 'Taoist' approach.

During the second century BC considerable criticism was voiced against the regime of Ch'in; but as yet this seems to have been directed against its methods and lack of restraint rather than against the principle of imperial government, vested in the authority of an emperor. The nearest approach to a critique of the principle of authoritarian government is seen in a passage of the *Huai-nan-tzu*, where the writer expounds a quietist or 'Taoist' view of government. The true function of a ruler, we read, lies in reigning by passive example rather than by initiating action. There is a warning against the potential evils and dangers of arbitrary power, and a call for the co-ordination of service rather than the imposition of demands. But the passage still assumes that supreme responsibility for the welfare and government of mankind on earth lies in the person of the ruler of the empire.

The dowager empress Tou, who died in 135 BC, had been known to favour a branch of Taoist thought known as Huang-Lao. Tomb no. 3, Ma-wang-tui, is dated at 168 BC, just at the time when her influence may have been at its strongest, and it

is of considerable interest that some of the manuscripts discovered in that tomb have a bearing on this mode of thought.
Several texts, hitherto unknown, were attached to the copies of
Lao tzu's classic, and they have been tentatively identified as
deriving from the Huang-Lao school. One of these has direct
implications for political theory, in a period for which information is noticeably lacking.

The book in question is entitled *Ching fa* and consists of nine
chapters. It may be regarded as a practical handbook for those
engaged in the art of government, and includes guides to the
techniques that a ruler needs to master in the execution of his
task. The text sees a place for the purposeful government of man
within a universal scheme of being; and it is by understanding the
order of nature (*tao*) that a ruler acquires true authority for the
exercise of his powers. While the sovereign is the sole source of
all commands, he must conduct himself so as to conform with
the model of heaven, and he must avoid certain artifices, such as
deception, that had been advocated by some of the authoritarian
schools. Temporal rule is seen as existing within the order of
nature, on the basis of certain constant values or criteria. There is
a marked mitigation of the idea of imperial government that had
been practised by the kings and emperors of Ch'in, in order to
enrich and strengthen the state, without reference to higher
ideals.

As far as may be told from the scanty evidence that we possess,
the political ideas of the Huang-Lao school lacked formulation or
precision, and in this way formed a contrast with orderly
prescriptions of the school known as legalist. It is hardly
surprising that its attraction seems to have declined from *c.* 135
BC, for that was the time when active, expansionist policies were
being adopted and growing attention was being paid to a
'Confucian' point of view and traditional texts of literature (see
Chapter 16). Alongside a view of sovereignty that derived from
Huang-Lao thought, it was Tung Chung-shu's more systematic
syncretism which came to be accepted as orthodox. This
formulation comprised a number of elements; there was a
reverence for the ethical ideals of Confucius and his followers and
an enhanced respect for Confucius' own personality; and while
harking back to the ideal aims of government as envisaged for the
pre-imperial age, Tung Chung-shu incorporated his belief in the
Five Phases as a theory of nature.

Tung Chung-shu applied his synthesis to the contemporary conditions of the Han empire, which were very different from those of Confucius' time or the era of the kings of Chou. His way of thought laid the foundations for what has come to be known as 'Han Confucianism', and from about fifty years after his death in *c.* 104 BC this came to be accepted as a model for statesmen and emperors. Sovereignty was seen as an integral part of the system of the universe, with the emperor bearing responsibility to heaven for the welfare of man on earth. Subsequently it could be suggested that the function of the emperor was shown symbolically in the Chinese character for king, i.e. *wang*, where a single vertical line is placed centrally to join three parallel horizontal lines. These stood for heaven, earth and man, and the vertical line was the link that bound them together.

The emperor is described as the son of heaven, like the kings of Chou before him. To enable him to discharge his functions thoroughly he has been endowed with special qualities by heaven which mark him apart from other mortals; and ideally he may be described as possessing saintly characteristics:

> The ordinances of heaven are termed destiny and these cannot be put into operation except by a man of saintly qualities. The fundamental substance of man is termed human nature, and this cannot be fulfilled save by cultural example and precept. Human desires are termed emotion and these cannot be moderated save by regulations. This is why the man who is a true monarch pays careful attention on the one hand to receiving the intention of heaven, so that he may conform with destiny. On the other hand he strives to educate his people intelligently, so that their natures may be fulfilled. He establishes correct norms for his institutions, distinguishing between the upper and the lower orders of humanity so as to preclude desire; and if he will devote himself to achieving these three aims, the fundamental basis of his being will be established.
>
> Man receives his destiny from heaven and is thereby pre-eminently different from other creatures. . . .

It is thus the responsibility of the emperor and his officials to provide for the welfare, education and moral improvement of man. They will inculcate and establish social hierarchies that will enable individuals to exercise to the full their own faculties, which distinguish them from the other creatures of nature. As in Huang-Lao Taoism, so here the sovereign must govern with the constant standards of heaven in full view, to whatever degree he may alter the means of achieving such aims in practice. In certain circumstances an emperor may be faced with the duty of eliminating evils that survive from the rule of a wicked predecessor; such was the case with the Han emperors, who had to replace the abuses of Ch'in's oppression with a humane administration.

The idea of the emperor as the direct instrument of heaven was developed in two ways which came to fruition towards the end of the western Han period. These were, first, the attention paid to the worship of heaven; and secondly, the elaboration of the doctrine of the mandate of heaven (*t'ien ming*).

It will be clear how the change of worship from the *ti* to *t'ien* in 31 BC (see Chapter 12) corresponded with the new concept of sovereignty as this had developed in western Han. Heaven was now worshipped as the bestower of the blessed right to rule, which had once been vested in the kings of Chou. Continuity could be claimed with that dynasty, while the kings and emperors of Ch'in, who had fought their way to their position by force, were to be regarded as interlopers. By worshipping heaven and establishing a direct link with the bestowal of sovereignty, the Han emperors could claim both continuity and legitimacy. So too could Wang Mang for his short-lived Hsin dynasty (AD 9–23), when the worship of heaven was finally accepted as part of the cults of state. Wang Mang's arrangements for ceremonies and rites and the terms of his edicts serve to demonstrate his insistence on the principle of heaven-blest sovereignty and his claim of continuity from Chou. It was in this contribution to the concept of imperial sovereignty that Wang Mang left a permanent heritage to China.

'The son of heaven acts as the father and mother of the people and is king of everything under the skies.' So runs a famous passage in the *Book of Documents* that was quoted by the compilers of the *Han shu*. It is a thought that runs through much of Confucian writing on the subject of kingship. The first full statement of the doctrine of the mandate of heaven is to be found in an essay of Pan Piao, of the first century AD, but the growth of the idea can be traced long before then.

The expression *T'ien ming* is seen in some of China's earliest writings such as the *Book of Documents*, together with the belief that heaven was ready to transfer its mandate from one individual or house to another in order to replace an unjust dispensation by a just one. During the long centuries of the *Spring and Autumn* and the *Warring States* periods the idea was not espoused or advertised much, for reasons that are easy to comprehend. These were times when no single leader could effectively claim to exercise undisputed rule; and at such times an assertion that heaven's mandate was essential for kingship would have become difficult to sustain and subject to ridicule. There are few references to the concept even in the idealist texts of Confucius and his followers.

From the outset of the Han dynasty there are signs of some acknowledgement that the foundation of the dynasty had depended on heaven's help. A far more positive attitude which emerged towards the end of western Han may be seen in the writings of K'uang Heng, whom we have already met in connection with the religious reforms of 31 BC. In a document of *c.* 45 BC K'uang Heng wrote that the duty of 'kings who had received the mandate' lay in transmitting their inheritance as a possession for ever. The principle that the beginning and end of a dynasty's rule depends on heaven recurs in a number of contexts, and received particular stress in the solemn pronouncement made by Wang Mang at his accession. Thereafter pretenders contesting the throne and the successful restorer of the Han dynasty (Kuang wu ti) all laid claim to be the true recipients of the mandate of heaven. In the account of Kuang wu ti's accession and the statements made on that occasion there is incorporated the principle that the will of heaven cannot be gainsaid in these matters; and the mandate cannot be left unbestowed without a recipient.

Pan Piao's essay on 'the mandate of kings' was written by an observer who had witnessed the rise and fall of the Hsin dynasty of Wang Mang and the restoration of the Han house in AD 25, following considerable dissension and civil warfare. He argued that true sovereignty was the lot of certain men to whom it had been apportioned by heaven. The gift of the mandate was attended by the appearance of auspicious omens; it depended on contact with divine powers; and it conformed with the cycle of the Five Phases. Only those persons capable of the office are chosen by heaven to receive it.

The invocation of omens played a significant role at most stages of Wang Mang's rise. But to demonstrate the legitimacy of his dynasty it was no less necessary to prove or assert conformity with the cycle of the Five Phases; for harmony therewith signified that a regime formed part of the universal order and possessed authority to rule mankind. A famous passage from the *Lü shih ch'un-ch'iu* (see p. 46) is an early expression of this link which may be dated to before the imperial period. Subsequently it was put forward that Ch'in had exercised its authority during that phase of the cycle that was symbolised by water, and initially the Han emperors were glad to maintain that they too ruled under this dispensation. But at various times it was proclaimed that a different element was dominant, thereby indicating that a new phase had started in imperial history. Thus the Han emperors adopted earth as their patron element in 104 BC, and Wang Mang retained this as his symbol (AD 9); the eastern Han emperors maintained that they were exercising sovereignty under the dispensation of fire (AD 26).

These changes were due to two reasons. First, there was a new view of which order of succession applied to dynastic change; and secondly there was a new urge to demonstrate that a regime had succeeded to power legitimately. When the Han empire adopted earth in place of water in 104 BC it was posing as the conqueror of its predecessor, in the same way as earth was conceived as conquering water. By the time of Wang Mang and the founder of the eastern Han house, different views were taken of the way in which the phases or elements succeeded one another; this was regarded as a natural process rather than as a response to forceful pressure (see pp. 70–1). Moreover, it was being held that, despite the pretensions made on behalf of first water and then earth, the Han dynasty had in fact risen and prospered under the aegis of fire, just as the kings of Chou had done previously. When Wang Mang chose earth, he had no intention of maintaining identity with the house that he had ousted; he wished to affirm that his dynasty was its natural and legitimate successor, in the belief that Han had existed under the aegis of fire; and just as earth was the natural successor to fire, so was he the natural successor to the Han house of Liu. When Kuang wu ti asserted that his own dispensation was blessed by fire, he was asserting his continuity with his forbears of western Han, and he was branding Wang Mang as an interloper.

By these devices, i.e. the claim to be the repository of the mandate and to conform with a dominant phase, it was sought to show that the exercise of sovereignty was legitimate and natural. In so far as Wang Mang's dynasty had been established by a break in imperial continuity and the Han dynasty had been restored after bloodshed and violence, it was all the more necessary for the successful contestants to pose as possessing their power legitimately rather than as having seized it by force. Two other questions were implicated here: hereditary succession, and the value of abdication.

While hereditary succession was regarded as the normal means whereby a king or emperor followed his predecessor, there were some occasions when the principle was brought into question. It was even manipulated sometimes, so as to ensure the succession of a candidate who would be malleable; authority could be cited from ancient writings to show that personal merit could be of equal importance to that of family relationship alone. Towards the end of the Han period, at a time of political instability, loss of confidence and abuse of institutions, one writer dared to bring the whole principle into question. This was Wang Fu (c. 90–165) whose reaction to contemporary conditions was to call for the reimposition of social discipline by means of firm legal sanctions. He believed that true leadership derived from personal qualities, and quoted examples of two types to prove his point; first, those whose merits had been outstanding without the benefit of family relationship; and secondly, those who had succeeded to a prominent position for just such reasons but had failed to show any ability.

As a further support for a newly founded house and as a means of showing that it was not a lawless dispossessor of a legitimate authority, it was claimed that the last incumbent had abdicated. This practice arose from the time of Wang Mang; it would hardly have been deemed necessary by the Ch'in emperors or the founders of Han. Wang Mang, we are told, received the instrument of abdication in the shrine dedicated to the memory of the founder of the Han dynasty, and the opening passage of Pan Piao's essay on the mandate of kings refers to the acts of abdication of the two paragon sovereigns of Chinese mythology, Yao and Shun. Their example was also cited in a document of AD 220, which derived from the succession of the house of Wei at the close of the Han dynasty. The document brings out a number of the principles that have been discussed above:

When the Han emperor realised that the greater part of the people had their eyes fixed in hope upon Wei, he summoned a meeting of his senior counsellors and made formal acts of notification and worship in the shrine dedicated to Kao ti. He commissioned Chang Yin, who held several official posts including that of imperial counsellor, to take his credentials and convey to the king of Wei the imperial seal with its sash, as a formal gesture of abdication. The emperor's rescript read as follows:

'The following message is addressed to the king of Wei. In ancient times the sovereign Yao abdicated in favour of Yü Shun, and Shun for his part delivered his charge to Yü; for the mandate of heaven does not rest in one place constantly, it reverts to one who is endowed with the qualities of the blest. In the alternate rise and fall of its fortunes, and as the generations have passed, the house of Han has come to forfeit its rightful place in the order of things, so that now, when the dynasty has passed to Our humble person, the times are marked by growing disruption and darkening gloom, and in the prevailing conditions of wickedness and injustice the world is being turned upside down. It is thanks to the holy qualities of king Wu* that relief has been brought to these evils on all sides and the whole civilised world has been purified. In this way has Our ancestral house been preserved in peace; it cannot be that We alone have been granted this blessing; it is surely destined that all Our subjects, far and wide in their many ranks, may enjoy its gifts.

'Let the king now in his majesty receive the heritage of former days and may his glory be shown forth in his qualities. May he restore the accomplishments of kings Wen and Wu† and bring a light to shine on the magnificent achievements of his late respected father.'

The rescript refers to the appearance of favourable omens. It continues in terms that deliberately evoke the solemn phrases in

* King Wu: i.e. the original leader of the house of Wei (Ts'ao Ts'ao), and father of the king addressed in the rescript.
† Kings Wen and Wu: the traditional founder kings of the house of Chou.

which the *Book of Documents* and other texts record the abdication of Yao in favour of Shun, and that of Shun in favour of Yü. The rescript concludes:

'The destiny appointed by the cycle of heaven rests in your person, and may you hold fast to the path of moderation as befits kings. [For, once there is distress and suffering in the area bounded by the seas],* the blessing of heaven will come to its eternal close. Follow with due care the great rule of life and nurture all the nations of the earth, that you may thereby in all solemnity accept the Mandate of Heaven.'

This document is but one of many which survive, in whole or in part, from the dynastic change of AD 220. It may be contrasted with the grandiloquent boasts made by the First Ch'in emperor on his accession four hundred years previously, or the flattering compliments paid to him (see p. 146). Comparison serves to show how the concept of imperial sovereignty had developed, from that of power which can be seized, to that of responsibility that is bestowed.

The development may be traced in other ways. There grew up a need for a formal show of reluctance that a candidate had to display before acceding to the wishes of his ministers to mount the imperial throne. In addition the religious nature of sovereignty came to be stressed. In the course of time it became more regular for a newly acceded emperor to pay his respects at the shrines of his ancestors. For Liu Hsiu, who acceded in AD 25 as the first of the emperors of eastern Han, and Ts'ao P'ei, first of the Wei emperors in 220, we hear of elaborate ceremonies which included the erection of an altar and a pyre, whose smoke conveyed to heaven a notification of the change of stewardship. A further development may be noticed in the attention to or exploitation of omens in connection with imperial destinies. From the time of Hsüan ti (reigned 74 to 49) onwards we hear of favourable omens which were said to predict the success of a reign or the suitability of a particular individual to become emperor. The classic cases of this practice concerned Wang Mang.

The growth of these political concepts affected the attitude

---

* The passage inserted here in parenthesis occurs in a fuller version of the incident than the one that is cited here. See *Analects* 20 'Yao yüeh' opening passage.

towards pre-imperial history, and engendered a nostalgia for the golden days of the past which recurs throughout the imperial period. This followed from the stress laid on heaven and the emperor's worship thereto. It was encouraged by the respect for the scriptural texts (see Chapter 16), many of which assumed or set out to demonstrate a moral superiority on the part of the kings of Chou. Similarly Tung Chung-shu's praise of Confucius implied agreement with an idealised view of the three pre-imperial ages of Hsia, Shang and Chou. In addition, the application of the theory of the Five Phases to dynastic sequences implied a cyclical view of time. It placed the contemporary regime or dynasty within the major context of a never-ending but ever-changing cycle; there could hardly be any concept of progress achieved in a linear manner.

Just as the kingdom of Chou was idealised as a dispensation blessed by heaven, so was the empire of Ch'in denigrated as that of an interloper; and in so far as those who restored the Han dynasty needed to justify their overthrow of Wang Mang and other pretenders, so too was Wang Mang characterised as a usurper. It is perhaps one of history's ironies that the regimes of Ch'in and Hsin between them did more than Han to initiate and forge some of the permanent characteristics of Chinese empire, i.e. an effective system of administration and a respected ideology. The successors of the first Ch'in emperor and Wang Mang could hardly have maintained their regimes without adopting the institutions and principles of the two powers that they displaced.

The orthodox view that the mythical sovereigns of the past and the historical kings of Chou were necessarily superior to the emperors of Han was contested by a rationalist whom we have met before. Wang Ch'ung argued that the Han emperors were no less capable, potentially, than their predecessors of bringing about an era of universal peace. Penetrating his opponents' home ground, he showed that the incidence of auspicious omens showed Han to be no less favoured than the exemplary regimes of the past; and he suggested that Han was superior in terms of material welfare and stability, the extent of its lands and the personal standards of its emperors.

The last word on the subject of sovereignty is left to a philosopher. At the close of the Han period, Hsün Yüeh (148–209) was striving to maintain that a sovereign had a proper place in the world which was not subject to abuse. He was writing in a particularly difficult situation, when the failure of the imperial system had been only too obvious, and an attempt to restore the dignity, nobility and respect of the Han house (AD 196) had ended by Ts'ao Ts'ao's assumption of control; and Ts'ao Ts'ao believed in the imposition of force rather than the value of ethical ideals. In contrast with some of his contemporaries, who were of an inferior intellectual calibre, Hsün Yüeh sought to identify those elements that are permanent in imperial sovereignty and to isolate the essential functions of an ideal emperor. He reached the interesting conclusion that an ideal ruler's first duties are those of conforming with the guiding principles and moral foundation of the state, and the advantages of the people he governs; only then should he be concerned with cultivating his own personal qualities and virtues. The reverse, however, holds true for officials, who must first satisfy their personal consciences that their motives are correct and may only then proceed to perform their duties of administering the people. Finally they may concern themselves with the basic principles of government. It is the prime duty of the sovereign to serve humanity; thereafter he may serve the gods.

14
The purposes of government

We may now consider how belief and theory, religious urge and intellectual achievement affected ideas regarding the purposes of imperial government. These stand revealed in certain telling symbolical actions taken by the emperor and his officials and in historical incidents. They may also be traced in the pronouncements of imperial edicts and in reports submitted by officials that are partly incorporated in the standard histories.

As far as may be surmised, the imperial government of Ch'in aimed at the enrichment and strengthening of the state; the maintenance of security in the towns, counties and farms of China; and the elimination of external threats to Chinese integrity. A specific objective of improving the lot of individual men and women would not have been admitted. Institutions had been established to provide effectively for the material objectives of wealth and strength. These were backed by a system of clearly defined rewards and punishments, which were intended to act as incentives to service and deterrents to crime. Political theory followed the conclusions reached by men such as Shang Yang or Shen Pu-hai or Han Fei; one of Ch'in's leading statesmen, Li Ssu, had been trained by Hsün Ch'ing. Political practice was a logical continuation of what had been the order of the day of the *Warring States* period, when contending kings or leaders had sought to outwit, conquer or take over their rivals. Had it been necessary to formulate the aims of the Ch'in imperial government, such a statement might well have included the principles that man requires organisation; that government exists to organise man; and that government is justified in applying coercion to do so.

Such principles were also acceptable to those Han statesmen who were of a modernist outlook. The major change that was accomplished in Han is sometimes described as the victory of Confucianism. This accompanied some of the developments that have been described in the foregoing chapters, and had any

160

statesman needed to define the objectives of government in, say, the first century BC, he might well have professed the aim of serving humanity, by providing for human welfare and improving living conditions. Such an ideology corresponded with the ideals believed to have informed the administration of the kings of Chou. It was espoused by statesmen of a reformist frame of mind in the western Han period and might well have been claimed as an objective of government under Wang Mang, and by scholars of the Old Text school (see Chapter 16). These ideas included the principle that human quality and potentiality may be improved by noble leadership; that moral precept and example are more effective than coercion; and that government is not justified in imposing force on individuals save in the last resort, or so as to protect them from evil.

How far these claims could be substantiated as elements of an imperial policy that was being actively implemented is a very different story, with which these pages are not concerned. But it must be noted that during the last century of Han a reaction was setting in against these ideals that was due partly to their failure in practice and the growing corruption and imbalances of the times. It was seen that effective government requires more co-ordination than had been achieved hitherto, and that there was too much scope for arbitrary or permissive behaviour, to the detriment of state and individual. In such circumstances a few men called for a reassertion of imperial purpose by a more stringent exercise of strength. In so doing, they were reverting to ideas that were more characteristic of the Ch'in and early Han governments than of those of the reformist statesmen and their promotion of Confucius' ethics.

Three men stand out for mention in this connection. Wang Fu (c. 90–165) advocated the impartial application of the laws of the empire to all its members, whatever their status or their power. Ts'ui Shih (c. 110–170) saw a need to adapt old principles to contemporary needs and to resist the retention of precedents for their own sake. He suggested a return to some very severe types of punishment that had long since been discarded, for therein he saw a means of curing the ills of the body politic. No less forcefully, Chung-ch'ang T'ung (born 180) believed that the imposition of authority would bring about the best measure of human good; he produced a set of practical suggestions designed to end current abuses and to improve China's wealth and strength.

In the Roman empire coins were used as an instrument of propaganda, advertising the achievements of government or the qualities professed by an emperor. The coins of the Ch'in and Han empires were cast more simply without embellishment, and were intended simply as a practical medium of exchange. But there were other means which served the same purposes, such as the selection of regnal titles for dating, or the choice of terms in imperial edicts. In addition there were certain symbolical actions whereby a Chinese emperor or government sought to proclaim its purpose and which sometimes ran in close parallel with the tone of the edicts. These included the personal part played by the emperor in agriculture or rites such as that of 'watching for the ethers', as will be described below.

Regnal titles (*nien hao*) were the means of enumerating years. Initially years had been counted from the start of each emperor's reign. At some point it was decided to do so by means of a term which would characterise the contemporary period. It was thus ordered that a specified year (either the current one, or its successor or sometimes its predecessor) would be known as year no. 1 of such and such a period, and the subsequent years would be enumerated in sequence. As the regnal title selected would appear in all official documents, its message would continually be brought before the eyes of statesmen, senior civil servants and junior clerks; no one who received a state paper need remain unaware of the mood or hopes of the government, or of its particular objects of pride.

During the latter part of western Han regnal titles remained in force for some four to six years, but in eastern Han they were sometimes retained for longer periods. Some of the titles were chosen to mark a moment of divine benediction or of religious activity. For example, Yüan ting (the first tripod) was assigned retrospectively to 116 BC, as a result of the discovery of the tripod in 113 BC (see p. 132) To 110 BC, the year of Wu ti's ascent of Mount T'ai, there was given the name Yüan feng (the first *feng* sacrifice). During Hsüan ti's reign (74–49 BC) the new attitude to phenomena as harbingers of good fortune was revealed in a unique series of regnal titles that commemorated these felicitous occurrences. Thus the years 61–58 BC were counted as Shen chüeh (the divine birds) 1 to 4; the term was followed by Wu feng (the five flights of phoenix, 57–54), Kan lu (honey-dew, 53–50) and Huang lung (the golden dragon, 49). A regnal title which was introduced for 28–25 BC commemorated the successful completion of operations to stem the ravages of the Yellow river; this was Ho- p'ing, the pacification of the river.

Regnal titles were also used as a declaration of faith in the start of a new era. This was seen most conspicuously in the choice of T'ai ch'u, 'the grand beginning', for 104–101 BC, and Shih chien kuo, 'the initial foundation of the state', which was adopted by Wang Mang after his enthronement in AD 9. Similarly an abortive attempt at dynastic renovation and rededication of 5 BC included the short-lived use of a grandiloquent title. Wang Mang used the same device to proclaim his regency, while the Han house still stood, in AD 6; and the title Chien wu (the establishment of valour) that was chosen after the restoration of the Han house in AD 25 remained in use for thirty years. For most of the eastern Han period, titles were largely chosen which bore a message of good will or felicity (e.g. Yung ho, 'Perpetual harmony', AD 136–41; Chien an, 'the establishment of peace', AD 196–220). A glance at the pages of Han history for some of these periods will show how, only too frequently, these pious expressions of hope or exercises in sympathetic magic were belied by the events of the years thus named.

Imperial edicts of western Han often link the implicit purposes of government with practical decisions, but with the development of a reformist attitude a concern for the care of mankind enters in. Edicts stress the need for the promotion of agriculture, and come to express an anxiety for the lot of suffering humanity, with a desire to care for the needy, elderly or lonely. Solemn utterances put into the mouths of emperors, sometimes still of a tender age, are often loaded with self-depreciation. They may affirm the need for an emperor to stand possessed of those qualities that fit him for his charge and enable him to extend his bounties liberally, or they may deplore an emperor's failure to live up to those standards. Some of these declarations of intent were proclaimed early in the days of the dynasty, when the acts of government were directed more to immediate material objectives than to an appreciation of moral virtues. Some edicts allude to an emperor's request for straightforward honest criticism; some take note of the occurrence of phenomena, whether they foretell good or evil, and seek to accommodate a government's behaviour or plans accordingly. The following are cited as examples of edicts of the western Han period:

178 BC

Whereas the work of the fields is the prime occupation of the world and the means upon which the people rely for their livelihood, We find that there are those of Our people who, while not devoting themselves to these prime tasks, occupy themselves with pursuits of minor importance; and as a result life cannot be sustained.

Deploring as We do that this is so, We shall in person lead Our many ministers of state to take part in the work of the fields as a means of encouragement; and We command that a grant shall be made to the people by remitting half of the dues to which they are liable in respect of the land and its produce.

163 BC

We are informed that for several years just passed there has been a failure of harvest, accompanied by disasters of flood, drought or pestilence. Deeply grieved as We are by these occurrences, in Our inept failure of understanding We have not ascertained the causes of these disasters; and We question whether there are faults in the manner that Our affairs are ordered or excessive measures in Our undertakings. Are We to suppose that the order of heaven has not met with obedience or that We have not acquired the gifts of the earth; that the affairs of man are all too often bereft of harmony, or that the demons and holy spirits have been abandoned so that they cannot enjoy their due meed of gifts? When We ponder how this state of affairs has been brought about, We ask whether the emoluments paid to Our officials are too lavish or whether there are too many of Our activities that bring no material advantage; and We are dismayed at the shortage of supplies for Our people.

The surveys of the land that may be ploughed show that its extent has not diminished and the counts that are made of the people show that their number has not increased. If we estimate the extent of Our territories in accordance with the number of individual persons We find that there is now more than there had been formerly; and yet there is a grave shortage of food. If We ask wherein the blame lies, We wonder whether it can only be that too many of the common people follow occupations that are of secondary importance, to the grave detriment of the work of the fields; that too much grain is consumed in the distillation of spirits, and that domestic animals are fed with grain too lavishly.

[The edict concludes with an order to senior officials to consider the problems that have been described and to present their conclusions, omitting nothing that may seem to be unpalatable.]

81 BC

In the second month of the sixth year of Shih-yüan [March to April 81BC], it was decreed that officials should make enquiry of those persons who, being of integrity, intelligence and learning had been recommended to serve in official posts. They were to ask to what hardships the people lay exposed. There followed the debate concerning the abolition of the monopolies of state for salt, iron and fermented liquors.

34 BC, third month [April]

We have been informed that when a monarch of blessed worth puts his kingdom in order, he makes clear what is approved and what is disliked and lays down what is to be chosen and what is to be rejected; and in so far as he upholds the ideals of respect and modesty the people raise the quality of their conduct. It thus comes about that when the laws are established there is no infringement thereof by the people; popular obedience accompanies the fulfilment of his ordinances.

Able as We have been to maintain the safety of Our ancestral shrines We have comported Ourselves with great care and trepidation, never daring to relax Our vigilance; but Our qualities are inadequate and Our understanding obscured, with the result that the guidance whereby We wish to improve Our people has been tenuous. As the *Records* have it 'That there are faults among the people is due to Us alone'.*

[The edict then orders the distribution of bounties in the form of a general amnesty, the bestowal of social and legal privileges, and material gifts of spirits and meat. There follows an injunction for greater and more intensive work in the fields and the silkworm farms, with less interference in these occupations by officials.]

---

* The citation is taken from the *Book of Documents* and is also cited in the *Analects*. See Dubs, *History of the Former Han Dynasty*, vol. II, p. 333, note 12.2.

The edicts themselves may order acts of bounty such as a general amnesty to criminals, the distribution of material gifts, exemption from taxation or the bestowal of a privileged order of rank. For the eastern Han period the philanthropic intentions of the edicts were sometimes supported by ceremonial and symbolical actions of the emperor and empress, undertaken as an example of charity or of personal exertion, or in order to initiate work that was needed throughout the empire. Reference has been made above (see p. 142) to the personal participation by the emperor or empress in some of these cults.

Certain activities took place at court for religious purposes, such as exorcism or purification (see p. 142). We may now consider other symbolical actions which were taken to ensure that decisions of government were in accord with the rhythms of the universal cycle and thus likely to achieve their purpose. Four examples of this type of activity will be considered, the regulation of the calendar, the observation of the ethers, the observation of the vapours and the eencouragement of rain.

In the days of a luni-solar calendar, it was continually necessary to determine the exact divisions of the year. In particular, it was necessary to stipulate which of the months would be long, at thirty days, and which short, at twenty-nine days, and to fix the point at which the intercalary month should be inserted, roughly once every three years. For unless these matters were regulated with reasonable accuracy, the calendar would quickly fall out of step with the march of the seasons. It is hardly surprising that Chinese governments which, as has just been seen, were wont to stress the importance of agriculture, assumed responsibility for regulating the calendar and distributing copies to officials. Indeed there is a reference to this duty in China's earliest traditions, which ascribe the practice to the mythical emperor Yao, and this story was reiterated at the close of the Han period by Wang Fu.

There was also a further motive behind the official attention paid to the calendar. Quite apart from the practical needs it was necessary to ensure that earthly and human activities would harmonise with the rhythms of the heavens. It was this motive as much as practical needs and the advances in astronomy which led to the introduction of revised and more refined calendars in 104 BC, at the start of the Christian era and again in AD 85.

The official practice of 'observing the ethers' was designed to note the arrival of successive stages of the universal cycle and to mark these points on a time-scale. Once the points were known, it would be possible to embark on actions appropriate to the season in question (e.g. the execution of criminals, which awaited the winter). While the energies (*ch'i*) of Yin and Yang were themselves invisible, it was nonetheless possible to observe their operation in material ways. Twelve pitch-pipes, carefully measured and sized to a scale, were buried; they had previously been arrayed in a circle in such a way that each corresponded with the month of the year and the spatial direction appropriate to the pitch in question. The arrival of the energy of Yin or Yang at a particular division of the circle, and thus at a particular division of time, would, it was hoped, be marked by the reaction of one of the pipes. For at that precise moment the invisible energy would exert pressure on the ash that lay within the pipe in question, causing it to be ejected.

The observation of the vapours was likewise a deliberate act undertaken by or on behalf of the Han emperors, and by private practitioners, to chart the progress of cosmic rhythms. Unlike the observation of the ethers by use of the pitch-pipes, this procedure was empirical, and as far as is known it did not result in the establishment of a formal set of criteria. It was believed that, invisible as the energies were, their presence could be inferred from the appearance of vapours of differing shapes and colours, to each one of which there could be attributed a prognostication for the future. This practice could well be classified as a form of consultation of an oracle, according to the distinctions that have been drawn above (see p. 91). It requires mention in this present context, in so far as it was sometimes intended to ensure the success of a government or an emperor's action. There were no less than twelve officials in the complement of the government whose special duty lay in watching for the vapours. It is possible that the practice forms one of the subjects depicted on a document found at Ma-wang-tui, which concerns prognostication from various climatic phenomena. The standard histories record a large number of incidents of watching the vapours between 164 BC and AD 195.

A striking instance of symbolism is seen in the ceremonies performed to encourage the rain to fall. There was a basic belief in the power of the dragon to produce rain by mounting upon the clouds. At times of need, prayers were held throughout the provinces; officials of senior and junior ranks took part, each standing in his rightful place according to grade and seniority. Clay models of dragons were set up, together with clay figures of dancing youths, in two rows; and these were changed every seven days, in accordance with precedent.

The *Huai-nan-tzu* alludes to this practice. It was evidently hoped that presentation of the model dragons would be sufficiently suggestive to bring about a fall of rain. According to Wang Ch'ung's *Lun-heng*, the philosopher Tung Chung-shu supported the observance. Wang Ch'ung's own opinion is perhaps ambivalent. He credits Tung Chung-shu with complete sincerity, as belief in the practice was quite consistent with Tung's view of the world. Wang Ch'ung himself seems to reject the practice as invalid, as it rests on a false view of nature.

A somewhat similar rite is recorded for the beginning of spring, when the people of the earth were to be encouraged to set to work with their ploughs, and officials of all grades took part in a ceremony which marked the end of winter. On this occasion clay models of oxen were set outside the doors together with ploughs; the rite is explained as a farewell gesture to the departing season of cold.

At the outset of this chapter we noted the existence of two major attitudes to the purposes of government: first, that which sought to strengthen the state, and which corresponds to 'Legalist' theory; and secondly, that which saw the duty of the state as lying in the protection and ennoblement of individual man, and which shared some of the ethical ideals of the 'Confucian' school of philosophers. We may now consider how these two attitudes affected the policies advocated by the statesmen of western Han and their interpretation of a government's duties.

The difference is seen in respect of both domestic matters and foreign policy. In very general terms, for the first seventy years of the Han dynasty policies were directed towards the consolidation of the state's authority and the re-establishment of social stability. Rather than initiate costly activities, governments refrained from entering into foreign entanglements. Then, from c. 130 BC, there began a period of intense activity in which the principles of Ch'in's imperial government were actively pursued and furthered. But a change in attitude is noticeable from at least 70 BC, when policies changed from a forward-looking expansion to withdrawal and retrenchment; the views of the reformists had gained ground at the expense of the modernists.

In addition to the evidence of practical measures, the difference of attitude may be seen in theoretical terms in the account of the debate staged in 81 BC, just at the time when expansionist policies had been brought into question. In domestic matters, modernist statesmen had used the system of bounties and rewards of state to stimulate effort and to reward service; but towards the end of western Han, state bounties feature as a means of demonstrating the virtues and philanthropy of an emperor and the ideals of sovereignty.

A similar contrast may be observed in the regulation of the economy. Wu ti's modernist statesmen had taken steps to control the minting of coin and to ease the distribution of staple goods. They believed that land tenure should be free of restriction; that cultivation of unworked land would be encouraged by private enterprise, and that this would result in increasing the government's revenue from the land. By way of contrast, they believed in bringing the iron and salt mines and industries under the supervision of officials who were entitled to employ conscript labour in the work of production and distribution. By this means the government would retain control of some of the staple necessities of life, direct them where they were most needed and collect any profits that might be forthcoming from these enterprises.

The very different attitude of reformist statesmen towards these matters discloses their different view of government and its duties. In a statement on economic policy of *c.* 44 BC Kung Yü argued that social imbalance derived partly from dependence on the use of money, and that it was no part of a government's duty to supervise the minting of coin or the direction of conscript labour to work in the mines. Earlier, Tung Chung-shu had stated the case against allowing land-tenure to grow unchecked, in view of the general poverty that a *laissez-faire* policy engendered. Right at the end of the dynasty this principle was translated into action by attempts (7 BC) to restrict the extent of land holdings. However, reformist statesmen rejected the principle of controlling the mines and working them with state-conscripted labour; they felt that such conscription could not be justified, and that in the mines there was a legitimate enterprise for private exploitation.

In foreign affairs, Wu ti's statesmen had advocated expansion by military means, in order to protect Chinese territory from invasion and in order to increase the country's wealth and strength; the task of implementing such a policy fell in the last resort on the shoulders of individual servicemen, working out their time as conscripts. Reformist statesmen reacted against the imposition of such burdens on individuals, and preferred retrenchment within China's borders to the deliberate extension of Chinese influence beyond. They believed that the alien should be won over to a Chinese way of life and to loyalty to the son of heaven on cultural grounds and by moral example rather than by military force; deployment of conscript servicemen for this purpose was unjustifiable.

The last word on the duties and responsibilities of a government may be left to one of the critics who took part in the debate of 81 BC. According to the account of that debate, the following speech reduced the spokesman for modernist government to abject silence:

Just as heaven has established the three great lights* of the sky to show forth guidance and warnings [to man], so does the son of heaven set up his ministers of state to bring an enlightened order to the world; and this is why it has been observed that the ministers of state form the pattern and example for all who live within the four seas, and the essential material elements for the spiritual improvement of man. Above they bear the duty of assisting a blessed and wise ruler; below their concern lies with bringing about a change to a more holy way of life. They act in harmony with Yin and Yang; they regulate human affairs to accord with the four seasons of nature; and they bring peace to all mankind. They nurture all manner of created things and provide a life of amity and concord for all men, unmarred by thoughts of hatred. Foreign peoples from all quarters submit to their virtues and their achievements, and there is no fear that anyone will rise in rebellion. It is the responsibility of ministers of state to bring this about and the duty of wise men to work for these ends.

* This expression is explained traditionally as referring to the sun, moon and stars, without further discrimination.

15

The regulation of man

It was a basic principle of much of Han thought to view the universe as an organic unity composed of the three interdependent elements of heaven, man and earth. It was therefore of just as much importance to Han philosophers to attend to the values, place and proper function of man as to the movements of the heavenly bodies or the processes of life and death on earth. Man must understand his place within this universe and he must find out how best to regulate his relations with his own kind. As in other subjects, so here four different attitudes may be discerned, that may be roughly described as Taoist, Confucian, Legalist and rationalist.

These attitudes may be summarised as follows. Man could be regarded as a creature of nature who must conform with nature's rhythms; or he could be seen as a creature who enjoyed superior powers to those of other creatures, whereby his character and personality could be ennobled. Others saw man as the agent or servant of superior temporal authority, whose efforts must be trained, disciplined and utilised as effectively as possible; to rationalists man was but one of the many creatures who inhabit the earth, whose merits depend on his actual performance and its results.

In their practical applications these views conflicted less than might be supposed, as the injunctions of one way of thought would often overlap with those of another. With the exception of the rationalist frame of mind, which first came to fruition and formulation under Han, these modes of thought could be traced back to the first flowering of Chinese philosophy. This had occurred mainly during the sixth to the third centuries BC, and had given rise to seminal thinkers (or texts ascribed to them) such as K'ung tzu (K'ung Ch'iu, Confucius), Meng tzu (Meng K'o, Mencius), Hsün tzu, Lao tzu, Chuang tzu, Shang Yang and Han Fei, to name but a few. But the conclusions expressed by such men were directed to the contemporary political and social state of China, which had not yet achieved unity. During the Ch'in and the Han periods, other thinkers succeeded in incorporating some of these views in theories that suited the new style of imperial government, with consequences that have been considered above in connection with imperial sovereignty (see Chapter 13). This chapter will consider the views of man as they are reflected in the concept of the laws of state and the trust in conventional behaviour (*li*); there are also implications on the subject of the following chapter, which concerns the 'scriptures'.

The establishment of regulations, punishments and sanctions, better described as 'the laws' than as 'the law', had grown up under the kings and emperors of Ch'in, on the basis of teachings ascribed to Shang Yang and Han Fei. In the course of lengthy processes, these were tempered by considerations of the ethical and humane values which were preached by Confucius and comprised basic guide-lines for the behaviour proper to given occasions. Such guide-lines or even rules for conventional behaviour were soon bound up with the choice of the 'scriptures', i.e. ancient texts that came to be associated with Confucius' own hand and which were chosen for prominent treatment in the processes of education thanks to their underlying ethical message. Written formulations of the conventions of behaviour were included in the canon of scriptures from the outset.

The laws of the early Chinese empires grew up as an instrument whereby an emperor and his officials proclaimed their decisions and implemented their will. They consisted of individual prescriptions and prohibitions which derived from the need to control, discipline and organise the population; they cannot be regarded as a statement of principles which stood beyond the authority of a particular ruler. As yet there was no determination to formulate basic ideas of justice or to provide a systematic account of the rights, privileges and obligations of an individual or the recognised authority of an official. The laws derived from expedient rather than principle; they could be used to establish a series of rewards whereby a king or emperor could encourage civil or military service; they could be used to impose punishments to deter persons from crime.

Fragments of the laws of the Ch'in and Han periods have come to light in some of the manuscripts found recently in tombs, and citations of these provisions have long been known in literature; but there can be no question of reconstructing a complete corpus. From these fragments it is possible to infer certain ideas of privilege and social hierarchy; but so far from depending on a preconceived notion of human values or qualities, these ideas had come about as a means of ordering a community. The fragments include texts of the 'Statutes' (*lü*) and the 'Ordinances' (*ling*), many of which are cast in negative form, e.g. as the statement of penalties that follow the infringement of stated rules or prohibitions. There are also a few texts of hypothetical cases in which an action and its consequence are described, as a means of guiding officials who administer the laws of the land.

In positive terms it may be claimed that the statutes and ordinances were directed to two purposes: some were designed to maintain the cosmic balance of the universe, by regulating seasonal activities and ensuring that those actions that destroy the balance are followed by countermeasures to restore it; others were intended to maintain social stability and political cohesion.

According to the histories, which may well be somewhat biased, early in the Han period critics were complaining that the laws of the Ch'in empire had been excessively complex and oppressive. It was the great boast of the founding emperor of Han and his advisers that at a stroke they had simplified the system of Ch'in, reducing it to three main provisions, and that they had mitigated the severities of its punishments. It is nonetheless likely that despite some formal changes and reduction of penalties, the concept of the laws remained unaltered, as a set of rules designed to prevent crime and to compel obedience to authority's demands for tax and service.

The place and function of the laws of state were brought into question at the time of the reassessment of ideas in 81 BC. The following exchange of views is recorded in the *Discourses on Salt and Iron (Yen-t'ieh lun)* that survives as a written account of that debate. The book discloses the contrast between those who upheld the system of laws and punishments as the most effective means of controlling the population, and those who believed that a nation should be led by precept and moral example rather than by discipline and force. The combination of the two metaphors of the steed and the ship of state which occurs in the opening sentence is maintained throughout this part of the dialogue.

The spokesman for the government: Measures of control are, as it were, the bridle and bit of the state, and punishments form its halyards and rudder. Even an expert horseman such as Wang Liang could not travel far without the help of bridle and bit; and however skilled a pilot might be he could not steer a ship through the waters if there were no halyards or rudder attached.

Han Fei said that those who suffer difficulties in maintaining hold of their states are unable to make manifest the force of its institutions, to control their subjects, to enrich their country or to strengthen their armed forces, and thereby keep their enemies in check and withstand difficulties. They are led astray by the arguments of the foolish scholastics and thereupon doubt the advice that is proffered by men of wisdom. They promote persons who are fickle or capricious in preference to those whose services are proven. To hope that a state may be kept in good order in this way is tantamount to trying to climb a height after discarding the ladder, or to control a runaway horse without using a bit. In the present situation the laws and punishments are indeed established and yet there are persons who infringe them. What could be expected if those laws did not exist? The result would inevitably be the breakdown of government.

The man of learning: Bridle and bit are the equipment that a horseman uses; given an expert horseman, the animal will be kept under control. The authority of the laws is the instrument for keeping a state in order; given a wise man, its people's ways will be improved. But if the wrong type of person is holding the reins, the horse will run amok, just as if the wrong type of person is at the helm the ship will be wrecked by turning turtle.

Some time ago, when Wu put [Sun] P'i in charge of the helm as chief minister the ship was smashed; and when Ch'in ordered Chao Kao to hold the reins the carriage was over-turned. If moral values and measures are rejected in favour of penal sanctions, there will be a repetition of the fate that overcame Wu and Ch'in.

It is an unchangeable principle, valid for all time, that the man who acts as ruler should take the three kings as his model; that the man who acts as chief counsellor should take his example from the Duke of Chou; and that the man who formulates measures of state should follow K'ung tzu. Han Fei paid no respect to the kings of old whom he denigrated; he did not conform with just institutions, which he rejected. In the end he fell straight into a trap, suffering imprisonment and dying as an alien in Ch'in. Basically he had had no conception of fundamental principles and only a small degree of discrimination – simply enough to do himself harm.

Li may be described as a system of behaviour devised to improve the lot of humanity and the quality of living. One of its functions was to establish a permanent framework for human activity that outlasts the frail and short-lived aspirations of the individual man or woman. *Li* derived from the moralist motives of a Confucian frame of mind, and was intended to inculcate a sense of ethical values. It would promote human welfare and eliminate discord; it would restrict excessive displays of emotion; it would stimulate the human capacity for good to the utmost.

The ethical values to which continual reference is made in this connection were mainly those of *jen* and *i*. As it was not the Chinese way to analyse ideas or to define terms, these expressions are best understood from their context in literature, mainly in the sayings of the master philosophers of the *Warring States* period. The terms correspond with the respect due to individual men and women as beings who are endowed with human rather than animal capacities, and to a sense of right or righteousness which would ensure that individuals are treated according to that principle. On this basis the provisions of *li* preserved those human relationships and social hierarchies that were thought to ennoble rather than to deprave. They enjoined ideal modes of conduct for rendering service to the gods, to deceased ancestors and to social superiors and inferiors. They laid down the forms of religious ceremonies and the protocol of a king or an emperor's court. They prescribed the conventional behaviour to be observed towards kinsfolk, friends or strangers, and between members of different generations of the same clan; and the *li* prescribed some of the disciplines of war.

Some of the earliest references and allusions to *li* are to be found in the *Spring and Autumn Annals*. This is a somewhat terse historical record that concerns the rulers of the many states of China during the period 722–481 BC. The book includes considerable detail of the behaviour thought to be suitable for such persons and between them, and of the formal means of retaining a correct sense of hierarchies. One of the reasons why this record has occupied so important a place in the Chinese tradition is the belief that it had been edited by Confucius and that it reproduced his ethical judgements.

Neither the minutiae of approved conduct nor the demands of ethical values were matters of prime concern to the kings, emperors or statesmen of Ch'in, who had established temporal power by the exercise of force rather than by hearkening to precept. But according to the standard histories, shortly after the establishment of Han there were some dignitaries who paid attention to these considerations. In a famous incident, an official named Lu Chia warned the first Han emperor that successful imperial government demanded different qualities from those needed to win control of an empire from horseback. It was consequent on this incident that Lu Chia wrote a short treatise (entitled *Hsin yü*) showing how the destiny of kings and emperors could not be separated from moral considerations.

Lu Chia's interview with the first of the Han emperors may be compared with a further event of much the same time. This was the formal specification of the correct modes of behaviour at court, that was ascribed to Shu-sun T'ung. His project was intended as a means of introducing a measure of courtesy and civilised behaviour to a court that included soldiers of fortune among its number. It was also intended as a way of laying down the correct marks of status that differentiated an emperor from his officials and his servants. It is reported, perhaps somewhat idealistically, that on the completion of this work the emperor remarked that at last he understood the full dignity and honour of his position.

The idea of *li* was vitally strengthened by the production of a number of treatises or compendia designed to formalise correct types of behaviour. Such books, of which three major examples survive today (the *Li chi, Chou li* and *I li*), were compiled either shortly before or during the Han dynasty. They lay down detailed regulations for matters such as dress, carriages or the funeral equipment approved for different social occasions. Of considerable significance is the stress that these compilations laid on precedent. In order to validate their rules, their origins were ascribed to the golden age of the earlier kings. In particular the practices that the books enjoin are attributed to the kings of

Chou; and in so far as Confucius had idealised that era for moral reasons, a strong link was again forged between *li* and the teachings of that philosopher.

This link was further strengthened by Tung Chung-shu (*c.* 179–*c.* 104 BC) whose contributions to Han thought have featured above in connection with both omens and imperial sovereignty. In respect of *li*, he not only emphasised the value and significance of Confucius as a teacher of ethical precepts; he also insisted on the value of the *Spring and Autumn Annals* as a guide to understanding contemporary events. The concern of that document with *li* was borne out in various commentaries to the work that were being promoted during the Han period (see Chapter 16).

The following passage, which is drawn from the opening part of the treatise on *li* and music in the *Han shu*, illustrates the ethical basis of *li* and its association with Confucius, together with the view that music fulfilled a similar function to that of the written prescriptions of approved behaviour:

Human nature comprises distinctions between the sexes and emotions of jealousy and aversion; it is for this reason that the holy men of old instituted the rites of marriage. It comprises a recognised order whereby old and young conduct their relations with one another, and it is for this reason that the holy men instituted the conventions for communal banquets. It comprises feelings of grief at the loss of the dead and a recollection of those who have long since departed; for this reason the holy men set out the rites of mourning and sacrifice. It comprises a desire to accord honour where it is due and respect to a man's superiors; for this reason the holy men instituted rules of procedure for audiences at court. For mourning, a limit was placed on undue weeping and posture, while allowance was made for song and dance on occasions of joy. These arrangements were sufficient to express the true feelings of properly balanced persons and to prevent a loss of moderation by those of evil inclination.

So, when the rites of marriage are abandoned, the correct relationship between the sexes will be weakened and crimes of sexual misbehaviour or depravity will increase. If the conventions for communal banquets are not observed, the correct order of old and young will be thrown into disarray and disputes will give rise to a large number of lawsuits. If the rites of mourning and sacrifice are discarded, the natural relations of kith and kin will become tenuous and there will be many who turn their backs on the dead and neglect their ancestors. When the rules of procedure for audiences and state visits are abandoned, the respective difference in status between ruler and minister will disappear, and the gradual process of the encroachment of power will set in. This is why K'ung tzu said 'There is nothing better than *li* for rendering a ruler secure and his people well-ordered; and there is nothing better than music for improving their customs and transforming their way of life.'

The rules of behaviour serve to moderate the people's feelings; music serves to bring harmony to their voiced expressions; administrative measures are used to induce certain types of behaviour and punishments are used to prevent other types of activity. The way of true kingship will be assured, provided that these four agents – the rules of behaviour, music, administrative measures and punishments – achieve their objectives without infringement.

By bringing order to human feelings, music attains some measure of uniformity; by regulating a man's relations to external matters, the rules of behaviour establish appropriate differences of attitude. Uniformity results in harmony and friendship; differences of attitude engender awe and respect. With harmony and friendship there is no hatred; with awe and respect there is no strife. The attainment of order throughout the world by the practice of modesty and yielding place to others may be attributed to the rules of behaviour and to music. These two ideals are practised together and form a single unity.

The intentions of awe and respect are difficult to observe; they are therefore displayed in the prescribed ways of offering a present, in declining or receiving a present; in the manner of ascending to a high place or descending; or in the conventions for sitting down or the formal salutation of others. The delights of harmony and friendship are difficult to express in material form; they are therefore brought out in poetry and song, in recitation and in speech, and by instruments such as bell or stone, pipe or strings. Music brings happiness to those who wish to show respect without involving material considerations; it lends beauty to feelings of joy without permitting an excessive indulgence in sound. This is why K'ung tzu questioned whether the rules of behaviour consisted simply in making expensive gifts of jade or silk, and whether music was no more than the sounds of bells and drums.

These are the fundamental principles behind the rules for behaviour and music; and this is why it is said: 'A man who understands the feelings of the rules of behaviour and music is able to be creative; whereas a man who comprehends the patterns of the two is able to compile a written record. Those who are creative may be termed saints, and those who draw up records may be described as intelligent. Intelligence and saintliness are terms used in respect of the abilities to record and to create.'

The foregoing passage dates from the first century AD, when the Confucian basis of society had been accepted as orthodox. The view of *li* and music as instruments of education and improvement had, however, not passed without criticism. It was a basic tenet of 'Taoist' thought that formal statements of moral values often detract from their own efficacy and defeat their ends. They give rise to the misapprehension that conformity to stated rules is sufficient to ensure good conduct, and they may thus encourage hypocrisy or greed. Wang Ch'ung had cited Lao tzu's view that *li* marked the tenuous nature of human trust and indicated the way to chaos. In setting out the dangers as well as the ideal advantages of the Confucian values, another writer had observed that while *li* was a means of expressing respect, it was likewise a means of encouraging laxity or indolence.

There were likewise thinkers of the Han period who were fully alive to the contradictory values of music. Music of approved styles was used in religious ceremonies of state; it was regarded as a means of moderating excessive emotion and harmonising man with other elements of the universe. But it was equally clearly recognised that certain forms of music were likely to excite base emotions and to stimulate passions that were best restrained. In *c.* 114 BC a special office had been founded with the function of collecting approved music and supervising performances, mainly on religious occasions. But as time passed it became clear that instead of concentrating on music that was fit for such occasions, the office was also concerning itself with the music of Cheng and Wei, which was regarded as debased and leading to licentiousness. From about 70 BC onwards successive attempts were made to eliminate such activities and to restrict the work of the office to its proper function. But the office was doomed. An edict of 7 BC ordered its abolition, on the grounds that its encouragement of the 'pop' music of Cheng and Wei was a mark of contemporary depravity. Over half of the 829 virtuosi in the employ of the office were dismissed; only those who performed old-style music at religious services or state occasions were retained.

16

The scriptures

Some of the most far-reaching decisions of Han governments, that affected many aspects of China's traditional heritage, are seen in the selection of certain ancient texts for special treatment as 'scriptures'. These decisions left a permanent mark on Chinese literature, scholarship and culture; they were intimately bound up with questions such as the choice of an orthodox philosophy for the empire, the view taken of earlier philosophers, and the formation of a syllabus of learning by which officials and statesmen would be trained.

That a 'literary policy' was in any way possible was due partly to the small extent of literature in the Ch'in and Han periods and the difficulty of circulating copies. As yet wooden strips formed the principal medium for writing, with silk being used somewhat exceptionally; and paper did not come into general use until the third or fourth century AD. Possibly the very scarcity of copies enhanced the value of the texts that were known, and a government that was concerned with its intellectual background would be quick to note how a few writings could exercise a disproportionately great influence, particularly if they were not countered by spokesmen for a different persuasion. The promotion or suppression of some writings could conceivably be the key to a government's authority and to the frame of mind of its officials.

Some of the earliest texts that are extant today (e.g. the *Book of Songs* and the *Book of Changes*) may include parts that date from *c.* 1000 BC or the next century or so. During the *Spring and Autumn* and the *Warring States* periods (770–221 BC), when the so-called hundred schools of Chinese philosophy developed, some of these early texts acquired a reputation for unquestionable wisdom. Particular respect was accorded to those writings believed to have been created or edited by Confucius, whose own teachings were being recorded by his pupils (as in the

Analects of Confucius or the *Mencius*). At much the same time the *Warring States* were giving rise to writings of a Taoist and a legalist nature, to name but two of the major schools of thought. A further feature of these days was the establishment of academies of learning which developed a particular interest or imparted a characteristic type of interpretation to some of these early texts. The best-known of these academies were situated in east China (the modern province of Shantung).

Antagonism to the ideals of these early writings, particularly those of a moralist nature, was only to be expected from the emperor and statesmen of Ch'in. A famous edict of 213 BC sought to translate this antagonism into action. It ordered the destruction of publicly held copies of those works that could be quoted by way of protest against the contemporary view of the state. The chief targets were the *Book of Songs* and the *Book of Documents*, by now irrevocably associated with Confucius' ethics and the moral purposes ascribed to the kings of Chou. Simultaneously steps were taken to prevent open discussion of such books, and considerable pressure was brought to bear on known teachers of their message. According to the histories, 460 such scholars were put to death. But it should be noted that books of certain categories were specifically exempted from destruction by burning; these were those that had a practical bearing on the conduct of affairs or matters of everyday life (e.g. treatises on medicine, divination and agriculture).

The effects of these measures cannot be known for certain, and it is likely that they have been subject to some exaggeration by critics of the succeeding generation. Our accounts of the incident derive from historians who were writing at a time when the Ch'in empire was subject to denigration and when the literary policies of the state were undergoing a complete change.

Shortly after the establishment of Han, an edict of 191 BC ordered the revocation of the Ch'in government's ban on certain types of literature. This was followed by attempts to recover some of the texts known or thought to have been lost, and the successful recovery of the text of the *Book of Documents*, in Wen ti's reign, formed good reason for instituting further searches of this type later in the Han period. But the principal innovations that introduced a new literary or scholastic policy may be dated from a series of measures undertaken in Wu ti's reign.

Until then, other influences than those of Confucius had been active at court. Wen ti (reigned 180–157), we are told, had favoured some elements of so-called Legalist thought, and his successor had not appointed to office those who were likely to be partial to the traditional mode of ethics associated with Confucius. The empress Tou, consort of Wen ti and mother of Ching ti (reigned 157–141), is described as being an adherent of Huang-Lao Taoism, and some of the statesmen who had taken a leading part in founding and forming the dynasty were of the same frame of mind. According to one passage in the histories, the death of the dowager empress Tou, which occurred in 135 BC, was followed by the rejection of Huang Lao ideas and certain Legalist ideas in favour of those imbued with traditional scholarship of Confucian style.

Already, before the death of the dowager empress, a memorial had been presented to the throne (141 BC) castigating those who had preached the views of Legalist thinkers such as Shang Yang, Han Fei, Shen Pu-hai and others; and the memorial was approved. A further step, which followed in 136 BC, was of crucial importance to the establishment of the Chinese tradition. Long before then there had existed an establishment of academicians among the officials. In this year it was specified that five of these posts should be concerned specifically with five '*ching*' or classical texts, i.e. the *Book of Changes*, the *Book of Documents*, the *Book of Songs*, the *Rites* and the *Spring and Autumn Annals*. To these five works these was added a sixth, which concerned music.

These books were largely concerned with the ethical ideals, interpretation of history and provisions for conventional behaviour that were the hallmarks of the Confucian view. By singling out five works for special attention by academicians, the edict not only founded the idea of 'classical' or 'scriptural' texts; it laid down for the remainder of the imperial period that those ideals would be regarded as orthodox. It formed the first step whereby these and similar texts of the 'Confucian canon' became textbooks with which Chinese officials were trained.

The academicians were responsible for concentrated study of the book in question and for teaching its lessons to pupils. Quite soon further steps were taken to strengthen the attention paid to this type of literature and to the adoption of its teachings. These included the foundation of an imperial academy, from 124 BC, wherein groups of fifty pupils were trained by the academicians and subsequently tested in their accomplishments. It is no

accident that at the time when these measures were being taken
to improve and regulate the education of future officials, the Han
civil service was expanding rapidly, with the growth of new
organs of administration. It is also no accident that Tung
Chung-shu was simultaneously formulating his own synthesis
of ideas, in which Confucius' ethics were combined with *wu
hsing* cosmology, and Confucius himself was being established as
a figure of outstanding significance in the Chinese tradition.
From its early beginnings in 124 BC the academy is said to have
grown dramatically, until it attained a muster of 30,000 pupils
c. AD 140.

Complications arose with the discovery of copies of some of
the early texts in slightly different versions and with varying
claims to authenticity. A distinction soon came about between
two types of text: those written in contemporary Chinese script
of the second or first centuries BC (*chin wen*), and those written in
archaic writing (*ku wen*). In chronological terms, it was the new
copies in contemporary script that had actually come to light
first; but it could be claimed that those written in archaic script
had a greater claim to validity owing to their apparent age and
seniority.

The contemporary script was the form of writing that had
been evolved and promoted during the Ch'in period. It was far
simpler than the archaic characters of the Chou kings and the
succeeding centuries of the *Spring and Autumn* and the *Warring
States* periods. The contemporary script suited the administrative
and educational needs of the Ch'in and Han empires, and the
attitude of those who hoped to strengthen and organise the state
for future greatness; archaic characters matched the mood of
those who looked to the past for examples of China's grandeur
and rejected the abuses or excesses of government that had arisen
in Ch'in and the first century of Han.

In literary and intellectual terms, the existence of different
versions of ancient texts posed two questions. In the first instance
it was necessary to decide which of the several versions should be
accepted as authentic. But bound up therewith was a second
problem, of choosing from several interpretations of the texts
and determining the precise message or doctrine to be sought
therein. There arose a polarised distinction between two points
of view dependent on the view taken of these matters; but the
divide was not sufficiently deep to prevent an adherent of either

the New Text or the Old Text school from retaining an interest in the books and teachings of the other.

From the incomplete information that is available today it would appear that the differences between the two groups of versions of these texts were slight rather than crucial, and many scholars have had cause to ask why the issues assumed such great importance. The reason may be more readily apprehended when it is realised how scarce the written word was in Han times and how valuable each newly discovered copy of a text would be. In addition the obsolete nature of the language of the texts compelled some attempt at interpretation, and it can easily be understood how violent and important controversy may have arisen. For, at their best, many of the interpretations offered can have been no more than speculative or subjective and recognisable as such; they were not backed by a systematic knowledge of the cultural and historical context of the books. Statements of the second and first centuries BC regarding the early beliefs of Shang or Chou, or the motives of their leading personalities, were put forward on their own merits, to meet with acceptance or rejection; they did not depend on scholarly investigation or the validation of hypothesis. If an analogy may be permitted, the situation would be comparable with a nineteenth- or twentieth-century study of recently discovered copies of Homer or Genesis, without the benefit of a systematic body of knowledge of Greek or Jewish cultural history.

In very general terms it may be said that the approach of the New Text school to early literature was characterised by an appeal to the supernatural rather than to natural explanations of the universe, and by an attempt to explain the texts of those early works by word-for-word literal exegesis; adherents of the Old Text school tried to ascertain the fundamental meaning and message of the books in human terms. The Old Text scholars emphasised historical fact and drew on precedent; they sought to find a synthesis rather than to speculate; and they were more open to the call of logic than to the warnings of portents. The New Text scholars required loyal obedience first of all to *ti* or to heaven; to the Old Text school, a man's first duty lay in loyalty to his earthly ruler. Scholars of the New Text school were established in official posts, and the opinions that they voiced were accepted as orthodox; many of the Old Text scholars lived and wrote in a private capacity and could afford to ignore any temptations to conform with orthodox dogma as a means of procuring promotion.

The limitations of the New Text school were described in the following terms by Pan Ku:

> In the past scholars were accustomed to till the fields and to provide for their families and it was only after three years that they would be conversant with a single work of the classics. They retained the principal lessons of its main content and did no more than familiarise themselves with the text itself. For this reason, despite the brevity of the time they spent on study the cumulative results in spiritual terms were considerable, and at the age of thirty the five classics were firmly established in their minds.
>
> In later ages the amplifications of the classics had deviated widely from the original meaning of those texts themselves. Men of wide learning had no thoughts of 'listening for instruction and leaving aside those matters of which they stood in doubt';* their main concern was with concentrating on subtle points of analysis so as to evade the real points of difficulty; and by their choice of a happy phrase or witty expression they split the main body of the text into fragments. As a result the comments on a passage of a mere five characters extended to twenty or thirty thousand words.
>
> Later, when these methods had been taken to even further lengths, young men who wished to master a single work of the classics would have to wait until their hair was white before they could discuss it. Scholars were quite complacent within the limits of matters in which they were well-versed, while denouncing any view that they had not heard of; and in the end they succeeded in deceiving themselves. Such was the terrible fate that overcame scholarship.

The approach of the two schools differed conspicuously in their treatment of the *Changes of Chou*. A further example concerns the historical chronicle entitled the *Spring and Autumn Annals*, whose pithy record of China's early history has exercised a profound influence on subsequent literary developments and political theory. The original terse record, which was written

* For this allusion, see Arthur Waley, *The Analects of Confucius* (London: George Allen & Unwin, 1938) p. 92.

from the point of view of the small state of Lu for the period 722 to 481, was believed to have been compiled or edited by Confucius; and it was maintained that by dexterous choice of subject matter, or expression, by the omission of certain details or the juxtaposition of others, a moralistic interpretation of history had deliberately been infused into a document of state. The text had given rise to two principal commentaries which were intended to explain the meaning of the work (entitled the *Kung yang* and *Ku liang* commentaries), and one independent set of annals (the *Tso chuan*) came to be closely related to it.

The preferences for the different types of commentary or treatment of the *Spring and Autumn Annals* illustrates the growth of different attitudes to early texts and the state's concern with these matters. Towards the end of the second century BC the government lay under the influence of modernist statesmen. Adherents of the New Text school were in favour and preference was given to the *Kung yang* commentary; this had been first compiled by the third century. A change came about in 51 BC as a result of a conference of scholars that had been assembled with the express purpose of considering questions of textual discrepancies and scriptural interpretation. It was then recommended that the *Ku liang* commentary, which probably dates from early Han, should be given pride of place. In making this recommendation the scholars were moving towards the Old Text point of view. Both of these commentaries are in the form of word-for-word explanations of the text, given as question and answer; both seek to read a moral lesson into the original chronicle.

A much more definite change in favour of the Old Text approach took place under the influence of Liu Hsin (died AD 23) just after the beginning of the Christian era; but, as will be seen shortly, this was by no means a permanent change as yet. It was Liu Hsin who deliberately brought the *Tso chuan* out of obscurity into prominence. This was an independent record whose additional information could be used to shed light on the events described so tersely in the *Spring and Autumn Annals* themselves. The close association now drawn between the two books was intended to explain the story on factual and rational grounds, rather than to refer a reader to an esoteric meaning or to the implicit intention of the saintly editor, Confucius.

The new approach to the *Spring and Autumn Annals* may be

compared with the production of the 'Ten Wings' as explicit explanations of the *Changes of Chou* (see Chapter 7). Liu Hsin's work was so successful that the *Tso chuan* came to be divided into separate passages that were then attached to relevant sentences of the *Spring and Autumn Annals*; and for long it was believed that the *Tso chuan* had originally been written directly as a commentary to the earlier chronicle.

This example of Liu Hsin's work should be considered in the wider context of the contribution that he and his father (Liu Hsiang: 79–8 BC) made to the literary history of China (see p. 4). As at the conference of 51 BC and a subsequent one of AD 79, their work of collecting and classifying literature for the imperial collection was the direct result of the official concern with an intellectual and educational policy. In the course of their work, Liu Hsiang and Liu Hsin formed single approved exemplars of texts, possibly by combining a number of wooden strips that came from different copies of a book, or by writing out new versions afresh. They drew up a list of the works included in the imperial collection, and they wrote brief descriptive notes regarding the extent and nature of the copies that had been submitted to them for examination. Above all they established categories of writings and intellectual distinctions that were long maintained in Chinese practice.

We have already had occasion to refer to this catalogue as a means of estimating the extent of writing that concerned the Five Phases at the beginning of the Christian era (see p. 43). We may now observe the figures given in the same source for scriptural works:

Title of principal work	Number of specialist writers	Number of fascicules or chapters
Book of Changes	13	294
Book of Documents	9	412
Book of Songs	6	416
The Rites	13	555
Music	6	65
Spring and Autumn Annals	23	948

A further type of literature came to be closely associated with the controversies between the New Text and Old Text schools.

This is a group of texts known as the apocryphal writings (*wei*), usually taken in conjunction with another category known as *ch'an*. The apocryphal writings provided their own arcane and heterodox interpretation of the 'scriptures'; *ch'an* writings were concerned with prognostications and may have included texts of the type mentioned above in connection with divination and oracles (see Chapter 9). The content of both types of writing appealed more to the minds of the New Text scholars than to the traditionalists of the Old Text school; it is partly owing to the popularity of the apocryphal texts and their value to the eastern Han emperors that the New Text school regained its influence early in the first century AD.

Surviving titles of the *ch'an* and *wei* literature show that it was once extensive, but the examples that we possess are often in the form of disjointed citations or allusions. It is likely that some of this material had first been formulated in the early part of western Han, although it may not have been committed to writing until some time thereafter. As commentaries to works such as the *Book of Songs* or the *Analects of Confucius* (*Lun-yü*), the *wei* professed to complement those early texts with pronouncements that were just as valid as those of the scholars whom the state sponsored. They constituted unofficial commentary that would counterbalance the opinions that were achieving official recognition as orthodox. From the surviving citations and texts it may be known how the subjects treated in the apocryphal writings corresponded with those discussed by Tung Chung-shu, for example, or in the 'Ten Wings'. They were concerned with many of the topics that have been considered in the foregoing pages, such as Yin-Yang and the Five Phases; natural phenomena and omens; the shape and size of the universe; the features of the earth and evolution of its creatures; the objects and operation of religious rites; music; mythical rulers of the world and dynastic sequences; the birth of Confucius and his contribution to humanity.

With the restoration of the Han dynasty in AD 25 the scholars of the New Text school regained a favourable position at court. They were ready to tolerate considerable attention to the apocryphal texts and did so from the strong position of acknowledged masters. Those of the Old Text school were criticising such writings for their excesses. The extent of writing produced by the New Text scholars was voluminous, mainly in the form of word-for-word or sentence-by-sentence exposition; but towards the latter part of the first century AD the vigorous protests of the Old Text scholars were beginning to have some effect.

Acute controversy led in AD 79 to a further assembly of scholars charged with the duty of reviewing the canon of scriptures and fixing its form. The meetings were held in the White Tiger Hall, and a written account of the discussions that took place shows that they may well have been concerned with minutiae of behaviour rather than with the principles that were at stake. In the event it would seem that despite the sharp protests of the Old Text school against the barren nature of New Text scholarship, it was the latter that remained supreme, while the Old Text school as yet failed to win recognition of its outlook.

That failure is illustrated by a further event. In AD 175 official orders were given for the texts of the scriptures to be engraved on stone, so as to provide a permanent copy of the approved versions. The work was entrusted to a scholar named Ts'ai Yung, and it was the New Texts that were chosen for inscription; some of the stones still survive.

However, at much the same time, extremes of controversy were being mitigated, largely thanks to the work of two famous scholars. Ho Hsiu (129–182) had been trained in the New Text school, but endeavoured to find a compromise by moving away from its extremes. Cheng Hsüan (127–200) had been a pupil of the notable Old Text scholar Ma Jung (79–166) and had thus been brought up in the Old Text tradition. He set himself to eliminate the differences between the two schools, and it was largely owing to the influence of this highly erudite man that petty differences faded into the background and a synthesis was reached which allowed for concentration on the more fundamental scholastic issues of the day. But even Cheng Hsüan, with his moderating influence, was unable to prevent the proscription of the apocryphal texts that took place just before the end of the Han dynasty (AD 220). Shortly afterwards the Old Text scholars were brought into prominence by their appointment to posts as academicians, and the posts reserved for teachers of the New Text school were abolished. These events have been described by one writer as marking the 'irresistible victory' of the Old Text school, and such a judgement may possibly be regarded as an overstatement. Nevertheless it may be noted that when the texts

190

of the scriptures were next engraved on stone, between 240 and 248, they included the Old Text version of the *Book of Documents* and that work whose acceptance was almost a touchstone of a scholar's persuasion – the *Tso chuan*.

References and notes for further reading

Unless stated otherwise, references to Chinese texts are to the *Ssu-pu pei-yao* edition. The following abbreviations are used.

BMFEA	*Bulletin of the Museum of Far Eastern Antiquities*
Bodde (Festivals)	Derk Bodde, *Festivals in Classical China* (Princeton: Princeton University Press and the Chinese University of Hong Kong, 1975)
Bodde (Myths)	Derk Bodde, 'Myths of Ancient China'; originally published in S.N. Kramer, *Mythologies of the Ancient World* (New York: Doubleday, 1961); reprinted in Chun-shu Chang, *The Making of China* (New Jersey: Prentice-Hall, 1975)
Ch'ien-fu lun	Wang Fu, *Ch'ien-fu lun*; annotated edition, including Wang Chi-p'ei's notes (Shanghai: *Shang-hai ku-chi ch'u-pan-she*, 1978)
Crisis and Conflict	Michael Loewe, *Crisis and Conflict in Han China* (London: George Allen & Unwin, 1974)
Forke	Alfred Forke, *Lun-heng* Parts I, II (Leipzig: Harrassowitz, 1907; reprinted, New York: Paragon Book Gallery, 1962)
Hawkes	David Hawkes, *Ch'u Tz'u The Songs of the South* (Oxford: Clarendon Press, 1959)
HFHD	Homer H. Dubs, *The History of the Former Han Dynasty*, Vols I–III (Baltimore: Waverly Press, 1938–55)
HHS	*Hou Han shu* and *Hsü Han shu* (Peking: *Chung-hua shu-chü*, 1965)
HNT	*Huai-nan-tzu*. References are to Liu Wen-tien, *Huai-nan hung-lieh chi-chieh* (original preface 1921; reprinted, Taipei: Commercial Press, 1969)
HS	*Han shu* (Peking: *Chung-hua shu-chü*, 1962)
KK	*Kaogu*
LSCC	*Lü shih ch'un-ch'iu*
Lun-heng	Wang Ch'ung, *Lun-heng*; references are to Huang Hui, *Lun-heng chiao-shih* (originally published Ch'ang-sha: Commercial Press, 1938; reprinted, Taipei, 1969)
MH	Édouard Chavannes, *Les Mémoires Historiques de Se-ma Ts'ien*; (originally published Paris: E. Leroux, 1895–1905; reprinted, Paris: Adrien-Maisonneuve, 1967)
SC	*Shih-chi*; (Peking: *Chung-hua shu-chü*, 1959)
SCC	Joseph Needham, *Science and Civilisation in China*, Vols 1– (Cambridge: Cambridge University Press, 1954–)
SHC	*Shan-hai ching*

Ways to Paradise	Michael Loewe, *Ways to Paradise* (London: George Allen & Unwin, 1979)
WW	*Wen wu*
YTL	Huan K'uan, *Yen-t'ieh lun*; references are to Wang Li-ch'i, *Yen-t'ieh lun chiao-chu*, Shanghai: *Ku-tien wen-hsüeh ch'u-pan-she*, 1958

INTRODUCTION

For the general intellectual development of China, see Fung Yu-lan, *A History of Chinese Philosophy*, Vols I, II, translated by Derk Bodde (Princeton: Princeton University Press, 1953); Wm Theodore de Bary and others, *Sources of Chinese Tradition* (New York: Columbia University Press, 1960); Burton Watson, *Early Chinese Literature* (New York and London: Columbia University Press, 1962); Wing-tsit Chan, *A Source Book in Chinese Philosophy* (Princeton: Princeton University Press, 1963); and Kung-chuan Hsiao, *A History of Chinese Political Thought volume 1: from the beginnings to the Sixth Century A.D.*, translated by F. W. Mote (Princeton: Princeton University Press, 1979). For the study of Chinese religions, see D. Howard Smith, *Chinese Religions* (London: Weidenfeld and Nicolson, 1968); Werner Eichhorn, *Die Religionen Chinas* (Stuttgart, Berlin, Köln, Mainz: Verlag W. Kohlhammer, 1973); and Marcel Granet, *The Religion of the Chinese People*, translated, edited and with an introduction by Maurice Freedman (Oxford: Basil Blackwell, 1975). For Chinese mythology, see Bodde (Myths); Bernhard Karlgren, 'Legends and Cults in Ancient China', in BMFEA 18 (1946), pp. 199–365; Wolfram Eberhard, *Lokalkulturen im alten China*, Vols 1–2 (Leiden: E. J. Brill, 1942); English translation, by Alide Eberhard, as *The Local Cultures of South and East China* (Leiden: E. J. Brill, 1968); and Noel Barnard (ed.), *Early Chinese Art and its possible influence in the Pacific Basin* (authorised Taiwan edition, Taiwan: 1974). For iconography, see Richard C. Rudolph and Yu Wen, *Han Tomb Art of West China* (Berkeley and Los Angeles: University of California Press, 1951); and Käte Finsterbusch, *Verzeichnis und Motivindex der Han-Darstellungen*, Vols 1, 2 (Wiesbaden: Harrassowitz, 1966, 1971).

CHAPTER 1

For the Taoist attitude, see Henri Maspero, *Les Religions Chinoises* (Paris: Civilisations du sud, 1950); Max Kaltenmark, *Lao Tzu and Taoism*, translated from the French by Roger Greaves (Stanford: Stanford University Press, 1969); and Herrlee G. Creel, *What is Taoism? And Other Studies in Chinese Cultural History* (Chicago and London: University of Chicago Press, 1970). For the Confucian view, see D. Howard Smith, *Confucius* (London: Temple Smith, 1973). For legalism, see Léon Vandermeersch, *La Formation du Légisme* (Paris: École Française d'extrême-orient, 1965). For Wang Ch'ung's views, as cited on pp. 13f., see *Lun-heng* 6 (Lei hsü), pp. 286, 299; Forke, Vol. I, pp. 286f., 294f.

CHAPTER 2

For concepts of the gods and the place of animals in their realm, see K. C.

Chang, *Early Chinese Civilization: Anthropological Perspectives* (Cambridge, Massachusetts and London: Harvard University Press, 1976), Chapters 8, 9. For *t'ien* and its relationship to man in the pre-imperial period, see Herrlee G. Creel, *The Origins of Statecraft in China*, Vol. 1 (Chicago and London: University of Chicago Press, 1970), Chapter 5 and Appendix C. For other aspects of early religious practice, see Henri Maspero, *China in Antiquity*, translated by Frank A. Kierman Jr (Folkestone: William Dawson & Son, 1978), pp. 93–168. For the deities depicted on the silk manuscript (p. 24 above), see Hayashi Minao, 'The Twelve Gods of the Chan-kuo period Silk Manuscript excavated at Ch'ang-sha', in Noel Barnard (ed.), *Early Chinese Art and its possible influence in the Pacific Basin*, pp. 123–68; and Michael Loewe, 'Man and Beast; The Hybrid in Early Chinese Art and Literature' (*Numen*, Vol. XXV, Fasc. 2, 1978, pp. 97–117). For imperial practices, see E. Chavannes, *Le T'ai Chan* (Paris: Annales du Musée Guimet, 1910).

For references to *ti*, see *Ch'u tz'u* 2.12b, 9.1b (Hawkes, pp. 40, 103); SHC 3.21a,b; LSCC 9.3b. For passages concerning the *shen* that have been translated or cited above (see pp. 20–1), see SHC 1.11a and 4.7b; HNT 4.13b, 14a. For further references, see SC 28.1370–71, HS 25A. 1206 and SHC 3.21b, 22a. The differences drawn between various styles of worship are described in YTL 29.204. For criticism of habits attached to mountain cults, see *Hsin-yü*, shang, (6). 11a. The passage regarding the ascent of the mountains is from the *Pao-p'u-tzu* (*nei*) 17.1a. For references and allusions to the hierarchy of the spirits, see HNT 4.12b and 4.4a; and *Ch'ien-fu lun* 26.358. For the twelve spirits who devour the ten influences, see Bodde (Festivals). pp. 81f.

CHAPTER 3

For studies of Chinese concepts of immortality, see W. Liebenthal, 'The immortality of the soul in Chinese thought' (*Monumenta Nipponica* VIII, 1952, pp. 327f.); Yü Ying-shih, 'Life and Immortality in the Mind of Han China' (*Harvard Journal of Asiatic Studies* 25, 1964–5, pp. 80–122); Joseph Needham, 'The Cosmology of Early China' (in Carmen Blacker and Michael Loewe (eds), *Ancient Cosmologies*, London: George Allen & Unwin, 1975, pp. 87–109); and *Ways to Paradise*.

The description of the five mountains or islands will be found in *Lieh-tzu* 5.3b (A. C. Graham, *The Book of Lieh-tzu: A new translation* (London: John Murray, 1960 p. 97). For the search for P'eng-lai, by the kings of pre-imperial China and by Wu ti (pp. 29), see SC 28.1369–70 and 1385 (MH, Vol. III, pp. 436f., 465f.). Ssu-ma Hsiang-ju's reference to the Queen Mother of the West (pp. 32–4) is in his poem *Ta-jen fu* (for references, see *Ways to Paradise*, pp. 94 and 149 note 38). The passage cited on p. 32 is from SHC 16.5b. The third century AD depiction of the Queen and her partner (p. 33) is from the reliefs of a tomb at I-nan (*Ways to Paradise*, p. 123, fig. 21). For the Yellow Springs (p. 34) see *Tso chuan* (Yin kung, first year; Harvard-Yenching Index series print p. 3, HS 40.2047 and HS 68.2938; and Han Nineteen Old Poems no.13 (Jean-Pierre Diény, *Les Dix-neuf Poèmes Anciens*; Paris: Presses Universitaires de France, 1963, pp. 32–3).

For the passages from Wang Ch'ung (pp. 35), see *Lun-heng* 20 (Lun ssu), pp. 871–73 (Forke, Vol. I, pp. 192–4); the translation follows the textual emendation of Huang Hui; the passage cited from the *Huai-nan-tzu* is from HNT 7.5a, b; the text of Chang Heng's *Ssu hsüan fu* is included in HHS 59 (biog. 49). 1914f.; see pp.1920, 1932.

CHAPTER 4

For the theories of the Five Phases and Yin-Yang, see Wing-tsit Chan (as cited under the Introduction), Chapter 11; Joseph Needham, SCC, Vol. 2, pp. 247–65; *Ways to Paradise*, Chapter 1. For the translation of the term *wu hsing* as 'Five Phases', see John S. Major, 'A Note on the Translation of Two Technical Terms in Chinese Science: *Wu-hsing* and *Hsiu*' (*Early China*, 2, Fall 1976, 1–3). For Taoist religion, see Max Kaltenmark (as cited under Chapter 1) Chapter V; Anna K. Seidel, *La Divinisation de Lao Tseu dans le Taoisme* des Han (Paris: École Française d'extrême-orient, 1969); Michel Strickmann, 'History, Anthropology and Chinese Religion' (*Harvard Journal of Asiatic Studies*, 40/1, 1980, pp. 207–48).

Citations from and allusions to primary materials are as follows. To the *Shu ching* (p. 38), 'Kan shih' (Bernhard Karlgren, 'The Book of Documents', BMFEA, 22, 1950, p. 18); to the *Shih-chi* (p. 38), SC 26.1256; to the *Shih-chi* (p. 43), SC 130.3290 (MH, Vol. I, pp. xv–xvi); from the *Huai-nan-tzu* (p. 44), HNT 8.1a; and (p. 46) from LSCC 13.4a.

CHAPTER 5

For mythological allusions to cosmology, see John S. Major, *Topography and Cosmology in Early Han thought*: Chapter Four of the Huai-nan-tzu' (unpublished doctoral thesis, presented to the Committee on History and East Asian Languages, Harvard University, Cambridge, Massachusetts, June 1973). Han ideas of cosmology are discussed by Joseph Needham, 'The Cosmology of Early China', in Carmen Blacker and Michael Loewe (eds), *Ancient Cosmologies* (London: George Allen & Unwin, 1975), pp. 87–109, and more extensively in SCC, Vol. 3, pp. 210f and Vol. 5, part 2, pp. 77f.

For research in early Chinese astronomy, see Needham, SCC, Vol. 3, section 20; Henri Maspero, 'L'Astronomie Chinoise avant les Han' (*T'oung Pao*, xxvi, 1929, pp.267f.) and 'Les Instruments Astronomiques des Chinois au temps des Han' (in *Mélanges chinois et bouddhiques*, 1939, no. 6, pp. 183–370 (Brussels, 1939); N. Sivin, 'Cosmos and Computation in Early Chinese Mathematical Astronomy' (*T'oung Pao* LV, 1–3, 1969, pp. 1–73); and Christopher Cullen, 'Joseph Needham on Chinese Astronomy' (*Past and Present*, Number 87, May 1980, pp. 39–53).

For citations from the *Yüan-yu* (p. 48), see *Ch'u tz'u* 5.1b *et seq.*, Hawkes, pp. 81, 83; from the *T'ien wen* (p. 49) see *Ch'u tz'u* 3.1b *et seq.*, Hawkes, pp. 46f. (lines 19–20, 15–16, 81–4 and 137–8). The reference to I the archer will be found in line 56 of that poem. Passages are quoted (pp. 50) from HNT 4.1a, 4.4a and 3.1b; a question from the *T'ien wen* (cited on p. 52) is from *Ch'u tz'u* 3.2b, Hawkes, p.47.

For statements about the shape of the universe, see HNT 3.2a, 15.3b and 7.2a. For the appearance of the number 12, see *Ch'u tz'u* 3.3a,b, Hawkes, p. 47; references to *Huai-nan-tzu* will be found in HNT 3.15a, 3.30a and 3.22b. For the symbolism of TLV mirrors, see *Ways to Paradise*, Chapter 3. For the names of the twelve animals, see *Lun-heng* 3 (Wu shih), pp. 139f. (Forke, Vol. I, pp. 105f.) and *Lun-heng* 24 (Chi jih) p. 990 (Forke, Vol. II, p. 398). For the twelve attendants in the Great Exorcism, see HHS (tr.) 5.3127 and Bodde (Festivals), p. 81. For theories of cosmology, see Shigeru Nakayama, *A History of Japanese Astronomy Chinese Background and Western Impact* (Cambridge, Massachusetts: Harvard University Press, 1969), Chapter 4.

The passage cited (pp. 54f.) on the *Kai t'ien* view of the universe is from *Lun-heng* 11 (Shuo jih), pp. 498–99 (Forke, Vol. I, p. 265; see also SCC, Vol. 3, p. 214). The quotation on p. 54 is from Cullen, p. 41. For Chang Heng's description of *Hun t'ien* (p. 55), see *Chin shu chiao-chu* 11.7b (SCC, Vol. 3, p. 217).

For archaeological discoveries, see KK 1977.6.407 (for the bronze gnomon); WW 1978.8.19 (for an early representation of the 28 Mansions); and WW 1979.7.40 for the earliest occurrence of the names of the 28 Mansions. For the *Han shu's* treatise on astronomy and its attribution to Ma Hsü, see HS 26 and HHS (tr.) 10.3215; for the *Shih-chi's* treatise see MH, Vol. III, pp. 339–412. For the manuscript that describes types of comet, see Michael Loewe, 'The Han view of comets' (BMFEA 52, 1980, pp. 1–31). For the observatory at Lo-yang, see KK 1978.1.54; for the Weaver and the Oxherd, see *Ways to Paradise*, pp. 112f.

CHAPTER 6

For mythological accounts of creation, see Bodde (Myths); for the significance of the seasonal meetings of partners, see *Ways to Paradise*, pp. 119f.; for man's relations with the animal world, see K. C. Chang (as cited under Chapter 2), pp. 174–96.

The passage cited on p. 64 is from HNT 20.1a; for the stories of P'an-ku and Nü-kua, see Bodde (Myths), pp. 24, 26, and HNT 6.10a. For the Queen Mother of the West's crown and the union of the two dragons, see *Ways to Paradise*, pp. 103–5 and 36f. The passage cited on pp. 66f. is from HNT 7.1a. For the *tsao-hua-che*, see HNT 7.5b (as cited on p. 68), 7.5a, 1.12b and 9.23a. For the allusion to the *Lieh-tzu* (p. 68) see Graham (as cited under Chapter 3) pp. 94f.

Wang Ch'ung discusses the destruction of Pu-chou in *Lun-heng* 11 (T'an t'ien), pp. 473f. (Forke, Vol. I, p. 250); he writes on spontaneity in 18 (Tzu-jan), pp. 775f. (Forke, Vol. 1, p. 92f.); for the passage cited on pp. 69f., see *Lun-heng*, p. 780 (Forke, Vol. I, p. 96). For the comparison of human beings with lice, see *Lun-heng* 3 (Ch'i-kuai), p. 152 (Forke, Vol. I, p. 322), also *Lun-heng* 25 (Chieh ch'u), p.1039 (Forke, Vol. I, p.535).

For references to transformation, see HNT 11.2b; *Lun-heng* 2 (Wu hsing), p. 55 (Forke, Vol. I, p. 326), for changes between frogs and quails or sparrows and clams; Lun-heng 3 (Ch'i-kuai), p. 152 (Forke, Vol. I, p. 322), for animals and human beings; and *Lun-heng* 16 (Chiang jui), p. 730 (Forke, Vol. I. p. 368), for various types of creature. The final citation is from *Lun-heng* 20 (Lun ssu), p. 871 (Forke, Vol. I, p. 193).

CHAPTER 7

A considerable literature has been published in recent years in regard to the *Book of Changes*; references given below are restricted to books which enable a

196

reader to consult the text, in English, and to a very few works of interpretation
that are backed by sound scholarship.

Probably the most easily available translation is that based on Richard
Wilhelm's work, i.e. *The I Ching or Book of Changes: the Richard Wilhelm
translation rendered into English* by Cary F. Baynes; Foreword by C. C. Jung; first
published in two volumes (London: Routledge & Kegan Paul, 1951). Reference
below is to the third edition, in one volume (London: Routledge & Kegan Paul,
1968). For a second translation of this difficult text, see John Blofeld, *The Book of
Change* (London: George Allen & Unwin, 1965). Considerable care is needed in
consulting these and other translations, in order to discriminate both between
the different elements of the *I ching* itself and between original text and
comment by modern translators.

For the different parts of the *Changes* and the titles of the 'Ten Wings', see
SCC, Vol. 2, pp. 304f. For comments on the original form of the *Changes of
Chou*, see Arthur Waley, 'The Book of Changes' (BMFEA 5, 1933, pp. 121–42).
For essays on the meaning of the text, see Helmut Wilhelm (a) *Change: Eight
Lectures on the 'I Ching'* (translated from the German by Cary F. Baynes;
London: Routledge & Kegan Paul, 1961); and (b) *Heaven, Earth, and Man in the
Book of Changes; seven Eranos Lectures* (Seattle and London: University of
Washington Press, 1977); and Julian K. Shchutskii, *Researches on the I Ching*
(London and Henley: Routledge & Kegan Paul, 1979).

The passage cited from the 'Ten Wings' on p. 77 is from the *Ta chuan* or *Great
Treatise* (also called *Hsi tz'u chuan*); for the Chinese text, see *Harvard-Yenching
Institute Sinological Index Series* (reprinted, Taipei: Ch'eng-wen Publishing
Company, 1966), p. 41. For another translation of the passage, see the
Wilhelm/Baynes translation, pp. 301f.

For Ching Fang, see HS 75.3160f (p. 3164 for the memorial of 37 BC). Ssu-ma
Kuang's appreciation of Yang Hsiung is expressed in his preface to the *T'ai
hsüan ching*.

CHAPTER 8

Portents and omens have been studied in the following works: Hans
Bielenstein, 'An Interpretation of the portents in the Ts'ien-Han-shu' (BMFEA
22, 1950, pp. 127–43); Wolfram Eberhard, 'The Political Function of
Astronomy and Astronomers in Han China' (in John K. Fairbank (ed.), *Chinese
Thought and Institutions*, Chicago: University of Chicago Press, 1957, pp.
33–70); N. Sivin, 'Cosmos and Computation in Early Chinese Mathematical
Astronomy' (*T'oung Pao* LV, 1969, pp. 1–73); Rafe de Crespigny, *Portents of
protest in the Later Han Dynasty* (Canberra: Faculty of Asian Studies, 1976); and
Michael Loewe, 'The Han view of comets' (BMFEA 52, 1980, pp. 1–31).

For the eclipse of 181 BC (p. 82), see HS3.99 (HFHD, Vol. I, p. 199); the
passage which describes the portents of 26 BC and 10 BC will be found in HS 27C
(a).1457 (see HFHD, Vol. II, pp. 385f.). For the edict of 109 BC (pp. 83–4), see
HS 6.193 (HFHD, Vol. II, p. 91). The passage which is given in paraphrase (pp.
84f.) will be found in HNT 8.1f. For Tung Chung-shu's statement of principle,
(p. 86), see HS 27A.1331; the edict cited on pp. 86f. is from HS 4.116 (HFHD,
Vol. I, p. 240). For the use of portents as a means of criticism, see Bielenstein.
Remarks on the events of 29 BC will be found in HS 60.2671 (Tu

Ch'in) and HS 85.3444 (Ku Yung). The citation from Ching Fang will be found in HS 27B (a). 1401; see HS 75.3160 for Ching Fang's early studies, and HS 8.262 (HFHD, Vol. II, p. 242) for the edict of 60 BC. For Wang Ch'ung's views, see *Lun-heng* 18 (Tzu-jan), p. 786 (Forke, Vol. I, p. 101).

CHAPTER 9

For the general subject of this chapter, see Léon Vandermeersch, 'De la tortue à l'achillée', in J. P. Vernant and others (eds), *Divination et Rationalité* (Paris: Editions du Seuil, 1974), pp. 29–51; Ngo van Xuyet, *Divination Magie et Politique dans la Chine Ancienne* (Paris: Presses Universitaires de France, 1976); and Michael Loewe and Carmen Blacker (eds), *Divination and Oracles* (London: George Allen & Unwin, 1981). A thorough study of the use of shells and bones in the Shang period is given by David N. Keightley, *Sources of Shang History* (Berkeley, Los Angeles, London: University of California Press, 1978). The methods used for casting stalks and the formation of hexagrams are explained in the Wilhelm/Baynes translation of the *I Ching* (as cited under Chapter 7), pp. 721f., and in Blofeld's translation (as cited under Chapter 7), pp. 59f. For the diviners' boards, see Donald J. Harper, 'The Han Cosmic Board (*Shih*)', in *Early China*, 4, 1978–9, pp. 1–10, and *Ways to Paradise*, pp. 75f.

For the rite practised for the discovery of the tortoise, see SC 128.3226; for the longevity of the turtle, see HNT 14.18b, *Lun-heng* 14 (Chuang-liu), p. 619 (Forke, Vol. II, p. 108) and *Lun-heng* 24 (Pu-shih), p. 995 (Forke, Vol. I, p. 182). The slow rate of maturity of the yarrow plant is mentioned in SC 128.3226–27 and *Lun-heng* 14 (Chuang-liu), p. 619; for methods of casting the stalks, see HNT 8.1b (note) and 17.3a, *Lun-heng* 24 (Pu-shih), pp. 997–98 and 1003 (Forke, Vol. I, pp. 184, 189). Ssu-ma Ch'ien's personal record appears in SC 128.3225.

The advice regarding the right time to enter the mountains (p. 96) comes from the *Pao-p'u-tzu (nei)* 17.1a, and the anecdote concerning Ming ti is recounted in HHS 49 (biog.39).1640. The fragments cited on p. 97 will be found in *Wu-wei Han chien* (Peking: *Wen-wu ch'u-pan-she*, 1964), p. 136, tracing 22. For the veins of the earth, see HNT 20.7a and 20.15a, and SC 88.2570 (for Meng T'ien); for the manuscript (p.98) see Michael Loewe, 'The Han view of comets' as cited under Chapter 8).

Accounts of divination are mentioned in connection with the imperial succession in HS 4.106 (HFHD, Vol. I, p. 225), *San-kuo chih* (Peking: *Chung-hua shu-chü*, 1959) 2.75 and HS 74.3143; for consideration of a girl's destiny, see HHS 10A.407–08 and HHS 10B.438; for the campaigns in the north-west, see HS 96B.3913 (A. F. P. Hulsewé and M. A. N. Loewe, *China in Central Asia*; Leiden: E. J. Brill, 1979, p. 107). The *Huai-nan-tzu* mentions occasions for divination in 15.22b and 5.14a,b; see SC 127.3222 for the choice of Wu ti's wedding day. Comments on the proper use or frequency of divination are found in *Ch'u tz'u* 6.1a *et seq.* (Hawkes, pp. 88f.); YTL 29.204; *Ch'ien-fu lun* ch. 6; HNT 8.1b, 20.3a. For the visit paid to Diviners' Row, see SC 127.3215; for Wang Ch'ung's views, see *Lun-heng* 24 (Chi jih) 985f., (Forke, Vol. II, pp. 393f.). Wang Ching's interest in divination is recorded in HHS 76 (biog. 66).2466; Chang Heng's views are given in HHS 59 (biog. 49). 1911f.

CHAPTER 10

See Arthur Waley, *The Nine Songs: A Study of Shamanism in China* (London: George Allen & Unwin, 1955); Hawkes, pp. 35f.; Hayashi Minao (as cited under Chapter 2); and Chow Tse-tsung, 'The childbirth myth and ancient Chinese medicine: a study of aspects of the *wu* tradition' in David T. Roy and Tsuen-hsuin Tsien (eds), *Ancient China: Studies in Early Civilization* (Hong Kong: Chinese University Press, 1978), pp. 43–89.

For the early reference to shamans (p. 104), see *Kuo-yü* 18.1a. Passages are cited from SHC 7.3a, 11.5a and 12.1a; for *Chao hun* and *Ta chao*, see Hawkes, pp. 101f.; Arthur Waley's views come from *The Nine Songs*, p. 14. For references to the Standard Histories, see HHS 18 (biog. 8).694; 11 (biog. 1).479; HS 25A.1225, 28B.1666 (for Ch'u), 28B.1653 (for Ch'en) and 28B.1661 (for Ch'i). For the establishment of shamans at Ch'ang-an, see HS 1B.81 (HFHD, Vol. I, p. 149) and HS 25A.1210–11, and for the disbandment of the complement, see HS 25B.1257. For the powers of shamans (pp. 106) see HNT 4.4b (for the *ling*), SC 107.2854, HS 60.2680; for the shaman's advice to the Red Eyebrow rebels, see HHS 11 (biog. 1).479. For the association of shamans with cures for illness, see HNT 16.19a, SC 12.459 and 28.1388 (MH, Vol. III, p. 472). Huang Pa's encounter is described in HS 89.3635; for Kao Feng, see HHS 83 (biog. 73).2769. For incidents in which shamans uttered imprecations (pp. 107f.), see HS 63.2760, HS 80.3325, HHS 42 (biog. 32).1448; for their use for this purpose by the Hsiung-nu, see HS 96B.3913 (Hulsewé and Loewe, *China in Central Asia*, p. 172).

For the ban on wayside shamans, see HS 6.203 (HFHD, Vol. II, p. 105); for Luan Pa, see HHS 57 (biog. 47).1841; for Pan Ch'ao's measures, see HHS 47 (biog. 37).1573; and for K'uang Heng, see HS 81.3335. For Sung Chün and *yin ssu*, see HHS 41 (biog. 31).1411f., and for the practice of *wu-ku* or *ku*, see *Crisis and Conflict*, pp. 81–90. Chang Heng's view is expressed in HHS 59 (biog. 49).1911.

For Wang Ch'ung's criticism, see *Lun-heng* 20 (Lun ssu), p. 875 (Forke, Vol. I, p. 196); 22 (Ting kuei), pp. 939, 942 (Forke, Vol. I, pp. 244, 246), and 25 (Chieh ch'u), pp. 1039, 1041 (Forke, Vol. I, pp. 535, 537). For other critical remarks, see YTL 29.205 and *Ch'ien-fu lun* 12.125 (also HHS 49 (biog. 39).1634). The comment on Lang I and Hsiang K'ai will be found in HHS 30B (biog. 20B).1085. For the three intermediaries of Wu ti's time, see SC.28.1384, 1387 and 1389 (MH, Vol. III, pp. 463, 470 and 477), and HS 25A.1216, 1219 and 1223.

CHAPTER 11

Aspects of the services paid to the dead are treated in the following works (see also those listed under Chapter 3): A. F. P. Hulsewé, 'Texts in Tombs' (*Asiatische Studien*, xviii/xix, 1965, pp. 78–89; Alfred Salmony, *Antler and Tongue: An Essay on Ancient Chinese Symbolism* (Ascona: Artibus Asiae, 1954); W. Bauer, *China and the search for happiness* (translated by Michael Shaw; New York: Seabury Press, 1976); and Michael Loewe, 'Man and Beast' (as cited under Chapter 2) and *Ways to Paradise*.

For the ceremony of invocation before burial, see Henri Maspero (post.), *Les Religions Chinoises* (Paris: Civilisations du Sud, 1950), p. 28; *Li chi* 13 (Sang ta chi

22).1a *et seq.*; *I li* 12 (Shih sang li).1a *et seq.* For details of the iconography of the eastern paradise, TLV mirrors and depictions of the Queen Mother of the West, together with illustrations, see *Ways to Paradise*. For the painting that dates from pre-imperial times (p. 118), see *Ch'ang-sha Ch'u mu po-hua* (Peking: *Wen-wu ch'u-pan-she*, 1973). The roof painting from Pu Ch'ien-ch'iu's tomb is shown as Figure 16 (*Ways to Paradise*, p. 102).

An article in KK 1981.1, pp. 51–8, discusses the various discoveries of jade-suits in recent years; for the discovery of the undecayed body of a Han King in *c*. AD 225, see *San-kuo chih* 28.771 note 3. For the symbolism of antler and tongue, see Salmony, *op.cit.*, and Hawkes, p. 105; for the engraved stele of AD 171, see *Hsi Hsia sung* (Tokyo: *Shoseki meihin sōkan*, series II, no. 28, 1960).

Prescriptions for choosing a suitable time and place for burial are given in *Li chi* 1 (Ch'ü li A).17b; *Li chi* 12 (Tsa chi A).3b; *Li chi* 12 (Tsa chi B).14a; *I li* 12 (Shih sang li).28b. For Wang Ching's view (p. 123), see HHS 76 (biog. 66).2466.

Literary descriptions of special tombs will be found in SC 6.265 (MH, Vol. II, p. 193; tomb of the first Ch'in emperor, died 210 BC); HS 68.2948 (Huo Kuang, died 68 BC); HS 93.3734 (as ordered for Tung Hsien, committed suicide 1 BC); and HHS 19 (biog. 9).718 (Keng Ping, died AD 90). For archaeological evidence, see KK 1972.4 pp. 2f. (site of a convicts' cemetery); Albert E. Dien, 'Excavation of the Ch'in Dynasty pit containing pottery figures of warriors and horses at Ling-t'ung, Shensi Province' (*Chinese Studies in Archeology*, Summer 1979, Vol. I, no. 1, pp. 8–55) and the following monographs: Tseng Chao-yü and others, *I-nan ku hua-hsiang shih-mu fa-chüeh pao-kao* (Shanghai: *Wen-hua pu, wen-wu kuan-li chü*, 1956); *Lo-yang Shao-kou Han mu* (Peking: *K'o-hsüeh ch'u-pan-she*, 1959); *Ch'ang-sha Ma-wang-tui i hao Han mu* (2 vols; Peking: *Wen-wu ch'u-pan-she*, 1973); *Ho-lin-ko-erh Han mu pi-hua* (Peking: *Wen-wu ch'u-pan-she*, 1978); and *Man-ch'eng Han mu fa-chüeh pao-kao* (2 vols; Peking: *Wen-wu ch'u-pan-she*, 1980).

For criticism of extravagant funerary practices (p. 125), see *Mo tzu* 6 (Chieh sang 25).4b *et seq.*, Burton Watson (trans.), *Mo Tzu Basic Writings* (New York and London: Columbia University Press, 1963), pp. 65–77; HS 36.1951; HS 50.2309; YTL 29.206–07; *Ch'ien-fu lun* 12 (Fu-ch'ih).154f., HHS 49 (biog.39).1636; and *Lun-heng* 23 (Po tsang) pp. 957f. (Forke, Vol. II, pp. 369f.).

CHAPTER 12

For secondary writings on the topics discussed in this chapter, see Édouard Chavannes, *Le T'ai chan* (Paris: Annales du Musée Guimet, 1910); Bodde (Festivals); *Crisis and Conflict*, Chapter 5. Primary sources for religious practice in western Han will be found in SC 28.1366f. (MH, Vol. III, pp. 430f.) and HS 25A.1210f. (for the pre-imperial tradition see HS 25A.1194f.; for Ch'in imperial practice, see HS 25A.1200f.). The translation of the hymn which is cited on pp. 128f. is from James Legge, *The Chinese Classics* (Hong Kong: Lane, Crawford; London: Trübner, 1871), prolegomena p. 119; for the Chinese text, see HS 22.1052.

For the first Ch'in emperor's ascent of Mount T'ai and his inscription, see SC 6.242 (MH, Vol. II, p. 140) and SC 28.1366 (MH, Vol. III, p. 430). For the discovery of the tripod in 113 BC, see HS 6.182 (HFHD, Vol. II, p. 71) and HS 25A.1225. For Wu ti's ascent of Mount T'ai, see SC 28.1396f. (MH, Vol. III, p. 495) and HS 25A.1233f. The principal reference for the Ming t'ang is HS

25B.1243; for the religious reforms c f 31 BC, see HS 25B.1253 and *Crisis and Conflict*, pp. 171f. Wang Mang's attitude to heaven is expressed in HS 99A.4080 and 4093 (HFHD, Vol. III, pp. 221f., 250). The suppression of shrines is described in HS 25B.1257; for Wang Mang's actions, see HS 25B.1270.

For Kuang wu ti's establishment of sites of worship at Lo-yang, see HHS 1a.27; HHS (tr.)7.3159, and Hans Bielenstein, 'Lo-yang in Later Han Times' (BMFEA 48, 1976). For Kuang wu ti's invocation of Hou t'u, at his accession, see HHS 1a.22; services are recorded in HHS 1B.69 and 84; for the ascent of Mount T'ai in AD 56, see HHS 1B.82, HHS (tr.)7.3164 and Chavannes (*T'ai chan*), pp. 158f., 308f.

References to the ancestral shrines of the imperial house will be found in HS 1B.67–8, HS 2.88, HS 4.108 and HS 4.126 (HFHD, Vol. I, pp. 124, 178, 228 and 257); HS 6.179, HS 7.229 and HS 8.243 (HFHD, Vol. II, pp. 67, 169 and 211); HS 50.2311; HS 68.2946 and HS 73.3125. For the occurrence of portents (p. 171), see HS 6.159 (HFHD, Vol. II, p. 33), HS 27A.1331 and Bielenstein (Lo-yang), pp. 55 and 114 note 259. For the elaboration and subsequent reduction of these services, see HS 8.243 (HFHD, Vol. II, pp. 210–11), HS 73.3115, and *Crisis and Conflict*, pp. 179f.

For the ritual occasions of eastern Han, see HHS (tr.)4.3101f., 3117f. The description of the Great Exorcism will be found in HHS (tr.)5.3127, and the translation of the passage that is reproduced here is from Bodde (Festivals), pp. 81–2 (reprinted by permission of Princeton University Press).

CHAPTER 13

For ideas of sovereignty in the pre-imperial age, see Herrlee G. Creel, *The Origins of Statecraft in China*, Vol. 1 (Chicago and London: University of Chicago Press, 1970). Translations of a number of passages which relate to Han ideas are given in de Bary, *Sources of Chinese Tradition* (as cited under the Introduction), Chapter vii. See also Carl Leban, 'Managing heaven's mandate: coded communications in the accession of Ts'ao P'ei, AD 220', in David T. Roy and Tsuen-hsuin Tsien (eds), *Ancient China: Studies in Early Civilization* (Hong Kong: Chinese University Press, 1978), pp. 315–41; and Michael Loewe, 'Water, Earth and Fire – the Symbols of the Han Dynasty' (*Nachrichten der Gesellschaft für Natur- und Völkerkunde Ostasiens/Hamburg* 125, 1979), pp. 63–8.

For the view that the kings of Chou ruled widely and effectively (p. 145) see Creel (as cited above). The quotation from the *Shih-chi* (p. 146) is from SC6.236 (MH, Vol. II, p. 125); for the views of the *Huai-nan-tzu* see HNT 9.1a *et seq.*, and for the symbolism of the character *wang*, see *Ch'un-ch'iu fan-lu* 11 (44).5a (de Bary, p. 163). Tung Chung-shu's views of sovereignty are carried in HS 56 (see especially pp. 2514f. as cited on p. 150, and 2498).

The concept of the emperor as the parent of his people is expressed in HS 23.1079; for Pan Piao's essay on the Mandate of Kings, see HS 100A.4207f. (de Bary, pp. 176f.); for K'uang Heng, see HS 81.3338; for Wang Mang, see HS 99A.4095 (HFHD, Vol. III, p. 255); for Kuang wu ti's accession, see HHS 1A.21–22. For the virtues of personal merit as against the claims of hereditary succession, see HS 68.2937 and *Ch'ien-fu lun* 4.36f.; for the formalities of abdication, see HS 99A.4095 (HFHD, Vol. III, p. 255) and *San-kuo chih* 2.62 (as cited on pp. 155f.), and Michael Loewe, 'The Authority of the Emperors of

Ch'in and Han', in Dieter Eikemeier and Herbert Franke (eds), *State and Law in East Asia: Festschrift Karl Bünger* (Wiesbaden: Otto Harrassowitz, 1981, pp. 80–111).

For Wang Ch'ung's views, see *Lun-heng* 19 (Hsüan Han), pp. 817f. and (Hui kuo), pp. 826f. (Forke, Vol. II, pp. 192f., 201f.). For Hsün Yüeh, see Ch'i-yün Ch'en, *Hsün Yüeh and the Mind of Late Han China* (Princeton: Princeton University Press, 1980).

CHAPTER 14

For the attitude towards the tasks of government in the Ch'in kingdom and empire, see Herrlee G. Creel, *Shen Pu-hai: A Chinese Political Philosopher of the Fourth Century B.C.* (Chicago and London: University of Chicago Press, 1974), and Derk Bodde, *China's First Unifier: A study of the Ch'in dynasty as seen in the life of Li Ssu* (Leiden: E. J. Brill, 1938; reissued, Hong Kong: Hong Kong University Press, 1967). The theme of modernist and reformist is discussed in *Crisis and Conflict*. For the reactions of the second century AD, see Etienne Balazs, *Chinese Civilization and Bureaucracy* (translated by H. M. Wright, edited by Arthur F. Wright; New Haven and London: Yale University Press, 1964), Chapter 13, 'Political Philosophy and Social Crisis at the End of the Han Dynasty'.

The texts of the edicts that are cited (pp. 163f.) will be found as follows: (a) for 178 BC: HS 4.118 (HFHD, Vol. I, p. 245); (b) for 163 BC: HS 4.127 (HFHD, Vol. I, p. 261); (c) for 81 BC: HS 7.223 (HFHD, Vol. II, p. 160); and (d) for 34 BC: HS 9.296 (HFHD, Vol. II, p. 333). For the regulation of the calendar, see Sivin (as cited under Chapter 5); Bernhard Karlgren, 'The Book of Documents' (BMFEA 22, 1950), p. 3 and *Ch'ien-fu lun* 18.250. For watching for the ethers, see Derk Bodde, 'The Chinese Cosmic Magic known as Watching for the Ethers' (in Søren Egerod and Else Glahn (eds), *Studia Serica Bernhard Karlgren Dedicata*, Copenhagen: Ejnar Munksgaard, 1959, pp. 14–35). For watching the vapours, see A. F. P. Hulsewé, 'Watching the vapours; an ancient Chinese technique of prognostication', in *Nachrichten der Gesellschaft für Natur- und Völkerkunde Ostasiens/Hamburg* 125, 1979, pp. 40–9.

For the encouragement of rain, see HHS (tr.) 5.3117; HNT 11.11b, 16.13b and 17.1a; *Lun-heng* 16 (Luan lung), p. 691 (Forke, Vol. II, p. 349); for rites at the end of winter, see HHS (tr.) 4.3102, HHS (tr.) 5.3129. Kung Yü's view of the use of money is set out in HS 72.3075; for Tung Chung-shu's view of landownership, see HS 24A.1137 (Nancy Lee Swann, *Food and Money in Ancient China*; Princeton: Princeton University Press, 1950, pp. 177f.); for attempts to restrict landholdings, see *Crisis and Conflict*, p. 269; and for an account of foreign policy in western Han, see Hulsewé and Loewe, *China in Central Asia* (as cited under Chapter 9), pp. 39–66. The passage cited on p. 169 is from YTL 20.145.

CHAPTER 15

For the Chinese concept of law and its provisions in Ch'in and Han, see Derk Bodde, *China's First Unifier* (as cited under Chapter 14); Derk Bodde and Clarence Morris, *Law in Imperial China* (Cambridge, Massachusetts: Harvard University Press, 1967); A. F. P. Hulsewé, *Remnants of Han Law*, Vol. I (Leiden: E. J. Brill, 1955), and 'The Ch'in documents discovered in Hupei in 1975' (*T'oung Pao*, Vol. LXIV, 4–5, pp. 175–217).

202

The main primary source for Ch'in and Han law is *Han shu* 23 (translated in Hulsewé, *Remnants*, pp. 321–422). For complaints about the severity of Ch'in laws and the reduction of Han law to three main provisions, see HS23.1096 (Hulsewé, *Remnants*, p. 333). The passage cited on p. 173 is from YTL 55.344 (following Chang Chih-hsiang's text). For Lu Chia's advice to the first Han emperor, see HS 43.2113; for Shu-sun T'ung's work, see HS 22.1030 and HS 88.3592. The passage cited on pp. 176f. is from HS 22.1027 (for a translation of the opening and closing sections of HS 22, see Hulsewé, *Remnants*, pp. 429–55). For expressions of distrust in *li*, see *Lun-heng* 18 (Tzu-jan), p. 784 (Forke, Vol. I, p. 100), and *Yin wen tzu* (Ta tao, hsia).13a. For differences in the types of music, the state's attitude thereto and the history of the Office of Music, see *Crisis and Conflict*, Chapter 6.

CHAPTER 16

For the main strands of pre-imperial philosophy, see Arthur Waley, *Three Ways of Thought in Ancient China* (London: George Allen & Unwin, 1939); for an account of the bibliographical work of Liu Hsiang and Liu Hsin, see P. van der Loon, 'On the Transmission of Kuan-tzu' (*T'oung Pao*, Vol. XLI, 4–5, pp. 357–93); for Han literary policy, see Tjan Tjoe Som, *Po Hu T'ung: The Comprehensive Discussions in the White Tiger Hall* (Leiden: E. J. Brill, 1949), Vol. 1, pp. 82–176. The most complete study of the apocryphal texts is to be found in Jack L. Dull, 'A Historical Introduction to the Apocryphal (Ch'an-wei) texts of the Han Dynasty' (dissertation presented to the University of Washington, 1966; unpublished). For literary measures of the Ch'in empire, see Derk Bodde, *China's First Unifier* (as cited under Chapter 14), pp. 80–4 and 162–6.

The primary sources for the literary history of Han are found in HS 30, HS 88 and HHS 79 (biog. 69) A, B. Edicts and memorials that concerned literary policies are found in HS 2.90 (191 BC; HFHD, Vol. I, p. 182); HS 6.156, 159 and 171 (141, 136 and 124 BC; HFHD, Vol. II, pp. 28, 32 and 54). For the recovery of the *Book of Documents* in Wen ti's reign, see HS 49.2277 and HS 88.3603. For the attitude of Wen ti and the empress Tou, see HS 88.3592f. For the foundation of the imperial academy and its growth, see HFHD, Vol. II, p. 24; Tjan Tjoe Som, p.88; HHS 79A (biog.69A).2545f. Pan Ku's criticism of the New Text school, as cited on p. 185 is found in HS 30.1723 (Tjan Tjoe Som, p. 143); for the statistics derived from Liu Hsin's catalogue, see HS 30.1703–23. Tjan Tjoe Som describes the contents of the apocryphal books in pp. 106–20 and the victory of the Old Text School on p. 165.

Glossary

Entries in this glossary are restricted to the principal persons and books to which reference has been made above. Where suitable, details are given of translations from Chinese works, biographical studies or monographs that are easily available. As far as possible the entries present generally accepted conclusions regarding the authenticity or authorship of texts and avoid matters that are subject to question.

For the formative personalities and writings of the pre-imperial period, readers are referred to J. J. L. Duyvendak, *The Book of Lord Shang* (London: Arthur Probsthain, 1928); Arthur Waley, *The Analects of Confucius*, and *Three Ways of Thought in Ancient China* (London: George Allen & Unwin, 1938 and 1939); Burton Watson, *Early Chinese Literature* (New York and London: Columbia University Press, 1962) and *Chuang tzu, Han fei tzu, Mo tzu* and *Hsün tzu: Basic writings* (New York and London: Columbia University Press; published in four separate volumes, 1963–4; reprint of the last three, in one volume, 1967); D. C. Lau, *Lao Tzu Tao Te Ching*, and *Mencius* (Harmondsworth: Penguin Books, 1963 and 1970); and Anne Cheng, *Entretiens de Confucius* (Paris: Éditions du Seuil, 1981).

Book of Changes, see *I ching*.
Book of Documents, see *Shu ching*.
Book of Songs, see *Shih ching*.
Chang Heng (AD 78–139)
  A specialist in astronomy and mathematics, Chang Heng contributed in a marked way to the application of scientific knowledge to practical problems, and he is credited with the construction of instruments such as an armillary sphere and a seismograph. As a man of letters he composed a number of prose-poems (*fu*), some of which describe the life of the capital cities of Ch'ang-an and Lo-yang. One of these compositions (*Ssu hsüan fu*) shows Chang Heng's capacity for a mystical approach to reality.
Chao hun, see *Ch'u tz'u*.
Ch'ao Ts'o (d. 154 BC)
  Ch'ao Ts'o served as an official at the courts of Wen ti (reigned 180–157) and Ching ti (reigned 157–141). As a statesman he advocated strong measures to enhance the powers of the central government and to reduce those of the subordinate kings, who had been invested with wide areas of territory in the northern and eastern parts of the empire. He also put forward positive proposals for countering the threat of foreign invasion and for increasing agricultural production. In the course of a major rebellion by some of the kings, and partly as a result of political rivalry, Ch'ao Ts'o was executed in 154 BC. In the sense that his political suggestions were designed to strengthen the empire, he may be regarded as a statesman of modernist views. He was also concerned in resurrecting from oblivion the text of the *Shu ching* (*q.v.*), which was later incorporated in the canon of scriptures.
Cheng Hsüan (AD 127–200)
  Cheng Hsüan had been a pupil of Ma Jung (*q.v.*). As a teacher in his own turn

he attracted a large number of disciples, and became a prolific writer whose comments and interpretation of the scriptural books have ever since been cited and respected in traditional Chinese scholarship. Together with Ma Jung and others he was responsible for the final ascendancy of the Old Texts School over the New Texts School.

Cheng lun, see Ts'ui Shih.

Cheng shih (Standard Histories)

Beginning with the *Shih-chi* (q.v.) there exists a total of twenty-five historical compilations, each of which sets out to treat the history of China within a specified period of time. As each of these periods is usually that of a dynastic house which reigned over all or part of the sub-continent, the series is frequently described as the *Dynastic Histories*.

However, the term *Standard Histories* is more accurate. In theory each one of the works is framed on the example of the *Han shu* (q.v.) with separate groups of chapters for imperial annals, tables, biographies and treatises. Not all the twenty-five works include chapters of all these types; some are not strictly limited to a single dynastic period; and in a few instances two standard histories have been written to cover one and the same period. For Ch'in and Han, the works in question are the *Shih-chi, Han shu* and *Hou Han shu*.

From the seventh century, compilation of these works became the responsibility of the state, which maintained a special commission of writers, led by a senior statesman, to do the work. In so far as these histories were written at the behest of a governing authority, they are necessarily marked by an inbuilt bias or prejudice.

For the compilation of these works, see Charles S. Gardner, *Chinese Traditional Historiography* (Cambridge, Massachusetts: Harvard University Press, 1938); W. G. Beasley and E. G. Pulleyblank (eds), *Historians of China and Japan* (London: Oxford University Press, 1961), Chapter 4; and Donald D. Leslie, Colin Mackerras and Wang Gungwu (eds), *Essays on the Sources for Chinese History* (Canberra: Australian National University Press, 1973), Chapters V, VI.

Chia I (200–168 BC)

Chia I is known as a young man of considerable brilliance who served at the court of Wen ti (reigned 180–157), and tendered positive suggestions for strengthening the administrative control of the newly established empire, its security and its economic prosperity. Statements of his views are included in the *Shih-chi* and the *Han shu*; a collection of essays ascribed to him, and including some of the material in the histories, is entitled *Hsin shu*. Doubts that have been cast on the authenticity of this collection have not been entirely sustained. Chia I was also a poet.

Traditionally Chia I has often been classed as a 'Confucian'; he would be better regarded as an exponent of methods of imperial government that rested on positive controls tempered by ethical considerations. In one of his most famous essays, he criticised the government of Ch'in for its excessive rigours and severities, in the hope that the Han emperors would avoid those very errors that had led to Ch'in's downfall.

Ch'ien-fu lun, see Wang Fu.

Ching Fang (probably 79–37 BC)

Ching Fang was known as a specialist in texts concerning the sixty-four hexagrams, and became a leader of one of four 'Modern Text' schools of interpretation of the *Changes*; the school is known under his name. He also paid considerable attention to natural phenomena of a strange type and their inherent meaning, and the views that he expressed in this connection are included in the *Han shu* and other texts. The importance of Ching Fang lies in (a) his attempt to interpret the sixty-four hexagrams within the major context of the natural rhythms of the universe, and his attempt to reconcile the cycle of sixty-four with other cycles; and (b) the development of various means of taking warnings from the oracles of nature. Ching Fang was involved in political disputes and executed after being accused of sedition. The *Ching shih i chuan* which is attributed to him is probably not authentic.

Ching shih i chuan, see Ching Fang.

Chiu ko, see *Ch'u tz'u*.

Chou i, see *I ching*.

Chou li (Institutions of Chou) and other texts

A number of codifications were made of the provisions of *li*, i.e. the conventional rules or guide-lines for behaviour, conformity with which was regarded by 'Confucian' thinkers as being the mainstay of social and political stability. To augment the authority of these works, traditional scholars ascribed to them a much greater degree of antiquity than may be warranted. While some of the prescriptions of the books may date to before the imperial age, many sections were written in the Han period and reflect Han practice rather than the way of life of Chou, as claimed. Four books should be distinguished:

(a) The *Chou li* (Institutions of Chou): an idealistic description of the institutions of government believed to have been adopted at the start of the Chou dynasty, in twelve chapters. Translated by Edouard Biot, *Le Tcheou-li ou Rites des Tcheou*, 2 vols, Paris, 1851.

(b) The *I-li* (Book of observances and ceremonial). The contents of this work (seventeen chapters) describe the proper behaviour at funerals, weddings, audiences at court and other family or court occasions. This may have been the work on *li* which was included in the scriptural canon. Parts of manuscript copies of the text have been found in a tomb which dates from the last quarter of the first century BC. Translated by John Steele, *The I-li or Book of Etiquette and Ceremonial*, 2 vols, London: Probsthain, 1917.

(c) The *Ta Tai li chi* (Records on ceremonial by Tai the Elder), a revision and abbreviation of an ancient work by Tai Te (western Han). Of 85 original sections, 39 survive.

(d) The *Li chi* (Records on ceremonial). 49 sections survive of this revision of Tai Te's work, which was compiled by his nephew Tai Sheng (Tai the Younger). Translated by S. Couvreur, *Li Ki ou Mémoires sur les bienséances et les cérémonies*, 2 vols, Ho Kien Fou, 1913.

Ch'u tz'u (The Songs of the South)

This is a collection of poems that derive from the culture of the Yangtse river valley, where the pre-imperial kingdom of Ch'u was situated. The oldest poems in the collection (including one that is entitled *Li sao*, 'On encountering sorrow') are ascribed to Ch'ü Yüan, an unsuccessful statesman who committed suicide towards the end of the fourth century BC. The latest poems in the collection are ascribed to Wang I (second century AD).

The collection includes some of China's earliest lyrical poetry. The content calls on the mythology and folklore of central China, and some of the poems express a mystic's approach to life. The religious background is best revealed in the two poems *Chao hun* and *Ta chao* ('Summons of the soul' and 'Great Summons') and a series that derive from shamanist practice (*Chiu ko*, 'The Nine Songs'). For translations, see David Hawkes, *Ch'u Tz'u: The Songs of the South* (Oxford: Clarendon Press, 1959) and Arthur Waley, *The Nine Songs: A Study of Shamanism in Ancient China* (London: George Allen & Unwin, 1955).

Ch'ü Yüan, see *Ch'u tz'u.*

Ch'un-ch'iu (Spring and Autumn Annals)

As a chronicle of one of the states that existed in China before the foundation of the empire in 221 BC, the *Ch'un-ch'iu* includes terse entries, in strict chronological order, for the events that concerned the kingdom of Lu over the years 722–481 BC. Much of the content concerns the ceremonies of religion and court, and the diplomatic or warlike relations between Lu and other states. The *Ch'un-ch'iu* was believed to have been edited by Confucius, himself a native of Lu. Of several commentaries or amplifications designed to explain its language and hidden meaning, there survive the *Kung yang chuan* and the *Ku liang chuan*. In 136 BC the *Ch'un-ch'iu* was included in the scriptural canon, with the addition of the *Kung yang chuan*.

At some stage, the text of what was probably an independent historical document, known as the *Tso chuan*, was separated into sections; these were severally attached to those entries of the *Ch'un-ch'iu* to which they were related or believed to apply. The *Tso chuan* was probably compiled in the third century BC and covers the period 722–468 BC. Its prose style was long respected as a model by Chinese writers of history. For a translation of the *Ch'un-ch'iu* and *Tso chuan*, see James Legge, *The Chinese Classics*, Vol. V, Parts I, II, *The Ch'un Ts'ew with the Tso chuen* (Hong Kong and London: 1872). See also Burton Watson, *Early Chinese Literature* (New York and London: Columbia University Press, 1962), pp. 37f.

Ch'un-ch'iu fan-lu, see Tung Chung-shu.

Chung-ch'ang T'ung (b. AD 180)

Chung-ch'ang T'ung was one of several men who deplored the decline and corruption that they saw around them (see e.g., entries for Wang Fu, Ts'ui Shih). He reacted partly by decrying the dangers of public life and seeking refuge in the mystical approach and poetry associated with Taoist thought. At the same time he gave vent to a sharp criticism of the political scene, while setting out a series of constructive proposals to solve administrative and legal problems. Dissatisfied with appeals to the force of tradition, like some of his contemporaries he saw the need for an authoritarian rule as a measure of reform. His original written work, in thirty-four sections, has been lost, but some of his essays are incorporated in the *Hou Han shu*. See Etienne Balazs, *Chinese Civilization and Bureaucracy: Variations on a Theme* (translated by H. M. Wright, edited by Arthur F. Wright), New Haven and London: Yale University Press, 1964, pp. 213f.

Classic of the Great Mysterious, see Yang Hsiung.

Classic of the Mountains and the Lakes, see *Shan-hai ching*.
Comprehensive discussions of the White Tiger Hall, see *Po hu t'ung*.
Criticisms of a hidden man, see Wang Fu.
Dialect words, see Yang Hsiung.
Discourses on Salt and Iron, see *Yen-t'ieh lun*.
Discourses of the States, see *Kuo-yü*.
Discourses Weighed in the Balance, see *Lun-heng*.
Disquisitions, see *Lun-heng*.
Fa yen, see Yang Hsiung.
Fan Yeh, see *Hou Han shu*.
Fang yen, see Yang Hsiung.
Five Classics, see *Chou li*, *Ch'un-ch'iu*, *I ching*, *Shih ching* and *Shu ching*.
Great Summons, see *Ch'u tz'u*.
Han chi, see Hsün Yüeh.
Han shu (History of the Han Dynasty)
  Being the first of the Chinese dynastic or standard histories proper, the *Han shu* covers the period from Liu Pang's accession as king of Han (206 BC) to the interruption of the Han dynasty by Wang Mang (first and only emperor of the Hsin dynasty, AD 9–23). The work was started by Pan Piao (AD 3–54) but the greater part of the 100 chapters was written by his son Pan Ku (AD 32–92), with a few chapters being attributed to his sister Pan Chao (AD ?48–?116). The history is arranged in four groups of chapters (imperial annals, tables, treatises and biographies). For whereas the *Shih-chi* (*q.v.*) is concerned with the history of both pre-imperial and imperial China, the *Han shu* covers part of the imperial period only; for this reason no group of chapters for hereditary houses is necessary.
  Much of the content of the *Han shu* corresponds almost exactly with that of the *Shih-chi*, but some material is retained uniquely in each work; for the second half of the western Han period (i.e. from *c*. 100 BC onwards) the *Han shu* is the sole primary chronicle. In addition to calling on official records, which it summarises, the work incorporates some writing that arose independently of the compilers, such as the treatise on astronomy and astrology (attributed to Ma Hsü) and the summarised catalogue of literary works in the imperial library, which had been the work of Liu Hsiang and Liu Hsin (*qq.v.*). For doubts regarding the relationship between surviving versions of certain chapters of the *Han shu* and the *Shih-chi*, see Yves Hervouet, 'La valeur relative des textes du *Che-ki* et du *Han-chou*' (*Mélanges de sinologie offerts à Monsieur Paul Demiéville*, Vol. II (Paris: 1974, pp. 55–76), and A. F. P. Hulsewé, 'The problem of the Authenticity of *Shih-chi* Ch. 123, the memoir on Ta Yüan' (*T'oung Pao* LXI, 1–3, 1975, pp. 83–147).
  The twelve chapters of imperial annals have been translated by Homer H. Dubs in *History of the Former Han Dynasty* (Baltimore: Waverley Press, 1938–55), and translations of a number of other chapters have appeared separately, e.g. Nancy Lee Swann, *Food and Money in Ancient China* (Princeton: Princeton University Press, 1950); A. F. P. Hulsewé, *Remnants of Han Law* (Leiden: E. J. Brill, 1955); Burton Watson, *Courtier and Commoner in Ancient China* (New York and London: Columbia University Press, 1974); and A. F. P. Hulsewé and M. A. N. Loewe, *China in Central Asia* (Leiden: E. J. Brill, 1979).

History of the Han Dynasty, see *Han shu*.

History of the Later Han Dynasty, see *Hou Han shu*.

Ho Hsiu (AD 129–182)

Regarded by his contemporaries as an outstanding scholar of the scriptural texts, Ho Hsiu preferred to avoid the cares of public office and to devote himself to scholarship. Nevertheless he was unable to avoid implication in political troubles. His best known contribution consisted of his explanations of the *Kung yang chuan* and other documents associated with the *Ch'un-ch'iu*.

Hou Han shu (History of the Later Han Dynasty)

Of a number of ventures aimed at compiling a standard history for the later or eastern Han dynasty (AD 25–220), the *Hou Han shu* survives as a principal work; it is in fact a composite book, deriving from two separate projects. The 10 chapters of imperial annals and the 80 chapters of biographies are from the hand of Fan Yeh (398–446); the 30 chapters of treatises (more strictly denoted as *Hsü Han shu*) are the work of Ssu-ma Piao (240–306), with a commentary by Liu Chao (first half of the sixth century); there are no tables in the extant book.

As compared with the *Shih-chi* and *Han shu* (*qq.v.*), the greater part of the *Hou Han shu* was written at a greater remove in time from the period which it records. It was, however, based on the *Tung-kuan Han-chi*, which was written during the eastern Han dynasty itself, and of which about a sixth part survives. For authorship and the process of compilation, see Hans Bielenstein, 'The Restoration of the Han Dynasty' (BMFEA 26, 1954, pp. 9–20).

Hsi tz'u chuan

Also called *Ta chuan*; one of the ancillary texts that forms part of the *I ching* (*q.v.*).

Hsin-hsü, see Liu Hsiang.

Hsin lun, see Huan T'an.

Hsin shu, see Chia I.

Hsin yü, see Lu Chia.

Hsü Han chih, *Hsü Han shu* see *Hou Han shu*.

Hsün Yüeh (AD 148–209)

Hsün Yüeh was perhaps the most original of a number of men who contributed to intellectual developments at a time of marked dynastic instability and political unrest. While adhering to a firm belief in Confucius' ideas of human ability and potential achievement, he saw the need to impose certain standards on society and for a discipline that would lead to the betterment of man. In the belief that the ideal of an imperial order would outlast the decline that he witnessed in practice, he tried to define the permanent elements necessary for a stable empire.

The originality of Hsün Yüeh's mind is revealed in the historical judgements of his *Ch'ien Han chi* and the theoretical essays of his *Shen-chien*. Of these works, the *Han chi* (thirty chapters; compiled after 196) is an historical record of western Han, set out in strict chronological order of the incidents reported; the *Shen-chien* (five chapters; written after the *Han chi*) is a collection of essays that discuss abstract principles such as the concept and organisation of man. There are two studies of Hsün Yüeh: Chi-yun Chen, *Hsün Yüeh (A.D. 148–209): The Life and Reflections of an Early Medieval*

Confucian (Cambridge: Cambridge University Press, 1975); and Ch'i-yün Ch'en, *Hsün Yüeh and the Mind of Late Han China; a translation of the 'Shen-chien' with introduction and annotations* (Princeton: Princeton University Press, 1980).

Huai-nan-tzu

Some time before 139 BC, Liu An (?179–122), king of Huai-nan, summoned scholars and specialists in a number of arts and sciences to discuss a wide range of intellectual problems. Those who attended the meetings came from varied backgrounds and the discussions drew eclectically on a number of schools of thought and opinion. In general the chapters of the *Huai-nan-tzu* which resulted from these conferences seek to place problems of human nature and the conditions of human existence within a universal context, whose underlying principle is *tao* or the order of nature. They also attempt to explain the patterns of the natural world and to explain how a perfect state of human government can be achieved. The book (presented in 139 BC) extends to twenty-one chapters and draws on elements of mythology as well as on some of the philosophical ideas of the time. There is no complete translation of the *Huai-nan-tzu*, but some chapters have been made available (e.g. John Stephen Major, 'Topography and Cosmology in Early Han Thought: Chapter Four of the *Huai-nan-tzu* (unpublished thesis presented to the Committee on History and East Asian Languages; Cambridge, Massachusetts: Harvard University, 1973).

Huan K'uan, see *Yen-t'ieh lun.*

Huan T'an (*c.* 43 BC – AD 28)

Serving as an official who was concerned with the state's attention to music, Huan T'an lived through the dynastic turbulence of the last decades of western Han, Wang Mang's dynasty and the restoration of Han in AD 25. As a critic of contemporary irrational beliefs (in particular the faith placed in the prognostication texts) he may be regarded as a precursor of Wang Ch'ung (see *Lun-heng*). His realistic approach to contemporary thought is shown in his protests against the excessive faith placed in the authority of Confucius and in precedents of the past. Fragments only of his essays (entitled *Hsin lun*) and other writings survive. See Timoteus Pokora, *Hsin-lun (New Treatise) and other writings by Huan T'an (43 B.C.–28 A.D.)* (Ann Arbor: Center for Chinese Studies, University of Michigan, 1975).

Huang-Lao Taoism

This term has been used somewhat loosely to refer to various philosophical theories that were current from the second century BC or possibly earlier, but which have been poorly documented in Chinese literature. Recently discovered manuscripts from Ma-wang-tui are believed to have derived from this branch of 'Taoist' thought, which was associated with the Yellow Emperor. The documents explain how the rule and organisation of mankind can best be accomplished within a universal context and according to metaphysical categories and ethical principles that are distinct from those of Han Confucianism (see Tung Chung-shu). For research in these documents, see Jan Yün-hua, 'The Silk Manuscripts on Taoism' (*T'oung Pao* LXIII, 1977, pp. 65–84); 'Tao yüan or Tao: the Origin'; and 'Tao, Principle and Law: the three key concepts in the Yellow Emperor Taoism' (*Journal of Chinese Philosophy*, Vol. 7, No. 3, 1980, pp. 195–204 and 205–28).

I ching (Book of Changes)

The earliest parts of this work, which are strictly termed the *Chou i* or 'Changes of Chou', are short pithy sayings or formulae which explain the meaning to be put on a hexagram that had emerged from the process of divination with yarrow stalks (or on the individual lines of the hexagram). These parts of the work, known as the *t'uan* (judgement) and *yao* (lines) may date from *c.* 800 BC. To these there have been added a variety of ancillary texts, written considerably later. These were intended to expound and explain the *t'uan* and the *yao* and to relate the whole subject of the 'Changes' and divination to philosophies that had been evolving from the fifth century BC onwards. These ancillary texts are known collectively as the *Ten Wings*.

The term *I ching* refers to the texts of both the *Chou i* and the *Ten Wings*. A silk manuscript that is dated before 168 BC carries some of the texts of these writings in the form that they had reached by then and which are slightly different from the received text of today. The 'Changes' was one of the texts singled out for special attention in 136 BC and thereafter incorporated in the canon of the scriptures.

Of the many translations and works on the *I ching*, three only will be mentioned here: *The I Ching or Book of Changes; the Richard Wilhelm Translation rendered into English by Cary F. Baynes* (London: Routledge & Kegan Paul, 1951, in two volumes; third edition 1968 in one volume); John Blofeld, *The Book of Change* (London: George Allen & Unwin, 1965); Hellmut Wilhelm, *Change Eight Lectures on the 'I ching'* (London: Routledge & Kegan Paul, 1961).

I-li, see *Chou li*.

K'an-yü, see p. 96.

Ko Hung, see *Pao-p'u-tzu*.

Ku Liang chuan, see *Ch'un-ch'iu*.

Ku Yung (died shortly after 8 BC)

A significant exponent of the view that heaven issues warnings to mankind by means of specially sent phenomena (see Tung Chung-shu), Ku Yung was known for his interpretations of such events. For this reason he was consulted in regard to the famous eclipse and earthquake of 29 BC (see Tu Ch'in). In the course of such interpretations, Ku Yung showed himself a fearless critic of the emperor (Ch'eng ti) and his behaviour, and sought to reform the licentious conduct and extravagances of the day. In 24 BC he issued a warning against the excessively adventurous undertakings with foreign states. In 9 BC he was appointed *Superintendent of Agriculture*.

Kung yang chuan, see *Ch'un-ch'iu*.

Kuo P'u, see *Shan-hai ching*.

Kuo-yü (Discourses of the States)

This is a chronicle of events (twenty chapters) reported to have occurred in the kingdom of Chou or in the principal states of the pre-imperial age. The incidents are dated at various times between the tenth and the fifth centuries BC, and the period that is described corresponds in part to that of the *Ch'un-ch'iu* (*q.v.*) and *Tso chuan*.

Li chi, see *Chou li*.

Li sao, see *Ch'u tz'u*.

Li Ssu (?280–208 BC)

Li Ssu was perhaps the most outstanding statesman who served the first of the Ch'in emperors, playing a leading role in the unification of 221 BC. The *Shih-chi* (*q.v.*) includes records of the advice that he submitted to the throne on a number of matters of practical organisation of the empire. He is also credited with proposals to standardise the system of writing, and to destroy copies of certain texts by burning, as a means of discouraging a scholastic attitude and a reverence for the past. Li Ssu died on the executioner's block, a victim of political intrigue. See Derk Bodde, *China's First Unifier: A Study of the Ch'in Dynasty as seen in the life of Li Ssu* (Leiden: E. J. Brill, 1938; reprinted Hong Kong: Hong Kong University Press, 1967).

Lieh-nü chuan, see Liu Hsiang.

Lieh-tzu

Authorship of this book (in eight sections) has been fastened on one Lieh Yü-k'ou. While it is likely that some of its parts may have been written as early as 300 BC, others may well date from as late as *c.* AD 300. The book is generally regarded as one of the basic texts of Taoist thought, including anecdotal and allegorical material, and being written from the point of view of a mystic. See A. C. Graham, *The Book of Lieh-tzu: A new translation* (London: John Murray, 1960).

Lieh Yü-k'ou, see *Lieh-tzu*.

Liu An, see *Huai-nan-tzu*.

Liu Chao, see *Hou Han shu*.

Liu Hsiang (79–8 BC)

In official life, Liu Hsiang served for a short period in a senior post reserved for members of the imperial family, i.e. that of *Superintendent of the imperial household*. A number of memorials which he submitted are included in the *Han shu* (*q.v.*), and show him to be a man of independent mind, ready to judge problems on their own merits rather than by rigid adherence to preconceived notions. The subjects upon which he tendered advice included foreign affairs, religious practice and the validity of scriptural texts. The *Han shu* also includes the interpretations that he put on a number of strange phenomena, and some of his writings reveal an interest in alchemy. In addition to his contribution to literature as author of the *Lieh-nü chuan*, the *Hsin hsü* and *Shuo-yüan*, Liu Hsiang played a highly significant part in literary history as a collector and collator of texts. After comparison of different copies, he formed exemplars to which he appended descriptive introductions, a few of which have survived. For this aspect of Liu Hsiang's work, see P. van der Loon, 'On the Transmission of the Kuan-tzu' (*T'oung Pao* XLI, 4–5, 1952, pp. 358f.).

Liu Hsin (d. AD 23)

As the son of Liu Hsiang (*q.v.*), Liu Hsin continued his father's work of collating the copies of books assembled in the imperial library. By compiling a catalogue of the books, divided into six major classes of writings, he laid the foundations of Chinese bibliography; and it is a summary of his descriptive notes and survey of literature that is incorporated as Chapter 30 of the *Han shu* (*q.v.*). As a protagonist of traditional values and writings, such as the *Chou li* (*q.v.*) and *Tso chuan* (see *Ch'un-ch'iu*), Liu Hsin provided valuable intellectual support for Wang Mang (emperor of Hsin, AD 9–23); but

being implicated in a plot against him, Liu Hsin was executed in AD 23.
Lu Chia (*c.* 225–145 BC)
  Lu Chia was one of the supporters of Liu Pang in his successful bid for
imperial power. The *Hsin yü* (in twelve sections) which is attributed to his
brush originated from the advice that he gave the emperor regarding the
prime causes of dynastic success and failure. Other writings have not
survived.
Lü shih ch'un-ch'iu (Spring and Autumn Annals of Mr Lü)
  Lü Pu-wei was a statesman who rose to high office in the kingdom of Ch'in
in the decades before the unification of 221 BC. He assembled a large number
of scholars and writers to serve at the court and a written version of their
statements of opinion was compiled as the *Lü shih ch'un-ch'iu*, in twenty-six
chapters (probably in 240 BC). The material represents the views of different
types of thought, and can hardly be classified within any single one. A
number of anecdotes are included to illustrate the principles expressed. For a
translation, see Richard Wilhelm, *Frühling und Herbst des Lü Bu Wei* (Jena:
Eugen Diederichs, 1928).
Lun-heng (Disquisitions; sometimes rendered 'Discourses Weighed in the
Balance')
  Writing in reaction against some of the prevailing opinions of the day, Wang
Ch'ung (AD 27–*c.* 100) was particularly anxious to disprove the theory of
heaven's deliberate interference in human and earthly affairs (see Tung
Chung-shu) and to dispel beliefs in the powers of the dead to harm the living
and other unjustified fears. In the *Lun-heng* he set out to explain the workings
of the world of nature on strictly systematic principles, insisting on the need
to collect evidence, to verify hypotheses and to apply scientific methods to all
observed phenomena. He stands out as a man of independent thought,
fearless in his rejection of accepted dogma and in his determination to reach
truth.
  All except one of the eighty-five sections of his main work, the *Lun-heng*,
have survived. They have been translated by Alfred Forke as *Lun-heng, Part I:
Philosophical Essays of Wang Ch'ung* and *Part II: Miscellaneous Essays of Wang
Ch'ung* (Shanghai: Kelly and Walsh; London: Luzac; and Leipzig: Harrassowitz, 1907 and 1911; reprinted New York: Paragon Book Gallery, 1962).
Ma Hsü, see *Han shu.*
Ma Jung (AD 79–166)
  Ma Jung enjoyed the reputation of a scholar and was also well known for his
somewhat eccentric behaviour. In public life he suffered for his outspoken
criticism of the influence exerted by some of the families of imperial consorts
on the conduct of government. He was a poet and commentator on a number
of works, including the *I ching, Shih ching, Shu ching* and the *Huai-nan-tzu*
(*q.v.*). Ma Jung was one of the scholars whose work and influence were
responsible for the final ascendancy gained by the Old Texts School.
Model Sayings, see Yang Hsiung.
Monthly Instructions for the Four Classes of People, see Ts'ui Shih.
Mu t'ien-tzu chuan (Story of Mu the son of heaven)
  The journey of Mu, king of Chou, to the west to seek the secrets of
immortality from the Queen Mother of the West has occupied an important
place in Chinese mythology and references occur in a number of texts. In its

description of this allegorical journey, the *Mu t'ien-tzu chuan* alludes to a number of details of geography and ritual procedure. The work probably derives from several hands, and the first four of the six chapters are regarded as being the most reliable. Various dates have been suggested for composition, and latest opinion places parts of the text in the middle of the fourth century BC. For translations, see Cheng Te-k'un, 'The travels of emperor Mu' (*Journal of the North China Branch of the Royal Asiatic Society* LXIV, pp. 142f. and LXV, pp. 128f., 1934); and Rémi Mathieu, *Le Mu Tianzi zhuan Traduction annotée Étude critique* (Paris: Collège de France, Institut des Hautes Études Chinoises, 1978).

The Nine Songs, see *Ch'u tz'u*.
On encountering sorrow, see *Ch'u tz'u*.
Pan Chao, see *Han shu*.
Pan Ku, see *Han shu* and *Po hu t'ung*.
Pan Piao, see *Han shu*.
Pao-p'u-tzu
    This collection of writings, in twenty plus fifty chapters, is attributed to Ko Hung (*c.* 280–340). The book reveals the mystical, quietist approach to life that is associated with Taoist thought and describes some of the observances and practices that evolved in Taoist religion. It includes a variety of valuable information that concerns the growth of science in China. See James R. Ware, *Alchemy, Medicine, Religion in the China of A.D. 320: The Nei P'ien of Ko Hung* (*Pao-p'u tzu*), Cambridge, Massachusetts: M.I.T. Press, 1966.
Po hu t'ung (Comprehensive discussions of the White Tiger Hall)
    This book sets out to be an account of the official discussions that were held in AD 79 regarding the texts and interpretations of the canonical books of the scriptures. Authorship is ascribed traditionally to Pan Ku, but some scholars take the view that it is a later production, of the third century. The book is of considerable value for a study of the New Text and Old Text schools controversy, and of the apocryphal texts. See Tjan Tjoe Som, *Po Hu T'ung: The Comprehensive Discussions in the White Tiger Hall*, 2 vols, Leiden: E. J. Brill, 1949.
Records of the historian, see *Shih-chi*.
Rites, books of, see *Chou li*.
San-kuo chih (Records of the Three Kingdoms)
    This book, compiled by Ch'en Shou 233–97, may be regarded as the nearest approach that we have to a standard history for the period of the three kingdoms (220–80), set up after the abdication of the last of the Han emperors. Its sixty-five chapters fall into three parts which concern the kingdoms of Wei, Shu-Han and Wu respectively. The commentaries to the *San-kuo chih* (principally that of P'ei Sung-chih, b. 372) cite from a number of other historical accounts or records of the period which have otherwise been lost. See Rafe de Crespigny, *The Records of The Three Kingdoms* (Canberra: Centre of Oriental Studies, The Australian National University, 1970).
Shan-hai ching (Classic of the Mountains and the Lakes)
    The book consists of a series of descriptive entries for some of the mountains and lakes of China; they describe their situation, flora, fauna and religious characteristics. The text draws on mythology and folklore and may have originated as notes that explained paintings of the places that are listed. The

first five chapters form the earliest part of this collection but the date of compilation is uncertain, being placed by some scholars at the end of the fourth century BC, by others in the Han period. Chapters 6–13 were almost certainly written during that period, some time before 6 BC, as they include geographical knowledge that could hardly have been available much earlier. Chapters 14–18 were added by Kuo P'u, a writer of the fourth century AD, who also supplied a commentary to the earlier chapters of the book. For details, see *Ways to Paradise*, p. 148 notes 11, 12.

Shang shu, see *Shu ching* and Ch'ao Ts'o.

Shen-chien, see Hsün Yüeh.

Shih (diviners' boards), see p. 98.

Shih-chi (Records of the historian)

Although some chronicles survive for some of the states that existed before the imperial period, the *Shih-chi* constitutes the earliest comprehensive history. The compilation was started by Ssu-ma T'an (d. 110 BC) and continued by his son Ssu-ma Ch'ien (?145–?86 BC), who is often cited as the author of the work. This extends to 130 chapters. From a very early stage it was realised that ten of these chapters had been lost and substitute versions were included. In compiling the history, Ssu-ma T'an and Ssu-ma Ch'ien were able to call on documents of state such as imperial edicts and the reports submitted by officials, which were later incorporated either in full or in summary.

The *Shih-chi* recounts the history of China from the origin of man until the contemporary period of Ssu-ma Ch'ien, and thus covers the mythological rulers, the many pre-imperial states and the empires of Ch'in and Han (up to the time of Ssu-ma Ch'ien's death). The chapters are divided into five groups (imperial annals, tables, treatises, hereditary houses and biographies). This arrangement (without chapters for hereditary houses) was adopted in the subsequent dynastic (or standard) histories, of which the *Han shu* (*q.v.*) should be regarded as the first.

The most valuable translations of the *Shih-chi* are: (a) Édouard Chavannes, *Les Mémoires Historiques de Se-ma Ts'ien*, Vols I–V (Paris: E. Leroux, 1895–1905); this work was reprinted (Paris: Adrien-Maisonneuve, 1967) with a sixth volume which includes (pp. 113–46) a list of other known translations of individual chapters (Timoteus Pokora, 'Bibliographie des Traductions du *Che ki*'); (b) Burton Watson, *Records of the Grand Historian of China*, Vols 1–2 (New York and London: Columbia University Press, 1961). For an account of the work and its compilation, see Chavannes, Vol. I, pp. i–lxi; A. F. P. Hulsewé, 'Notes on the Historiography of the Han period' (W. G. Beasley and E. G. Pulleyblank (eds), *Historians of China and Japan*, London: Oxford University Press, 1961, pp. 31–43); and Burton Watson, *Ssu-ma Ch'ien: Grand Historian of China* (New York: Columbia University Press, 1958).

Shih ching (Book of Songs)

According to one tradition, this book, which forms the earliest anthology of Chinese poetry, was compiled by Confucius. There is a total of 305 poems, which include lyrics, folksongs, hymns for formal occasions and some erotic pieces. By the Han period, the ancient musical setting for the poems had already been lost, but the collection retained great respect owing to its association with the past and the interpretation of some of the poems as the voice of popular protest against misgovernment. The work (known in a number of recensions) was included in the scriptural canon formed by the edict of 136 BC. For translations, see Arthur Waley, *The Book of Songs* (London: George Allen & Unwin, 1937); and Bernhard Karlgren, *The Book of Odes* (Stockholm: Museum of Far Eastern Antiquities, 1950). An account of the contents of the book will be found in Burton Watson, *Early Chinese Literature* (New York and London: Columbia University Press, 1962), pp. 201f.

Shu ching, also called *Shang shu* (Book of Documents)
This book consists of a collection of separate prose documents that purport to be pronouncements or solemn undertakings of sovereigns of the mythological period and leaders or kings of the Hsia, Shang and Chou periods. Some of the pieces are of undoubted antiquity, and the assembly of this collection was attributed to Confucius. During the Han period the book probably comprised twenty-eight sections of the received text of today, whose further twenty-six sections were included only from the third century AD and should not be regarded as being authentic. The statements of the book were long revered and exploited as authority for the exercise of kingship or the practice of other institutions of state. The book was included in the scriptural canon formed by the edict of 136 BC. For a translation of the authentic parts of the book, see Bernhard Karlgren, 'The Book of Documents' (BMFEA 22, 1950, pp. 1–81).

Shuo-yüan, see Liu Hsiang.
Songs of the South, see *Ch'u tz'u*.
Spring and Autumn Annals, see *Ch'un-ch'iu*.
Spring and Autumn Annals of Mr Lü, see *Lü shih ch'un-ch'iu*.
Ssu hsüan fu, see Chang Heng.
Ssu-ma Ch'ien, see *Shih-chi*.
Ssu-ma Hsiang-ju (b. *c.* 179 BC)
A native of west China, Ssu-ma Hsiang-ju served at the courts of Wen ti and Ching ti, and was concerned in the steps taken to extend Han influence towards the south-west. Ssu-ma Hsiang-ju made an outstanding contribution to literature in his development of the *fu* (prose-poetry) form. A number of his compositions which have been incorporated into the *Shih-chi* and *Han shu* reflect aspects of his career at the court and his personal experiences. See Yves Hervouet, (a) *Un poète de cour sous les Han: Sseu-ma Siang-jou*; and (b) *Le Chapitre 117 du Che-ki (Biographie de Sseu-ma Siang-jou) Traduction avec notes* (Paris: Presses Universitaires de France, 1964 and 1972).
Ssu-ma Piao, see *Hou Han shu*.
Ssu-ma T'an, see *Shih-chi*.
Ssu-min yüeh-ling, see Ts'ui Shih.
Standard Histories, see *Cheng shih*.
Story of Mu the son of heaven, see *Mu t'ien-tzu chuan*.
Summons of the soul, see *Ch'u tz'u*.
Ta chao, see *Ch'u tz'u*.
Ta chuan, see *Hsi tz'u chuan*.
Ta Tai li chi, see *Chou li*.
Tai Sheng, see *Chou li*.

Tai Te, see *Chou li*.

T'ai hsüan ching, see Yang Hsiung.

'Ten wings', see *I ching*.

Ts'ai Yung (AD 133–92)

Ts'ai Yung was a scholar known for a number of accomplishments, including proficiency at astronomy, astrology and music. As a student of scriptural works, he became aware of the prevalence of a number of textual discrepancies, and along with others suggested (175) that authentic versions should be engraved on stone, as a permanent record of the approved text. Fragments of the tablets, which survive, may preserve examples of Ts'ai Yung's own handwriting; large numbers of scholars made their own copies of these approved works in the form of rubbings. Ts'ai Yung was a writer of poetry, epitaphs and historical writings, nearly all lost. There survives a small treatise on Han protocol and institutions entitled *Tu tuan*.

Tso chuan, see *Ch'un-ch'iu* and Liu Hsin.

Ts'ui Shih (*c.* AD 110–70)

Of a long treatise written by Ts'ui Shih on government (*Cheng lun*) only those parts which were incorporated in the *Hou Han shu* survive. In those essays, he argues that the political weakness and laxity of behaviour of the day required a radical type of reform which could be achieved by introducing a stringent discipline and severe punishments for crime. Ts'ui Shih was also author of the *Ssu-min yüeh-ling*, (Monthly Instructions for the Four Classes of People), which sets out a practical schedule for agricultural and other tasks, the conduct of social relations and the observance of religious functions. See Balazs (as cited under Chung-ch'ang T'ung), pp.205f.; Christine Herzer, *Das Szu-min yüeh-ling des Ts'ui Shih Ein Bauern-Kalender aus der Späteren Han-Zeit* (Hamburg: 1963); and Patricia Ebrey, 'Estate and Family Management in the Later Han as seen in the *Monthly Instructions for the Four Classes of People*' (*Journal of the Economic and Social History of the Orient* XVII, 1974, pp. 173–205). For Ts'ui Shih's family background, see Patricia Buckley Ebrey, *The aristocratic families of early imperial China: A case study of the Po-ling Ts'ui family* (Cambridge: Cambridge University Press, 1978).

Tu Ch'in (*fl. c.* 35 BC)

Although Tu Ch'in's grandfather and father had served in senior positions in government, Tu Ch'in did not achieve high office. In political matters, he is known for the strong arguments which he voiced (33 BC) against Chinese involvement with foreign states that lay at a remote distance from the empire. He gained a high reputation for his interpretation of strange phenomena, in which he rarely failed to espy a political or dynastic connection. A famous example in which his views were consulted was the coincidence of a solar eclipse on 5 January 29 BC with an earthquake whose shock was registered in the imperial palace. For Tu Ch'in's part in government, see *Crisis and Conflict*, pp. 243f.

Tu-tuan, see Ts'ai Yung.

T'uan, see *I ching*.

Tung Chung-shu (*c.* 179–*c.* 104 BC)

Although Tung Chung-shu never served in a senior capacity in Government, he exercised a major influence on the development of Chinese political thought. By forming a synthesis of cosmic theory, the principles of imperial government and the ethical ideas associated with Confucius, he laid the foundations of orthodox 'Han Confucianism' that dominated imperial philosophy and statecraft for some centuries. He believed in the interaction of heaven, earth and man, and the operation of the eternal cycles of Yin-Yang and the Five Phases. He saw a place for centralised imperial government as an integral part of a major cosmic system, provided that it was operated with fairness and leniency rather than by means of harsh oppression, and provided that the emperor was of sufficient stature to fulfil his major obligations within that system. A firm believer in heaven's communication of warnings to mankind by way of strange phenomena or miracles, Tung Chung-shu attracted the later criticism of sceptics such as Huan T'an (*q.v.*) and Wang Ch'ung (see *Lun-heng*). The *Han shu* includes the texts of several submissions that he made to the throne together with his pronouncements upon strange phenomena. The authenticity of the independent *Ch'un-ch'iu fan-lu* which is attributed to him has been called into question.

Tung-kuan Han chi, see *Hou Han shu*.

Wang Ching (d. *c.* AD 85)

Wang Ching made a specialist study of astronomy and some technological subjects, and became known as an expert in connection with problems of water control. With the help of conscript labour allocated to him by the government, he successfully supervised a project to bring the Yellow river under control (AD 69), making a topographical survey as part of his work. His successful career as an official closed with his tenure of a provincial governorship. Wang Ching also expressed an interest in various methods of divination and attempted to correct some of the current misapprehensions on the subject.

Wang Ch'ung (AD 27–*c.* 100), see *Lun-heng*.

Wang Fu (*c.* AD 90–165)

Wang Fu is known as a critic of the social disorders, economic imbalances and political weakness of the times in which he lived. He reiterated the need to concentrate on agriculture rather than the provision of luxuries for the enjoyment of the privileged few. He saw the cause of contemporary troubles in the choice of officials by favouritism rather than according to merit. Protesting strongly against the prevalent injustice, corruption and oppression, Wang Fu realised that the ethical ideals that he valued could not be put into practice without the imposition of laws and punishments. Some of his essays are included in the *Hou Han shu* (*q.v.*); a fuller collection is in the independent *Ch'ien-fu lun* (Criticisms of a hidden man; thirty-six chapters). See Balazs (as cited under Chung-ch'ang T'ung), pp. 198f.

Wang I, see *Ch'u tz'u*.

Wu ching (Five Classics), see *Chou li, Ch'un-ch'iu, I ching, Shih ching* and *Shu ching*.

Yang Hsiung (53 BC – AD 18)

As a philosopher and author, Yang Hsiung may be described partly as a precursor of Wang Ch'ung's rationalism, and partly as an exponent of the power of the mysterious. In his prose-poems (*fu*), which are expressed in a wealth of imagery, he contributed to the establishment of a literary genre. In the *Fa yen* (Model Sayings; thirteen chapters), he expounded the view that human nature includes a mixture of both good and evil elements; these essays are set in dialect form. In the *T'ai hsüan ching* (Classic of the Great Mysterious; ten chapters), Yang Hsiung set up a system of eighty-one tetragrams as an alternative scheme to the sixty-four hexagrams of the *Chou i* (*q.v.*) and as a means of divination and recognition of the stages reached in the process of cosmic change. In a further work (*Fang yen*, Dialect Words; thirteen chapters) which is attributed to him, there is a comparison of the expressions used in different dialects, but doubts have been cast on the authenticity of this book. See David R. Knechtges, *The Han Rhapsody: A Study of the Fu of Yang Hsiung (53 B.C.–A.D. 18)*, Cambridge: Cambridge University Press, 1976.

Yao, see *I ching*.

Yen-t'ieh lun (Discourses on Salt and Iron)

An edict of 81 BC ordered senior officials to examine and report on the causes of popular distress and suffering. According to the *Yen-t'ieh lun*, which purports to be an account of the ensuing discussions, the issues raised ranged over major questions of principle and policy and concerned most of the contemporary intellectual and political controversies. The book (in sixty sections) is cast in dialogue form, in which two contending parties participate. As one of the first questions to be brought forward for discussion was the value of the state's monopolies of salt and iron, it is from that subject that the title of the book derived. The work is attributed to Huan K'uan and was probably compiled within two or three decades of the edict and subsequent debate. There are signs that the account of the debate is biased in favour of those critics of the government who favoured an ethical and moralist outlook rather than a materialist view of the proper task of a ruler.

A summary of the issues raised and the arguments presented appears in *Crisis and Conflict*, Chapter 3. A translation of sections 1–19 of the work was published by Esson M. Gale, *Discourses on Salt and Iron* (Leyden: E. J. Brill, 1931), and of sections 20–28 by Esson M. Gale and Peter. A. Boodberg in the *Journal of the North China Branch of the Royal Asiatic Society*, Vol. LXV, 1934, pp. 73–110. These have been reprinted in one volume by the Ch'eng-wen Publishing Company, Taipei, 1967, under the title *Discourses on Salt and Iron*. A recent translation of select parts of the text has appeared as *Chine, An −81 Dispute sur le sel et le fer Yantielun*, présentation par Georges Walter (Paris: Lanzmann et Seghers, 1978).

Yin ssu, see pp. 109.

Emperors of the Han Dynasty

Name	Title	Acceded	Died
Western (Former) Han			
Liu Pang	Kao tsu (Kao ti)	202 BC	195
Liu Ying	Hui ti	195	188
(The empress Lü)	*	188	180
Liu Heng	Wen ti	180	157
Liu Ch'i	Ching ti	157	141
Liu Ch'e	Wu ti	141	87
Liu Fu-ling	Chao ti	87	74 (5 June)
Liu Ho	—	74 (18 July)	74 (deposed 14 Aug)
Liu Ping-i	Hsüan ti	74	49
Liu Shih	Yüan ti	49	33
Liu Ao	Ch'eng ti	33	7
Liu Hsin	Ai ti	7	1 BC
Liu Chi-tzu	P'ing ti	AD 1	6
Liu Ying	(infant emperor during Wang Mang's regency)	6	8
Hsin Dynasty			
Wang Mang		9	23
Eastern (Later) Han			
Liu Hsiu	Kuang wu ti	25	57
Liu Yang	Ming ti	57	75
Liu Ta	Chang ti	75	88
Liu Chao	Ho ti	88	106
Liu Lung	Shang ti	106 (13 Feb)	106 (21 Sept)
Liu Yu	An ti	106 (23 Sept)	125 (30 April)
Liu I	Shao ti	125 (18 May)	125 (10 Dec)
Liu Pao	Shun ti	125	144
Liu Ping	Ch'ung ti	144	145 (15 Feb)
Liu Tsuan	Chih ti	145	146
Liu Chih	Huan ti	146	168
Liu Hung	Ling ti	168	189 (13 May)
Liu Pien	Shao ti	189 (15 May)	189 (demoted 28 Sept)
Liu Hsieh	Hsien ti	189	220 (abdicated)

* During this time two infants successively held the formal title of emperor.

Addendum to further reading

A number of works published subsequently to this book concern its subject matter. They include: Michèle Pirazzoli-t'Serstevens, *The Han Dynasty* (New York, 1982); A.F.P. Hulsewé, *Remnants of Ch'in Law* (Leiden, 1985); *The Cambridge History of China volume I: the Ch'in and Han Empires*, ed. Twitchett and Loewe (Cambridge 1986; a supplementary volume is now in preparation); A.C. Graham, *Disputers of the Tao* (La Salle, 1989); Michael Nylan, *The Canon of Supreme Mystery* (Albany, 1993); and *The Five "Confucian" Classics* (New Haven and London, 2001); three volumes of *The Grand Scribe's Records* (a translation of the *Shih chi*, edited by William H. Nienhauser; Bloomington and Indianapolis, 1994, 2002); Donald Harper, *Early Chinese Medical Literature* (London and New York, 1998); Geoffrey Lloyd and Nathan Sivin, *The Way and the Word: Science and Medicine in Early China and Greece* (New Haven and London, 2002); Roel Sterckx, *The Animal and the Daemon in Early China* (Albany, 2002); Marc Kalinowski, *Divination et société dans la chine médiévale* (Paris, 2003); Charles Le Blanc and Rémi Mathieu, *Philosophes taoïstes II: Huainan zi* (Paris, 2003); and the present author's *Early Chinese Texts: a Bibliographical Guide* (as editor: Berkeley, 1993); *Divination, mythology and monarchy in Han China* (Cambridge, 1994); *A Biographical Dictionary of the Qin, Former Han and Xin Periods* (Leiden, 2000); and *The Men who Governed Han China* (Leiden, 2004).

Index

An asterisk * indicates an entry which will be found in the glossary

222